Love,
Naturally

Also by Sophie Sullivan

Ten Rules for Faking It
How to Love Your Neighbor
A Guide to Being Just Friends

Love,
Naturally

A Novel

Sophie Sullivan

ST. MARTIN'S GRIFFIN
NEW YORK

To all the women in my life who inspire me, lift me up, and make me a better human. More importantly, thank you for accepting me when I'm not at my best. I appreciate you.

First published in the United States by St. Martin's Griffin, an imprint of St. Martin's Publishing Group

LOVE, NATURALLY. Copyright © 2023 by Jody Holford. All rights reserved. Printed in the United States of America. For information, address St. Martin's Publishing Group, 120 Broadway, New York, NY 10271.

www.stmartins.com

Library of Congress Cataloging-in-Publication Data

Names: Sullivan, Sophie, 1976– author.
Title: Love, naturally : a novel / Sophie Sullivan.
Description: First edition. | New York : St. Martin's Griffin, 2024. |
Identifiers: LCCN 2023032998 | ISBN 9781250875839 (trade paperback) |
   ISBN 9781250875846 (ebook)
Subjects: LCGFT: Romance fiction. | Novels.
Classification: LCC PR9199.4.H6454 L68 2024 | DDC 813/.6—dc23/eng/20230721
LC record available at https://lccn.loc.gov/2023032998

Our books may be purchased in bulk for promotional, educational, or business use. Please contact your local bookseller or the Macmillan Corporate and Premium Sales Department at 1-800-221-7945, extension 5442, or by email at MacmillanSpecialMarkets@macmillan.com.

First Edition: 2024

10 9 8 7 6 5 4 3 2 1

And in the middle of my chaos,
there you were.

One

A DECEPTIVELY SUNNY SUNDAY

Relationships were a back-and-forth, a seesaw of give-and-take, a money-up-front, rewards-at-the-end sort of venture. Presley Ayers repeated this in her brain as her boss bemoaned her upcoming week off, going so far as to hint that maybe she didn't want to move up from associate concierge at La Chambre Hotel. She did. She very much did. She wanted to move up and move on. One day. For now, she just wanted Ms. Twain, no relation to Mark, to stop making herself out to be a martyr for switching around some shifts.

I've been planning this for months and asked for the time off. Not my problem you forgot, lady.

"I'm assuming it won't be a problem when I want you to work extra shifts to make up for this when you return," Ms. Twain said, staring down her nose through her thin wire-framed glasses.

She had willingly jumped through every other hoop, but now Presley simply smiled. "You know I'm always willing to take extra shifts, Ms. Twain. I thought I'd given you enough notice when I booked my holiday in April. I apologize." She crossed the index and middle fingers on her right hand in her pocket. She wasn't sorry. She just didn't want to be fired. Biting her lip kept her from saying any of the words floating around in her brain.

This woman was a primary source of Presley's sleepless nights. Emmett, her boyfriend of almost eight months, had once mansplained that this was how the game was played. If she wanted to be a success, she needed to show it, not just say it. If she didn't, someone else would want it more. She didn't know how anyone could think she wasn't ambitious, since she'd spent most of her waking hours, and many when she should have been sleeping, at this hotel for the past three years.

"Are you headed out of town? Are you completely unavailable?" Ms. Twain made a note on her calendar, then looked up at Presley from behind the desk where she sat.

"Yes, ma'am. I'm taking my boyfriend to a fishing lodge as a surprise birthday present." Give and take. Things hadn't been great lately with both of them working so much and their schedules not matching up. The little time they did spend together was generally with Emmett's work friends. But this gift would show him she listened, paid attention to the little things. It would be the nudge he needed to take them more seriously. Maybe even consider moving in. That was the endgame. At thirty-one, she'd thought she'd have her professional and personal life cemented by now. Or at least one of them.

Ms. Twain wrinkled her nose, her thinning gray brows pushing together. "Do you fish?"

Not even in the supermarket. "No. But he does." *And it will show him I can get behind his hobbies and interests.*

The woman regarded her for several moments, making the back of Presley's neck sweat. "There's a seminar in a couple of weeks, the beginning of July, for senior hotel staff. Typically, we recommend one to two assistant staff associates to take part."

Presley sucked in a breath. She knew all about it, having been passed up for it twice in three years despite her stellar track record with guests and growing persona as one of Great Falls' local influencers. "Oh?"

Ms. Twain sat up straighter in her high-back chair. For two generations, she and her family had owned the three-and-a-half-but-striving-for-four-star hotel.

"Is this something you'd be interested in?"

Refraining from nodding her head like a cartoon character, she went with, "Absolutely."

Ms. Twain nodded. "Very well then. I'll take that into consideration."

Pulling her hands from the pockets of her pleated black dress pants, Presley curled her fingers into her palms, then loosened them. She didn't like playing games, especially since she proved herself daily, but it didn't stop her from smiling as wide as she could.

"I'd really appreciate that. I know I'd do an excellent job."

As she left the office, her flats felt wobbly, her heart felt full, and her stomach twirled like a ballerina on a roll. Her phone rang as she exited the hotel and climbed into her new-to-her Honda Civic. Practical and pretty. That was her sweet spot. She'd just topped fifty thousand followers on TikTok and Instagram by playing to her strengths. Fancy was nice, but affordable was necessary.

She'd already packed. Emmett was meeting her at the coffee shop located just before the airport. They'd share pie, like they had on their first date, and then she'd show him the tickets and they'd park in long-term and board the plane. She was doing her best not to think about how small the plane would be. A new airline that catered to short flights had offered her two tickets in exchange for promo. At the time, she hadn't had a destination in mind, but this worked perfectly. *As long as the plane does, too.* A short bus ride would take them to a ferry, which would bring them to their final destination, Get Lost Lodge. *Set a goal, make a plan, achieve success.*

Her phone buzzed through the Bluetooth as she drove in the direction of the airport. *Don't say you're going to be late, Emmett.* As a lead advertising exec, he often worked long hours, including weekends and nights.

She pressed ACCEPT on her steering wheel, hoping this time it worked. Her car often glitched in the electronics department.

"Hey," Rylee's voice said through the speakers, just a hint of static punctuating the word. Best friends for half a decade, they knew the best and worst about each other. They'd both come a long way since working at a little boutique hotel in Great Falls, Rylee as a line cook and Presley as a bellhop. There'd been an almost instant connection that couldn't be contained to only working hours.

"Hey. I'm on my way. My stomach won't settle down."

"I know you have everything because you're you, but are you sure you're ready for this?"

"I am." It hadn't been easy to arrange this surprise getaway. Emmett was particular about his space and his things. He never slept at her house, and lately, she hadn't been spending a lot of time at his. But bit by bit, she'd snuck out some boxers, T-shirts, sweaters, and other necessary items to pack his bag. One of his friends helped a bit when Presley confided her plans. The lodge provided fishing rods and whatever other accessories went along with fishing.

"You're sure?" She heard the worry in her friend's normally chill-as-cucumber-eye-patches voice.

Presley knew Rylee wasn't asking about her covert packing skills but more the whole "great outdoors" piece. She was known online and in person as someone who could recommend a five-star restaurant off the top of her head. A woman with connections to cheap theater tickets and knowledge of the best times to visit the museums. She knew Great Falls city center because she'd grown up in it, but she'd never spent much time hugging trees or planning picnics.

As a kid, she'd begged to sleep outside once, so her parents had let her sleep on the balcony of their apartment. She'd woken up freezing, scared, and uncomfortable. But this wasn't that. She would spend time on the beach, soaking up the June sun, letting the fresh air work wonders on her skin while showing her followers that vacations didn't have to be pricey to be enjoyable. Not something Ms. Twain would approve of, but since the woman refused to listen to any of her ideas for the hotel's social media, Presley did her own thing.

Infusing her voice with a confidence she didn't fully feel, she said, "I'm excited. I'm being spontaneous and adventurous."

Rylee laughed. "With only a couple of months' planning to put it all together."

True, but it was still one of the most impromptu things Presley had ever done. Emmett often complained when she wanted to make plans for a Friday night on Monday, telling her sometimes he just liked to see how things went.

"He's going to be so surprised. When he was working to secure the Get Lost account, he kept saying he wanted to go there. There's a little town on another island about a ten-minute ferry ride from the lodge that we can explore. There's a craft beer tour and little shops. And at the lodge there's hiking, fishing, canoeing. Plus, there's the beach and swimming."

She knew she was repeating herself, but it was almost like a checklist, a way to remind herself that she'd thought this through. When she'd asked Emmett about a trip to New York to see some plays, he'd said that was definitely not his thing. Well, this wasn't hers and she was still doing it. Give and take.

Presley turned right at the light, the butterflies now doing jumping jacks in her stomach.

"It sounds awesome. Let's just hope he appreciates it. I've never seen him do any of those things here, so don't be afraid to do some of what you want on this trip, too."

Presley knew her friend worried that she did a little too much of the giving in her relationships. Particularly this one. Presley loved her best friend, but Rylee was the queen of one week or less, no strings attached, and multiple dating apps. Her bestie was working her way up to head chef at a popular downtown restaurant and didn't want to be tied down. If a person started to truly fall for Rylee, she ended things. Presley, on the other hand, had always been a full-meal-deal relationship person. She didn't mind making allowances or being flexible with her life, because she wanted to share it with someone.

This would be worth it. Emmett would love it, they'd reconnect, and they'd maybe even talk about their next steps. Together.

After promising to text Rylee, Presley hung up just as she pulled into Slices Pie Shop. She parked, got out, smoothed out her button-down blouse, and picked a little piece of lint off of her pants. Slinging her purse over her shoulder, she headed for the entrance. Emmett's car wasn't in the lot yet, but he'd be here any minute. She was craving the strawberry rhubarb they'd had on their first date.

As she slipped into a booth and ordered a pop for each of them, along with a slice of pie, she thought about how they'd met. His company had held a weekend conference at La Chambre Hotel even though the firm was local. It wasn't uncommon. Companies rented rooms, set up workshops, and let their staff bond for a couple of days over free food and drinks. Presley was almost in charge of the team-building activities. That is, she planned and executed them but received none of the credit.

Whatever. It had been a great success personally and professionally. He'd asked her out on the second evening, and after work they'd come to this diner, sat in this booth, and shared her favorite pie.

"Here's your drinks. Pie will be out in a minute," the waitress said.

Emmett came through the door as Presley was putting his present on the table. It didn't look like much in its black trifold packet, but she had a lot riding on this. Those butterflies were backflipping like divers off the high diving board now.

His blond hair was perfectly styled; not one hair dared to move. His blue eyes sparkled, and every time he leaned in for a kiss, Presley breathed deep, wrapped herself up in his scent, not entirely sure what it was but enjoying it all the same.

He slid into the booth as the waitress came back with one piece of pie and two forks. He gave her one of his shining grins.

"Hey. Would it be too much trouble to get lemon meringue instead?" Emmett asked.

The waitress glanced at Presley, raised her brows a little. She felt silly for wanting the romance of sharing the same type of pie they once had, so she smiled at the woman. "Lemon is my second favorite."

Once he opened his gift, the pie wouldn't matter.

The waitress took the plate and went to get the other dessert.

"Sorry I'm a couple minutes late." He took a long drink of his pop. He was fidgety. She could feel his knee bouncing from across the table.

He seemed to be looking everywhere but into her eyes. *We'll reconnect on the trip.*

"No worries." Presley reached for his hands. "Happy birthday."

He met her gaze, his smile a little tight around the edges, and pulled his hands back. "Thanks. Listen, about tonight."

The waitress showed up with two plates of pie. "Here's your lemon." She set it in front of Emmett and looked at Presley as she slipped the original piece in front of her. "It's already sliced, so it's on the house."

Simple, random acts of kindness could not be outdone. "Thank you so much."

The waitress's gaze softened. "It's just pie, hon."

Not to Presley. It was memories and the start of something special. The waitress wandered off to help two new customers.

Presley tapped her fingers on the packet. "I have your birthday present here."

Emmett was a few bites into his pie. "Thanks," he said around a mouthful. "Some of the guys want to go for drinks tonight."

Her smile slipped. "But you said no, right?"

He shrugged. "Figured a couple drinks wouldn't hurt. It is *my* birthday."

The butterflies got tangled up in each other like they'd had a few drinks of their own. "Of course, but I told you I had something special planned and it starts tonight."

He sighed. "You always do that, pin me down. I say yes because I feel like I have to and then you're upset when I bail. And I'm not bailing. I know it messes with your precious scheduling, but I'm just saying we'll meet up later tonight. Okay?"

She pushed down her irritation, reminded herself he didn't actually *know* what she had planned. She picked up the packet, tapped it against the table. "Not really."

Her pie was forgotten when she caught his look of irritation, which he made no effort to hide. "Pres." That's it. That's all he said—the first syllable of her name—and then he just stared at her. A typical Emmett tactic.

It's fine. Everything is fine. It's okay. She pushed the packet toward him. "I think you'll be happy to skip drinks for this."

He grabbed the packet, opened it up. Presley held herself impossibly still, watching him as he looked over the information, his eyes widening. The airplane tickets, a little brochure for the resort, and a couple of fun doodles she'd done of them fishing and relaxing on the beach were inside.

Emmett looked up, locked his gaze on hers. "You bought me a vacation?"

Mostly. She nodded, her head feeling like one of those bobbleheads. "Yes. We need to be at the airport in an hour. Do you remember how much you talked about going to this place? It has everything you wanted. We'll fish, hike, sunbathe, swim. Not a museum or play in sight."

She expected him to laugh, as they spent a fair amount of time arguing over what to do with their weekend evenings and disagreeing on what counted as fun.

His brows scrunched. "This is that place we didn't get the account for?"

Uh-oh. Hopefully that didn't bring up bad vibes, but the owners had pulled the account for reasons that had nothing to do with Emmett or his team.

"Yes, but just because you aren't doing their marketing and advertising doesn't mean it won't be fun, right? We'll have a great time and you can finally check it out."

"We?"

Okay, the butterflies were starting to resemble unstable pigeons in her stomach now. One tripped, the others all following suit like dominoes.

"Of course. I worked everything out. The guys know, so they probably didn't even mean it about tonight, because Paul was the one who helped me get your time off, and I have the week as well. It's ten days, actually, but your boss was great about it. Mine not so much, so I might be working some triples when we get back, but it'll be worth it."

Emmett's gaze shuttered. He was good at his job because he had a great poker face. Even Presley couldn't get a good read on him sometimes. "Pres. This is cool. I mean, it looks like a great time."

There it was. The gratitude she'd hoped for. The "my girlfriend kicks ass and I should up my game, give her a drawer at my place, maybe even suggest we live together" energy she'd been after.

"Ten days . . . together . . . away . . . that's . . ." Emmett's voice trailed off.

"Amazing? Spectacular? A dream come true?" Her excitement amped up her pitch and she had to remind herself to take a breath.

"Too much."

All of the energy coursing through her stopped like someone had pulled the plug or switched off the power. "Excuse me?" In her periphery, she saw the waitress almost approach then veer right and sidestep their table. *Smart move, lady.*

With another heavy sigh, Emmett let go of the packet and lifted one arm so he could rest it along the back of the booth. He'd done that eight months ago, too, on their date. But her shoulder had been just underneath and he'd scooted a little closer.

"I just don't think we're there. A couples' vacation? I love this. It's great. You're a sweetheart for being so thoughtful. But this has guys' trip written all over it. I think that much forced proximity might, you know, be a bad thing for us."

She said nothing. He kept going. "At this stage. Maybe we could try a weekend away sometime. An overnight at a bed-and-breakfast. I don't know. Ten days is a lot."

"What?" The word came out as a raspy whisper.

He lowered his arm, folded his hands together, and leaned in. "Can you imagine us in each other's space for ten days?"

Her nod was slow. She had spent time doing just that. "Yes. It was supposed to be a prelude. An idea of what it would be like if we moved in together."

The horror on his face should have sent her running. But Presley liked to really nail a coffin closed. "Clearly, that idea doesn't impress you."

"Look, this is fun. What we have. It's good. But it's not till-death-do-us-part."

A strange smile tipped her lips. "Oh, I don't know. I kind of feel like killing you now just to see."

He laughed too loud. "See? You're fun. You're funny. But you've got to admit, you'd drive me crazy if we were stuck together for ten days."

"'Stuck'?" The word trembled. For some reason, her brain flashed back to all of the spring and summer breaks when her parents would quietly argue in their bedroom about who would bring Presley to work with them. Each of them acted like they were happy to do so to her face, and she knew they loved her, but she'd always felt like . . . a burden.

"This is a great birthday present, Pres."

Her spine stiffened as she pushed against the hard plastic back of the booth. Both of her brows lifted. "Seems like it."

He covered one of her hands with his. It was clammy. "It *is*. But a real gift is all about the recipient, right?"

Tears blurred her vision just a little as the effort it had taken to coordinate and execute this surprise flipped through her head. "It was definitely all about you."

"Then I should get to pick who I want to go with me."

Her heart might have actually stopped in her chest. Pulling her hand back, she sat up straighter. "What? Are you nuts?"

Emmett looked around, then at Presley. "Keep your voice down. No, I'm not nuts. If I was, I'd go on a ten-day vacation with the woman I'm seeing."

Presley's temples throbbed and she swore she heard a sharp crack. Probably the last of her patience. "'Seeing'? What the hell is that supposed to mean? This isn't high school. We've been together for eight months. I thought we were moving forward."

Again, he looked around like the few customers in the diner were watching the show. "We are. Just clearly not in the same direction. This is fun and all, but my idea of a vacation doesn't involve being nagged for ten days to keep you busy and entertained."

The sharp breath she sucked in made her cough. Those tears spilled over, but at least now she could blame them on choking. She took a sip of her pop, grabbed her purse, and stood up.

"You are a complete ass. I can't believe I thought we had something special."

He looked up, his expression guarded. "To be fair, you think everything is special. You see what you want to see and read too much into things, Pres."

She kept the bad words flitting through her brain to herself, leaned over, grabbed the packet, and tucked it in her purse. "Well, this will be easy to read into: you now have tonight and the rest of your life free and clear to do whatever you want. We're done."

"Stop being dramatic. Where are you going?"

Her lips curved. "On the vacation of your dreams. Alone."

She hurried toward the door, briefly locking eyes with the waitress, who had clearly heard everything. When Emmett tried to follow, the waitress stopped him.

"Excuse me, sir, if you leave without paying, I'll be forced to call the police."

She heard Emmett swear, but it gave her time to get to her car. Small kindnesses—even if they were just an extra few seconds of space to breathe and toss her idiot ex's bags onto the cement of Slices' parking lot. As a bonus, she got to see Emmett's stunned expression as his bag burst open and the contents spilled out.

Two

Presley's stomach roiled like angry waves as she stared at the boat meant to take them to the lodge. She didn't really remember the bus ride from the airport. She'd watched through the window as buildings, cars, and people whipped past without actually seeing anything. She'd gone through the motions like she was on a human assembly line and somehow ended up *here*. The details of it were foggy at best, but she would sure as heck remember this part. After experiencing the bus with wings that the airline called a plane, she hadn't thought it could get worse.

It was one of many things she'd been wrong about today. *You see what you want to see.* Well, she did *not* want to see this. Or get on it. The boat seemed too small to be called a cruiser. She couldn't keep hesitating on the pier like she was about to walk the plank. A tall, dark-haired guy with mirrored sunglasses stood behind her like a reminder that she could only go forward.

When she was little, she'd asked her parents if she could sleep over at a friend's house. They'd said yes, but when she'd woken in the middle of the night, wanting nothing more than to go home, they'd told her she had made her choice and they'd pick her up in the morning. Follow-through was an Ayers family must. She'd made her choice. The person behind her was ready to go. She just needed to do it first.

"Let me help you," the boat captain offered, extending his hand.

Did people have to go to school to operate boats? *They must. Of course they do. It's a vehicle. You need a license to drive a vehicle.*

"I promise you, it's safe," the guy behind her said in a low, steady voice. He must have leaned closer, because the chill running through her body lessened for a fraction of a second—whether from the warmth of his tone or from his body heat, she didn't know. The pleasant scent of his cologne, or maybe just his soap, worked like smelling salts bringing her back to life.

It got her on board. Even though the deck felt more like an extension of the wobbly dock than a boat, she made it to the closest seat. There was a small hard-shell canopy at the front of the boat, but Presley's chill returned, and she didn't want to move, even if it meant her fair skin would burn. Leaning her back against the padded leather seat cushion, she hugged her large travel bag to her chest.

The ferry terminal was smaller than she had expected, with only a few boats docked. One boat had cars being loaded onto its lower bay while passengers walked up a ramp to a higher level. In the distance, an impressive bridge stretched across the sky. Because she was unable to see the beginning or end from where she sat, it gave the illusion of being suspended, even with its concrete pillars and cable lines.

She closed her eyes as the captain started the engine. The gentle rocking didn't feel soothing, but the crisp air, even with the breeze, did. *You can do this. Breathe. You're fine.* She'd never considered herself boat averse, but the day was catching up with her. Or, because she was a city girl, her body was accustomed to less choppy forms of travel than those she'd experienced today. Despite that, she was glad she hadn't planned a road trip to the northern tip of Michigan, where she was now. Free airline tickets for the win. At least she wasn't out the cost of the second flight. And once she'd boarded, she couldn't change her mind like she would have in a car.

When she opened her eyes, her gaze caught on the man across the boat, the one whose voice had steadied her nerves a minute earlier. He had one ankle crossed over the other while he leaned back against the side of the boat like waves didn't dare affect his stomach.

He wore a lightweight dark gray bomber jacket with dark jeans.

Between that and the shades, he made her think of a movie star playing a pilot. A blue duffel bag rested near his sturdy black boots. Cataloguing little details about him allowed her stomach to settle. Her breathing evened out, her pulse settling somewhere near normal. His hair was the color of medium-roast coffee. Not that she drank medium-roast coffee. She preferred tea, wished she had some. His eyes were probably the color of tea. Unlike the other four passengers, a husband and wife and two guys talking about how epic this trip would be, he didn't have much in the way of luggage. Maybe he was only staying a couple of days. His slightly too long hair was being teased by the wind.

Thinking back to the brochure tucked inside her purse, she remembered the passenger boat was a twenty-foot cruiser. The lodge apparently had two additional boats, but this might be the only one she boarded. The engine hummed as they pulled away from the dock, heading in the direction of what appeared to be nothing but water.

"I'm Grayson. Glad you're sharing your vacation with us. Let me tell you about the area. It's believed that hundreds of shipwrecks lie beneath these waters," the captain, who'd greeted them at the bus, boomed over his microphone as they set off.

Great. Awesome. Please don't let us be one of them. The woman standing with her husband on whatever the left side of the boat was called pointed to the water, then said something in her husband's ear. He touched her lower back. Casual affection was Presley's favorite. She loved the idea that one person reached out for another without thought just because the urge to be closer was always there. Hovering.

"It's one of the largest freshwater lakes in North America," the captain continued.

Presley worked to drown out the guy's voice by finding a focal point, something that would distract her from absolutely everything. The knees of the guy with the duffel bag seemed like a safe bet. When her gaze moved up, she saw he was watching her as well. Maybe he was using her as a way to not throw up, too.

One of the men asked if they could grab a rod and throw out a line right this minute. Mr. Steady On His Feet lifted his glasses onto his head and rolled his eyes, and it almost made her smile. Of course, any movement at all felt like a threat, so she was careful.

The boat swayed, the water choppy from the wind, as the captain continued to share facts and history about the lake. Despite the strong breeze, the sun shone overhead, trying to warm her. The problem was, she was cold from the inside out.

Presley clutched her bag tighter and tried to breathe through her nose. The hotel had hosted a mindfulness seminar a few months back and she'd picked up numerous supposedly calming tricks. Notice five things you can smell, see, hear, feel. Breathe in for four, hold it, and out for five. It seemed to work for her erratic heart rate but not her nausea.

"The lodge is about forty-five minutes from Mackinaw City, where we picked you all up, but we only come to this terminal once every two weeks or so. When we need supplies or guests want to explore off the island, we take a smaller cruiser to Smile, which is one of the smaller islands to your east. It's home to about five thousand people, but it's growing into a little tourist community of its own, with charming shops, delicious food, and interesting folks. It's only an eight-minute boat ride from Get Lost," he said, pointing. "It's got a fun history. My family and I grew up there, and even though it's not far from the big city, I can tell you firsthand that it seems like a world of its own. Fun fact: the town was meant to be named after its founder, Ernest Simel, but the sign makers misspelled his name. His wife loved it so they let it stand."

She didn't like that they were leaving big-city hotels and shopping malls behind them, but if she got desperate and needed a respite from the great outdoors, she could handle a ten-minute torture trip. So much for ever going on a cruise though. Her stomach tilted, and she swore she could feel every wave as if it washed over her.

"Water is a bit choppy today," the captain said.

Presley wished she had gum. *Is that just for planes?* The knees she was keeping her gaze on uncrossed and bent before coming her way. Presley looked up as he crossed the deck, a piece of brown paper in his hand. When he stopped right in front of her, she had to remove one hand from her bag to protect her eyes from the sun. He'd lowered the shades, so she couldn't answer the tea-colored question yet. She felt his perusal, down past her white knuckles clutching her bag and back up.

He held out a brown paper bag. Presley scrunched her brows, waiting for an explanation. His stubbled jaw was tight and she couldn't read his expression.

"In case you need to throw up," he said.

In all fairness, his voice lacked any judgment, but it didn't make her feel better. Was she that obvious? She worked to loosen her fingers, her shoulders.

"I'm fine," she said, hating that even when she was trying to be strong, she clearly showed weakness. Even to strangers. She couldn't read her boyfriend of eight months, and this stranger had sized her up in a glance. But she didn't need to be rude, so she tacked on, "But thank you anyway."

He stood there and Presley did her best to ignore him. Not ignore-ignore, because she was human, and with the windblown hair, strong jaw, and straight nose, he was really good-looking. He was also, probably, trying to be nice. She appreciated that. But there was no way she'd admit to the possibility of needing that bag. He handed it to her, waited for her to accept it before returning to his previous spot against the railing. She also appreciated the way he resumed his stoic position so she could use his knees again for the rest of the journey. She tucked the hopefully unnecessary item into the pocket of her own bag.

Presley tuned back in to the captain's voice around the time he said they were coming up on the lodge. Emmett had been so excited about possibly getting this account. She'd read reviews and looked at photos online when he'd talked about visiting there months ago, but then the clients backed out, decided they didn't need a new marketing team. When Presley was thinking about what to do for his birthday, the lodge bounced back into her mind. The name sounded charming and cute.

"Hopefully you've received our emails and notifications that our lodge is under construction. The ownership has recently changed hands, and while we still have amenities to offer, there are some restrictions to guest services and excursions."

As the boat slowed near a long dock with one other boat moored, she saw a wooden sign that read: GET LOST. God. If only.

Email. Her email. She'd used her personal email to book everything because she had a habit of leaving her work email open on her laptop for ease of use. Ms. Twain liked to send frequent updates and suggestions. She had *not*, in fact, checked her personal one recently. *Doesn't matter. As long as they have clean beds, hot water, and leave me alone, I'll be fine.*

"The email said you're working on the cabins," the woman called out, keeping a hand on her extremely large hat so it didn't blow away.

"That's right. They need some repairs and updating," the captain said, looking over his shoulder with a nod. "We'll be in close quarters because of that, but the lodge has plenty of space and everyone has rooms there. You guys are in for a great trip. If you love fishing, outdoors, hiking, and campfires, you are in the right place."

Presley groaned and let her head drop down to her bag even as she considered picking up the paper one, pride be damned. She was so in the wrong place.

Three

Presley hadn't spent a lot of time outdoors in places other than the city, but she couldn't deny the beauty of what lay before her as she stepped—nearly stumbled—off the dock. Or maybe she just liked solid ground more than she realized. It was like a painting worthy of a high-end art gallery, with trees of every variety, ones she couldn't put a name to even for money, creating walkways and paths in all directions. Two guys in ball caps and plaid jackets fished from the edge of the sand. She didn't know much about the whole process, but she wondered if they could catch anything in the shallows. If so, she definitely wasn't swimming. Sand in her toes was one thing. Fish kisses were an absolute no. In the distance past the guys were a couple of cabins with decks that looked out onto the water.

She followed the others as the captain led them along the aging cobbled walkway, being careful of the missing and cracked stones. Past a few trees taller than La Chambre Hotel, the grounds opened up to reveal a massive log lodge that no picture in a brochure could accurately depict. Some Paul Bunyan had chopped down actual trees, plunked them together, and built a monstrous structure. A real-life Lincoln Log house.

"This is the lodge. To the left are more cabins. They're nestled into the trees, but all of them have a spot where you can see the water, whether it's from the front or back porches or a side window. We hope when you visit us again, they'll be open for business," Captain Grayson said.

The lodge looked like it had been carved into the base of the mountains, even though they had to be far away. She felt like she'd been dropped into another world.

I'm in Jumanji. I might not make it out. She giggled, earning a look from the big-hatted woman who held her husband's hand.

"You all right, dear?"

She'd planned a trip, ignored her nagging instincts, and was now here alone. "All right" wasn't the best description, but she nodded, not trusting her voice. Too bad she'd trusted her stupid heart. Something between pain and irritation bounced around in her chest like a rubber ball. Those hard ones that kids whipped at brick walls.

The captain talked about trails, hiking, and not venturing out alone as they continued toward the main house. She looked up for a split second, just to see the way the clouds played with the peaks of the mountains, where the sun was dipping low, and caught her foot on one of the broken cobblestone pieces.

She was on her way down when strong hands gripped her hips from behind. Heat and delicious pressure shot through her clothing, along her skin, chasing away a chill that had been with her all day.

"Careful," Brown Paper Bag Guy's gruff voice murmured.

Swallowing the sudden moisture in her mouth, Presley looked over her shoulder. "Thanks."

His eyes were *not* tea colored. They were a brown so dark they almost looked black. A ring of hazel around the edges made them seem even darker.

The captain's voice pulled her back. He stood on the steps of the lodge looking at them all. He was a handsome man. Dark hair, strong jaw, dressed in a blue button-down and khaki pants, he definitely looked the part of an outdoor guide. While the guy behind her looked like a poster model for being sexy in the great outdoors, the captain was more polished.

"My sister will get you all settled in your rooms. Her adorable helper is my niece. Our chef should have snacks set up in the dining room. We'll let you settle into your rooms, but if anyone would like a tour of the lodge and grounds, I'll be leading that at eight P.M. Until then, thank you for joining us here at Get Lost Lodge."

As they shuffled in, Presley couldn't help but wonder if Emmett would have loved this place as much as she'd thought. Sure, he'd have dropped his bag and hit the beach, maybe even with a fishing rod. Rylee's words echoed in her head: *I've never seen him do any of those things.* He'd canceled several weekend plans for fishing time with the guys over the course of their relationship. *You see what you want to see.* Even if he didn't love fishing with the guys as much as she'd believed, he would have enjoyed this. The image of his face when he'd realized he wouldn't be going on the trip at all curled her lips upward. That in itself was worth the boat ride.

Presley smiled at the little girl who stood behind a woman's hip. Her red hair fell forward even with the little butterfly barrette she wore. Her mom—who had to be the captain's sister—had her own auburn hair tucked into two braids. Makeup free, wearing camo shorts and a shirt that read WELCOME TO THE JUNGLE, she looked like she could model outdoor wear with Mr. Hot Hands who'd kept her from falling.

"Welcome," she said. "I'm Jillian, but you can call me that, Jilly, or Jill. This is my daughter, Olivia. Welcome to the lodge."

The little girl tugged on her mom's shorts until Jilly bent at the waist, listened, then stood again. Her lips quirked. "My apologies. This summer, Olivia would like to be called Ollie. Please let us know if we can get you anything."

Half the little girl's face beamed. The rest stayed hidden behind her mom. Presley met Jillian's gaze and found it, like her tone, friendly. If things had gone as planned, maybe she would have befriended this woman while Emmett kept himself busy with all of his favorite things. Instead, Presley decided she was going to consider this a self-care trip and do only the things *she* felt like. She'd share on her socials, promo the airline that gave her the tickets, and talk about the benefit of low-key lounging. Maybe even take a hike. Hell, she might even try fishing. After she slept for twelve hours straight.

She waited patiently for Jilly to assign those in front of her to their rooms, smiling at the way Ollie assisted, all while trying to ignore how aware she was of the man standing behind her.

"Presley Ayers," Jilly said, looking at a clipboard as the husband and wife and the two guys headed up the stairs to the right for their rooms. She glanced behind Presley, then met her gaze. "It says you're a party of two."

With a tight smile, Presley shook her head. "Change of plans. Party of one." She didn't want anyone's pity, so she forced her smile to widen. "Now I get the bed to myself."

"Oh," Jillian said too brightly, like she understood what Presley was really saying. "Okay. No worries. I'll just make note of that." She jotted something down on the clipboard.

Presley tried to see what she wrote, hoping it wasn't something like: *Watch this one, she's out of her element.*

"You're down here on the main level. Room one," Jillian said. Ollie handed Presley a key.

"Thank you," Presley said, her throat thick with tears she refused to shed.

She moved as quickly as possible, grateful for the open layout of the lodge. Room one was along the left side, under the stairs that led to the second floor. Once she was inside her room, her chill took on new meaning. The space was downright *cold*. She could hear the AC fan and feel the temperature settling on her skin like a layer of ice.

Tossing her bag and purse on the bed, she went to the thermostat, rubbing her arms briskly. It read forty-four; winter temps indoors at the end of June. Presley shivered, punched the UP button. The digits moved, but as soon as she took her finger away, it returned to the same number. She tried pressing the OFF button, but nothing happened. *Okay. Give it a minute to warm up.*

She went to her bag and pulled out an oversized hoodie. She'd forgotten that she had wrapped lingerie inside of it. Black and purple lace undergarments tumbled onto the bed. They definitely wouldn't be getting used. Pulling the sweatshirt over her head, she grabbed the folded blanket at the foot of the bed and wrapped it around herself.

Seating herself in the middle of the mattress, she crossed her legs, tugged the blanket tight to her body, and pulled her phone out of her purse. It was still in airplane mode. Once she changed that, going from no Wi-Fi to guest Wi-Fi, emails and notifications poured in.

The first text made her laugh out loud.

Ms. Twain

Can you work this Saturday? We're short-staffed.

Tossing the phone, she fell back into the pillows, stared at the white popcorn ceiling. Ten days to herself at a lodge where the highlighted feature was getting lost in nature. Nature. The place with the bugs and bears and itchy plants.

Looking from side to side, she took in the room. Simple. Clean. Closet beside the door, dresser with an old television on it. *Please, Camping Gods, have Netflix.* The door to the bathroom was slightly ajar but she didn't have the energy to go check out the tub.

Starting to shiver, she pulled the comforter around her, snuggling into the surprisingly comfortable bed. Curling onto her side, burrowed like a hibernating bear, she waited for the tears to come. They'd likely freeze when they did and she'd be surrounded by icicles. Little Emmett-I'm-an-idiot icicles.

Ten days. She'd become one with nature, make a plan for moving forward, spend time doing what she wanted, maybe find a new hobby.

Everything would be okay. Presley hadn't been much older than Ollie when she realized people didn't make good choices just because you hoped they would. Or because you'd have chosen differently in their shoes. She'd grown up forcing herself to put a happy spin on things that disappointed her. Maybe Emmett was right about that part. In *Pride and Prejudice,* Lizzy Bennet said to her naive sister: *All the world are good and agreeable in your eyes.* Maybe it was time to take the rose-colored glasses off.

This trip was a chance to figure out what she really wanted, because she'd been plodding along to some imaginary finish line, obviously not paying attention to the signs. She'd thought she and Emmett were happy, that she was on the fast track to promotion—told herself at every turn that things would work out. When they didn't, she told herself they would next time. She thought of Ms. Twain asking if she wanted more responsibility even as she watched Presley take on more and more at the hotel. It'd be easy to blame others for not listening to her, but it could be she needed to start listening to what *they* were telling *her.*

She shut her eyes and let the images of how she had thought this week would go sift through her mind like a slideshow. Then she imagined a garbage can and envisioned herself dumping all of those images into it. She was a blank slate, an empty photo album. How she filled it was up to her. Whatever she chose, she'd be wiser. Stronger. A better version of herself. One who wouldn't have been caught off guard by Emmett's behavior because she would have seen it coming. *Look out, world, there's a new version of Presley Ayers coming your way. Get ready. This Presley camps.*

Four

This ought to be interesting, Beckett Keller thought as he watched the gorgeous, preoccupied woman head for her room. He'd left enough space between them that he didn't hear whatever his sister said to her, but he'd noticed Jilly's scrunched face. Something was up with the wary-eyed traveler. He winked at his niece, Ollie, then leaned down and asked what room he got.

"You're silly, Uncle Beck. You sleep in your own bed."

The kid meant the bed here at a cabin his brother, Grayson, kept for him. At the moment, he had more than one bed to choose from, since he hadn't given up his apartment in Smile. When Gray had asked if he'd help out with the lodge, Beckett jumped on board. He was at a crossroads in his own job at a sporting goods store in Smile, trying to decide if he wanted to accept a promotion that included relocating or pull a complete one-eighty and do his own thing. He'd taken all of his vacation time so he would have the next five weeks to figure out an answer.

He hadn't planned to stay on the island, but the entire place was a to-do list. As soon as they fixed one thing, another went. But they dealt with it. That's what family did. His brother had walked away from his divorce with a broken heart and the lodge. Gray was determined to get one of them back on track, and since he wanted nothing to do with putting himself out there again, the lodge was his focus.

Which meant Beck and Jilly were by his side doing their best to help him stop it from going under. Not an easy task, since it had been well on its way when the deed transferred hands. Beck tried to split his time almost evenly between the island and the mainland, but travel, short as it was, was wearing on him.

"Are we roasting marshmallows tonight?" Ollie bounced on her toes. Jilly shook her head.

He grinned. Bugging his kid sister had changed over the years in delivery but it still felt good. He held his fist out for Ollie. "You got it. You're my favorite date."

Ollie clapped, jumping up and down while Jilly called him a jerk with just the narrowing of her eyes.

"Why didn't you drop your things at the cabin?" Jilly asked, shutting the door now that all the new guests had arrived.

He shrugged the duffel farther onto his shoulder. He should have, but he'd been staring at the back of the woman ahead of him, certain she was going to trip over the rocky path. She looked like she might pass out. He'd seen seasick people before, more than his share. The woman clutched her bag like a lifeline and shook a little when she'd stepped onto dry land. Despite not being at her best—he assumed she wasn't always seasick—she had an elegance and grace that caught his attention like a fist to the gut.

Beckett had been too wrapped up in concern for her to drop off his things. "Wanted to see my sister and niece."

Jilly laughed. "Sure." The phone rang behind the front desk. She raced to answer it but didn't beat Ollie.

"Hello? This is Ollie. What can I help you with?"

Beckett's heart melted as he watched his sister gently remind his niece that only the adults answered the phone. Moving around the huge log front desk, he dropped his duffel and picked up Jilly's ever-present to-do list. No matter how quickly he returned to the lodge, there was always a ton of shit to be done. His personal to-do list was getting longer as a result, but the lodge's needs were more pressing.

Ollie grabbed her iPad and moved to the little table-and-chair set they'd put out for her. Grayson was so grateful for Jilly and Beck's help, he'd have built Ollie her own command station if she'd wanted it.

With parents who worked long hours, the three siblings had grown up raising each other. They'd always counted on each other. Which was why he hadn't confided in his siblings about the possible promotion. Could he call it that? Brian, who ran the sporting goods store on Smile, wanted to open a second location, thinking Beckett could run it. But it would mean moving to the mainland. The actual mainland, more than a few hours from his siblings and niece. They'd encourage him to do it, but the truth was, Beckett didn't know what he wanted. Keeping busy between the two places let him put off making the decision.

While Jilly booked reservations, he checked the tours she'd scheduled. They were operating at half capacity. At one time, this lodge and a few other islands around them had been more than bustling. Like most things, tourism could ebb and flow.

Gray had met Lana, his ex, almost twenty years earlier when her dad bought the lodge, then named something else, on a whim for his wife. Nothing like a little vacation property as a birthday gift for the woman he loved. A lot of the smaller islands were privately owned or developed into exclusive retreats for the wealthy.

From time to time, Lana and her family would come stay and she'd cruise over to Smile in a boat Daddy bought her, looking for fun. They'd all been teenagers, and Beckett and Grayson—Jilly usually had her head buried in a book—were used to teen tourists coming in and out of their lives. They'd both had their share of summer crushes and the kind of heartbreaks that came from falling fast and hard in the way that was uniquely dedicated to being young. Gray and Lana had shared more than a couple of summers making heart eyes at each other—a fact Beckett had loved to goad his brother about. But time, distance, and life had made her just another summer crush until Lana had come to Smile for a girls' weekend about six years ago. She and Grayson had reconnected. Fallen in love. Gotten married.

With Gray going to work for Lana's dad as a general manager for his chain of pharmacies in Chicago, he was too busy to visit much.

The lodge was mostly forgotten by all of them. Until Lana asked for a divorce and her father had hired the world's sharkiest lawyer to make sure Gray walked away with nothing but a run-down piece of property and a few memories.

Still. Grayson had remembered it fondly and in far better shape than it was when the divorce was finalized and they all came to take a look.

"Okay," Jilly said with a sigh as she hung up. "We need to get at least one cabin up and running. I told that guy I'd call him back, but really, I'm just stalling. We can't house a party of six right now without splitting them up." She looked at Beckett, who was still going over the chores.

Beckett tapped the clipboard against his leg, mentally picturing the layout and condition of their largest cabin. "When's it for?"

"He wanted middle of July. That's only three weeks away."

Beckett looked at the list again, grabbed a pen, made a few notes, then looked back at his sister. "See if they can swing first week of August. I'll move some stuff around and get cabin four ready."

Cabin four was the largest and the only one that could accommodate a party that size. They had four cabins in total, but Beckett and Gray used two of them, with Jilly and Ollie staying in the family area of the lodge. The lodge itself had ten rooms. He might be able to get one cabin ready, but more than that was beyond his scope of abilities in that time frame.

Ollie came over and opened a drawer between Beckett and Jill. She pulled out a dried fruit strip that looked gross to him. She definitely deserved marshmallows later.

"Beck, that's a lot. We need to get two of the lodge rooms painted, and there's three to furnish in total."

She was telling him things he already knew. Two of the lower rooms had water damage on the walls from years back. They'd had them re-drywalled but were saving money by doing the cosmetics themselves. There'd been no furniture in most of the rooms when Gray took over a little more than six months ago. Slowly and surely, one room at a time, they were getting there.

Jilly continued, her checklist in her head. "That puts us down three rooms in here. Lots of people want a bank of rooms, or at least side by side, which we can't offer yet. I feel stuck between trying to bring in more people and us not being ready to do that. I'm trying to learn about Facebook ads, because other businesses I've talked to said those were successful for them. But if that works, where will we put people?"

Her breath accelerated. He started to tell her it would be okay. They'd figure it out. They both knew these were platitudes, but generally, they were true. She carried on before he could say anything. "I feel like if we don't have the lodge up and running at max capacity, we'll never catch up. We need to be logical and sequential about this. Intentional. I say we do one thing, then move on to the next. This building first."

Ollie ripped her snack open. "We're bleeding money." She shook her head like a miniature adult.

Both of them looked down at her, Jillian with her mouth open and Beckett with a loud laugh.

The front door to the lodge swung open and, as Grayson strolled in looking exhausted but smiling, the husband and wife who'd just arrived came down from their second-floor room. Beckett worried the weight of Gray's divorce would be replaced with that of getting the lodge up and running. He'd missed having his brother close by and wanted to help make this work.

"Back to work, kid," Beckett said to Ollie. He grabbed the clipboard, nodded at his brother and left the people-ing to his siblings. "That's my cue to leave."

"Don't be so antisocial," Jilly said, her greeter smile easily gracing her lips as she turned to the couple. "How are you settling in? Can we get you anything?"

While his sister tended to the guests, he met Gray in the center of the large lobby. It was a gorgeous building, with stained-wood walls and thick, sturdy beams creating a vaulted ceiling. At night, when they lit the fire and turned down the lights, he could almost smell the history of the wood. Of course, there were usually too many things to do. By the time he got that moment of quiet or solitude to really breathe it in, he was ready to fall face down on his bed.

"Hey. How's things?" Gray asked. A few days' growth shadowed his jaw.

"Good." *Talk to him about the other store.* If he took it, the money would be good, but he'd be starting over, somewhere else. "Brian is good with me using my banked holidays to play out the rest of the summer." *And then he told me he wondered if I want to help him grow his business by managing a new store.* "It was nice to sleep in my own bed for a few nights." Not that he'd slept much, since decisions and ideas plagued his brain. He'd been toying with the idea of opening his own bike rental place on Smile. Most tourists came by ferry, some on their own boats. It would give an option other than walking through their quaint little town. He was surprised someone else hadn't beat him to the punch, but this was his shot to make his own way doing something he loved in the town he loved. But he'd worked at Brian's Sports since he was a teen and felt a loyalty to the man almost similar to the one he did to his family.

Beckett remembered renting bikes and touring one of the islands with his family one summer. He was about twelve and hadn't been stoked about the idea, but it turned out to be one of his favorite memories. Smile was the perfect place to offer something like that, and he could be the guy who did it. It would even tie in to the lodge, but he didn't want to stress Gray out with the thought of taking on more responsibility. Beckett had some savings; he'd priced things out for a start-up rental shop. But every time he thought to follow through, he got sidetracked with helping others.

"Tevin called." Grayson ran both hands through his dark brown hair. His brother was older by two years, but they shared a lot of the same physical traits: height, hair, eyes. They looked like their father, and Jill looked like their mom. "The cruiser needs a couple more parts. He won't get it back to us until next week." Tevin worked on the mainland and Smile as a mechanic and all-around handyman. He was also a friend of theirs, so if he could get it back sooner, he would.

"Mom and Dad are coming in July. Dad will be able to look after the boats and take care of some of the other maintenance."

"Okay. You heading to your cabin?"

"Yeah. I'll drop my stuff, then I want to take a look at cabin four. Jill has possible renters."

"We're not ready."

He shook his head, gave his brother a light shove. "Which is why I'm going to look at it. I need to fix a couple spots on the dock." He thought of the woman in room one. "And the pathway has some loose stones."

"Okay. You're good for the tour tomorrow?"

"I am."

Gray clapped Beckett on the shoulder and, knowing his sibling well, Beckett felt the gratitude in it. They were all tired. But it would pay off. They'd keep working together and all of them would get where they wanted to be. For him, right this minute, that was between the sheets right after something to eat and a cold beer. But he hadn't even reached the exit when the front desk phone rang again.

Five

Presley couldn't blink. She was positive her eyes had a thin sheet of ice coating them. Adding the sheet to the two blankets bundled around her did nothing to stop the shaking.

She padded to the door, shuffling beneath the weight of the down comforters, which she had thought would be warmer. She hoped whoever was knocking knew how to sweet-talk her thermostat, because she'd tried everything, including googling "how to turn off AC" with the make and model number of the controller.

When she pulled the door open, her stomach and heart lurched in sync. Like they were fist bumping at the sight of the good-looking guy from the trip over. No amount of seasickness could have blocked out the zip of energy she'd felt when their eyes connected on the boat. Or when his hands gripped her hips. His eyes made her think of dark chocolate, decadent and tempting. They were gorgeous. Intense. It was almost enough to warm up some of the chill. Almost.

"Hi," she said, breathily. Was that a puff of air?

"Hi."

Oh wow. Okay. This staring contest couldn't keep happening. She'd had hours to realize that Emmett was an ass. A completely selfish, narcissistic ass. But that didn't mean she could jump into some vacation fling. For one thing, that would require removing some blankets. Unless they were incredibly inventive. *It would warm you up.* She wasn't really into sex for staving off hypothermia though. Not that he was offering. Didn't matter. She didn't do flings. Did she? City Presley might not, but maybe Country Presley did. Maybe her brain was frozen.

She should probably try moving her mouth. Make sure it still worked. "Listen." What was she even going to say?

His dark brows bounced up. He was, in fact, listening. Closely. Like he cared about what she might say. How had she missed the fact that Emmett never looked at her that way.

In her job, the direct route was typically the best. "You are an extremely good-looking man, and I am positive I will regret not acting on this . . . heat between us. Trust me, I'm an icicle under all these blankets, so I could really use some heat." She leaned on the doorframe, her body heavy.

His gaze widened. He put a fist to his mouth, coughed, then lowered it. "Excuse me?"

She was muddling this all up. She was a modern woman. She could be up-front. If she couldn't, she wouldn't have even made assistant concierge. Besides, being part iceberg made her numb to embarrassment.

Gripping the bedding between her breasts, she looked him up and down before settling on those sexy eyes again.

"Maybe I'll feel differently in a day or two and we can have dinner or something, but it's been a bad day. A really bad day." And while he looked like he'd know exactly how to fix it, she was not letting go of the blankets.

He inhaled deeply, let it out. She watched the rise and fall of his Henley-covered chest. It was defined even through the shirt. Wow. Okay. Maybe she should pull herself together. The best way to get over someone was said to be get—

"I'm here to fix your thermostat. I'm Beckett Keller. My family owns the lodge."

Presley nearly choked on the air as she stepped back. It was looking like embarrassment might heat her up faster than anything else. And no, she was clearly not immune, because holy icicles, she could feel her face turning redder than Ronald McDonald's nose.

She couldn't force words out. She tried but nothing would come. Backing up, she pointed to the thermostat as she shuffled, hit the bed with her calves and then just plopped down on it.

He gave a tight smile and a quick nod, coming in and going to the wall where the digital thermostat was located.

Presley felt like she was back on the boat, being tossed around in the waves. Her stomach was revolting against her decision to speak out loud. She really had a gift for misreading situations.

Beckett worked for the lodge. His family owned it. He wasn't a guest like her. She'd just thrown herself at one of the owners. Or rather, informed him she wasn't going to throw herself at him. Yet. There was low, and then there was slither-on-the-ground, roll-in-the-dirt low. There was literally nothing else, short of the curtains, to burrow under.

She must have groaned louder than she thought.

Beckett turned sharply, looked at her. "You okay?"

Fan-freaking-tastic. She nodded, stared at the carpet, willing him to fix the thermostat and leave. *Fix it and leave. Fix it and leave.*

His dusty work boots padded into her view. She felt his gaze and wrestled with the desire to look into it.

"Your name is Presley?" His voice had a hint of kindness and a bucket full of salve.

Deep breath. Tipping her head back, she looked up, found him staring down. "Yes."

"You won't be able to stay here tonight. I don't know what's wrong with it, but it's more than I can fix."

She continued to stare at him, fixated on his lips. Not just because they were full and looked soft. They were telling her something she could understand. In this particular moment, everything felt like more than she could fix.

At this, he bent his knees, crouched in front of her. "Presley, I don't mean to pry, but are you okay? You seem like you're in shock."

Considering this, she flattened her lips and nodded. "That's a good word for it. 'Shock.' Or I'm just frozen." What he had said registered, and she sat up straighter. "Wait. Where will I go? Is there another room? Do I have to get back on the boat to get to a hotel?" She really didn't want to go back on that boat right now. Maybe in a couple of days. Or never.

The smile he gave her calmed the waves wanting to rise in her chest. "Can you give me two minutes? I'm going to sort that out right now."

Presley shrugged, gave him a wry smile. "I'm not going anywhere. My feet are frostbitten."

At this, he laughed. "I'd say you're not quite there yet. I promise to get you out of here before that happens."

When he left, leaving the door open, she realized that she trusted his promise more after only knowing him six minutes than she had Emmett's after eight months. She'd lived every day wondering what would tip them over the edge of "not together." After the first month, she'd felt off-balance with him. Like she'd needed to work to keep him. Like he was worth the work. Her parents always said their incredibly secure and happy foundation took effort, just like anything that was worth having.

In the back of her mind, she knew she'd let her absurd timeline and need to show she could balance a successful relationship and a career dictate her happiness. If she wanted to reach her work goals, marry, and have at least one child before thirty-five, it didn't leave a ton of time to start over. She sighed. *Foiled by my own determination.*

Beckett reappeared in the doorway with Jilly, the woman who'd greeted them. His sibling? He'd said they were his family. Maybe his wife? Sister-in-law? Captain Grayson was part of all of this.

"Hi, Presley," she said, her smile so genuine it felt like a hug. "I'm so sorry for the inconvenience. We're going to get you set up in a cabin. I'm also going to refund the first couple nights of your stay."

Presley's brain was a bit fuzzy. It didn't operate well in frigid temperatures. Jilly rubbed her arms as Presley remembered something. "I thought none of the cabins were available?"

"Oh, Beckett—"

Beckett stepped around her, cutting off her sentence. "—just realized there is one. It's not the Ritz, but the air and heat work."

She'd stayed at the Ritz in Chicago once. It was decadent. Jilly looked at Beckett but said nothing. He picked up Presley's bag. Jilly came to Presley's side. "Let's get you settled."

"I got her," Beckett said. "Go finish checking on dinner."

Jilly gave an encouraging smile. "There are snacks in the dining room. I can put something together for you and bring it down to the cabin. If you're up for it, dinner will be at seven, but if you'd prefer a quiet night, I can also bring your meal to you."

Nose scrunched, Presley searched her brain for a polite way to say she wasn't up to that much socialization at the moment.

"Jilly, I got her. Go."

Doing as her possibly-husband-or-brother-or-who-knew said, Jilly left.

Beckett picked up Presley's purse off the bed, then froze. Presley watched his jaw tighten as he stared at the mattress with only its fitted sheet. Well . . . not *only* that. Cold brain cells made her slow. She followed his gaze to the purple and black lace underwear and push-up bra. *Ahh.* Thank goodness she could count on embarrassment to further thaw her out.

Risking the chill, her hand shot out, grabbed the items and pulled them inside her blanket fortress.

He cleared his throat, then gestured for her to lead the way out the door. They stopped in the main room, a wide-open area used to welcome guests. The lodge was a strange kind of opulence. Usually, when she thought of that word, she pictured gilded ceilings, oversized artwork in gold frames, and marble-tiled entryways. She hadn't thought the term could be used for something that was also rugged and rustic. It was an amazing amalgamation of styles. The website photos didn't do it justice.

The high cathedral ceiling had to be at least twenty feet above them. Staircases ran up both sides of the large room, their design again merging rustic with elegant. A huge chandelier hung down over the registration desk, and to either side were hallways that Presley suspected led to the kitchen and dining areas. She couldn't recall all of the amenities, but she knew there was a hot tub. A bowl of fruit and a plate of assorted granola bars sat on the reception desk, easily accessible to guests. Presley wasn't so far out of it that she couldn't note and appreciate these little details. They mattered.

"You want to off-load those blankets? It's pretty warm out here," Beckett said. He stopped, setting her bag on one of two couches that faced the large stone fireplace. An oversized chair rested between them, and a coffee table in front displayed an array of magazines. Very inviting. They had something similar at the hotel.

"Presley?"

She looked at him. She liked the way her name sounded coming from Beckett. She'd always hated "Pres." What a dumb nickname. She could maybe support "honey" or some other term of endearment, but "Pres"? *Stupid Emmett.* Too lazy to even say her whole name.

Beckett stepped right in front of her so she had to tip her head back. When his hands came to her . . . well, where her shoulders probably were under the layers, she sucked in a breath. She wanted to step into him for a hug.

"I promise, it's not cold out here, okay?" His voice was gentle and firm at the same time.

She let the blankets slide off of her and found that he was right. When his thumb grazed her forearm, her synapses sparked, like an engine sizzling to life. In her head, she heard the crackle of flames. Judging by the look on his face, he didn't feel it, because his lips turned into a very deep frown.

"You really are freezing. I'm so sorry." His brows furrowed in concern.

"It's okay," she said, happy to feel the warmth emanating from his body.

"It's not. Come on."

They were quiet as she followed him back toward the dock. The scent in the air was different than she was used to. Fresh. Cleaner, with a hint of water and a variety of flower blooms. Before reaching it, they veered left to a little cottage set behind the one she'd seen when they arrived. It was tucked behind foliage, overgrown flower bushes, and a few trees. It was simple but charming; aging, weathered brick went halfway up the otherwise wood walls, stopping at the windows. Below the smaller window to the left of the porch, there was an empty planter box. It could use a coat of paint and some flowers, but it was cute all the same.

Lights were on inside, the glow of them shining through the bigger window to the right of the door. Beckett rushed up the stairs before her, opened the door, and then stepped back so she could go first.

It was . . . well, lived-in, for a place they hadn't planned to rent. It smelled like . . . dryer sheets. Beckett set her bags down on a small couch. She turned in a circle as he shut the door. It was an open-living-area floor plan, with a few doors leading to what she expected were the bedroom, bathroom, and a closet.

Beckett ran a hand through his hair. It stood up a little, making Presley smile. He'd seemed so confident and self-assured on the boat, all laid-back and casual. Not so much now. He caught her staring and gave her a strange look. *Uh-oh.* Maybe her smile was at the I'm-so-tired-I-resemble-a-creepy-stalker stage. She knew she had it in her.

He pointed. "Bedroom, bathroom, closet. There's a tub if you want to warm up. I just need to do a check of all the areas to make sure . . . nothing was left behind."

He walked toward the bedroom while Presley moved farther into the house. She heard him rustling around in the other room as she peeked out the front window, smiling at the view of the water. It really was pretty if she wasn't *on* it. Moving slowly around the room, she confirmed one of the doors led to a small bathroom with a tub-and-shower combo. It was basic but clean, with a small washer and dryer stacked in a corner. Walking back toward the couch, she noticed a blue bag by the bedroom door. One very much like she'd seen at his feet on the boat.

Realization dawned like another fist to the face. How many of those could she take today? He came out of the bedroom, no surprise, with a couple bags. Giving an uneven laugh, he said, "They left some stuff."

This man had been kinder and sweeter to her than the man she'd worked into her stupid timeline. Tears threatened, making her throat feel thick. "This is your place. This is your house."

He froze. "It's . . ." No other words followed.

Presley shook her head, went to her bags. "No. I'm so sorry. I absolutely cannot take your home. Listen, is there any way I can get to the mainland tonight? Or is there anywhere else to stay on the island?"

He shook his head, dropping his bags on the ground. "No. This entire island is the fishing lodge. We're only ten minutes from Smile. There are places to stay there. If you want me to, I'll take you back tonight."

Just the thought of the boat made her stomach roll.

Beckett laughed. "That look on your face suggests it's not your favorite idea. Please stay here, Presley. It's not a big deal. I can bunk with my brother or on Jilly's couch."

She shook her head, clasped her fingers together. One side of Beckett's lips tipped up.

"We'll get the AC fixed. This is temporary, saves you from being on the water and will make us very happy that we were able to find a workaround. We're just starting up. This is actually our first season, and we really don't want unhappy guests."

"Your whole family runs this place?" She was genuinely curious.

"It's my brother's." Something sparkled in his gaze, a hint of mischief that warmed Presley's skin. "If you leave, he'll worry about bad Yelp reviews or something. You'd be doing us a favor if you'd stay. And there's no cost. You wouldn't want Grayson to stress out over you leaving, would you? Think of the ripple effect that might have."

Her stomach pitched at the word "ripple" and his grin widened, like he knew the impact of that particular word. "What effect might that be?"

That grin turned almost playful—and boy did that up the hot-guy factor—as he walked closer. "If you leave, he'll take it personally. He'll be in a funk. That'll worry my sister and niece."

"Jilly and Ollie?"

He nodded. "Grayson is doing his best to make this place a success.

Mix-ups and screwups happen. It's our job to fix them so the guest has the best stay possible. Please, let me fix this. If I don't, my brother will be unbearable."

His predicament, however much he was overselling it, was one she was familiar with. Pleasing guests was her full-time job. Beckett let out a deep sigh, tucked his chin, and used those eyes on her.

"Do you have siblings, Presley?"

She shook her head. Short of Rylee, she often felt like she had no one. When she was little, she'd asked her parents if they would ever give her a brother or a sister, and they said no. Their lives were perfectly balanced, they said. Another child would throw things off-kilter.

Her lips quivered. She did her best to focus on the man staring at her intently. "Unbearable, huh?"

"You have no idea." Beckett's grin widened. "He'll make my life hell."

Her lips quirked. "That doesn't seem fair."

Beckett shook his head, his gaze pinning her to the spot. "It's not. I know you don't know him, but he's a good guy. We're really serious about making guests happy. Let me make you happy?"

Those words slipped over her heart and squeezed.

Beckett took her silence as a positive. "I know it's a bit messy, but it's warm and cozy."

She nodded slowly, looked around again. He stepped closer. "There's food in the fridge, and not just the well-balanced stuff Jilly makes Ollie eat." Bending a bit at the waist, he leaned closer still, sharing the woodsy, alluring scent of his cologne. "I have chips. And chocolate." The last word came out as a whisper.

She bit her lip, staring at him. "If I'm taking your place, I don't want any free nights."

He stood up straight, grinning like he'd won. "That's Jilly's area. I'm not the money guy."

She laughed, more charmed by him than his place, which felt welcoming and homey. "What guy are you?"

Beckett's expression turned serious. "The one who wants to see everything work out for everyone. Please, stay here."

She nodded, beyond touched by his words. "Thank you."

"No problem. I'm not sure what's going on in your life, Presley, but I promise you, we're going to make sure you have a fantastic vacation." He turned and grabbed his bags, hefting one on each shoulder.

When he started for the door, fear seized her. The lodge was one thing. There were other people somewhere in the place, maybe even room service of some sort. There was activity, noises to remind her she wasn't alone. In the city, she often opened her window at night so the sound of traffic could lull her to sleep. Here, something might crawl through that window. Were there bears out here? Other creatures? More rodent-related ones? She was way down at the far end of the property by the water. Away from everything else. Everyone else. If she screamed would anyone even hear her? *Cabin in the woods? Hell, no.* That was a freaking horror movie for a reason. "Beckett!" She didn't mean it to come out quite so shrill.

He started, turned to face her. "What is it?"

Let the humiliation just keep coming. As much as it pained her, it was better than the alternative, and she'd never see these people again. Who needed pride? *"I'm scared" sounds so childish.* Swallowing the lump in her throat, she did her best to push down the fear, which was probably irrational. "Do you think you could stay? For a while?" There. That wasn't so hard. He'd probably think she was hitting on him again, but she'd take that over watching him walk out the door. Lesser evils. This trip might be full of choosing between them.

Six

Beckett stood in his own doorway looking at a woman who belonged on the cover of one of those fancy fashion magazines. Even with the day she'd clearly had—maybe she lost her job, split up with someone, lost a bet, who knew—she was beautiful. Her dark hair was coming loose in several areas, little wisps dancing across her pale skin. Her eyes were a soft, whimsical shade of blue, and a man could drown in them as easily as Lake Michigan.

He could feel the nerves and anxiety pumping off of her very being. She'd asked him to stay but he had a feeling that what she really meant was that she didn't want him to go. There was a distinction between the two, and he was positive a woman like this would be careful to word the request properly.

Despite this hunch, he got the sense that she wasn't the type to ask for help often. There was an inner steel that shone through in her resolve to say what she needed. That hint of vulnerability called to him nearly as much as her attempt at covering it up.

He dropped his bags, surprised by how much he wanted to comfort her; put her at ease. "I've got some time." He stared at her, went with his gut. "It's safe here, Presley. I promise you." He didn't know why he was so sure his word would mean something to this woman.

She nodded, her gaze darting around, not settling on him. "I know. I'm sure it is." Her gaze came back to his, locking him in. "But."

He didn't pride himself on being able to read people. That was another one of Jilly's things. With Presley, though, something spoke to him. Made him understand all the things she didn't say with that final syllable.

Huffing out a sharp breath, he went into his standard mode of operation. He wasn't the money guy or the people person. He was the problem solver. "I'm starving. It's been a long day and I haven't had a chance to eat. You like steak?"

Her expression softened, relaxed, and any fool—and he knew he was one for staying, getting sucked in—could see the gratitude shining there. She nodded.

Going to the fridge, he pulled out the steak he'd remembered to ask Jill to thaw out for him. He noticed the vegetables, fruit, condiments. His sister had stocked his fridge. If Beckett was the fixer in the family, Jilly was the caregiver. He grabbed a beer, held it up to Presley.

She nodded, walking closer. "Thank you."

"You know how to make a salad?" Why did his words feel garbled in his mouth?

A small smile, a little hint of magic, graced her lips. "I didn't go to school for it, but I'm familiar with the process."

Damn. Gorgeous, alluring, and funny? He should head to Grayson's or Jillian's. The last thing he needed was to get caught up in a guest. Not only didn't he have any time in his schedule, he wasn't a big fan of goodbyes or watching people leave. His significant other was sleep, and they rarely saw each other lately.

"Good. Bowls are in there. Grab the lettuce and veggies you like. There's a cutting board in the drawer." He pointed to the various spots. If he was shaking off the kind of day that she seemed to be, he'd want to keep busy.

Without a word, Presley set her beer down, grabbed what she needed, and got to work.

He dug into a drawer for the lighter. "If not salad making, did you go to school for something else?"

She turned her head, smiled at him. It almost hit her eyes, and he figured when it got all the way there, it was going to stop him in his tracks.

"Business and hotel management."

If Beckett were the kind of guy who believed the universe listened, he'd think she had landed in their laps for this very reason.

"Do you like it?"

His hand finally closed around the lighter as her gaze locked on his. She looked so thoughtful, it made him want to know more.

"Most of the time. How about you? Is the fishing lodge your dream job?"

He couldn't stop the bark of laughter. "Not particularly, no. But I do like many aspects of it. I'll go start the grill."

She said nothing as he walked out to the back deck. The air was cooling off, the sun sinking further into the lake. He loved the peacefulness of it. They'd grown up in Smile. It wasn't exactly a bustling city. Hell, it was barely a city. But he'd never known the quiet that existed here on this island. Once he started the grill, he walked to the edge of the deck, leaned on the railing, and called Jill to tell her he was sticking around for a bit.

"How long is 'a bit'? You know you can't sleep with her, right? She's a guest. We're not that kind of full-service resort." Jilly's tone was a blend of humor and one hundred percent serious.

Beckett whipped around like somehow Presley could hear his sister's words through the phone. He ducked his head. "What the hell, Jilly? I'm just trying to help her settle in. I think she didn't want to be alone."

"But she doesn't know you."

He sighed. No. She didn't. But that hadn't stopped her from asking or him from willingly agreeing. "Listen, she asked me to stay. She seems vulnerable. I'm going to make her some food and get her settled. If she feels more comfortable after dinner, I'll come sleep on your couch."

"Okay. Ollie is already on her way down there. You can send her back."

Beckett looked out at the water again, letting it soothe him. It was beautiful here. Every cabin needed work, the boats were money pits, some of the guests were needy and demanding, but damn, this place was perfect. Or it could be, if it wasn't falling apart. He shook his head. They'd make it work.

"Beck?"

"We'll see," he said into the phone.

"Sorry to throw all this at you."

"Not your fault. Call Tevin and see if he knows someone for the AC. I thought it was a good thing each of the rooms had their own controls. Might end up being a pain."

"Already called him. And he got the part for the boat early, so it'll be back day after tomorrow."

"I'll text you later."

They hung up. Beckett scraped the grill, his stomach growling loudly. He turned on his row of twinkle lights—Ollie's special touch. It made him smile when the railing of his small porch lit up. In the yard, there was a small firepit with chairs around it. When the guests were all tucked in, the four of them would sit around the fire and just hang out. Soon, his parents would be here and would join them at the fire.

They should be renting this cabin out, but they weren't exactly bogged down with reservations. Which was both good and bad. They needed reservations to make money and they needed money to make repairs, but they couldn't fully accommodate guests while they still had those needs. If there were more than two things, was it still a catch-22?

The lodge had ten rooms between two floors. Including Presley's room, they had four booked, three out of commission, and three just about ready for guests. Grayson and Beckett could double up in one cabin as soon as they got some work done on the two they were in. They'd thought bunking in one each would allow for them to do some repairs and updates after the day ended. But instead, by the time they were ready to call it a day, they were exhausted.

Fully running and at max capacity, they'd turn a profit. They just needed to get there.

Feeling a wave of excessive fatigue, he let himself back into the cabin. He froze when he saw the sight before him.

"I told Uncle Gray I want to plant a garden. We should be able to grow some of our own food," Ollie, who stood on a stool he kept for her, said as she washed lettuce.

"I've never grown my own anything. I can't even keep houseplants alive," Presley said, chopping peppers.

"Mom says you have to baby them. She babies everything. Especially me."

Even though Beckett was looking at her profile, he could feel the fullness of Ollie's smile. Presley had a soft look in her eyes, like she was enchanted by his niece. It made his heart shift in his chest.

"Hey," he said, announcing himself before he shut the door.

"Uncle Beckett, you stole one of the guests," Ollie said, shaking the lettuce and getting water everywhere.

Presley flinched, and he started toward them, but then she laughed and he stopped in his tracks, because holy hell, could a woman's laugh curl inside a heart and make it beat faster?

She tipped her head back with her laugh. "You're giving me a lettuce-water shower."

Ollie stopped, giggled, and looked at Presley. "Sorry."

Presley shook her head. "It's okay. Why don't you grab some paper towels and we'll dry it?" She looked at Beckett. "We couldn't find a salad spinner."

He frowned. "A what?"

Ollie shook her head. "To dry the lettuce, Uncle Beck. Mom says you still need to be domesticated."

Heat rushed to his cheeks. "I'll be sure to thank her," he said as he watched Presley bite her bottom lip. He arched his brow at her, a dare to laugh. Her lips quivered but she held strong. Little sparks flickered in his stomach, interest he didn't need and hadn't felt in a long time stirring.

"I'm going to grab the steaks. You staying for dinner, Ollie?"

"I'm just here for the marshmallows. I already ate. Chef made me mac and cheese."

"Chef likes you," Beckett said, grabbing the steaks, a plate, and a fork.

"He let me help make it."

He smiled at his niece. Chef Shane, like most other people, was charmed by her outgoing, mini-adult personality. The chef was an older man who'd been cooking for the lodge for close to fifteen years. When they'd taken over, it was actually the one part of the business running smoothly. Though they had a small room for him off the kitchen, his husband traveled back and forth each day to drop him off and pick him up. The men had each other but not much in the way of other family, so they tended to treat all of the Kellers like their own kids.

Or grandkids. "You'll be running this place before long." Looking at Presley, ignoring the little clutch in his chest, he asked, "You're okay?"

She nodded. "I am. Thank you."

"You're welcome."

He realized, even though he'd wanted nothing more than the night to himself, that he meant it.

❧

They ate around the tiny table that had come with the cabin. Ollie begged to stand even though he told her she could have his seat. She nibbled on small bites of steak even as she chatted nonstop about the guests, the grounds, finishing first grade, her mom and her uncles.

When she started a story about how Beckett almost fell into the lake last week, he interrupted her. "You should ask Presley something about herself, kid."

Ollie stood straighter, her face a mask of concentration like she was trying to come up with the best question possible.

"Tell us about yourself, Presley."

Presley smiled and started to talk. Ollie interrupted with a barrage of questions. "Are you married? Do you have kids? Do you like to fish? How old are you? Mr. Dayton is sixty-seven."

Beckett ground his teeth together to avoid letting out a sigh. Bernard—Bernie—Dayton, a guest who'd been with them for about four days now, was about the only person Beckett knew who could out-talk his niece.

"Is he someone special?" Presley asked as she cut a tiny piece of steak.

Ollie shook her head. "Nope. He's just a guest, but mom said all guests are special. But he likes to ask a lot of questions."

That was an understatement. The old guy was likable, funny even, but he liked to talk and ask questions, and when Beckett was fixing things, he enjoyed pointing out how to make other improvements. He'd booked a room through the middle of July, so they were trying to make his stay worthwhile and enjoyable. He didn't seem to mind that other guests weren't frequent. "Like someone else I know. You didn't give her a chance to answer, Ollie."

Ollie ducked her head. "Sorry."

Presley leaned over, squeezed Ollie's arm. "Don't apologize. You're delightful. Let's see, what did you ask? I'm not married, no kids, no siblings either. I have a best friend who has probably texted me a hundred times today. I don't like to fish. At least I don't think I do. To be honest, I never have. I'm thirty-one."

"Uncle Beck is the big three-oh."

Presley's laugh got him again, making his chest feel too tight. He liked the way she looked smiling at his niece, talking about herself, and sharing a meal with them. Usually he avoided guests because he ran out of things to say, but with her, he didn't feel the need to fill the empty space with words.

"You're older than him," Ollie noted.

Before Beckett could mention something about manners, Presley nodded her head, met his gaze with a smile and then looked back to Ollie. "I guess I am. How about you? Any husbands, girlfriends, boyfriends, pets?"

Ollie giggled. Beckett wasn't sure he'd ever had a dinner that was in turn nerve-racking and completely enjoyable at the same time.

"None. But I'm trying to convince Uncle Grayson we should get a goat. It would help with the lawn."

"You're right. But it might eat your garden," Presley said, stabbing some lettuce with her fork.

She didn't seem to have much of an appetite. Beckett was nearly finished with his dinner and still hungry.

"Your steak okay?"

Her smile was tired. "Yes. Thank you. I guess I'm not that hungry."

"You have to eat something, because you can only have marshmallows if you eat all your dinner."

"That rule doesn't apply to adults, kiddo," Beckett said.

Ollie frowned dramatically. "I can't wait to be an adult."

Presley's quiet smile widened, but her gaze was sad. "Don't wish it away, sweetie. It's not as great as it seems."

She looked down at her food. Beckett felt a surprising urge to find the guy—because it had to be a guy; or it could be a woman, but definitely a romantic relationship—who'd made her feel this way and have a little chat. Other than his family, he didn't often feel protective of people. There was something about Presley he worried he wouldn't forget after her visit.

A knock at the door surprised them all. Jilly entered, poking her head in. "Anyone seen a red-headed brat about this high?" She let her hand hover near her knees.

"Mom," Ollie said, drawing the word out. "I'm taller than that."

Jilly came all the way in, carrying a large brown paper bag. "Maybe a little. Did you invite yourself to dinner, Peanut?"

"She helped make it," Presley said.

"I did, Mom. I'm earning my keep."

Jilly laughed with the others but also rolled her eyes. "You have got to stop quoting Gramps, honey."

Gramps wasn't actually Ollie's granddad. He was the mayor of

Smile and spent most of his days wandering the town, checking in with store owners and shopkeepers. He was writing a book about the history of Smile and could talk about it for days. Gray and Beckett joked that they should put Gramps and Bernie in a room together and see who ran out of things to say first. He was a good man, helpful and reliable, but the post of mayor had become an almost figurehead position. With residents eager to pull in new and return tourists, there'd been talk of replacing him, but no one had the heart.

She came in further, removed her shoes. "How are you doing, Presley?"

"I'm good, thank you. I feel bad about taking over Beckett's space."

Jill waved her free hand dismissively. "He doesn't need much. Don't worry about that. I'm just going to make sure you're all stocked up on toiletries. Beck, you did the bed, right?"

"I did. I don't think we need anything in there." Beckett gestured toward the bathroom with a thumb over the shoulder.

He pushed his chair back from the table, scraping it on the hardwood floor. "I can check."

"Sit. Eat. Entertain. I'll switch out the pillows. Come help me, Ollie."

"Yes, Mom." Ollie followed Jilly.

Presley stabbed her fork into some lettuce but didn't lift it. He should go check on cabin four, see what needed to be done first. No doubt Bernie and Ollie would offer to help. He had other things to do tonight and he really wanted to get some sleep, but he didn't want to go. He didn't want to leave Presley here, looking sad and seeming lonely.

She stood, surprising him out of his own thoughts. "Thank you for dinner. For sharing your space, your time, and your family with me."

She picked up her plate and took his, but didn't move from the table. She stood there, looking at him like she didn't quite understand.

"You're welcome. It's nothing, really."

Her smile was sad. "Sometimes what people think is nothing can be everything to someone else."

Those words echoed in his ears. *Everything to someone else.* If she'd been that to anyone, what kind of idiot would let her go? He didn't even know her and he could tell she was special. Seeing the way she interacted with Ollie and the way she held her head up despite obviously having been knocked down said a lot about her character.

Beckett had more questions than answers. Fortunately, before he could really tangle himself up in this woman's problems, his niece came bounding out of his bedroom announcing that marshmallows could wait no longer.

Seven

Presley was low-key mortified by her neediness but convinced she did an excellent job hiding this on the outside. She had a practiced smile and manner that came from years of having a job focused on pleasing people and attending to their every whim no matter how many times those whims changed.

She didn't have an issue being alone. But alone in her apartment building was a way different vibe than alone in a creepy cabin. Okay, fine: it wasn't creepy, but it was still removed from everything else. She'd give in to her weaknesses tonight, but tomorrow started Operation Suck It, Emmett. She was going to throw herself into this trip and do every single thing offered on the lodge's website. She might not like the outdoors or hiking, but this family, these people, were amazing, and she had no doubt they'd do whatever they could to ensure a great vacation.

"You up for roasted marshmallows?" Beckett asked. He held up a bag of huge ones.

"Actually, if you don't mind, I'd love to take a shower, put on my warmest clothes, and crawl into bed."

She wasn't imagining the heat that flashed in his gaze when she said "crawl into bed." Even though she was in no state to act on it, nor did she think he'd take advantage, it soothed her wounded pride to recognize and acknowledge it. It bothered her to realize just how long it had been since she'd felt wanted. She'd allowed that to happen by looking at a bigger picture and not seeing what was right in front of her.

"Of course. Yes. Absolutely."

They both stood there for a moment, and she wondered what he saw when he looked at her.

"But you're staying, right?"

His smile was soft, genuine. "For sure. I promised marshmallows."

Just then, Ollie came bounding out of the bathroom with a smile. "Marshmallows!"

Jilly laughed. "Awesome. She really needs the sugar."

Ollie grabbed the bag from his hand and zipped out the back door.

Jilly stood near them. "You have everything you need. Fresh towels, toiletries."

Presley did her best to make her smile as genuine as Beckett's. "Thank you. I appreciate you both."

"We appreciate your flexibility. A good night's rest will make things look better in the morning. That's what our mom says, anyway," Jilly said, then added, "I'm going to go check on Ollie." She left them alone, sending her brother a look that Presley couldn't interpret.

He tucked his hands in his pockets. "Listen, my couch is just as good as Gray's. Would it make you more or less comfortable if I slept on it?"

She could kiss him. And not just because he was good-looking and sweet. She didn't want to socialize, but she didn't want to be alone here either. Somehow, he read her better than her ex. What had she been thinking? Clearly, Island Presley was much more aware of Emmett's true self. It was like breaking up with him had pulled the cloak off her own skewed vision of him.

"I want to say I'm fine. Usually, I have no issue being alone, and I know you don't know me, but you've already been so kind, so I hope it won't make you feel weird if I take you up on the offer of you staying. Sleeping on the couch. Or I could take the couch." She didn't care. She just wanted to put today in the past.

Beckett pulled his hands from his jean pockets, shaking his head as he stepped closer. "Absolutely not. I've got no problem staying, especially if it makes you feel better. But I'll take the couch."

She could only nod. She'd felt more like crying today than all the days of the last year combined.

"If there's anything you need, anything I, or we, can do, please ask."

He looked so heartfelt, the dam nearly broke. Breathing deeply, she did her best to keep her emotions in check so she didn't embarrass herself further.

"Presley?" He bent his knees, locking his eyes on her in a way that made her feel like he could see her.

She raised her brows, her words caught in her throat.

"Are you okay?"

She bit her lip.

He put a hand on her shoulder and she closed her eyes, absorbed the warmth of the caring, friendly touch.

She opened her eyes to look at him. "Just a breakup. Nothing major. I'll be okay, and I promise you won't have to babysit me the entire time."

He hadn't moved his hand, and Presley really didn't want him to. Little whispers, like static electricity, moved outward from where he touched her. "That guy?" he whispered, holding her gaze and, sadly, dropping his hand. "He's an idiot."

She laughed. "I could be the idiot."

He shook his head. "Nope. You're a good person."

Tilting her head to the side, she studied him. Funny; she had thought the same about Emmett. Maybe her radar was faulty. "How do you know?"

He smiled, stepped back. "You said 'thank you' even though I think I insulted you with the paper bag."

Presley's chest felt like an overblown balloon was popped with his words. The pressure eased out of her rib cage and shoulders and nearly made those tears fall. She blinked rapidly.

Beckett pointed at her. "I'm going to teach you to fish."

"I don't really eat fish."

His grin was quick. "You don't need to eat it. You can toss it back."

Presley stepped back so she wasn't tempted to curl back into him. "What's the point of that?"

"What's the point of window-shopping?"

"You've got me there." This man was way too easy to talk to.

"Uncle Beck, Mom says we can't stay late," Ollie called through the door they'd left open.

Presley smiled. "You have a wonderful family."

He nodded. "They're pretty great. I should go help."

She didn't want to keep him. She'd already intruded enough. "Thanks again."

"My pleasure, Presley. Sleep well."

She watched him walk away and wondered how on the worst day of her life, she'd landed somewhere she'd never choose to go on her own and it had ended up being exactly what she needed. *Not what. Who.* That was even more surprising.

❧

Presley crawled into Beckett's bed and tried not to think too much about the fact that it was Beckett's bed. With her phone, her iPad, and her e-reader beside her, she snuggled into the pillows. Even with the bedding freshly laundered, she could smell the scent of him—woodsy and fresh—around her. His room was bare basics: the bed, dresser, a small desk, and a closet. No pictures on the walls, a few books stacked on the nightstand on the other side of the bed. She looked at them, appreciating his reading tastes. She enjoyed a couple of the same authors—Harlan Coben and Sandra Brown. She didn't read a lot of nonfiction, but the copy of *How to Be a Grill Master* made her smile.

The shower had worked miracles. She was clean, warm, and a little bit closer to being herself again. Her hair was drying on top of her head as she faced reality and picked up her phone, swiped it open. She'd tucked it away when keeping her fingertips warm had taken precedence over feeling connected.

Texts, app notifications, and emails waited, but she went directly to the one that mattered most. Rylee had left over fifty messages. Everything from GIFs and jokes to threats about what she would do if Presley didn't make contact immediately.

There was absolutely no point putting it off. She pressed Rylee's number and waited for her to answer.

"Where the hell have you been? I was fifteen minutes from booking my own flight to find you," her bestie said instead of hello.

At this, the vehemence, worry, and love in her friend's voice, Presley's tears broke free. It surprised her to realize most of them fell out of feeling stupid and naive. As she related the entire story to her friend, it finally hit home that a person could see the good in something as long as they didn't blind themself to reality.

"I'm going to wedgie him," Rylee said when Presley finally finished.

Laughter escaped, sharp and unexpectedly. "Stop."

"I'll pay someone to do it."

God, she loved her friend. "Someone big and scary?"

"Yes. I'll google options. We don't use the wedgie as payback nearly enough these days. It was a classic for a reason. What an ass. I didn't like him, but I still had some hopes for him."

"You didn't like him at all?" Presley wondered why she'd ignored that, but, even as she asked, she knew the answer.

"All I want is for you to be happy, to have the kind of relationship you deserve. He wasn't going to give it to you because he was too worried about himself. Do you need me to come there?"

Presley sat up so quick, her e-reader tumbled off her lap. Fortunately, it was still on the bed. "No! Of course not." She would *not* put anyone else out.

"What do you mean 'of course not'? I'm here if you need me."

"I know. I appreciate the offer more than you know, but I'll be fine." She was already better than she'd expected to be. She didn't need to disrupt any more lives because of her rose-colored glasses.

"Okay. If you change your mind, I'm there."

She thought of Beckett, Jilly, and Ollie. "Thank you. I'm going to learn to fish. And hike. I'm going to try everything and make the absolute most of each day. Then, I'm going to lie around and read, paint my nails, and swim in the cove. I'm going to ignore all of my work texts and just relax."

"She's seriously texting you?"

"Repeatedly. Like we didn't have a conversation where I told her I was out of town."

"You need another job."

"I can't deal with that today."

"No. Of course. I love you, Presley. You're the best person I know."

"Thanks. Back at you."

They hung up and Presley tried to get into the romance she was reading, but her mind kept wandering to all the signs she'd overlooked. Her parents had raised her to be independent mostly because they wanted their independence. She thought of calling them now. If they weren't at work, they were together, so she'd reach both of them if she reached out. But her mom would tell her it clearly wasn't meant to be and problems didn't get solved by moping about them. Her dad would make agreeing noises regardless of whether there was anything to agree with.

"You're fine. You're always fine. This is just a small detour." She looked around the room again.

Scooting down in the bed, she put her book aside. She turned the lamp off and lay in the darkness. Little stars twinkled on Beckett's ceiling, and for some reason, it delighted her. Had he put them there? It was funny to think he went to sleep every night looking up at these. They weren't real, but she made a wish anyway.

It would have surprised her to know she went to sleep with a smile on her face.

Eight

Her internal clock woke her even before the sun peeked through the slats in the blinds. She loved mornings, the start of a new day. Today, especially. Today was the start of a new road. One she hadn't traveled before. A new Presley Ayers.

Getting out of bed, she pulled on a pair of yoga pants, brushed her hair up into a high ponytail, threw on a cute T-shirt she'd found at L.L.Bean, and slipped on some socks. The cabin was definitely warmer than her first room, but it still had that "should I get out of bed?" cold that greeted every morning.

Taking her phone off its charger, she opened the blinds quietly and looked out at the lake, glistening like it'd been covered in pixie dust. She took a picture, added a couple of filters, posted to Insta. TikTok was the popular kid in socials these days but she stayed loyal to her Instagram fans because that was where she started.

Her followers had grown slowly and organically. When a local celebrity influencer followed her and shared one of Presley's posts in her story, she'd gained several thousand followers. She liked TikTok, utilized it, but she liked the not-having-to-perform aspect of Instagram.

Slipping out of the room, Presley stopped when she saw Beckett's large body sprawled out on the couch. A blanket was draped partially across him, but most of it pooled on the floor where one of his sock-covered feet rested. The other was up on the arm of the couch. He still wore the Henley from the night before, but he'd changed into sweatpants or pajama bottoms. She couldn't quite tell which.

Her fingers twitched at her side. He had the kind of hair that begged for a woman to run her hands through it. *Not your hands. Not you.* She padded lightly past the couch and into his kitchen. As quietly as possible, she set about making her charming and sexy host a thank-you breakfast.

The tension in her shoulders eased when she accidentally banged the pan against the stove and he didn't wake up. She found vanilla, her secret ingredient, in his cupboard and wondered if Jilly put it there. Did he like to cook? God, she could just imagine him baking cookies with Ollie. He was so good with her.

By the time the French toast was sizzling on the stove, she'd loosened up enough that she wasn't thinking about the gorgeous man sleeping on the couch. Instead, she was thinking about all of the things she was going to embrace moving forward.

Grabbing her phone from the counter, she angled herself for a perfect selfie with a pretty plate of the powdered-sugar-covered, golden-brown bread. Extending her arm as far as she could, she used the point-five option. She'd make a TikTok later in the day, but right now, she didn't feel like talking. Right now, she just wanted to capture the moment.

She tagged the airline in the photo when she shared it to her story, thanking them. Her caption read, "On my own again. Woke up in paradise." Smiling, she tagged the lodge and added a couple of hashtags, including #GetLost.

A sound spun her around, and she nearly squealed and dropped her phone when she realized Beckett was standing. She saved the phone, but the top piece of toast went flying, leaving a powdered-sugar trail in its wake.

She couldn't look away from him staring at her. His gaze was bleary and he looked a little confused. His hair was mussed, one hand shoved in the locks. He blinked several times and everything inside her clenched. She pulled in a deep, slow breath. He was sexy as hell in the morning. She hadn't thought the bulky, outdoorsy type was her jam, but wow.

"Coffee?" That one word was rough.

Putting her phone and the plate of food down, she quickly grabbed the piece of bread from the floor and tossed that one in the trash.

Grabbing a cup for the coffee, she poured some as he padded, not so lightly, over to the table and sank into a chair. "Cream?"

"Black."

She bit her lip to keep from grinning as she set the coffee in front of him. His brows furrowed as he stared at the cup, then up at her. She grinned. Why hide the smile? He was gorgeous and adorable.

"Did my bed suck?"

She raised her brows, unsure where he was going with this. "No. Why?"

"Then why aren't you still in it? It's six A.M."

She laughed, delighted by his lack of affection for the morning. "I was excited to start my day. I made you breakfast."

"Flying French toast?"

She laughed, then remembered the other ones on the stove. "Oh, shoot." She hurried back to flip them. A little dark, but not charred. Turning the burner down, she went to the fridge. She'd seen some fresh berries. Grabbing them, she ran them under water.

"Why are you whistling? Why are you happy in the morning?"

Presley hadn't realized she was making any sounds. She looked back over her shoulder, smiling at him. "Why wouldn't I be? I had a great sleep and woke up to a happy and cordial host." She left out the word "sexy," but she thought it.

He gave a rough laugh, sipped his coffee. "Sorry. Mornings aren't my thing. That smells delicious."

She dried the berries and grabbed plates and some jam, since he didn't seem to have syrup. Turning the stove off, she plated the rest of the French toast with berries on the side.

Presley set her own coffee on the table before bringing over the plates.

He jolted a bit, like he was surprised to see food materialize in front of him. "You shouldn't be making me breakfast. We provide breakfast and food at the lodge."

She hesitated before sitting. "Is it okay that I used your groceries instead?"

His gaze woke up. "Of course." He gestured to her seat. "Please, sit down. This looks and smells incredible. I'm sorry. I'm not a real human before coffee."

"I disagree. You're fantastic, and I truly appreciate you letting me stay here last night. More than that, I'm grateful you stayed. I slept better for it."

His gaze warmed. "Happy to have you. You're an easy guest. My bathroom is cleaner than when you went in."

She laughed, cut her toast. "Sorry. Habit."

They ate in a surprisingly comfortable silence. She didn't feel the need to fill the quiet. Instead, she relished it. When he finished, before her, he pushed his plate forward and leaned back in his chair. "That was awesome. Thank you."

"My pleasure. It's the least I could do." Her phone pinged, once, twice, three times, so she reached over, switched it to silent.

"What are your plans for today?" he asked, getting up to refresh his coffee. He brought the pot over and topped hers up as well.

"Thank you," she said, thinking about what Ollie had said about him needing to be domesticated. He seemed just fine to her.

He set the pot back and joined her at the table as she finished up her breakfast. "So? Plans? How are you doing?"

He was so tentative when he asked, but she felt really good today. Emmett was an idiot. Presley's desire to make the best of a bad situation had gone too far this time.

"I'm good. I bought this trip for my boyfriend—ex-boyfriend—thinking it would show him I could support his hobbies and interests. He wanted to bring someone other than me."

"Someone else?"

She nodded, pushed her plate away. "Yes. Not a woman necessarily. Just someone 'less demanding and difficult to entertain.' Someone he could have more fun with."

"See? I was right. He's an ass." Beckett tapped his fingers on the table.

"I don't think you called him that."

His grin was wide awake now. "I did in my head. I love that you came without him."

She smiled. "Not only that, but I'm going to try new things, enjoy myself, and relax."

"You're in the right place for all of that. If you'd like to start with a hike, I've got to take a group up to one of the lower summits this morning. It's a breathtaking view. Definitely photograph worthy."

"Perfect. I'm going to go up to the main house to talk to Jilly. I really appreciate you letting me stay here last night. There's no need to comp the stay though."

"It's pretty standard." He shifted in his seat, averted his gaze.

"I'm a hotel concierge. I know it's standard for some things, but I'd say you upgraded me quite nicely to make up for the inconvenience."

She'd comped plenty of stays in her time at the hotel. They didn't do it for slight inconveniences. That was worth a free meal at the hotel restaurant. Besides, from what she'd seen of the lodge in person and what Gray had said, they needed the money.

He held both hands up. "That's Jilly's department, but be warned, she's stubborn and unlikely to be swayed. She's had ample practice standing her ground." He picked up his coffee again. "A concierge? That sounds like a cool job. I bet you're good at it."

Presley nodded. "I am." Even if she was underappreciated. Looked like there were more parallels between her professional and personal lives than she'd let herself admit.

Getting up, she started to take their plates, but Beckett stood as well. "Don't even think about it. You cooked and you're my guest."

"Uninvited guest."

Did he move a little closer, or was she just imagining it? Her breath hitched when he lowered his chin. "I'm sorry for your day yesterday, but I'm not sorry you're here. Without him."

An unfamiliar burst of energy . . . awareness danced through her entire body. She wanted to take a close-up picture of his eyes just so she could study the details. Memorize them.

"See you later?" Shit. Did she sound breathy? *Chill. You're totally chill.*

"Absolutely."

He held her gaze a moment longer then started the kitchen cleanup. Sexy, kind, great with kids, and he cleaned? So this was where the perfect men were kept. Good to know.

Hiking was a unique kind of hell. It looked all picturesque in people's lying, stupid Instagram photos, but her ass, calves, and feet were killing her. Dead. The skin on her feet, the little that was left, was being rubbed raw by her socks. They felt wet, and she wouldn't be surprised if it was with blood as well as sweat.

This shouldn't hurt so bad. One Black Friday, she and Rylee spent a solid twelve hours on their feet, racing from one sale to the next. More than once, she'd closed down bars dancing on three-inch heels. How was that not preparation for anything life threw at her? The only reason she was able to continue putting one foot in front of the other was pride.

Mel, the woman who'd been on the boat yesterday with her husband, Richard, kept stopping—because, yes, despite being at least ten years older, she was ahead of Presley—to make sure she was doing okay.

How were people supposed to talk and walk uphill at the same time? That should count as a city girl Olympic sport.

Her toe caught on an exposed root, but she managed to stop herself from falling flat. Though maybe if she fell, they'd leave her here, go on without her. *Save yourselves.* Beckett was at the front of the group, and though his voice traveled back to her as he told them about the area, the words weren't registering in Presley's brain. Something about the view. It was beautiful. She could acknowledge that without snarling. The trees, the sun, the view of the lake. *Blah, blah, blah.*

Smacking her arm, she looked for the bug that had landed on her. Sweat dripped in uncomfortable places. She couldn't even do some calm breathing because she was working too hard just to catch her breath. She smacked her arm again. What the hell kept landing on her?

How was this fun? Maybe it got more fun the more a person did it? Who would do this again? Because everyone else did, she took a few photos with her phone. She'd been getting notifications from her morning shot so she switched the settings, turning off the constant alerts. She was used to her photos getting attention, but today her friends and followers might be wondering if she'd been abducted from the much flatter streets of her city. Her socials, TikToks, reels, and posts tended to share her love of luxury at an affordable price. Hiking was free, but somehow, Presley had a feeling every bit of her body would be paying a hefty fee this time tomorrow.

She wouldn't be posting a selfie of this excursion. A few great lake shots, maybe. If she looked at her reflection she'd cringe or cry. When she worked out in any capacity, her cheeks resembled tomatoes. There was nothing dignified about this.

Beckett strolled over and sat on the log beside her without even checking for bugs. Presley kept standing even though her back ached. She didn't trust the wood not to have ants or some other insidious creature.

"You feeling okay?"

She smiled as widely as she could. "Definitely. This is amazing. Breathtaking. I can't believe I haven't done more of this. I have been missing out." Oh. Her lungs were going to suffer for offering up that many words at once. Was it normal for a person's heart to beat so hard? She pressed her hand to her chest. Way too much action happening in there. Did they have medical care here? Were any of them licensed in first aid? Did a person have to be licensed or certified? She frowned, wondering how good Smile's medical services were.

Beckett stood up, pulled his backpack off his shoulders, and dug through it. Pulling out a beach towel, he laid it on the log.

"Sit down before you fall down. I won't tell anyone you hate this."

She sank down beside him and groaned quietly. It felt like her body wept in relief, but it was probably just more sweat. "I'm hot and sticky."

He smirked, which would have made her blush, but with the incline, who could tell? Small mercies.

"Not much of a hiker, huh?"

"I think I wore the wrong shoes," she said, trying to find the part of her that saw the good. But that part of her did not like being sweaty.

Beckett looked down at her expensive (even with the sale she'd found) hiking shoes. "Please tell me you've worn them before."

She shook her head. Not exactly something she'd wear to work, shopping, or on a stroll through the park by her apartment. Strolling— another sweet spot.

He winced. "We'll wind it up after everyone has a snack."

Presley leaned closer. "Do not end this early because of me."

Beckett smiled at her, like they were old friends. "I'll take the blame. I actually have to work on one of the cabins today, so I'd like to get back."

"I can hack it." She sat up straighter. She wasn't a wimp. She was just out of her comfort zone.

"Did you get your selfie?" He grinned in a sweetly teasing way that reminded her he'd woken to her taking a picture of herself.

"No. I'm a mess." She started to put her hand up to her face but he stopped her.

"You're beautiful. Your cheeks are flushed like you're happy," he said, leaning in close enough to speed up her pulse. That was saying something, since her heart was already beating like a hopped-up humming bird. This close, she saw flecks of green in his dark gaze. "Even though you're secretly miserable."

She laughed, her lungs slowly beginning to function again. "It's not horrible, I guess. I think I just need less of an incline and some athletic clothing." Maybe more breaks.

He held out his hand. "Phone."

"Beckett."

He shook his head. "Come on. Give it up. You'll want evidence you did it."

Presley shook her head and dug her phone out of the side pocket of her pants. Beckett pressed the camera and held it up. In the view, she saw the sparkle in his gaze and the hint of one in her own. She *was* flushed, her cheeks a rosy pink, but he was right about it making her look happy.

"Okay if I'm in it with you?"

When she turned her head to answer, it brought their faces close. Really close. She heard the click but it didn't register. She was too busy trying to breathe while her heart flip-flopped.

Their gazes stayed locked and Presley felt her heartbeat in the base of her throat. His eyes were every bit as captivating as the view.

"Presley?" he whispered.

Right. Picture. "Absolutely. I'll tag you when I post it," she said, hoping her voice wasn't all breathy.

He laughed, turned toward the camera. "I'm not on social media. The last thing I need is to have more people to answer to."

Presley turned her head to face the camera, butterflies fluttering. She smiled, her gaze glued to his in the reflection of the screen.

When he pressed the button, the moment was captured. She wouldn't need the photo to remember it though. Beckett Keller was quickly etching himself into her life in ways she wouldn't soon forget.

"Aren't you two the cutest. I was so worried about you yesterday," Mel said, adjusting her wide-brimmed hat as she came over. Her dark skin showed a subtle sheen, but her clothes didn't look wet or uncomfortable. Her selfie would be gorgeous. It was clear from her smile down to her well-worn shoes that she'd done this before.

"I'm doing better today," Presley said.

"Looks like you are, too, son," another gentleman said.

Presley didn't know his name, but he'd chatted with Beckett, or *at* Beckett, for most of the hike.

He winked at Presley, then looked at Beckett. "Guess when you said there were no women here it's because you were keeping the good ones for yourself."

Beckett fumbled the phone, nearly dropping it before passing it back to Presley. "We should get back. Jilly and Ollie will have an afternoon snack and drinks waiting for all of you."

Guilt tugged at her chest. He was being so kind and she'd made him the focus of attention. She didn't have to be his best friend to know it wasn't a spot he'd enjoy, any more than she enjoyed hiking.

"What was your name again?" Presley asked the gentleman as she stood.

"Bernard Dayton. Call me Bernie. And you are?"

Presley remembered Beckett mentioning him. "Presley Ayers. I'm a novice hiker. Would you mind if I walked down with you?"

He gallantly held out his bent arm. "It would be my pleasure, lovely lady."

The others closed up their packs and got ready for what she hoped would be a much easier walk. Beckett caught her gaze. He was smiling. He mouthed, "Thank you." At least now he could walk down without this man's constant ramblings.

She laughed to herself when she realized she hadn't completely altered her stance from yesterday. All relationships were a bit of give-and-take. He'd given her a place to land. She'd give him some peace and quiet.

Nine

Beckett was man enough, and honest enough with himself, to admit that, in no time at all, Presley Ayers was imprinting on him like a permanent tattoo. Definitely not one of those fake ones Ollie loved to put on, the ones that wash away in a few showers. It was rare that he found a connection with someone so easily. Usually, he engaged enough to be polite until he could find a way out of a conversation. End of story.

He did his best to keep from turning around to check on her. She hadn't broken in her damn shoes, so she was definitely going to be sore. She did *not* like hiking. Chuckling to himself, Beckett made sure to point out the other trails so people could head out on their own. Six of the eight guests had joined in. The other two guys staying here had come for the fishing only.

He'd talked to Grayson this morning, and they were meeting at cabin four before dinner to take a look at how to best fix it up. Two of the cabins needed only minor repairs and probably could have housed visitors, but they'd all worried about being able to see to their guests' needs if they spread them too far apart. Plus, he and Gray needed somewhere to sleep. Beckett had woken to a detailed email regarding costs for bikes should he choose to go that route. His savings would help, but he'd applied for a small business loan. Next time he was in Smile, he needed to swing by the bank and chat with the manager. But it was hard to get information without people sharing his business. Smile was big enough that you didn't know everyone but small enough that word traveled fast. He also needed to think about location.

He needed to chat with Gramps about one of the lots the mayor owned just up from the water. Or he could consider a brick-and-mortar establishment rather than a kiosk/open-air type deal. A few of the shops along Smile's water's edge had been empty since he was a kid. But he needed to do a walk-through, see what needed updating, think about accessibility. He needed to figure out what he actually wanted so he could talk to his siblings. Because the idea of running his own sporting goods store also held its own appeal. Especially since Brian had offered him a buy-in option. It was just the distance. Did he want to uproot his life?

One of the guys, Bo, came up beside him, carrying a big-ass stick. He'd arrived yesterday with a friend for a three-night stay.

"You the one taking us fishing tomorrow?"

"I am. Gray, my brother who picked us up yesterday, prefers being on land."

Bo laughed. "He owns the place, right?"

Beckett nodded.

"The guy who owns a fishing lodge prefers not to fish?"

Smiling at his walking partner, he clarified. "He loves fishing. Just prefers to do it from the shore." Which was fine with Beckett because he loved taking people out on the water, though he'd prefer doing it at dusk rather than dawn. He also loved hiking and didn't mind leading the hikes. He'd briefly thought of mentioning to Gray that they could do some overnight tent trips to the summit, but he didn't want to put more on his brother's plate.

The walk down didn't take as long as the trip up. He stopped in front of the lodge, waving at Ollie, who was sitting between Grayson's legs on the mower, pretending to drive. They really needed to hire some help, but they were trying to do as much as they could on their own for now. He hoped that once their dad showed up, he'd have some ideas. After all, his parents had raised three kids on minimum-wage jobs and given them a good life. There had to be a life hack in this somewhere. A licensed mechanic, his father would be able to help with the boats and upkeep on the mower and the quads. Their mom promised to help with check-ins and the front desk, which would free Jill up to learn more of the marketing and publicity side. *If you get the small business loan, you could give Gray part as an investment and ask him to join with you on the bike rental shop.* His stomach tightened. Shit. He really needed to figure out what he wanted so he could set it in motion. Standing still was only going to make him lose out.

"Okay, head on in. Enjoy the rest of your day, and those of you who are fishing with me tomorrow, I'll see you at six A.M." Even saying it aloud hurt. That time of day was only okay if he was still up from the night before. That hadn't happened in a long time. He was too old for that shit now. He liked a firm mattress, a good night's sleep, and quality coffee.

"You, my dear, are a gift," Dayton said to Presley as they walked arm in arm.

Beckett noted that she was limping a bit and wondered if she already had blisters. He didn't second-guess his worries over her physical welfare. She was a guest. That's it. Their whole objective was happy guests. Though he'd never felt like picking Dayton up to save his sore feet.

The older man stopped them in front of Beckett, turned to Presley, and kissed the top of her hand. "Great chatting with you, Presley."

"You, too, Bernie. I'll see you at dinner."

"It's a date."

She laughed as her eyes came to Beckett's. "I guess it is."

He looked at Beckett, his grin cheekier than usual. "Life is short. You snooze, you lose."

Holding back his own laughter and hiding how close to home that comment hit, Beckett nodded. "That's fine. I have one of my own. She's quite a bit shorter than Presley, here, but she's quite the conversationalist."

Mr. Dayton belly-laughed and looked out at Ollie and Grayson on the mower. He turned back to Beckett. "I think I've met your companion as well. Very enjoyable. I look forward to tonight."

Oddly enough, even though he usually avoided dinners with the guests, Beckett found himself looking forward to it, too.

When Dayton went back into the lodge, Beckett looked at Presley. "Come on. Let's take care of your feet." He nearly held out a hand but stopped himself. *Guest. Guest. Guest.*

She made a face. "What? My feet are fine."

"Mm-hmm. Sure they are." He crossed his arms over his chest, appreciating the way her gaze followed the movement. At least he wasn't the only one who was hyperaware of whatever this connection between them was. *Nothing. It's nothing.*

"I'm perfectly capable of taking care of myself and my feet, thank you very much."

He shook his head, all too aware of the way just her hint of a smile lit something inside of him. "Fine. When you're done being stubborn, there's a first aid kit under my bathroom sink." He waved and started off toward the uninhabited cabins. If he stayed, he'd try to convince her that she should let him take care of her. She probably wasn't used to people watching out for her, which was none of Beckett's business. The last time he'd had a serious relationship, one that included thinking more about another's needs than his own, she'd left, telling him there was nothing for her in Smile. He wondered, at the time, what the hell he was to her, then decided he was better off alone.

"Wait, where are you going?" Presley fell into limp-step beside him.

"I need to look at a cabin and see what I can do to get it ready for six guests."

"Mind if I come?"

Something flickered in his chest. "Not at all."

There was a gentle breeze coming in off the water. It felt good after the hike, but he couldn't wait for a long, hot shower. He glanced at Presley. Which he should definitely take at the lodge. Shit. He hadn't thought about today or tonight. Would she feel more comfortable after the first night? *Should text Jilly and see if Tevin is coming to fix the AC.*

"Now that we're back, the hike seems less awful," Presley said, pulling a bottle of water out of her small pack.

Beckett laughed. "I think my sister said something similar about Ollie's birth."

Presley tipped her head back with a soft, carefree laugh that suited her personality and made him want to get closer.

He could easily become addicted to making Presley laugh. His phone rang just as they approached cabin four. He put a hand on her arm before answering and gestured to the steps, which were broken.

Proud of himself for ignoring the flash of heat from touching her skin, he answered, "What's up, Jill?"

"Have you checked Instagram?"

His brows drew together. "Why the hell would I check Instagram? I don't have any of those apps. That's your area."

"You, my tech-averse big brother, are getting some serious attention. We've been tagged over three hundred times this morning alone. People are sharing your morning photo and you've put Get Lost Lodge on some sort of singles' map."

He shook his head. "What the fu—" He broke off and looked at Presley, who was watching him with keen interest. He tried to curb his language for Ollie's sake, but every now and again, words slipped. "What's a singles' map? What does that even mean? What photo?" He hadn't ever posted a photo to anything. Other than texting, emails, and a few games, he didn't use his phone that much.

Presley's face scrunched adorably. She pulled her phone out of her pocket, tapped her fingers on it.

"Ask Presley to show you," his sister said into the phone as Presley covered her mouth with one hand, her gaze going impossibly wide.

"Fine." He hung up without saying goodbye and stared at Presley, who was backing up slowly. "Something I should know?"

She winced and nodded at the same time. "Um. So, I have a fairly small following compared to other influencers."

"Influencers?"

"Yeah. People who promote stuff, get free stuff? Have a certain vibe and run with it?"

She had a certain vibe all right. Even with his brain tripping over Jill's call, his skin was humming with awareness.

"You're a hotel concierge. Not an influencer."

She nodded, bit her lip. "I am. But I also love a really good deal and sort of gained a following for it. Which is cool, when you think of it. I got the flights to Mackinaw for free."

He stopped moving, arched his brow, waited.

Presley's chest rose and fell with quick inhalations. "Anyway, I have a couple of bigger-name followers, including actress Lucy Layne."

What the hell was she talking about? "The reality TV star?" He didn't live in a cave.

She nodded, looking so happy with herself. "Yeah. Sometimes she reposts my stuff. Like today!"

"Okay," he said, drawing out the word, unsure why when he was in the claws of apprehension he still found her cute.

She grinned wider. "I woke up with the intention of making the most of this trip and sharing it all on my socials. Starting this morning."

He stepped closer. "With a photo?" What did this have to do with him?

"Funny thing. It was just supposed to be me and some French toast. You remember I made you French toast?"

He smirked, resisting the urge to grab the phone. "Fondly."

"Well, who knew you were in the background?"

"Okay." Again, he drew the word out. He was a zombie in the morning. He'd just woken up, wondering why his cabin smelled so damn good. *How was that only this morning?*

Presley put a hand on her chest. "I mean, I *didn't*. I wouldn't post someone's photo without permission or knowing them."

"Show me the phone, Presley."

She started backing up again without even lifting her feet, like she was moonwalking away from him. "The thing is, normally I get lots of likes. People like my content. A thousand is pretty average, but sometimes, usually when Lucy shares in her stories or on some of my Tik-Toks, that number is bigger. I'm not actually an influencer. I just like to share stuff."

His stomach crunched like the gravel path under his feet. "Presley."

"Once I posted a picture of my matching manicure and pedicure at this place that has wicked deals. It got a ridiculous amount of attention. They thanked me for the increase in business with two more freebies. Funny, right?"

It didn't feel funny. "Presley I-don't-know-your-middle-name-but-I'd-use-it-if-I-did Ayers."

She gave a high-pitched laugh, and damn it, that was cute, too. "Marie. It's Presley Marie Ayers."

Beckett fought his grin. "I'll remember that for next time. Phone, Presley."

She turned it around. There she was, smiling, no makeup, beyond gorgeous with her hair all piled on her head, a plate of the best French toast he'd ever had in her hand. He leaned closer. He was in the background. He'd just rolled off the couch and stood up, trying to remember why he was on the couch. She'd caught him mid-stretch. His Henley had ridden up, showing his stomach, and his muscles were bunched, his head down a bit like he was being coy or modest or some shit. Several comments were visible under the picture.

Who's the Hot Mountain Man?

Yes please. I'd have that for breakfast any morning.

Hello. I'll take the nummy dish behind you, please.

What the hell? Nummy dish? Who talked like that?
The next person had a blue check mark. Lucy Layne.

Sexy Morning Mountain Man FTW. Get it girl.

Get what? Jesus. People were forward.

He looked at Presley. "What's an 'FTW'?"

Her shoulders sank. "For the win."

"This doesn't seem so bad." He leaned closer, his brows shooting up when he saw "view all 2,073 comments." "Who are all the comments from?" Was his voice squeaky?

She shrugged. "It's really not that many. I have just under fifty thousand followers. So what's that? Like four percent?"

"Sexy morning mountain man?"

Presley laughed loudly. "Yeah. Lucy is funny."

She sobered, frowning and casting her gaze down. "I'm so sorry."

He shook his head. So what? It was a photo on the internet. No one cared. It would go away by the end of the day. Reaching out, he squeezed her shoulder, then reminded himself he should try to avoid touching her. Touching her made him want to pull her close, maybe see if she smelled like his body wash or if she'd chosen the no-name lodge stuff Jilly bought.

"It's okay. Not your fault. At least I wasn't full yawn or in boxers, right?"

Looking up through lowered lashes, she gave a half smile. "If you'd been in boxers, you might have broken the internet."

Ten

She was sticky and hot in an awkwardly uncomfortable way, and still, her body buzzed with a delectable kind of tension. Guilt over parading Beckett around the internet doused it a bit, but honestly, it was like the high of finishing the hike had her wires all wonky.

Beckett's gaze didn't help the overheated factor. Presley stepped back, wanting to give him some space but also wanting to erase the distance between them entirely, which was definitely not a good idea. Engaging in a fling with sexy Hot Mountain Man was not on the agenda.

He sighed and turned away from cabin four. "Let's go get you cleaned up and I'll meet Gray here later."

As sweet as it sounded to have him "help her clean up," she suspected it would involve a lot of not-so-sexy whimpering when she finally took off her boots.

"You stay. I'm a big girl. I can take care of myself. I'm really sorry for the post. I can remove the photo, but . . ."

"It's already out there?"

She nodded, and guilt washed away the last of the tension. She'd been nothing but trouble for him so far today.

Beckett put a hand on her arm, squeezed gently. "Stop worrying. It's okay. Jilly will probably get a bunch of emails asking about rooms and availability."

"Which you can't really accommodate right now," she said on a sigh before realizing she was walking beside him back to the cabin. As he'd suggested. Sneaky.

"There's that saying—all publicity is good or something, right?"

Turning her head as they walked, she studied his profile, his strong, full jaw shadowed with a couple of days' growth. "Almost word-for-word," she teased.

He turned his head so they were looking at each other, which made both of them grin. They probably looked pretty goofy walking like that, but he didn't seem to care and, right now, neither did she. She could not have predicted that twenty-four hours after walking away from Emmett, she'd feel this light and . . . happy. Hell, she'd never imagined she could feel this carefree without knowing for certain what was next. *You do know. A shower. A glorious, hot shower.* Alone.

Beckett unlocked his cabin and she walked ahead of him, stepping into the open space. It was cozy despite not being fancy. A small corner fireplace would warm the entire place and be perfect for snuggling up on the couch. She turned and found Beckett staring at her.

"You have things to do. I'm going to shower, and tonight I'll chat with your sister about getting out of your space."

He inched just a touch closer and she had to stop herself from closing the distance. Presley was impressed with her ability to keep her focus on his face and not the way he looked in his track shorts. His calves suggested he liked more than hiking. Maybe soccer? His dark green hoodie said GET LOST in the top left corner, and Presley imagined it'd be cozy to snuggle inside of, too. Preferably while he was wearing it.

Maybe hiking overactivated her estrogen or dopamine or something. Fresh air, nature's aphrodisiac? *No. That would be Beckett. According to me and the internet.* Would it be so bad to *really* enjoy her vacation? She couldn't imagine when her next one would be. Presley had a feeling Beckett Keller would be one hell of a memory.

Like he was struggling to read her thoughts, thank goodness, he narrowed his gaze. "I'm going to put together a snack. You're going to shower and wash the hike off of yourself. Then I'm going to cover your feet in Polysporin and Band-Aids."

Okay, clearly too much fresh air made her frisky, because that sounded far too sexy coming out of his mouth.

She swallowed, couldn't look away. "I don't remember reading anything about the lodge offering that kind of service." She was trying to lighten the pressure building between them. Hopefully it wasn't one-sided.

"This has nothing to do with the lodge." His eyes changed, she realized. Little flecks of gold stood out when his gaze flickered with obvious interest. Nope. Not one-sided.

"Oh."

Beckett reached out, his finger slowly moving toward her cheek. She sucked in a breath, her eyes widening in anticipation. The pad of his index finger trailed over her skin, along her cheek, her jaw. Her tongue darted out, wetting her lips. His eyes flared, his jaw tensed.

"Go shower, Presley. Let someone do something for you."

Oh, she could think of many things she wanted him to do for her. To her. With her.

She nodded quickly, a real-life Presley bobblehead. "Shower," she whispered.

One side of his mouth tipped up in a knowing smirk.

❧

Every muscle in Presley's body ached, even after the hot shower. Dressing in the yoga pants she'd bought specifically for the trip and a pale gray hoodie, she took the time to dry and straighten her thick hair. She was procrastinating on purpose. Asking Beckett for some kind of hookup was so far out of her comfort zone, it didn't even reside in the same stratosphere. Not even Camping Presley had that much confidence. Plus, she'd reduced him to a hashtag that Lucy Layne would likely share. It wasn't her hashtag; she didn't even know the person who'd used it, but it was too good—and too accurate—for Lucy not to snap that up and share it. Not the best way to the heart of a guy who didn't even have Instagram. *You don't need a way to his heart. And he doesn't need your baggage.* Her shredded feet now felt like a strange kind of penance for bringing someone into her haphazard plan.

Guilt and embarrassment over the photo slowed her movements. It wasn't her fault. Logically, she knew that. She'd posted a picture. She hadn't even known he was behind her looking all gorgeous with that sexy expanse of naturally tanned skin with just a light dusting of hair around his navel, heading down from tight abs. She had to admit, when she'd studied the photo in detail, he had flexed his arms perfectly. It looked like a setup shot.

Here's me in a cabin with breakfast and a random hot guy. She laughed at her reflection in the mirror. Rylee had texted that she'd left out some rather important details of the trip so far. Her estimate was about six feet two of sculpted details.

The Wi-Fi on the hike had been nonexistent, plus there'd been the whole possibility of dying due to lack of oxygen, so Presley had been beyond shocked by the number of notifications on her phone when they got back to the grounds of the lodge. When she'd opened Instagram to show Beckett, she hadn't really paid attention to the stupidly high number of responses—she had been focused on those first few comments that had had them both turning red.

Presley had a full-time job and a plan to move up the ladder. She didn't intend to gain followers or increase her online presence. It was just a by-product of wanting to share things with a wider circle. She obsessed over proving herself to Ms. Twain, not algorithms. Basically, she wanted the same thing online as she did off: genuine connections.

Maybe the internet had been craving a Hot Mountain Man post to take their minds of the world's problems. Beckett definitely fit the bill.

Finishing up her hair, she left the bathroom to find Beckett, his sock-clad feet up on his sturdy wood coffee table. The smallish TV had a baseball game on mute.

His eyes came to her immediately, tracking over her slowly before landing on her face. "How was the shower?"

She clasped her hands together, unsure what to do with them. "Good. Really good." Doing her best not to limp, she made her way over to the couch.

It was obvious he noticed. "Stay here."

She sank down, saying nothing, because not staying there, at least for a few minutes, was not an option. He went into the bathroom, came out a minute later with a white case.

Setting it down on the coffee table, he sat down, leaving some space between them, and gestured to her foot, then patted his knee.

Presley laughed. "I don't think so."

"Stop being so stubborn."

"You're not touching my feet, Beckett." She shoved her hands in her hoodie pocket.

"Are they ticklish?" His lips quirked.

"Yes, actually. But that's not why."

Moving slowly, clearly giving her the option to stop him, he reached down for her foot, set it on his knee. "Baby steps."

"Seems appropriate, given I'm waiting for you to leave so I can cry like a baby about how much I hate my new boots."

Beckett grinned, put a hand on her ankle. *Oh, great. Now ankles are erogenous?* He opened the first aid kit and pulled out a rectangular box, then a second before grabbing a small tube of cream.

"You bought great boots. You just needed to wear them in. You know, like warming up before a run." He kept his hand on her ankle like he was letting her grow accustomed to the weight of it. News flash: she would not. It made her want him to forget her feet and slide that hand all the way up.

Presley frowned, unable to quiet the buzzing in her gut that was especially tuned in to his touch. "By the time I warm up, I'm too tired to run. That's why I prefer yoga."

He chuckled. "I'm going to remove your sock."

"Ew."

His belly laugh made her short of breath. Even his laugh was sexy. It was the kind that would make a person work to hear it again and again.

"I've bandaged Ollie's feet. I got you."

Despite his large hands, his touch was gentle and soothing. He looked at her foot, studying it, before setting it down on his knee again and preparing a cotton pad with cream. She squirmed when it touched her foot, making him look up at her through lowered lids.

"You're in pretty good shape. Just a few sore spots on the pressure points. I'll put this on, some Band-Aids, then wrap your foot in some gauze. Extra padding and your sock will stay clean."

"This is going above and beyond," she said, her voice unintentionally throaty.

He carried on with his task, his face a mask of concentration. "You like your job?"

"Very much. I work for a boutique hotel. I'm hoping to get into management eventually, but it's a long ladder."

"Worth it if you love it, I guess." He placed a wider bandage on the arch of her foot, which ached less once he put on the cream.

"Do you love your work?"

Beckett looked up, grabbed another Band-Aid. "I work at a sporting goods store in Smile. I enjoy it a lot." He ripped open the package, dabbed some ointment on it. "Actually, I have a chance to run my own, but it would mean moving a few hours away."

Moving a pillow behind her back, she watched as he took care of the next sore spot. "Is it a chance you're going to take?"

When his gaze caught hers, she sucked in a sharp breath, the question feeling much larger than she had intended.

"I don't mind taking chances," he said quietly, one hand resting on her ankle, one on her foot. "But I'm not sure yet. I'm trying to weigh my options."

She nodded, words stuck in her throat while something different lodged in her chest. Something a lot like longing.

He slipped her sock back on, lifted her other foot.

"What are your options?"

Beckett pulled her second sock off, his lips firming into a straight line.

"I'm sorry. That's not really any of my business." She felt the urge to yank her foot back.

Shaking his head, he cut her a quiet smile. It felt intimate. Like he didn't give it to everyone.

"No. It's okay. You're really easy to talk to. It's kind of dangerous."

She laughed, gestured to her feet. "Yeah, that's me. All kinds of scary until you put a slight incline in my way."

His thumb dug into her arch as he turned her foot a bit and it felt so good she almost groaned out loud. "It was a good incline. It's not surprising you're sore. You should have told me you hadn't hiked before."

"I should have, but I figured Bloomingdale's and Macy's on Black Friday when the escalators aren't working counted."

Another laugh that sent shots of lust straight to her belly.

"It should. For hiking and bravery. Back to your question, my other options are staying at Brian's in Smile while I keep helping my brother. Or I could take an entirely new path, open a bike rental shop over there. It would have tandem bikes, singles, even four-seaters for families." He shrugged, suggesting it wasn't all that important, but his tone said otherwise.

"That one lets you stay close and do something you like. Or it sounds like you like it. I'm not into that kind of torture, but to each their own," she said, clamping her jaw closed when his touch tickled.

"You're right about that. Macy's and Bloomingdale's sound terrifying."

"Well, if you ever try it, I will be there after, ready to take care of your feet and bring you a beer."

He grinned, finished up, and closed the medical kit. "Is that your way of asking for a beer?"

She laughed again. She had done that more in two days here than she had in weeks and weeks with Emmett. Something to dissect tonight while she stared at the ceiling wondering how to build the courage to ask Beckett if he'd be at all interested in a short-term thing.

"No," she said. She picked up the Band-Aid wrappers, rose from the couch, and did her best to walk normally. It was better, but it still hurt like crazy.

He joined her in the kitchen, washing his hands, then passing her the towel when she washed hers. It was then that she noticed the small board of snacks: strawberries, crackers, some cheese, almonds, peanuts, pretzels, and grapes. Her chest constricted like she'd tied a rope around it and pulled.

When was the last time Emmett had done something sweet for her? Why had she been okay with so much less than she deserved?

"You okay?" Beckett shifted closer.

Presley turned, but he was so close, she nearly plastered herself against him.

"I will be. Thank you for being so incredibly sweet."

The softness of his smile, the understanding in his gaze, untied the knots around her heart.

"Don't tell anyone. I have a sexy mountain man persona to maintain."

Maybe asking for a fling was too far outside her comfort zone, but in that moment, Presley wanted something far smaller that would mean even more.

She stepped into Beckett, put her hand on his chest, let it slide down to his waist as she moved closer. As if they'd practiced, they swayed into each other, her arms going around his waist, his coming around her back.

As the embrace soothed her in ways no first aid kit ever could, she smiled against his chest. "Your secret is safe with me."

Eleven

Presley's phone continued to ping with endless notifications, so she put it back on silent and decided to go up to the main house a bit early, see if she could chat with Jilly. Beckett had given in to the hug for a few blissful seconds before stepping back, looking at her like he wasn't sure where she had come from, and stammering out an excuse to leave. He'd pointed at the snacks and told her to eat and that he'd see her later.

So, clearly her seduction skills were lacking. *You weren't trying to seduce him.* She'd honestly just wanted a hug. And she was right; that sweater with Beckett *in* it? Perfect for snuggling.

A full sit-down meal was served in the dining room each night at seven. Breakfast and lunch could be there as well, or on the go, if preferred. Beckett mentioned that two evenings a week they took the boat to Smile, where guests could try the local fare.

Outside, the air had cooled, and even though she couldn't see them, she knew there were bugs just flitting around waiting to land on her. She swiped her hand through the empty space. Nothing. She started to do it again but caught herself, realizing she looked ridiculous waving her arms as she walked. She tugged the zipper on her sweater up as far as it could go, resisting the urge to tuck her head into the hood. A sweet, pleasant smell emanated from the flowers, the water, and the breeze.

A couple of guests fished off the dock and Presley wondered if they'd stayed there all day. The sound of their laughter seemed to echo off the still water. The scent of freshly mowed grass danced on the breeze. Ollie sure was cute, riding along with her uncle like a miniature caretaker.

Careful on the path, Presley wondered if they'd thought of putting in more flowers, walkways, and perhaps even some rock gardens. Ollie's idea for growing some of their own food was a great one. Herbs, at the very least, would be a nice touch. More than once, Presley had suggested to Ms. Twain that they offer personal touches like flowers in the rooms or even specialty chocolates, sort of like DoubleTree offered cookies. Her ideas were "taken under consideration."

Hammering caught her attention, pulling her away from the stairs leading to the lodge. Wandering down the side of the house with a different view of the water, she saw the door to cabin four was open. Not wanting things to be awkward between them, Presley figured she'd pop in, say a breezy hello, and then go see Jill. This Presley would pretend to be chill. City Presley laughed in her head at the very notion. Moving slowly because her feet were killing her—after Beck had left, she'd added about ten Band-Aids to her feet—she eased up the steps. Inside, she found him on his hands and knees with his head up the chimney.

"Little early to be watching for Santa," she said.

He jumped back in his crouch, losing his balance and landing on his butt. Presley bit her lip to keep from giggling.

"You scared the hell out of me." His smile let her know he wasn't mad.

"I'm probably not your favorite guest today, huh?"

Beckett stood up, brushed off his shorts. He had some soot on his cheek. His hair was a mess. He still wore his hiking clothes. No wonder he slept so hard; the man never stopped.

"Depends. You Instagram a shot of me looking up that chimney?" His lips quivered.

He was playing, but guilt still made another notch in her heart. "Of course not. I mean, your butt is Instagram-worthy, but I told you, I wouldn't do it on purpose."

Heat rose from the base of her neck when his brows arched. She should steal some more Band-Aids and tape her mouth shut.

"I'm not sure if having an Instagram-worthy butt is a compliment."

Going with it, because what choice did she have at this point, she nodded. "Definitely. But regardless, I hope I'm not causing you to hide out."

He pursed his lips, pretending to think about it. "You ask less questions than Ollie."

She tapped her fingers against her legs. "Is that a compliment?"

He shifted his hand side to side like he was somewhere in the middle on the whole thing, but the amusement in his gaze settled her nerves.

They both started to speak at the same time. He gestured to Presley, for her to go first.

Beckett nodded and they stood across from each other, staring until she had to say something. "I'm sorry. About the photo, the comments, all of it. And I'm sorry if I made you uncomfortable with . . . the thing."

His chin dipped and he stared at her. "'The thing'?"

Argh. He was going to make her spell it out. "You know. The hug."

"Well, which was it? A hug or a thing?"

"You're teasing me." She pursed her lips together.

Beckett stepped closer. "I am, because there's nothing to apologize for, Presley. And trust me when I say you're a wonderful guest. Sweet, accommodating, and an excellent cook."

With his easygoing tone, her shoulders relaxed to a near melting point. He walked over to the small table in the kitchen, and even though it was a fairly big place, the room felt smaller, more alive, with him in it. Like his cabin, it was an open concept, but quite a bit bigger, with more doors and a set of stairs leading up to a loft.

"It's fine, Presley. Honestly, Jill is thrilled. She said the phone has been ringing nonstop. We've got some of the rooms booked into the end of September. The last two callers asked if this was the Hot Mountain Man Lodge, so I think Gray is considering renaming the place."

Laughter escaped. "It's not a bad idea. Definite marketing possibilities."

"How do your feet feel?"

Like I beat them with jagged hammers and lit them on fire. She averted her gaze, wandered to the worn, plaid couch. "Good. They're great. Can't wait to go again."

"We could do a short after-dinner one," he suggested.

Her gaze zipped to his. "Funny. No, thanks. So, what's happening with this cabin?"

Beckett looked around, then back to Presley. "I need to fix the stairs to the loft. There's room for two up there, with two bedrooms down here and a pullout. Jill pulled all the bedding from every cabin when we took over and washed it all, but some of it was so old it disintegrated. We've been working on prepping one room at a time in between guests and all of our schedules. She doesn't want to give up on the chance to rent this place for a week."

"It looks like it's in decent shape."

He nodded and walked closer to her, making it harder to focus on the conversation.

As surprising as it was, she couldn't remember being this viscerally attracted to anyone. Ever. But more than that, she liked him. And his family. She was on day two with them and already felt included. The homey, family feel was something sorely lacking in big hotels.

Beckett shoved his hands in his pockets, like he didn't know where to put them. "It is, structurally. That doesn't make it fit for guests. Even if I get a deal on furniture, the bedding is pricy. We weren't ready to outfit an entire cabin yet." He pointed to the stairs. "I need some wood, but the stairs are an easy fix." He pointed to the bathroom. "I need a part for the sink and a better showerhead." Then to the kitchen. "Two of the cupboard doors are cracked, but I have some wood glue, so I think I can fix them, maybe even paint them. It's not much, but it's time and money. The fridge and stove are decent, but even with a deposit on this place, it doesn't cover all we need."

Ideas swirled in her brain. When she was in Hospitality Management School, she'd entertained the idea of running her own bed-and-breakfast. La Chambre had been her practicum placement and she'd never left, instead slowly working her way up the ladder. Well, up a couple of low rungs. The idea of her own place was always in the back of her mind. She had several notebooks filled with pictures, ideas, recipes, room concepts. They were fun to look through and a great stress release on days when she felt like no one listened to her at work. When she'd opened one this morning, she'd clearly fugue-doodled on the plane, because there were all sorts of little drawings that hadn't been there before. It was a cheaper version of stress release than a massage.

A creative outlet, since she couldn't have one at Le Chambre. Even there, she did more than she got credit for, which was why Ms. Twain hadn't stopped texting. If the hotel, a staff member, or a guest had needs, Presley knew how to meet them. She ended up being a private concierge for many returning guests, which her boss told her was a compliment— but sometimes, it ended up feeling like a punishment.

Beckett sighed heavily beside her, and she could feel his exhaustion.

She didn't want to cross any lines, but he'd touched her feet, so she figured some boundaries had already been pushed. Besides, she couldn't say nothing. "Have you guys checked out Your Stay?"

He looked at her. Shadows haunted his gorgeous eyes, making them seem darker. "What?"

Presley smiled. "It's a wholesale website for everything you could possibly imagine needing at your hotel, inn, or bed-and-breakfast. They have a partner auction site. I spend hours on there. My mother used to say if I spent the same amount of time on dating sites, I'd be married by now." She shrugged off the itch between her shoulder blades. She knew her parents loved her, but sometimes she wondered if they were proud of her. They'd only met Emmett a couple of times, and she'd been disappointed by their lack of interest in the status of their relationship. *Why does it matter? Gives you less to explain now that you've broken up.* She refocused on Beckett. "But I got a raise out of finding new bedding for an entire floor when the hotel decided to make it the luxury level."

Beckett's jaw dropped slightly. She wanted to reach up and wipe the soot from his cheek. Maybe let her hand linger, like he'd done earlier.

"What kind of prices are we talking about?"

She looked around, mentally calculated. "What size are the beds?"

"We'd have to take from the lodge rooms and storage, but we'd do a double in the loft, a double sofa in here, two twins, and a queen."

"Bet you I could get you bedding for the entire cabin for around a hundred bucks." If shopping were a sport, she'd be a gold medal champion. When she retired from that, she'd be a sought-after coach, teaching others how to find the best deal. She would be placed in the Shopping on a Budget Hall of Fame. It was her true calling in life, and if she could figure out how to get paid for it, she'd be a bazillionaire.

"No way." He shook his head.

Presley grinned, bounced her brows as she held out a hand. "Bet?"

He eyed her skeptically with a hint of teasing. "What's on the line?"

Their palms slid together and she was surprised they didn't *hear* the sparks firing between them. His grip reminded her of his hands on her hips when she'd almost fallen.

"Rumor has it there's a hot tub."

Beckett pulled her just a little closer, his gaze lit with amusement. "Fact, not rumor, and one of the things that actually works well around this place. Knock on wood." He knocked on his head, making her laugh.

"I prefer my hot-tubbing without an audience. I mean, with another person is fine, but I don't really want to soak my poor feet with Bernie present."

"Thought your feet were fine."

"Lies we tell ourselves, Beckett."

He laughed, loud and carefree. "If I can get you an hour in the hot tub without any other guests, you'll outfit this entire cabin with bedding."

She pointed at him. "Sheets. Sheets for every bed. Pillowcases, too, but comforters and blankets will be more." It would take some time, but the deals on Your Stay were so awesome, it was worth the effort. Especially when it wasn't her money and she was helping someone.

"That's fair. Let me talk to Jill, but I'm pretty sure you have a deal."

She held out her hand again. He shook it and she recognized the interest she felt mirrored. Magnetic energy and chemistry were not the goal of this trip. Just a handy side benefit she might need to think more about.

Pulling his hand back, he cleared his throat, stepped back. "I need to go shower before dinner."

"Question?"

His lashes lowered slightly. "Yeah?" His voice came out husky.

"You okay if I post the hiking picture?"

The desire cleared from his gaze with his laughter. "Sure. Just don't tag it 'Hot Mountain Man.'"

Presley laughed. "Are you sure?"

His cheeks turned a subtle shade of pink. "Positive."

"I'll see you at dinner," she said.

He left her there in the cabin. It was nice. She liked the simplicity of it. Functional. People came here for the outdoors, but they wanted to retire to a comfortable, cozy spot. For someone like her who had less interest in the outdoors, it wasn't too rustic. More ideas tumbled through her mind about how to maximize space, little things they could add to spruce the place up with minimal cost, but she didn't want to overstep.

Pulling her phone from her back pocket, she opened her photos to post a couple of hike pictures, but as she scrolled through, her heart gave a painful hiccup.

There was a picture of Beckett and Presley staring into each other's eyes. Their mouths were close, their heads bent toward each other, and the desire between them vibrated off the still photo. He'd snapped it before they had their camera faces ready. She couldn't take her eyes off of it. All of it. The way he looked at her like she was something special, the way her own energy seemed to pulsate in the picture despite being more physically exhausted than she could remember ever being. They looked like old friends or something more, something deeper, but definitely not like two people who'd only met the day before.

Giving herself a second to regain her breath, she scrolled to the safer photo, posting it to Instagram and once again tagging the lodge. She'd do a TikTok in a day or two, after she got her bearings and maybe took a trip into Smile. Beckett might not love the attention, but if she could help their lodge, it was a good cause. Plus, he didn't have social media, so it shouldn't bug him.

She had over a hundred new followers, and her picture of Beckett in the morning continued to gain traction by getting shared on stories and added to reels. She followed the lodge, seeing that they—Jilly—had already followed her. She had several DMs but closed the app. She'd deal with that and emails from Ms. Twain later.

Aside from the blisters, this trip had been nothing like she expected.

While she was a born planner, nothing could have prepared her for any of this.

Twelve

"I'm telling you, Jill, this site is crazy," Beckett said into his phone on the walk back to his own cabin. He'd managed to get dust and soot all over himself. "Three sets of five-hundred-thread-count sheets just went for thirty-four dollars."

Jilly made happy noises over the phone, probably looking at some of the same things he was while they talked. "Why would anyone sell this stuff so cheap? Oh, these are hotel brand. The starting bid is two dollars. What the heck?" She'd logged onto the site as soon as he'd told her about it. He wanted to get on his own laptop and check things out, but just glancing through it on his phone had revealed a treasure trove.

"Overpurchasing? They don't match existing decor? Who cares? It's legitimate and we need stuff." Beckett shrugged even though she couldn't see him. Who cared why, if it was legit?

"This is amazing. Presley is amazing."

Beckett said nothing to this because he couldn't disagree and didn't want to verbally admit to anything his sister would use to start playing matchmaker. He wasn't sure he'd ever wanted to kiss a woman as much as he had wanted to kiss Presley at his place. She'd burrowed right in, fitting into the crook of his arms, against his chest with an ease that felt *right*. And a woman who was leaving in eight days wasn't someone he needed to fall for. Unless they didn't fall but simply . . . explored.

"I'm going to go look up bedding for all of the rooms. You're coming up for dinner, right?"

He felt the tremor of anticipation roll through him. Not something he usually felt about dinner with the guests. He didn't mind it, but he didn't necessarily look forward to it. Until Presley. "I am. We should ask Chef to serve Presley's French toast."

"The way you look at her, I'm surprised you'd want to share," his sister said, laughter in her tone.

Beckett didn't take the bait. "I need the hot tub shut for maintenance tonight," he said, letting himself into his cabin.

"Oh no. What's wrong with it? It was fine earlier."

"I just need to check it out. Did Tevin find someone for the AC?"

His cabin was cleaner than when he'd left it. It was weird sharing his space with someone. Especially a woman. Stranger still? He sort of liked it. He'd had a couple of serious girlfriends but never lived with any. The time he'd thought he wanted to try, she'd said yes, but only if they lived anywhere but Smile.

"Someone's coming tomorrow. Should be fixed by the time you get back from the fishing trip."

"Okay. I need to head back to Smile tomorrow night for a couple days."

"I thought you were on vacation?"

Beckett grabbed a beer, then headed for the bathroom and started the shower.

"I am, but I have other things to tend to. I'll swing by Mom and Dad's place, make sure things are good. I need to take Adam for comics. I told Gramps I'd stop by the Outdoor Association Meeting and talk about the lodge. And I want to swing by my place for some more clothes."

"Sounds good."

They hung up. He stripped down, tossed all his clothes into the hamper instead of on the floor, and climbed into the hot spray. He sighed out loud with the pleasure of it.

Damn, he was tired. He could ease his own stress by telling his brother and sister what was weighing on his mind, but he wanted to figure it out first before he got their input. He was easily influenced by their opinions and needs. As an adult, a capable one at that, he should be able to make a decision without asking for their blessings or thoughts. But every time he felt like one path was "the one," he thought about another and it became a loop in his head.

Beckett had chosen the smoother, predictable path more than once in his life, and he worried he was doing that now. Staying at Brian's while helping with the lodge was the simplest option with the least amount of change. But he'd know, in the back of his head, that he could have more. Like one of the other two attractive options he was thinking about.

Since they were kids, he and his siblings had handled everything together: homework, bullies, chores, all of it. Their parents were awesome, hard workers who loved the three of them and supported them at every step. As kids, they hadn't realized how hard their parents had to work to give them a good life, but they'd been raised to take care of each other.

When Jilly's ex left her alone with a kid, they'd gone down to Pittsburgh and brought her and Ollie home to Smile. She didn't love moving back in with their parents, but it worked out well, only a few years later, when Mom and Dad bought an RV to travel.

When Gray's marriage went south, they rallied again. Poor guy lost his high-paying job at his father-in-law's company, his wife, his house, his friends. On paper, being gifted the lodge in his otherwise dismal settlement looked good, but the amount of work the property needed was unexpected. Gray came home, and Beckett and Jilly stepped up and stepped in to support their brother. Now they were together again, and Beckett didn't want to wreck that. But he also wanted more. What he knew for sure was that he loved his family and his hometown. Which should take managing the second shop, hours away, off the table. He'd never had any real desire to be anywhere else permanently.

In high school, Beckett had loved sports and math. He'd gotten a scholarship to University of Michigan, gotten his degree in business, and come right back home. His job at Brian's made him happy and didn't stress him out. He didn't have a lot of needs. But now, it felt like he was ready for some elusive next step. He just didn't know what it was yet. Maybe a house instead of an apartment. His own roots instead of helping someone else plant theirs.

After showering, he dressed in jeans and a light sweater. Opening his sock drawer, he saw his swim trunks and wondered if Presley wanted *any* company tonight. Then he wondered how the hell he'd keep his lust reined in if he saw her in a swimsuit. She was a guest. One who had a whole life she was getting back to in eight days. She didn't like the outdoors. She was on the rebound. And he didn't have five seconds to himself most days. He sighed heavily and shut the drawer.

❀

He should have shown up earlier. As he slipped into the dining room, hoping to draw as little notice as possible, he saw that Mr. Dayton had already taken the seat beside Presley. On her other side was Ollie. Beckett swallowed a laugh. Presley was being chattered at on both sides.

"Hey," Grayson said, coming into the dining room after him.

They all tried to join the guests for dinner a couple of times a week. They wanted to be part of the experience, but not in anyone's face. Some of the guests thrived on the interaction with others and some of them wanted their own space. Not that there'd been a ton of guests. They'd taken over in the offseason, after all. But things would pick up. Especially now.

"How's it going? I feel like I've barely seen you," Beckett said.

There were ten of them tonight. Grayson had just dropped the guys who'd been staying in room four back on the mainland.

"Good. The boat is back. Tevin cut us a break. Pretty sure he's into Jill."

Beckett frowned, catching his sister's gaze as she came through the swinging door that connected to the kitchen. She carried a huge platter of hamburgers, already on the bun. Both brothers headed for the kitchen.

"About time you two showed up," Jill said as they passed.

Beckett pushed through the door first, wondering if there was any way of getting some help for the kitchen. They were all running themselves ragged. Chef was icing a somewhat crooked cake. The taste and the chocolate he was spreading all over it would make up for the presentation. He was a short, roundish man with hip, dark-framed glasses, his skin tanned from enjoying the outdoors and weathered from age. He kept his graying brown hair up in a bun. His smile was too big for his face and his laughter was the kind that made others want to join in. He kept the meals simple, family style, and served promptly each night before he cleaned up and left. They'd considered doing the cooking themselves, but Gray and Beckett sucked at it, and Jilly didn't have the time. Plus, he felt as much a part of the lodge as the stone fireplace and wooden beams. One of the sturdier parts.

"Ahh! Good. Everyone is here. Family should eat together," Chef said.

"We wish you'd join us," Gray said.

Beckett laughed. Gray tried to get him to join every time, but the man always said no.

Chef chuckled. "No, no. Louis and I eat dinner together every night. He cooks for me, if you can believe it."

They believed it, because he told them every time they asked him to join and because Louis was every bit as in love with Chef after twenty years together as Chef was with him.

Beckett picked up a platter of hamburger fixings while Gray grabbed a bowl of crispy potato wedges.

Beckett's stomach growled as his brother commented, "Smells good."

He wondered how often Gray forgot to eat.

"Jilly has the burgers," Chef said with a smile, going back to his cake.

They brought out the dishes and set them in the center of the table. Ollie was showing Presley how to fold her napkin into a strange-looking shape. Mr. Dayton chatted with the couple who'd shown up with Presley. Bo and Morgan, the two guys who also arrived yesterday, were arguing over something to do with fishing.

Beckett met Presley's gaze and did his best to ignore the little loop de loop thing his stomach did. Before he could head to his seat on the other side of Ollie, Grayson grabbed his arm.

"You okay with everything that happened online?"

Beckett felt his cheeks warm. He shrugged off his brother's hand. "It's fine."

Gray's gaze, similar to his own, twinkled, making him look younger and happier than Beck had seen in a while.

"Better than *fine,* according to the comments," Gray teased.

"Sit down, you two." Jill gave them both a look that reminded Beckett of their mother.

When he sat next to Ollie, she gave him her napkin. "Hi, Uncle Beck. I made you a napkin flower."

He took it and kissed her head. "Perfect. Just what I was hoping for."

Presley continued to fold her napkin, then tossed it forward. "I can't do it."

Ollie giggled. "Mom says I have a unique talent."

Jilly looked over from across the table. "For many things."

People talked over one another, sharing the meal like a huge family. Beckett took it in, listened, chatted with Ollie while reminding her to chew with her mouth closed. His sister sent him a couple of grateful grins.

When they sat with the guests, inevitably, questions about the lodge came up.

"Saw you poking around cabin four. You opening them up soon?" Bernie asked as he added lettuce and tomatoes to his bun.

Gray scooped some potatoes onto his plate before he looked up. "We need to make sure everything is in good shape before we do. I only took over six months ago. I'm still finding my footing."

"Summer is your moneymaker. The more space you have available, the better off you'll be. The old adage 'you have to spend money to make money' is a favorite for a reason," Bernie said. He took a big bite of his burger, then mumbled around it, "Just as good as I remember."

Jill picked up the pitcher of juice, poured herself some. "We sort of like this intimate setting of having all the guests close. Are you fishing tomorrow, Mr. Dayton?"

Beckett hid his smile behind a roll. His sister was a master of redirection.

"It's what I came for, and I hear we've got a newbie with us," he said, looking at Presley.

"I can help you fish," Ollie told her.

Presley smiled at both of them. "Thank you. I'll give it a shot, but I think I'm better suited to sunbathing than fishing."

"You can do both," the older man said, chuckling. "I plan to."

"Other than hiking, are there more activities we can do here at the lodge if we don't want to fish each day?" Mel, the woman with the many large hats, asked.

Jilly looked over, set her juice down, glanced at Beckett and Grayson.

"What sorts of activities do you like, Mel?" Presley asked easily.

Mel cut her burger into fourths, picking up one little wedge. "I enjoy hiking and fishing, actually, but I didn't have anything particular in mind."

"Melly doesn't like to let a conversation lag," Richard said fondly, smiling at his wife with obvious affection. "How about you, Presley? What do you enjoy?"

Beckett couldn't say why their eyes connected effortlessly, like they'd already been seeking each other, but they met and locked like a needle slid right into a groove.

"Shopping," she said, ducking her gaze with a smile as the others laughed.

"Mom likes shopping, too," Ollie said.

Presley grinned at his niece. When she reached out to smooth down a wayward lock of Ollie's hair, Beckett's heart muscles tightened.

"I also like yoga, walking on flat ground"—she shot Beck a mock glare—"swimming, paddleboarding, finding good deals, and posting them online. I enjoy reading, and I absolutely love to cook."

"I can confirm you are excellent at cooking," Beckett said, picking up his glass of juice.

"The famous French toast," Grayson said with a lopsided grin.

"I'm not sure it was the toast getting all that attention," Presley said, her cheeks turning a pretty shade of pink.

"Uncle Beck is a thirst trap," Ollie said as she set her napkin on her plate.

Beckett nearly spat his juice all over the table.

"Olivia Anne Keller. Where did you hear that?" Jilly set her fork down.

Grayson's mouth hung open for a full second before he stood abruptly. "I think Ollie and I will grab the dessert." He reached out a hand for Ollie and the two of them made their escape.

Jilly took a deep breath. "I thought with school being done for the summer, she'd have only good influences. I forgot my potty-mouthed brothers."

Beckett had to work at holding the laughter in. "What'd I do?"

The rest of the conversation stayed light and fun as the guests shared little details about themselves and Beckett snuck glances at Presley. It didn't hurt his feelings one bit that every time he looked her way, she was looking back at him.

Gray and Ollie returned with the cake and serving plates. "If you don't mind, we'd appreciate if everyone can scrape their plates and stack them on the trolley," Gray announced. "Beckett will be leaving at six A.M. There'll be oatmeal, cereal, and granola bars available for breakfast and sandwiches at lunch. I'm heading to the mainland at noon if you'd like to do some sightseeing or shopping. Also, the hot tub is closed tonight for repair."

The guests did as asked, complimenting the food as they left the room. Mel and Richard headed to the lobby, which doubled as a larger movie viewing area if people didn't want to watch on the smaller tele-visions in their rooms.

Jill left to finish turning over one of the rooms, and Ollie trailed after her.

Presley cleared her plate, setting it on the trolley as Chef came to collect the dishes.

He smiled widely at Presley. "Oh, hello again. I hope you enjoyed your meal."

"It was delicious. I haven't had a burger in far too long. And that cake. You need to share your recipe." She was so at ease with conversa-tion, regardless of who it was with.

Unless it was with him when she was flustered, he thought with a smile.

Chef looked at Beckett. "Maybe we can do that on one of her video reels." He looked back at Presley. "My husband and I have followed all your socials for months now. Louis used the discount you posted on TikTok for a gorgeous new Sherpa rug."

She laughed with delight, the sound sending a punch of hunger straight through him.

"Oh, that makes me so happy. Thank you. I'll be sure to follow you back. You know, a Sherpa rug would look great in the main room in front of the fireplace."

It took him a second to tune back in to the fact that they were both looking at him.

"Oh. I don't know. You can ask Gray and Jilly about the reel. I'm sure they'd both love it. More buzz, right?" Then he realized he'd missed Presley's suggestion. "I'll ask Jill about the rug."

"Maybe we can get Beckett to help with breakfast. He can go shirt-less." Chef Shane said the words in a deadpan voice, but the glint in his eye gave away his humor.

"Very funny," Beckett said, watching Presley's gaze darken.

"Time to clean up," Chef announced, turning the trolley toward the door, leaving them alone.

When she came back to sit down beside him, Beckett could only stare, unsure if he'd imagined the wave of lust in her gaze. Presley smiled innocently, naturally, at him. "What?"

"Do you charm everyone you meet?"

Presley's eyes widened even as her mouth formed a little O. Beckett reminded himself not to look at her mouth. Too tempting.

She nudged his shoulder, the heat of her hand all but searing him, and he realized he ought to jump in the lake tonight instead of thinking about the hot tub.

"Hardly. Trust me on that one."

He felt the absence of her hand, so he leaned in, inhaled the sweet, subtle scent of Presley and his own body wash.

"I'm afraid I can't do that when evidence points to the contrary." His gaze wandered to the delicate spot where her neck met her shoulder and he thought about pressing his mouth there to feel her pulse.

Shit. He really needed to redirect the conversation.

"Maybe you're just easily charmed," she said in a breathy voice.

He laughed too loud. "I'm not. There's just something about you, Presley . . . Marie Ayers."

She tipped her head back and laughed. "There it is—but I don't know if that was a middle-name-worthy moment."

Beckett couldn't stop himself from leaning in farther, though he knew he should put distance between them. "I like the way your whole name sounds."

Their gazes locked again, and this time, his heart fishtailed, moving frantically like it was trying to stay afloat in all the unexpected feelings.

"His idea for doing a couple of reels is a good one. Another way to bring positive attention to the lodge. If you ask for a deposit with bookings, which I noticed you don't, it would bring in money for some strategic marketing." She winced. "I'm sorry. Talk about overstepping. You probably think I'm a—"

He didn't know what she was going to say, but the truth left him on a sharp exhale, cutting her off. "I think you're magic."

Presley sucked in a breath, and it felt like they were exchanging air. His for hers and back again. He didn't even realize he was moving closer until Gray came back into the room, followed by Jilly.

Beckett and Presley both startled, and suddenly, he didn't want to meet about the lodge or hang with his siblings. Every tiny particle of what made him whole wanted nothing more than to be alone with Presley.

He stood, looked at his siblings. Jilly sat with her notebook, the one she treated as though it held all the winning plays for a Super Bowl game. Gray met Beckett's gaze with a questioning glance.

"Listen, can we reschedule? I've got to get up early. I need to check the hot tub, and Presley is coming with me." Not his most subtle moment.

Jilly's expression of surprise was a contrast to Grayson's smirk.

"Sure. Presley, the AC guy will be here tomorrow so we'll have you out of the cabin soon. Unless you'd like to stay there, no extra cost, and Beckett could bunk here," Grayson said.

Presley wouldn't pick up on it, but Beckett heard the playful challenge, the tease in his sibling's tone.

Presley looked up at Beckett, her hand brushing his as she stood. "Oh. No, I don't need to do that. Things are . . . fine the way they are." She bit her lip. "I mean, until the AC is fixed. Then, of course, I'll get out of your space." She looked at him and he saw the want mirrored in her beautiful blue eyes.

He wanted her *in* his space. All up in it.

"No rush," he said, his voice thick.

His siblings were going to tease him like hell as soon as they got him alone.

"I'm going to go play a game with Ollie, then," Jilly said with a sly smile.

"Thanks for helping my brother check the hot tub, Presley. He could use the backup."

Beckett shot Grayson a warning glance, but the jerk just laughed and followed their sister.

"Subtle," Presley said under her breath.

When she looked at him, she was smiling.

"What can I say. I'm a man of many skills. Stretching. Subtlety."

Presley's laughter danced over his skin.

"I stole more of your Band-Aids," she said as they walked out of the dining room and down a hallway that led to a sunroom with French doors leading outside to the hot tub.

"Whatever you need, it's yours," he said.

Then he realized what he had said. All the other decisions plaguing him fell away. He knew exactly what he wanted. At least for the next eight days.

Thirteen

Presley slipped into the hot tub with a low groan, the water greeting her aching feet and tired muscles like a welcoming friend. Behind the lodge was an entire bounty of beautiful grounds. Double glass doors off of a sitting room in the lodge opened to a stone path, which led to a set of stairs nestled in a space between trees. The steps led to a raised, boardwalk-style patio surrounding the entire hot tub, letting people sink down into it. It was interesting to her, the way some of the amenities were top-notch and others were in great disrepair. Whoever had been in charge of this place before Beckett's family had clearly had their priorities.

At the moment, as the heat and jets massaged, she was thrilled the hot tub had been on the top of the upkeep list. Beckett was right about the twinkle lights adding to the ambience, as he'd called it when he showed her his backyard. She smiled. A few lanterns hung from the trees, creating a soft, romantic feel, elevated by the stars beginning to poke through the gaps in the canopy of trees.

Because she was facing the lodge, she saw Beckett come from around its side, along the path that led from the front grounds to the back. He wore a pair of patterned board shorts and a T-shirt.

Presley's pulse ramped up, competing with the strength of the jets, as his long, lean legs closed the distance. She'd truly thought she was a suit-and-tie girl, but the way he wore casual clothing made her rethink her entire stance on what was attractive. Holding steady at the top of the list, currently, were his smile, the way his eyes crinkled in the corners, and the way he looked at her when she spoke.

"You still sure you're okay if I join?"

She had a fleeting curiosity about whether he'd hooked up with any other lodge guests before shooing it away. The only thing that mattered was right this minute. Presley needed a break from thinking about the past or future. Right now, she just wanted to sit with Beckett under the stars. "I hoped you would." How was it only yesterday she'd shown up here? It seemed like a lifetime ago.

Beckett grabbed the back of his shirt, yanked it over his head, and tossed the shirt on the deck. Presley swallowed, willing herself not to drool at the sight of his low-key six-pack—it suited him in the way that it made it obvious he worked out while still being understated, like a shy six-pack. She smiled at the thought. Then her mouth went dry as her gaze caught on the perfect V his muscles made and the way his shorts hung low on his hips, making her mind and gaze wander. *Good lord*. No wonder the internet was loving him. He looked like one of those romance book cover models, all smooth, tanned skin and toned muscles. If she snapped a picture right now, she'd end up with a blue check mark.

He slipped into the water, letting out a deep sigh. Little noises—she didn't want to think about the creatures making them—sounded in the distance.

Beckett leaned his head back and rested it on the edge of the tub. "God. Why don't I do this more often?"

Presley was grateful his eyes were closed so she could keep staring. He was like art. Sculpted and molded by hard work, determination, and an underlying gentleness that could shatter her already weak defenses. "I'm guessing you don't get much of a chance."

Sitting up, he nodded, meeting her stare. "I don't. We've been running hard since Grayson got this place. We keep saying we'll catch our breath when we're caught up, but every time we turn around, there's more to do."

They sat a few minutes in the quiet and she wasn't sure if she was responsible for erasing the distance between them or he was but they'd drifted closer. This spot here, this moment, felt like perfection. Like it was worth everything in the last forty-eight hours to get right *here*. What a strange twist of fate. Presley spent so much of her time planning, trying to get things just right, that she'd never sat back and let the universe take over. *Well done, Universe. I should leave you in charge more often.*

Beckett gave her a soft smile. "Too bad you don't have your phone. This would be Instagram-worthy, right?"

She laughed. If he only knew. "It absolutely would." She hesitated a second, ran her palms over the surface of the water, watching the bubbles pop. "I'm glad not to share this though."

The way he held her gaze made it feel like he could see inside of her soul. She wondered if he felt it; the connection. And it wasn't just *him*. It was this place bringing her to life. She had a dozen ideas to jot down in her notebook for this place and wanted to work up the courage to run them by him. It wasn't really any of her business. Plus, the other piece of her wanted her working brain to shut the hell up.

"Thank you for showing me that site, Presley. Jilly bought enough linens to outfit all of cabin four. I can't thank you enough."

Warmth buzzed through her, over her skin. "I'm so glad it worked out. If you guys are open to it, I have some other ideas I could share with you. Sometimes fresh eyes and someone with a background in the industry can smooth the way."

The usual response she received—at work, or when she offered Emmett ideas for his campaigns—was a quiet, somewhat condescending smile. She wasn't prepared for the impact of Beckett's happy, open grin.

"I'd love that. Let me talk to my siblings."

Quiet fell between them. Presley felt her heartbeat in her ears and in little pulse points all over her body.

With her head still lowered, she turned a bit, meeting his gaze with lowered lids. "It's beautiful out here."

He smiled, and Presley got stuck looking at his lips.

She cleared her throat, pushing herself to think of something different than where her mind was headed. "Has Grayson thought about selling?"

Beckett shook his head. "I asked him about it right after the divorce was final. I think he's channeled his feelings of failure into making this succeed. That sounds weird, I know, but I don't think he can handle this falling apart right now, too."

Presley understood the idea of not wanting to let one more thing fall through the cracks. "I'm sorry. That's hard." She let her hand drift along the water. "Why bikes?"

Happiness flashed in his gaze, making him appear younger, more relaxed. "When we were kids, we went on a trip to one of the smaller islands. We rented bikes and rode around the entire place, camped for a couple of nights. It was awesome. I was twelve. I think it's that time in life right before everything becomes incredibly confusing."

She nodded, liking the way his tone softened when he talked about his past. "Before the teen years wreak havoc on the brain. Your family seems pretty special."

He nodded. "What about yours?"

Safe subject. "We're close but not like yours. I'm an only child. My parents are very committed to their jobs and each other. They love me, but I was raised to be independent. Self-sufficient."

Beckett copied her movements with his hand on the water, and their fingers floated close together.

"Sounds lonely."

Her gaze snapped to his, and the word "lonely" tumbled around in her head. It occurred to her that she'd felt lonelier in the last few months of being with Emmett than she had before they'd begun dating.

"I had lots of hobbies."

"You still do, from what I can tell." Their fingers grazed in the heated water.

"Yup," she said, her voice catching a bit. "And I have a best friend, so no loneliness for me even without siblings." *Who you trying to convince? Him or you?* "She offered to come here when she didn't hear from me for the first several hours."

"A friend like that is every bit as good as a sibling. When you'd do anything for them or vice versa, what more could you need?"

Presley had a list of things she'd like. Things she wanted. But he was right. She didn't *need* more than she had.

"You've got two built-in best friends, I guess. What do they think about the bike shop?"

Beckett let his gaze wander to the trees. "I haven't told them." He turned on the bench, which brought them closer. "I love it when I'm here. It isn't my dream, but it might be Gray's. I want to give him a chance to figure that out before I decide what to do. I don't want him to be swayed by what I need. My obligation to family sort of trumps everything."

She'd taken high school science, so she knew that her heart couldn't actually grow in her chest without it being a serious medical condition, but holy hell, his words, the conviction in his eyes, and the sincerity of his tone made her chest tighten uncomfortably.

She reached out, touched his arm. "My best friend always tells me I can't sacrifice my own happiness for others. In the end, no one ends up happy if you don't."

He smiled, soft and slow and incredibly sexy. Maybe more so because she didn't see this smile when he was surrounded by people. "Your friend sounds smart."

Presley laughed. "She is. And feisty. You'd like her."

Beckett drew in a breath, making his chest, which she was trying not to study, rise. "I like *you.*"

It was a wonder she heard him with the jets, the erratic thumping in her ears, and the way his voice lowered to that husky timbre. It sent a shiver over her skin even though they were sitting in a hot tub.

"I like you, too." Which was bizarre, considering she'd planned to be here with another man. *Thank you again, Universe.*

"But you're hurting," he whispered.

Presley smiled. "My feet, maybe. But surprisingly, not my heart."

His smile was quiet in the glow of the lights but it lit her up inside. "I knew you lied about your feet."

Silence stretched between them, her hand on his arm, their gazes locked on each other. She definitely hadn't come here for this, but she was tired of ignoring the signs that were right in front of her.

Beckett Keller wanted to kiss her and she wanted the same. So she leaned forward, grateful he met her halfway. The heat of the tub, the heady scents of almost-summer wafting around them, and the softness of his mouth against her own made the kiss dreamlike.

She sighed into it as she moved closer and one of his hands cupped her cheek. The water lapped between them. She put her fingers on his wrist, not able to wrap them all the way around. Beckett's mouth moved over hers, gentle and sweet. Presley leaned closer, needing more. Needing him. Her other hand moved to his shoulder, her fingers digging into his skin just a little. He let out a sharp breath against her lips, their eyelids fluttering open for just long enough to scorch each other with want, then his free hand whipped around her waist, stroked up her back, stopping when his fingers touched the back of her neck under her hair. His forearm braced her against his body, locking them closer even as he turned the kiss deep and insistent. Their lips met over and over again. Ragged breaths, his tongue touching hers, retreating, teasing. When he changed the angle, tipped her head back a little against the cradle of his hand, he stole her breath. He could have it. She'd gladly give him that and anything else he wanted in this moment. Her own hands moved into his hair, her fingers tangling in the strands. It was soft, his body hard, and his mouth made her dizzy with desire.

When they parted, they were both breathing heavily. His forehead rested against hers as they regained some semblance of composure. Not that she wanted it—she'd trade feeling calm for his mouth on hers any time. How had she thought she knew what kissing was when, clearly, she'd been missing out until this moment?

"Wow." His voice was full of reverence.

Presley's heart bounced around in her chest, excited by this new development. "I'll say."

She loosened her grip in his hair, but only a bit. She liked the feel of it between her fingers. His hands stroked over her skin, up her back and down, along her outer thigh with a gentleness that made her feel precious. His choppy breathing matched hers and their chests rose and fell together. Letting her own hands drift down, she gripped his shoulders, sighed when his lips touched the underside of her jaw.

"Uncle Beck," came a shout just before Ollie rounded the corner.

They moved back from each other like the other was on fire. In a cute little swimsuit, her red hair in braids, bouncing like her steps, Ollie announced, "Mom says I can go fishing with you."

She hurried up the deck steps, stopping at the edge of the tub. She looked down at the two of them with so much excitement, Presley couldn't help her laughter.

"Mom made me shower before I came out. Did you guys shower? I beat Mel at Chutes and Ladders."

Jilly, in a navy-blue swimsuit, her hair piled on her head, rounded the corner. "Oh." She stopped when she saw them. "I'm sorry. I thought you'd be out later tonight. Ollie, we'll do this tomorrow."

She felt Beckett's embarrassment even without looking at him. "Don't be silly. I'm actually going to go. That hike did me in, and if I want to become a master fisherwoman tomorrow, I need some sleep."

Ollie lifted her arms so Beckett could lift her into the tub. He did so with a fun splash, making the little girl laugh.

"I'll put the worms on for you, Presley," she said, jumping up and down in the tub.

Jill sent Presley an "I'm sorry" look that was unnecessary.

Giving Beckett's sister a subtle headshake, she looked at his niece. "I would love that. You can be my expert." When she stood, her legs weren't entirely sure they were up to the task of holding her steady.

"Hey. I thought I was teaching you," Beckett said, finally meeting her gaze.

"We can share, Uncle Beck."

Jill covered her laugh with a cough and looked at her brother. "Yeah. You can share."

"Awesome," Beckett muttered. "You sure you need to go? Did you want me to walk you back to the cabin?"

"I'm fine on my own," Presley said after climbing out of the tub and grabbing a towel. She slipped on her flip-flops. "Enjoy your family time."

She walked back to the cabin, her brain and body buzzing. That kiss was as shocking as her being here on her own. Life was full of moments that changed a person, pointed them to new choices. She already knew that. But for years now, she'd chosen the safe path. The path she believed would lead to the end results she craved. She'd pushed realities aside for the fairy tales she spun in her own mind. She believed she could turn what existed into what she wanted.

With this trip, she hadn't chosen safety. She'd dropped herself right into the middle of a world she wouldn't choose. And she felt more like herself than she could ever remember. It begged the question she hadn't even considered: Who the hell was Presley Ayers? And what did she want?

Fourteen

Fishing was . . . *fun*. She knew her hair was all over the place and her cheeks were cold to the touch, probably bright red from the wind. She wore an oversized sweater under the ugliest life preserver ever invented. She'd stolen two pair of Beckett's socks to protect her Band-Aid-covered feet, but that made her shoes so tight it counteracted her intentions. Regardless, Presley bounced on her toes like Ollie, gripping the rod with determination and using the exact positioning Beckett suggested. The sun was out but the air was cool, and the gentle rocking of the boat lulled her this time rather than making her want to puke.

Ollie stood beside her, her hands wrapped around the railing as she tried to peer over. Beckett had thrown the anchor into what felt like the middle of the world. All they could see around them was water. It was unbelievably peaceful and oddly exciting at the same time.

Beckett joined Presley and Ollie at the starboard side—look at her, learning the lingo. Mel and Richard were on the port side, while Bernie was on the bow. Bo and his friend Morgan had taken the dinghy to go farther out. They were a tiny speck in the water.

"Uncle Beck, can I go in? Can I please?"

"Not while people are fishing, kiddo. You'll scare the fishies."

Ollie laughed at this. "Okay. Can I take my jacket off?"

Beckett shook his head. "You like when your mom lets you come, right?"

She nodded, her little chin bouncing up and down rapidly.

"Safety first, sweet pea. For all of us." He tapped his own life jacket, then gestured to Presley's.

"But the water is quiet," Ollie said. It was as close to a whine as Presley had heard from her.

"Things can change in an instant, Olivia." His voice was so serious. Ollie's eyes went wide at the use of her whole name. Beckett crouched. "You're our favorite person. Safety matters."

Ollie threw her arms around Beckett, not an easy feat since they both had on orange life vests. Presley's heart warmed right along with her skin. They were the absolute sweetest. He was so genuine with her, speaking to her in a way that didn't negate her age but didn't treat her like a baby either.

"Why don't you go see if anyone needs bait or drinks?" He set her down and stood up.

"Okay. Can I have a pop?"

He laughed. "It's eight A.M."

She stared at him. He nodded and she took off, starting to run, but then, like she could hear her uncle's voice in her head, stopping to walk. Fast.

"You are so good with her," Presley said, eyes fixed on the water. Why did knowing that, *seeing* it, make her feel so much?

"She's a great kid."

"She is. Any chance I'll catch anything?"

Presley had secretly worried she'd be bored or seasick but instead was enjoying the morning immensely. It would be incredible to catch something and post a photo, but the thought of sharing wasn't pulling at her like it usually did. Maybe because she'd had so many comments and DMs, it felt overwhelming. She ignored most of them when she'd posted a picture of the boat before they boarded. She'd tagged the lodge and added a couple of fun hashtags, like #FishOutOfWater #GreatAdventure and #GetLost. Several comments asked for more of Hot Mountain Man, but she didn't want to do that to Beckett. Posting a great big fish though? That would be awesome. Definitely not something she'd typically do. She'd laughed and sent a simple "No" to Ms. Twain, who'd texted to ask if she was working for a rival company. Clearly, more people followed her than she had thought.

Beckett leaned his forearms on the railing beside her and her pulse sped. She did her best to keep her focus. Just like she'd done her best to crawl into bed last night, pretending to be asleep when she'd heard him come in. Just like she'd tried not to think about the way his mouth had felt on hers, the slide of his tongue, and the pressure of his hands moving over her skin.

"Mel and Richard caught three trout but put them back. Too small. If you catch a big enough one, we can use it for dinner."

Presley scrunched her nose. "I don't know about that."

Beckett bumped her hip with his. "City girl."

"Absolutely. Though I'll happily admit, so far, this is fun."

She turned her head to see him watching her, their bodies touching along their sides.

"Wait until you catch one. It's a total high," he said, his voice low, making her feel like it was just the two of them out here.

She wondered which would rank higher: kissing him or the feel of actually catching something and reeling it in. She suspected not much would top Beckett's kiss.

Like he could read her mind, his face inched closer, his eyes open and on hers like he was seeking permission. She did her best not to shout *Yes, please,* instead playing it cool and leaning into him as well.

This kiss was like the cool, fresh breeze: soft, alluring, and very welcome.

She didn't want to think too much about what she was doing kissing a man she'd only known for two days. For once, she wanted to follow what felt good. No end goals. Just now. She'd had enough of real life. It had brought her here. Maybe there was a reason.

Her grip on the rod loosened as her body turned into him on its own, settling into him and seeking more. Her arm jolted, and for a second she just thought he was *that* good with his mouth, which inspired all kinds of ideas.

He pulled back, eyes wide. "You've got something."

She made a little humming sound in the back of her throat. "So do you," she murmured breathily.

He chuckled, his hand reaching out to grab the rod. "No. A fish. Turn your body, brace your feet."

He moved behind her as her kiss fog cleared. She didn't have time to be embarrassed—she'd fixate on it later—because her rod was bending.

Beckett nudged her right hand with a tap. "Reel. Fast. That's it. Keep going—lean back into me, not forward."

He surrounded her. It was difficult to identify where the sense of euphoria came from once the fish broke the water, flipping and twisting. The scent and feel of Beckett enhanced the moment and she kept reeling, pulling the fish up farther and farther. Her arms strained as the fish fought, her heart rate revving up like an engine.

Letting her go, Beckett grabbed a net, leaned over the edge of the boat. "Try to bring him in line with the net."

She did, but the fish fought for his life with everything in his scaled body. He flopped and pulled, spinning in crazy circles that yanked Presley's arms at their sockets.

"You got it. I'm going to cut the line, okay? Bring him in?" He pulled a pair of scissors from his back pocket. That didn't seem safe, but who was she to judge?

The rod shook, the line swinging, making the tip bounce. Presley stepped back away from the railing, trying to pull the fish closer. She tripped over Beckett's shoe, her arms going up over her head, the fish flying through the air, still attached to the line for a second before it broke free, landing with a thud and then slipping along the deck of the boat, right to Ollie's happy feet. The little girl didn't miss a beat as she leaned down, grabbed him in both hands, and held him up.

"We got one!" She turned with a wide smile and faced Richard, who had his phone out in front of him, filming.

The fish flopped and flinched in Ollie's hand, jumping right out. Presley could only watch as the fish hit the deck again, determined for his life to go on. Beckett hurried forward while Ollie bent at the waist, pointing her finger at the fish.

"You're being rude. Accept your fate, fishy," she scolded.

Beckett laughed, "It's fight or flight, kiddo. He's giving it his all." Beckett scooped up the fish, dropping it in the net. "Look at this beauty!"

He turned to Presley as she hurried forward. "Look at this. Your first catch!"

The fish continued to flail in the net. Presley's throat went tight. "Let him go."

"What?" Ollie yelled.

"That's our dinner!" Richard called with a hearty laugh.

Presley shook her head. "Please. Let him go."

Beckett regarded her carefully, handing her the net. She took it, leaned over the rail, feeling his presence directly behind her as she shook the net, turned it upside down. As the fish splashed back into the lake, a gasp escaped Presley's lungs.

She turned, net in hand, and flung her arms around Beckett. "That was amazing. I just couldn't keep him."

"You didn't need to. Sometimes all you need is the catch." He squeezed her tight, lifted her off the ground, then, like he remembered they weren't alone, let her go quickly, stepping back from her.

Presley crouched, looked at Ollie. "I'm sorry. It didn't feel right to keep him when he wanted to go home so bad."

Ollie reached out and patted the side of Presley's head. "It's okay. Uncle Beck says if you want to keep it you got to clean it, and I don't want to do that part at all. It's gross."

Presley laughed, the sound cutting off when Ollie threw her little arms around her neck, squeezing tight. Her heart filled and soared like a balloon with no limits.

The little girl let go and looked up at Beck. "Everyone's done fishing. Can we swim?"

He frowned. "That water is cold, Ollie."

She frowned back at him. "You'll go in the hot tub with me?"

He hesitated, then gave a curt nod. "Tomorrow."

"Today." She folded her arms across her chest with a grin.

Beckett reached out and tapped her nose. "Don't push it, kid."

Bo and Morgan climbed back onto the boat, laughing about the entire thing, which they'd watched from afar. Richard played the video and Mel put an arm around Presley, telling her how great she was.

Presley looked around at this group of strangers and couldn't believe she'd been dreading this trip. It wasn't just Emmett's signals she'd ignored. She'd disregarded her own. The world, like this group of people, seemed open and ready for Presley to explore in a whole new way.

She didn't want to think about the end of the trip, but she knew that when it came, she might not be the same person who'd shown up slightly broken. While it had seemed like the worst thing at the time, now she could put herself back together however she chose.

Fifteen

Gray didn't put up any sort of fight when Beckett said he'd take the boat to Smile. After spending the morning with Presley, after staying awake thinking about the way she felt against him, he needed some space. If he didn't get away from the delectable feel of Presley's mouth, the sweet scent only she carried, and the way her laughter made him feel like a different man, he was going to end up with a broken heart. Which made zero sense, since he'd only known her for two days.

He'd briefly thought, when he realized his attraction to her got stronger by the second, that he could propose a short-term thing. After a couple of nights exploring the insane chemistry between them, she'd leave, and he'd go back to figuring out his life. But the only thing he'd figured out was that where Presley was concerned, he couldn't get close to her without wanting *more*. And not just physically. If he let himself dive in, telling himself he could deal with temporary, he'd end up wanting something that couldn't happen. That would only make him even more unsure of where he was headed than he was at this moment.

Presley was the kind of woman who made a man commit one hundred and ten percent. Obviously not the idiot she'd been with, but any guy with a brain. That couldn't end well for him. Not with a woman who was gone in a week. *You kissed. She didn't propose marriage.* Maybe he was blowing the feelings out of proportion, but he couldn't stand being the one left behind again.

He'd had a taste of that when his high school sweetheart had moved away, wanting bigger, better, and all-around more. Smile was where Beckett wanted to live out his days. He loved walking through town and saying hello to people he knew. He liked that neighbors and friends counted on him. He didn't know everyone, but it felt like everyone knew him, and for a guy who spent most of his adult life being single, it made him feel less alone. Like he had a purpose. Sure, people knew the bad stuff—the shit he'd done in high school, like trying to pull a senior year prank only to have it blow up in his face. Too many people knew that he'd proposed to his high school girlfriend, thinking it would get her to stay. It was hard to date in a place where rumors flowed like coffee at Starbucks. Hell, it was hard to live in a town that didn't have a Starbucks. But he loved it here. *And yet, you're considering leaving.* He'd always assumed he'd grow old in Smile, but it occurred to him, between Brian's offer and Presley Ayers, that maybe he was being shortsighted. Maybe he needed to rethink his plan. Be braver. But not because of love.

Look what love had done to his siblings. They were different versions of themselves, and maybe that was great in some instances, but not necessarily in others, because in the core of who he was, a fling wasn't for him.

Beckett wanted a home, a partner he could share a life with. That life included the lodge for as long as Gray was determined to make a go of it. What it didn't include was falling for a woman on the rebound.

With everyone settled, he grabbed his duffel, like a coward, and headed for the speedboat. He was on it, ready to pull out, when Mr. Dayton stepped on the dock, moving quicker than usual. None of the other guests had been interested in leaving the lodge grounds.

"Hang on, son." The old man came his way, a duffel in his own hand. He held it up. "Wasn't sure how long you were leaving for so I came prepared."

Speaking of things he didn't have time for. "Mr. Dayton, I'm actually staying over on the mainland tonight. Tomorrow as well." He needed to get some things done or the opportunity would slip away. He should definitely say bye to Presley, but he knew if he got too close, he'd ask her to come with him. Or stay just to be with her.

"Fine by me. I like to mix it up."

Beckett stared at him. What was he supposed to do? "Where will you stay?"

Mr. Dayton smiled and reached a hand out for Beckett to help him aboard. "Don't you worry about me, Beckett, and for God's sake, call me Bernie. I never have trouble finding a place to hang my hat."

Laughing, Beckett helped the man aboard. The sun was holding steady in the sky, but the air was cool, and the world felt quiet. Beckett loved that feeling. As he started to back the boat out of its slip, he saw Presley coming out of his cabin. Jilly would move her back up to the lodge tonight. The AC issue was an internal spliced wire. Easy fix if someone knew what they were looking for. Beckett felt uncomfortable with the fact that he'd considered putting off his trip to the mainland if Presley had to stay in his cabin alone. The sun caught her hair as she tipped her head back and looked up to the sky.

The spot right below his ribs tightened.

"She is a looker. Sweet girl, too. Funny. Reminds me of my wife. Makes me miss her more," Mr. Dayton said, following Beckett's gaze, then sitting in one of the padded seats.

Space. That's exactly what he needed. From everyone. He needed to sort through the list of things weighing him down right now. He should have known the quiet wouldn't last. This old man really did have Ollie beat for most talkative.

"What are you tending to on the mainland? You have a job? You kids are running yourselves ragged."

Beckett kept one hand on the wheel as he adjusted his ball cap. "I have a few errands to run. I work at a sporting goods store, but I'm on vacation. It's hard taking over a business, but we'll get there." He didn't really want to get into specifics. Gray wanted to make a go of it, so that meant they'd do what they could to help him. *And if you told them about your choices, they'd help you make one.* One major life decision among them felt like enough for now.

"Beautiful place. Someone didn't appreciate it before they gave it to you," Dayton said behind him. His voice easily carried over the wind.

Beckett didn't disagree with that understatement, so he just nodded.

"My family owned it a long time ago," Mr. Dayton said after an unusual spell of quiet.

Beckett's hand slipped on the wheel, jolting them a little. He gripped the wheel but looked at the old man. "What?"

Mr. Dayton, looking like he was imagining another time, smiled into the distance. Beckett recalled how he'd sighed into his bite of burger the night before. *As good as I remember.*

The man's lips twitched as he rubbed his jaw with a wrinkled hand. "Before your time. I was just a kid. We used to spend our summers there. Then hard times hit, everything got sold off. I've been coming back for the last five years. Thought I might buy it, but it wasn't for sale. It's changed a lot. The cabin beside the one you're fixing up? It was the only one when I was a boy. It was mostly trees and animals. My brother and I used to stay in tents, as did most people who visited. Even needing repairs, it's a lot fancier than it was." He chuckled.

Beckett glanced back once again. "That's really amazing. I had no idea. I thought you knew the woods well." He turned back, easing off the throttle.

Another laugh, this one ending with a bit of a cough. "I knew them without all that trimmed greenery and the shortcuts. Been lost more than once in those woods."

"I'm glad you keep coming back," Beckett said. A strange feeling of nostalgia lodged in his heart. He couldn't explain it. How could he miss something that wasn't ever his?

They said nothing else for the remainder of the trip but Beckett couldn't wait to tell Gray, Jill, and Presley. The thought made his hand slip again. Not Presley. She wasn't part of his circle, because his circle was already jammed tight. A few kisses didn't equate a life together. What the hell was he doing getting all wrapped up in a woman just because she made his heart feel like it was full of sunshine?

Once they docked, Beckett headed for his car. He glanced at Mr.

Dayton. "Can I give you a ride somewhere?" If he used to visit the island, he was likely very familiar with the surrounding area. Smile, Michigan, was a tourist town. In two weeks, the town would be overrun with them. Beckett would be grateful for the island refuge.

"Nope. I'm good, son. You take care, and I'll make my own way back."

Like they'd been lying in wait, Anderson Keddy swung into the lot, got out of the bright green Mini Cooper they used as a cab, and greeted Mr. Dayton. Catching sight of Beckett, they waved.

"Hot Mountain Man! Almost time for a trim, buddy," Anderson yelled across the lot. They held up a lock of their own wavy, brown-blond hair in case the message was lost.

Beckett groaned. Mr. Dayton chuckled. *Awesome.* Anderson was also the hairdresser and barber for most of the locals. Beckett lifted a hand in an acknowledgment he didn't want to give, then hurried toward his car.

Slipping inside the stale-smelling, warm vehicle, he started it, then got the windows down for fresh air.

Beckett headed for his apartment. He'd do some laundry, repack, make sure nothing was growing a new life in his fridge. It was Tuesday, so Adam would be waiting to go to the store and get his groceries. Adam was a twenty-two-year-old gaming wizard who lived across the hall from Beckett. The kid was beyond shy but liked Beck. He was still learning how to navigate the world on his own, having lost his parents in a car accident a few years back. On the cusp of becoming an adult, he'd been catapulted into a life he couldn't have predicted.

The town took care of their own. When Adam sold his childhood home, unable to stay there with all of the memories, he'd moved into Beck's building, and the two had struck up an unlikely friendship.

A hot shower in his own apartment, one where he could actually turn around without touching the sides, soothed a lot of the kinks in his neck. He grabbed his wallet, keys, and phone and headed out the door. Before he could knock, Adam's door swung open.

"You were almost late," Adam said.

Beckett laughed. "Which makes me on time."

Adam stepped out into the hall, locked his door behind him. He had his reusable shopping bags in the backpack he wore.

They took the stairs down and walked out to Beckett's car without chatting. Once inside, Adam triple-checked his seat belt. Every time he did, it made Beckett's heart feel like it had claws jammed in it.

"Did you decide yet?" Adam asked, awkwardly trying to pull his phone out of his pocket around the confines of the seat belt.

"No." Beckett shook his head, realizing that his confidant was a twenty-two-year-old kid who wouldn't even go to the grocery store alone. He shrugged off the uncomfortable feeling. Adam was nothing if not impartial and exceedingly blunt. He also knew more about bikes than anyone other than Beck and looked at a situation from interesting angles.

"You might lose money the first year, but in the end, I believe you'll be successful enough to make it worth it. Especially if you choose a lot over a building and partner up with your brother to offer excursions. Have you told him yet?"

Beck shook his head. "No. And there's something I haven't told you."

Adam turned his head. "Tell me."

Taking a deep breath, keeping his gaze on the road, he told him the final piece of the puzzle: "Brian says I could buy in to the store, open a second location in Whitney."

"Whitney is a ferry ride and three-hour drive."

Yup. Adam knew his facts. "I know. But I'd be part owner."

Beckett pulled into the parking lot of his favorite deli. When he cut the ignition, Adam was still staring at him.

"If you open a bike shop, you'll be full owner." Adam grinned.

Laughter bubbled up in the space between them. Unlike Beckett, who added unnecessary roadblocks and layers to his own thoughts, Adam boiled it down to the simplest of points. And usually, he was right.

"There is that," Beckett said, opening his door.

Adam met him at the front of the car, his backpack on even though they were just grabbing lunch. "Put a note on the community board."

Nerves formed an alliance in Beckett's gut. If this wasn't something he wanted to keep on the down-low, he'd do just that. There was very little Maureen, who owned the General Store, didn't know. People used her wall-sized chalkboard as a community forum, asking for things, offering them, and sharing whatever information they wanted out there. Even if no one in the store found out, Maureen was Louis's older sister, which meant Chef would find out. His siblings would know within the hour.

Beckett started to clap Adam on the shoulder before remembering he didn't like to be touched without warning. Dropping his hand, Beckett just smiled at him. "Let's leave it for now."

The deli was in a strip mall with a couple of drive-through restaurant options—nothing recognizable. That would be too mainstream for Smile. The quickest options were Triple W's, which stood for Wally's Wonderful Wings—way too long to put on a sign—or Big Burgers. Smile was a step back in time with its false-fronted buildings painted ridiculously bright colors. Even the strip malls joined in on the fun decor.

As he and Adam walked into Angelo's, his phone buzzed with a text from Jill; it was a list of some things they needed.

Inside the deli, the tables were busy but there was no line up at the counter. His stomach growled, overshadowing the unease he felt from being stared at by the couple near the window.

Mrs. Angelo smiled at him from behind the counter. He didn't know her other than to recognize her, but she'd run this place since he was a kid. Her grayish brown hair was piled on her head and wrapped in a scarf. Her flower-patterned shirt poked through a white apron. She reminded him a bit of his mom with her friendly smile and assessing gaze.

"Beckett. Adam. How are you boys?"

Adam stared at the menu. "I'm good. I'll have a pastrami on whole grain, Dijon mustard, tomatoes, lettuce, pickles, and pepper."

"Please," Beckett reminded, shooting Mrs. Angelo a smile.

"Please." Adam went back to looking at his phone.

Mrs. Angelo nodded, her eyes soft. "How's your family?"

Beckett smiled, the muscles in his chest loosening. *See? Not everyone wastes time on the internet.* "We're good. Working hard, but we're okay with that."

When she winked at him, he thought he'd imagined it until she leaned in with laughter in her eyes. "But not all work, right? You and that pretty girl are having some fun?"

"Hot Mountain Man," Adam muttered, his eyes still on his screen.

Son of a . . . His mouth refused to work, but she didn't seem to mind. She waved away her own question and said, "What can I get for you?"

Ordering an Italian meat sub with a bag of chips, he listened to the chatter of the diners and watched as Mrs. Angelo whipped up a delicious-looking sandwich, humming to herself. When his gaze landed on a sign at the end of the counter reading WE CATER, he wondered about outsourcing. Presley really was rubbing off on him. *Do not think about Presley and rubbing in the same thought.* Though he did a great job, Chef was getting older. What if he couldn't keep making the commute? Plus, what if catering saved on food waste by ordering exactly what they needed depending on the number of guests? Not for dinners, but it might help with the other meals.

"I'm curious—" he started, clearing his throat like a nervous high schooler.

"That's a good thing in a person," Mrs. Angelo said with a wide smile.

Beckett laughed, enjoying the sparkle in the older woman's gaze even if he was the subject of some teasing.

"Not that he's asked," Beckett started, being sure to word things carefully. "But to make it easier on Chef, I'm curious about low-maintenance lunches, like sandwiches and salads, being brought into the lodge." Just an idea. A way to ease things up. They could even cut back Chef's hours.

Shane hadn't asked for that and none of them had discussed it yet, but Beckett knew Louis wanted more time with his husband. It was good to think ahead.

She set the mayo down, nodded her head. "Us old people don't like to admit when we need to slow down. It's a good idea, especially with Louis retiring."

Beckett nodded. *That* had been on the community message board. There was a big party later this summer to celebrate Louis's career as a teacher at Smile Public School, where he had taught PE for the last forty years.

"We're just looking to simplify a little."

"How often were you thinking?"

Not a no. "I'd need to chat with my sister and brother if you're open to it." Mrs. Angelo catered and ran a busy shop, a successful business. She knew how to turn a profit.

"It's only ten minutes from the dock to the lodge. We could organize custom orders depending on the number of guests you have. We'd just need to know first thing how many and what types of sandwiches. Your brother is back and forth daily, so pickup wouldn't be an issue. Are you looking at lunches only?"

Excitement hummed in his veins as he looked at the glass case full of baked goods.

"Breakfast options would be great as well."

She finished making the sandwich, wrapped it. "You talk to your siblings and I'll talk to my husband and daughter. I think we could work something out."

Beckett hadn't expected it to be this easy. "That would be great." He grabbed a pen by the cash register and a napkin, jotted his number down. "This is my number."

Mrs. Angelo put the sandwiches up on the countertop.

"Are you hiring for the summer season?" Mrs. Angelo asked as Beckett paid for the meals.

Adam sat at a table waiting.

"We're running on a low budget. We could definitely use some help, but we don't have a lot of free cash."

She nodded and Beckett told himself he didn't need to be embarrassed. Business ventures took time. Especially one that wasn't his own. Their own. He might prefer to keep to himself more than Jilly, but he knew that these people, the town of Smile, or a good portion of them, were rooting for his family.

"My nephew, he needs . . ." She pressed her lips together, the wrinkles at her eyes creasing deeper. "How can I say this politely? Some direction. Some focus. You still do guided hikes?"

"We do." Beckett wasn't sure how he had ended up being the main tour guide. Despite his enjoying them, the hikes cut into a lot of other things.

"He's coming to stay with us for the summer. He'll work here, but we don't want him to have idle time. What do you think about letting him lead some hikes? The fresh air, it's good for young people."

Smiling, Beckett thought about Presley's first hike and then the joy on her face when they'd gone fishing today. "Even if they don't realize it. "

"Yes." She stared expectantly.

"I'll speak with my brother. Meanwhile, if you could get your nephew to email a résumé to the lodge?"

"I can do that."

He said goodbye, high on the success of the conversation. It didn't escape his notice as he and Adam ate their sandwiches that the person he wanted to share this with was Presley. She had a keen business sense and had helped the lodge within twenty-four hours of being there. She'd get a kick out of his quick thinking. He could picture the smile on her face when he told her and knew, right then, that he was in big trouble.

He'd need to keep his distance if he wanted to keep his heart. There was no other choice: no more kissing Presley Ayers.

Sixteen

The rapid-fire texts from Ms. Twain made it impossible to pretend life didn't exist outside the island. Seeing no other choice, she pressed her boss's contact on the phone.

"Finally, you call me back." No "hello" or "thank you."

Presley sank down on the front porch. She pulled her sweater around her to ward off the morning chill. The bed in the lodge was more comfortable than the one in Beckett's cabin, but somehow, she'd woken this morning earlier than usual with a restlessness she couldn't shake.

"Ms. Twain, I am on vacation. On an island. With spotty cell service and boat access only."

"The Shefflys are staying with us. She says you always get them the best dinner reservations."

The aftereffect of tossing and turning last night was feeling especially snippy this morning. At least where her unappreciative boss was concerned. Presley's mind kept wandering to Beckett and how he hadn't said goodbye. How he hadn't said . . . anything. Not that he needed to. He didn't owe her anything. But she couldn't ignore the little stitch between her ribs when she thought about it.

"Presley?" Ms. Twain's tone was sharp.

Right. The Shefflys were repeat guests who preferred to have Presley as their personal concierge. "Yes. She likes to try new things but he prefers old favorites."

"Everything I suggest, she argues. You can make bookings from there?"

Mel, Richard, Morgan, and Bo set up bocce ball on the lawn. Even though she was a morning person, it was too early, in Presley's mind, for games that required focus. She'd never played, but she'd seen it before. Her parents were more museum and open-air market people than lawn game enthusiasts. They were high-rise apartment people who loved having a great selection of restaurants within walking distance. Presley had ended up the same without giving it any thought. She'd never had a reason to think outside that particular box.

Frustrated that her boss had broken the tranquility that seemed to come with the island lodge, she bit back her sigh. "Yes. I'll do that. How many nights are they staying?" The porch creaked behind her.

"Six more."

"I'll take care of it and email the information," Presley said.

"Breanna is filling in for you. It'll be a mess when you return."

"I'm sorry." Because what else could she say?

"You'll be back at work in a week. The management training seminar starts the next day. I've registered you for it."

Presley sucked in a breath even as Jill sat next to her, a GET LOST mug in her hands. "You did? Thank you. That's fantastic."

"You miss it, you lose out."

"Yes, ma'am."

They hung up and Presley realized the only thanks had come from her. She looked at Jill. "Other than dinner, I don't think I've seen you sit down."

Jill smiled. "I have to make myself."

"These moments must be nice," Presley said, setting her phone beside her. Booking reservations for one of her favorite couples wouldn't take long. She had long-standing relationships with several of the chefs and shop owners in the hotel's neighborhood. "When people are content and doing their own thing."

"They're perfect. We've spent so much time just trying to keep up that we, especially my brothers, never get a moment to sit and appreciate it."

"Are you happy to be here?"

Jill didn't answer right away. "I am. It's not where I thought I'd be. Professionally or personally."

Presley could certainly relate to that.

"I feel out of my element," Jill continued. "That can be overwhelming, but I love it when I'm here."

Jill's gaze was soft as she looked out at the grounds, and Presley was surprised by how much she connected with Jill's thoughts and words. There was a lot to love about the place.

"Do you live in Smile when you're not here?"

Jill took a sip of her drink. "I'm on leave from my job. Have been for a while. I'm living in my parents' place. Originally, I was going to get Ollie settled and then find a place. But they decided to travel, Gray got this place, and, well, she loves it. She thinks she's one of the managers." She laughed, and when she spoke of her daughter, everything about her relaxed.

"She could grow up to be a great one," Presley remarked, leaning back on her hands.

"Maybe then she can tell me how to make more money come in than out." Jill winced. "Sorry. You're too easy to talk to. That wasn't very professional."

Presley went with her gut, which had definitely led her wrong more than once. But not enough so that she was ready to stop trying.

"If you don't mind my overstepping, there are ways to simplify. You guys just need a solid chunk of time to wrap your head around it."

Jill looked her way. Her blue gaze was shadowed with fatigue. "What do you mean?"

Birds sang out from the trees. Presley figured her opinion could easily be ignored, so she didn't mind giving it. "You have an eclectic group of people here. Who do you *want* to cater to? What clientele do you want? If you're happy with the wide variety, rather than say, people solely interested in fishing, then you move to the next step. What do those people need when they're here? What's the best way to easily meet everyone's needs?"

"You make it sound easy."

Smiling, Presley shook her head. "Not at all. But there are some shortcuts and hacks I've learned in the last few years that take the pressure off of the host and put it on the guest to choose what they want, to help them be responsible for their own time. Also, I can help you with Facebook ads and such. If you want. I'm pretty good with marketing."

Jilly nudged her and Presley's chest grew warm. Other than Rylee, she didn't have a lot of friends.

"I'll say. You put us on the map with a post. I just got a booking for this afternoon from some women who want to meet Hot Mountain Man."

Presley had to bite her lip to keep from laughing. It had funny elements, but not always when real people were involved.

Laughter came from down by the lake. Ollie and Grayson had their pants rolled to their knees, headed toward the group on the lawn.

"She's a great kid." Presley had thought she was headed in *that* direction, too. Looking at Grayson with his niece, the way he put a hand on her hair to ruffle it and teasingly ran from her when she swatted him for it, reminded her Emmett had always had this little edge to his tone when he said the word "kids." Why had she let herself be so blinded?

"She's the light of my life. Theirs, too, I think. She's so good for Beck and Gray. She brings out a softer side of both of them." Jill waved at her daughter, who came running toward them.

It was the perfect opening to ask whether Beckett would be returning today, but she didn't want to show her cards. Not to his sister. Not even to herself.

"Hey, Presley," Ollie said, launching herself at her mom.

"Hello, there. What were you and your uncle Grayson up to this early?"

"We were building sandcastles."

"One of us was," Grayson said, joining them on the steps. "The other was seeing how much water could stay in the moat." He smiled at Presley. "Good morning. Did you sleep well?"

"I did. Thank you. The room is much more comfortable now." She preferred the cabin even though the room was nicer, but she strongly suspected that was due to the cabin's inhabitant.

"Glad to hear it." He looked at his sister. "I have to head over and grab the new guests this afternoon. I called Beck and asked him to come back sooner, so he should be here by lunch. I'll be back before dinner," Grayson told his sister.

"Remember the garden," Ollie said, pulling out of her mom's hug, where she'd been still for almost a whole three minutes.

"What garden?" Jill squinted up at her brother.

"Ollie wants to try to start a garden off to the side there," Grayson said, pointing to the left side of the lodge, where patches of dirt and grass shared space with the walkway to the backyard.

"Oh, honey. I don't have time for a garden today," Jill said. "I need to get the rooms ready."

The thought of dirt and worms sent a shiver up Presley's spine, but she was here, and it sounded a hell of a lot better than hiking. "I'll give it a try with you, Ollie. If that's all right with your mom and your uncle."

Both adults looked her way in surprise. It was Grayson who spoke. "You're a guest. You don't need to work."

"Oh. I don't think that counts as work. I'm going to try bocce ball, too. And I tried hiking. It's part of the experience, right?"

Gray gave her a warm smile that made her feel . . . included. Accepted.

"She wants to!" Ollie jumped off the step and stood in front of them with her hands on her hips. "You're supposed to give the guests what they want. Mom says."

They all laughed. Jill poked her daughter in the belly, making the little girl laugh. "Not exactly what I meant, cutie."

"I really don't mind as long as you know it'll most likely resemble upside-down grass in a weird shape more than a garden. I'm better at making reservations and getting a great deal on show tickets."

"Those skills shouldn't be undersold, my dear," Mel said as she wandered over to join them. She wore a different hat today, though this one was every bit as large. Her dress was a rust-brown, flowy one that made her look like she was at a tropical beach rather than a lodge.

Speaking of, Presley needed to book some reservations. She stood up as Ollie informed the other guest of their plans.

"Gardening is good for the soul. Mind if I help?" Mel asked.

"I feel awkward putting our guests to work," Grayson mumbled to Jill.

Mel shook her finger at him. "Nonsense. No one is doing anything they don't want to. Now, Ms. Ollie, let's see what kind of tools you have."

Presley really liked Mel. She was soft sophistication, adaptable like an indoor-outdoor chameleon.

"I need to take care of something, then I'll join you guys. Jill, if you have time later, I could show you a couple things for advertising. But only if you want."

Jill's lips flattened before she nodded. "Only if *you're* sure. You really don't have to."

Presley loved the idea of being able to share some of the things she knew. Especially with people who appreciated it. "I want to," Presley said, looking forward to it. The company. Not the dirt. Or the worms. She said a silent prayer that there wouldn't be anything worse buried in there.

❦

Worms were the least of her worries. There were some creepy-crawlies in that dirt that would haunt Presley's dreams. After the first couple of squeals, one crab-walk away from an offending critter, and landing on her ass by tripping over a trowel, she got herself under control. At least from the outside.

By the time the sun was high in the sky, she was nearly comfortable with Mel's instructions. They'd gathered a bunch of hand-sized rocks from the entrance to the hiking path and brought them back to the front of the lodge. Mel guided, but also helped. They used the rocks to create a flower bed along the front of the house. It was a lot of rocks, but the effect was charming. Mel suggested they paint them at a later date. She'd shown them how to turn the earth, something Presley hadn't even known was necessary. They pulled weeds, smoothed over the dirt, made a list of things they'd need, and started cleaning up their mess. It was hard but surprisingly rewarding.

"That looks fantastic," Beckett's voice said from behind her just as she was swiping a strand of hair off of her forehead. Gardening wasn't nearly as sweaty as hiking, but it wasn't easy either.

Presley didn't love the way lust pooled low in her belly just from the gravelly tenor of his words. Nor did she appreciate the way her heart full-on lurched in her chest when she faced him.

Those aviation sunglasses were blocking his gaze, but she knew it was pointed right at her.

"Uncle Beck. We need to grab some seeds. We're going to plant stuff. Look what we did." Ollie grabbed his hand and pulled him closer.

"We worked hard. I'd say we earned some iced tea, or possibly something stronger," Mel said, winking at Presley.

"Like coffee?" Ollie asked.

The three adults laughed. "Sure," Mel said.

"Why don't you and Mel go check with Mom and see what we have?" Beckett said.

Mel gave them a knowing look before taking the little girl's hand and heading off toward the lodge. The others had scattered a while ago. Presley couldn't believe how long it had taken to create a little garden that they hadn't even planted anything in.

Refusing to think too much about how good Beckett looked, or how easy she was to walk away from without a goodbye, she picked up the trowel, shovels, and garden gloves they'd found. "I should return these to your shed."

"I'll go with you," Beckett said.

They walked quietly to the shed that was housed on the side of the lodge. Anticipation and uncertainty poked at Presley's skin, throwing her off-balance. There was another outbuilding farther back on the property—kind of like a barn but not quite as big. Beckett opened the door and held it for her while she put the tools back on the workbench.

When he closed it, locked it up, he shoved his hands in his pockets, and Presley's stomach plummeted. She could hear the speech now: *We shouldn't do this, act on whatever this is between us. Kissing you was a mistake. You're making too much out of nothing. Like you always do.*

"I thought if I stayed away last night, I'd come back with a clearer head. But one look at you and I forget all of the reasons I shouldn't kiss you."

Presley sucked in a breath. As far as apologies went, that was damn good. It just didn't erase the "but" she worried would follow.

She swallowed, glanced at his lips before meeting his eyes. "You have reasons?"

He stepped a little closer, brought his hand to her cheek. Instead of cupping it, he rubbed the pad of his thumb over her cheekbone. It was about the least seductive thing he'd done. Her emotions were ping-ponging, smashing one way, then the other.

When she furrowed her brows, looking up at him with her nose crinkled, he laughed. "You have dirt all over your cheek."

She'd forgotten about everything that had happened before this minute. She was a mess. "I need a shower."

His eyes lit up like she'd struck a match in the dark. Clearly, he didn't mind what he saw. "You're leaving in a few days."

She nodded slowly. He dropped his hand. "Six. That's a few doubled."

"Exactly," he said with a wry grin.

Presley laughed. "Well, we have the math figured out."

He shook his head. "You seem like the kind of woman a guy doesn't get over."

Her heart muscles tweaked. "I have it on good authority that's not true." She meant it to be funny. Self-deprecatingly funny.

Beckett's gaze heated in an entirely different way. "No. You don't. That loser doesn't count."

She sort of loved how protective he was on her behalf. Like the waitress that day. On her side even without all of the facts.

"You're right. On both counts. I'm leaving and he was a loser. But I'm here for less than a week and I like you, Beckett. I came here thinking I was going to hide away in my room, watch Netflix, and eat my feelings. Instead, I've met awesome people, caught a fish, hiked, and even gardened."

"Not what you expected, huh?"

Nothing was like she expected. Or planned. His hands were now clenched at his sides in tight fists. Her own fingers itched to touch him, run her hands over his chest, up into his hair. She'd never felt this level of attraction and wondered if it was because of the fleeting factor. Or the getting dumped factor. Or so many other factors she didn't really want to examine right now.

Which of them had moved closer? It was hard to tell, but they were nearly front-to-front now. It wasn't one of her best ideas, but the ones she had thought were great hadn't worked out all that well either, so why not try a little something different? Something she hadn't written down in her planner.

Presley's pulse thrummed steadily at the base of her neck. "I didn't expect you."

"Back at you. But I don't know where that leaves us," he said with a hint of sadness.

She nodded. She wouldn't push. "Wherever we want it to, I guess. I'm going to get cleaned up. Maybe I'll see you later." *Idiot. Of course you'll see him later.*

"Presley." Her name on his lips could become one of her favorite things, and it had nothing to do with how sweet or sexy he was but instead was because he said it like she mattered. Like those two syllables meant something to him.

"Hmm?" Her throat grew thick but she forced more words out. "If you're around later, maybe we can hang out." Look at her sounding all breezy as a storm brewed in her chest.

A low growl left him and his hands unclenched, reached for her. "This might be a slippery slope, but something tells me you're worth losing my footing."

He leaned down, pressed a soft kiss to the tip of her nose that didn't match the way he held her; the way his fingers dug deliciously into her hips. The duality made her senses spin. "Not maybe. I *will* see you later."

He walked away, leaving her staring after him, her hands a little shaky, her heart jumping like a jackrabbit on speed. She still wasn't sure what she thought of the great outdoors. She didn't know if it was okay to get lost in a man's eyes after only a couple of days. But nothing made her want to back up or back down. She'd learned that having a solid plan didn't always make something pan out. Maybe it was time to stop being so careful. Stop thinking before she acted. Beckett made her want to do nothing more than feel. Everything. He made her want to go barreling down that slippery slope headfirst. She might end up buried under an avalanche of hurt, but as he'd said about her, she got the feeling he'd be worth it. More than that? She was worth the leap.

Seventeen

Under the hot, strong spray of the shower, Presley made a decision: if she had less than a week with Beckett, she would make the most of it. She sensed his hesitancy and even understood it, but she was tired of waiting for perfect moments to seize the day. She wanted to seize the day and the man. If he'd have her. No labels, no rules, no expectations.

By the time she joined the others in the dining room, the sun was high in the sky, shimmering through the tall windows.

Mel and Ollie were folding napkins at one end of the table while Jill put out plates and cutlery. They were clearly in the middle of a conversation.

"In the past, this place has been open year-round. I'm not sure what Grayson plans for the winter, but I'll have to go back to the mainland."

"I want to stay here," Ollie said. "Hi, Presley. Want to make napkin swans? Mel knows how to do everything."

Mel and Jill laughed. Mel pressed a kiss to Ollie's head. "You are just the sweetest thing." She glanced up at Presley. "I was a kindergarten teacher for twenty-five years. I simply have a lot of tricks up my sleeve. Speaking of which, did you get things sorted out for your boss?"

Presley looked at Jill and grinned, then back at Mel. "Nothing gets by you. I was able to arrange all of the reservations so she wouldn't have to."

"I wish I could be as organized here as you seem to be from afar," Jill said.

"It's just because I've done it before. You guys are doing a great job with the lodge. You'll find your own groove." She hoped she hadn't added more pressure by offering help or suggestions. It wasn't her place. Maybe she should grab a book and go back to her vacation for one. She considered it for one second until Ollie came over to show her the swan she'd made.

"This one is yours." Ollie beamed. The little neck flopped forward.

Beckett walked into the dining room with Mr. Dayton. Both were smiling. Presley's stomach gave a little jump when their gazes locked.

"What's everyone up to here?" Beckett asked, strolling over to pick up Ollie, his gaze still on Presley.

"We made swans for dinner," Ollie said.

"I'm not eating swans, kid."

Ollie laughed. "Napkin swans!"

Beckett jostled the little girl, making her laugh more. "I'm not eating napkins either."

"You're silly, Uncle Beck."

Presley's heart nearly melted into a puddle when the little girl curled into his neck and just rested her head against him.

Beckett leaned his head on Ollie's, glancing at Presley again. "No swans for you?"

She shook her head. "Let's just say I have other talents."

His gaze heated and she realized the double entendre of her words, felt her cheeks flush.

Jill shot her brother a sly grin that had Presley looking down at her hands to avoid both of their gazes. Setting the table went quick with everyone helping. Mel went to check on Richard. Mr. Dayton followed, likely heading to his own room.

Voices and commotion came from the front of the lodge.

Jill hurried around the table, still grinning as she snagged Ollie's hand. "That'll be Gray with our check-ins."

In the silence, Presley second-guessed the decision she'd come to alone in the shower. Nerves tumbled inside of her. So, they'd kissed. Twice. She wasn't twelve, so that didn't make him her steady boyfriend. She was only here less than a week.

He stepped closer, his hair disheveled in a sexy, careless way. "How'd you sleep last night?"

Had he thought of her like she had him? "Good," she said, nodding, lacing her fingers together. "Really great. Not too hot, not too cold."

Beckett smirked. "Glad to hear it, Goldilocks." He picked up a lock of her dark hair, let it drift through his fingers.

The sound of laughter, loud and voracious to the point of exaggeration, came from the lobby.

Beckett frowned. "I should go help with guests. See you at dinner?"

She nodded. When he left, she stayed in the dining room, willing her heart rate to settle. She had no idea how to account for the barrage of feelings he inspired in her. She'd been with Emmett for almost eight months, been working toward moving their relationship forward, and not once had a subtle touch, a look, or a smile from him lit her up like a bonfire inside.

More laughter and some interesting sounds came from the lobby. Hanging out in her room until dinner, alone, seemed like the most sensible idea. At least then she wouldn't make a fool of herself staring at Beckett while his siblings looked on. Doing her best to move through the lobby like a ghost, she kept her head down as the laughter and loud voices continued.

"Presley!" Beckett's voice was nearly frantic.

Her head snapped up, and she saw him surrounded by three women. Two were around her age, one was older, and they all looked similar enough that she'd guess they were family. Mother and daughters. The mom, a tall, willowy Goldie Hawn look-alike, was running her hand down Beckett's chest. He couldn't stop her with the number of bags in his hands.

Jill looked like it was taking serious concentration for her not to laugh.

Grayson was leading two guys up the stairs with their bags.

"You are every bit the mountain man your social media advertised," the older woman said.

Presley stood still, biting her bottom lip as Beckett's cheeks brightened.

"I don't have social media, ma'am."

"We saw you on Instagram. Who was the genius that decided to use you for marketing?" one of the younger women, whose hair fell lushly over her shoulders, asked.

His lips thinned, and he took a step back and met Presley's gaze with an imploring one of his own. Her eyes widened. She gave him a shrug. What was she supposed to do? Sure, she'd gotten him into this, but he was the one with the six-pack!

Jill stepped around Beckett and gestured to Presley with an interesting grin. "His girlfriend. Presley."

His *what?* Her eyes couldn't open wider.

He smirked at Presley, wasting no time in confirming his sister's fib. "That's right. My Presley. I mean, my *girlfriend*. My Presley." His eyes pleaded. There was a hint of desperation in his tone.

Presley shuffled forward, unsure what she was supposed to add to this moment. "It was an accident, really."

The women turned her way, giving her a once-over. One of them reminded Presley of a wicked stepsister with a more pleasant smile. "Girlfriend? The hashtag was #HotMountainMan. Not #CoupleGoals."

"Gabriella," the had-to-be-mom said, her tone sharp like she was dealing with a petulant child.

Jill grinned, looking suspiciously like she was trying not to laugh as she moved behind the counter.

"Come here," Beckett said, his gaze set on her. When she hesitated, he lifted his brows—which seemed to be a family parlor trick—and added, "Sweetheart."

Presley bit her lip, while Jill had the good grace to cover her laugh with a cough. Presley moved to Beckett's side with more than a little apprehension. Catfights weren't her thing.

"Welcome to Get Lost Lodge," Presley said, standing as close to Beckett as she could with all the bags in the way.

"Thank you. We're excited to be here," said the other woman. "I'm Libby, and this is Gabby, and our mama, Chantel. We were already planning a girls' getaway when a friend of a friend told us about this place and your Hot Mountain Man. We checked out the website, thought it looked like a little slice of heaven, and decided, why not?"

Libby was more polished, more professional, and somewhat familiar, though Presley couldn't place her. She probably followed her on TikTok or something.

"Well, my family and my *girlfriend* and I are very happy you could join us." Beckett reached out, shifting the bags to find and grasp Presley's hand. Gabriella, still pouting a bit, leaned across the counter, addressing Jill. "Any others as fine as him around here?"

"The captain was a cutie pie," Libby said. Her mother nodded.

Presley wanted to remind these women that Beckett and Gray were men. Humans. Not objects they could get their paws on. Irritation and an odd feeling of protectiveness rose up inside her, overheating her skin. "There are a number of wonderful guests, and Smile is only a short trip away. Rooms one and two connect, don't they?" Presley had realized the door she thought led to a closet in her room actually joined the room beside it.

Jill's brows arched even as her gaze narrowed. "They do."

Now or never. She'd packed up all her stuff after the shower, hoping she'd have the nerve to tell Beckett she'd rather stay with him.

"We have them in rooms two and five," Jill said slowly, eyeing Presley. "Those are the ones I was able to get ready."

Grayson descended the stairs, Bo and Morgan behind him. They took obvious notice of the women, putting on smiles and straightening their shoulders. Presley would have laughed if the tension in the air wasn't poking her like a hot stick.

"We recently had the guest check out of room one. Didn't we, Beckett?" She'd wanted to dive in. Seemed like now was a good time. Putting on what she hoped was a great girlfriend smile, she stared up at Beckett, putting one hand on his biceps.

His smile loosened, widened. "That's right. I'll just take these to room one and unlock the connecting doors, and that'll make your visit with us even better," Beckett said, his smile more genuine.

When he started for the room, Presley, still holding on to him, naturally fell into step beside him, muttering under her breath, "I need to grab my bags, but otherwise the room is clean."

He looked down at her. "You packed up your room?"

Looking away, she stared at the door, using her key to open it. Jill was talking to the women and the guys, including two new guests who had joined the little group.

Beckett chuckled under his breath. "Not going to tell me why you packed your things when you're staying another six nights?"

They went into the room, and Beckett put everything on the freshly made bed. She picked up her bags, which she'd left by the door, and sent Beckett what she hoped was a haughty glance. Not that she had much of a soapbox to stand on now.

"Maybe I'm leaving."

The door shut behind them, giving them a second of privacy. He used that second to close the distance between them. Presley backed up into the wall, anticipation humming along her skin at an alarming rate.

Fisting his hands in her hair, Beckett lowered his chin. No hesitation now. There shouldn't have been so much satisfaction in that. He leaned down, so close she could taste his breath against her lips. It made her crave more. "Are you?"

"Maybe."

His gaze lowered, his body pressing in. His lips twitched. "Presley Marie Ayers."

She laughed, tilted her head. "Well played. Does it matter?"

His gaze went impossibly dark. "It matters."

They held each other's stares, neither of them saying anything. "I would think, as my boyfriend, you could guess my plans."

His grin came lightning fast. "My *hope* is that you're staying in my cabin."

"We don't have a lot of time," she said, reminding him of his earlier concern.

His breath fanned her face, his body molding itself to her own. He nodded, like he was making a decision. "Then I guess we'd better make the most of it."

She liked the idea and the way he said that. Very much. A knock sounded on the door. They jumped apart as Jill opened it.

"Guess you two got lost in here," she said, her voice loud.

"Nope. Just making sure everything is all ready." Beckett picked up Presley's bags as the women filed into the room.

"Whose are those?" Gabriella asked, crossing her arms under her breasts, lifting them while at the same time showing off a tanned and toned midriff.

Beckett looked at Presley, who looked at Jill.

Jill walked forward, took the bags. "Another guest's. Wrong room. I'll take these."

Beckett and Presley walked out of the room, her hand in his, into the lobby. Jill closed the door to room one and followed them, setting the bags down by the front desk, where Grayson and Mr. Dayton chatted.

With his hands on his hips, Gray looked at the group, his gaze lingering on Presley and Beckett's clasped hands. "What's going on?"

Presley looked at Jill, who looked at Beckett, who was looking at Mr. Dayton. Morgan and Bo stood grinning at everyone. Ollie came down the stairs, Richard and Mel behind her. She'd adopted them, so it would seem.

"What'd we miss?" she asked, rushing up to them while the couple took their time.

Beckett sent his sister a wide grin. "Yeah, Jill. What'd they miss?"

Jill's cheeks went a pale shade of pink. "I was helping *you*. Presley, I'm sorry. That was unprofessional, to say the least. I just didn't want Beckett to feel uncomfortable, and they were . . . a lot. Calling you his girlfriend just happened. I'm sorry."

In all honesty, Presley wasn't overly upset about the idea. "Don't be. I could do worse," she teased, bumping Beckett's hip with her own.

Grayson said, "Girlfriend?" He looked at Beckett.

Beckett slipped his arm around Presley's shoulder, and she knew she shouldn't dwell on how good, how *right,* it felt. "It's new."

Ollie looked like Mickey Mouse himself had come straight from Disneyland to invite her to lead the parade. The little girl grabbed the front of his shirt, yanking on it as she jumped. "You have a girlfriend, Uncle Beckett? Is that why you two were kissing on the boat yesterday?" She looked at Presley along with everyone else.

The weight of all the stares pushed on her rib cage and Presley did one of the two things she always did in highly stressful situations. Her default was going into the zone and doing what needed to be done, like getting to the island on autopilot. The backup default was a tad more embarrassing. At least at the moment. In all moments. Any of them.

Presley let out a sharp breath and started to laugh. Hysterically.

Eighteen

They'd broken his fake girlfriend. To be fair, it was amazing she hadn't fallen apart, in any way, already. Beckett might not know her well, *yet,* but he knew she'd been holding herself together every second of the day since he'd first laid eyes on her, and probably in a lot of the moments before that. In the last four-plus days, she'd broken up with a long-term boyfriend, traveled out of her comfort zone, learned she didn't love boats, tried several new things, and been inundated with him and his family. Now this. Even someone with as much bravado and grace as Presley Ayers had to have a breaking point.

Beckett, Grayson, Jill, Mr. Dayton, Bo, Morgan, Ollie, Mel, and Richard watched as she bent in half, tears streaming down her face, giggles erupting from her mouth.

She tried to speak but couldn't—she just kept waving her hand in the air and resuming her giggling. Eventually, they all joined in, because the days and nights lately had exhausted them and laughing felt really freaking good. Even if it was somewhat maniacal.

Several moments passed before they wiped tears from their cheeks, straightened out their posture, and pulled in several deep breaths. Surfacing from her laughter, Presley seemed to take a sharp turn into embarrassment.

"I'm so sorry. I don't know what came over me. I think I'm just completely overwhelmed. So much has happened, and—" She stopped. Inhaling deeply, she held her breath, then let it out. "I'm sorry."

"Don't apologize. That's the best laugh I've had in a long time," Mr. Dayton said.

"Me, too," Grayson said.

"No clue what we're laughing at, but it felt good," Morgan said.

"Adults just don't laugh enough," Ollie added.

Gray scooped her up. It was as if the laughter had lightened his load. Beckett looked at Presley with what he was sure was an expression of awe. This woman was magic. Maybe one little peek behind the curtain wouldn't hurt.

"Let's table the girlfriend conversation and talk in the dining room." He couldn't be mad at his sister. Presley was going to be in his cabin, his life, and, hopefully, his arms, for the next six days. Those women had made him feel like an all-you-can-grab buffet. Jill had simply gone on the defense for her brother.

Beckett looked at Mr. Dayton and gave him a subtle nod to let him know he was included in the chat. In between trying not to think of Presley, he'd had some other ideas last night and wanted to share them with Jill and Gray. Mr. Dayton knew the history of the lodge better than any of them.

"We're going to fish off the dock until dinner," Morgan said as he and Bo went on their way.

"Ollie, what do you say we go water your garden?" Mel took his niece's hand, and Beckett's heart pinched. He couldn't wait until his family was all together. In a way, he'd made at least one decision. He couldn't leave them behind. Not even for a stake of the company. He still wasn't sure if he'd open a bike shop, but he wouldn't be opening a new store for Brian.

"There's nothing in it yet," Ollie said.

"Nope, but you want to get the soil ready," Richard said.

"If that's okay with your mom?" Mel looked at Jill, who nodded.

❧

In the dining room, which seemed to serve as their meeting space more often than not, they all sat around the long, rustic wood table. His mother was going to love it. She was going to refinish it after watching a dozen YouTube videos, and then she would love it.

Jill spoke first. "Our Instagram account for the lodge has over one thousand new followers. Someone reposted the photo on Twitter and TikTok. We don't have TikTok, but I've seen a few videos." Jill looked at Beckett like she couldn't quite believe what was happening because of a photo. That made two of them. "Our online booking site crashed because of traffic."

Beckett grinned. No time like the present to move forward.

Presley tapped her fingers on the table. She didn't meet Beckett's gaze but clearly spoke to him. "I really didn't mean to make you an Instagram meme or household name."

"Don't even think of apologizing, Presley," Grayson said. "We've had a few requests from other accounts to advertise their products. Outdoor apparel companies in the area, a shoe company with a new hiking boot, and a beverage company. They're not only willing to pay but willing to provide free merchandise and promotion."

Beckett's head swung to his brother. "What?"

Grayson nodded. "Our DMs on Instagram have exploded. I've been sorting through them. And those women talked about you the entire trip over. One of them is a lifestyle blogger? I don't even know what that means, but I think it's good."

Beckett ran a hand through his hair, almost at the same time as his brother. Though he suspected Grayson's action was one of relief. Beckett's was not. He wanted to get them on the map in an entirely different way. One that had nothing to do with his abs on a social media app.

"Not to make things worse, but I really think it's in your best interest to capitalize on your momentum. If you do Instagram live, maybe even a giveaway of some sort, you could keep your numbers up," Presley said, lowering her gaze.

He reached for her hand on her lap, closed his around it. "As long as it's not *me* going live, that's a good idea. Like Shane's idea to post you two making French toast. We could make it a signature dish." Even if they catered, they could still have some specialties. And he knew, no matter how many days she was here, he'd never be able to eat the breakfast food without thinking of her again.

Jill grinned. "That would be fun. Ollie and I could do it. Maybe a live walk-through, what we offer, that sort of thing." She looked at Presley. "What do you think?"

"Now is the time to act. I know that might mean investing more money in repairs than you have up front, but it'll have a big payout if you can book up for the entire summer. I have a notebook full of ideas I've been jotting down." Presley ducked her gaze again. "It's just something I do when I'm trying to occupy my thoughts. I didn't sleep well last night and I made a list of things that would be easy to do but make a big impact for you guys. If it's not overstepping, I could share it?"

Beckett squeezed her hand. Not overstepping. Another *step* in the right direction, even though it was one more reason he might regret getting close. She was going to leave an empty space in each of their hearts.

He glanced at Presley, whose hair hung loose around her shoulders. Why had he thought he could stay away from her when he only had limited time? A man didn't *not* fish at all just because he only had a short stretch of time to do it. Beckett's life was all about small pockets, little moments in between the noise to fully embrace what made him happy. He hadn't found anything that made him as happy as this woman. He wasn't sure where he'd land in any area of his life, but he knew he'd regret not taking a chance, even a brief one, with Presley. He thought about the look in Mr. Dayton's eyes when he spoke about his wife. Beckett wanted a lot of things. He did not, however, want a lot of regret.

Nineteen

Mr. Dayton lingered, listening like a wise sage, nodding now and again. Beckett figured there was no harm in sharing the connection since the man still sat comfortably and made no move to leave.

"You'll never guess whose family owned this place way back in the day," Beckett said, leaning against the chair, his shoulders relaxing.

Grayson, Jill, and Presley looked his way, waiting for an answer without guessing.

Mr. Dayton chuckled. "That would be me." He lifted one hand like he was in school, then lowered it.

"No way," Jill said, delight lifting her features.

"How long ago was this? Has it changed a lot?" Gray folded his arms on the table and angled his body toward the older man. One of the great things about his brother was that he was willing to put in the work, but he didn't let pride get in the way of success. Beckett needed to tell them about Mrs. Angelo, the deli, and her nephew. *And the damn bikes.*

"Oh my. I was just a boy. Over fifty years ago. Come on. I'll show you something."

They followed him out of the dining room. Ollie left Mel to the watering, joining them as they went down the lodge steps, taking the older man's hand. Beckett's parents' most recent trip was the longest one they'd taken. They'd worked their entire lives, sometimes more than one job each, and now, they were finally getting the retirement they deserved. But it would be nice when they got back. Ollie missed her grandparents, and the siblings missed them as well.

They walked to cabin three, nestled in the trees with a great view of the water. Mr. Dayton turned, gripping Ollie's hand. "Got a key?"

Jill rushed up the steps, used her master key, then stepped into the house, holding the door open. Everyone else followed. It was musty. This one had no furniture. Grayson and Beckett thought it might have been used as a staff quarters, because there'd been a bunch of sleeping bags and beer cans when they first took over. What was left behind didn't seem like a setup for paying guests. Looked more like a frat flophouse.

"Stuffy in here," Mr. Dayton said, looking around the room with a hint of a smile on his face.

He dropped Ollie's hand and they watched as he took in the bachelor pad cabin. With one small closet and a tinier bathroom, this one would need a pullout couch; maybe a rollaway bed. Beckett would have to check Presley's site and see what he could find.

Walking to the stone fireplace that trailed up the wall, Dayton knelt down, using the wall as support. He pulled a handkerchief from the pocket of his shorts.

"What are you doing?" Ollie asked, peering over his shoulder.

He was clearing the dirt and dust from the corner where the stone met the wall.

"Check this out, Ollie-girl."

She peered even closer. "'BD was here,'" she read.

Beckett grinned, surprised by the emotion that rose up. "This is the one that was yours."

Dayton looked back over his shoulder with a bittersweet smile. "It was. Some of my favorite memories are in this cabin."

Grayson stepped forward to lend a hand as the guy started to get up. Dayton brushed off his knees.

"This is such a cool thing, Mr. Dayton. I love that you have happy memories here," Jill said, moving forward to squeeze his arm.

Some guests weren't just guests. Beckett knew that this crew—Dayton, Richard, Mel, and even Bo and Morgan—was special.

Dayton's smile turned cheeky. "Got in trouble for that. Took me forever to etch it in and even longer for my mom to stop being mad."

"I love that you have history here," Gray said.

"Can I scratch my name in?" Ollie asked.

Presley laughed when he, Gray, and Jill all said no at the same time.

Ollie frowned and asked to go play on her tablet. Jilly kissed her head and answered, "Just for a little while."

Ollie dashed to the door, calling out on her way, "Okay, Mama. Bye, Mr. Dayton."

"See you soon, Ollie."

She took off like she couldn't wait to leave, and they laughed at her enthusiasm. Gray wandered the room, probably wondering, like Beckett, how much it would cost to outfit the place. They needed the cabins more than ever. Jill had her phone volume on low, but Beckett could hear it pinging constantly.

"Did you come here with your wife ever?" Presley asked Mr. Dayton, who stood staring out the window to the water in the distance.

He smiled at her. "I did. For our fiftieth anniversary, four years ago. Wasn't the same as I'd remembered it. The year before I came without her, and now, I find myself wishing I'd never left her side while I still had her here."

Presley lowered her head, but Beckett could feel her sadness. Or maybe it was his own. He couldn't imagine falling in love, never mind losing the love of his life. A little voice buried deep in his brain struggled more with the idea of finding her and willingly letting her go.

"We can't go back. I bet she'd be glad you're here now," Jill said, flanking his other side.

Mr. Dayton squared his shoulders, turned his back to the window. "She would. I spent most of my life worrying about making money. I loved that woman more than anything else. I mistakenly thought I could prove that by giving her everything. All she ever wanted was me. Now I just want to be in places that remind me of her and of good times I've had."

"I think that's a really great way of honoring her," Grayson said, his voice suspiciously gruff.

"I'm glad you think so, son. Because I want to buy this cabin."

Beckett blinked several times. Had he heard that right?

"It's not for sale," Gray said hesitantly.

Obviously not deterred, Mr. Dayton stepped toward Grayson. "I know you think that, but you should hear me out."

Gray sent a glance to Jill and him. They both gave subtle nods. Presley cleared her throat. "Maybe I should go." She started to back up.

"I have no secrets. Especially from Beckett's *girlfriend*." The older man's gaze danced with mirth.

Beckett's cheeks warmed when Presley met his gaze. "Sorry." But he wasn't. Not entirely.

She shook her head, then looked at Mr. Dayton.

"Go ahead, Mr. Dayton," Jill said.

Like he was dressed in a three-piece suit in a boardroom—Beckett could almost picture him in his glory days—he held one hand at his middle, addressing them like he'd prepared this speech.

"It's easy to see that you kids are finding your feet. We can help each other. I want to purchase a piece of my past. If I give you fair market value for this cabin, as it is now, you'll have cash up front, which will give you some breathing room, and I'll secure a vacation home that lets me be where I want but means I don't have to do all the work for the grounds or anything else. Let's be clear—I can afford a cabin that isn't run-down, and one with a better view, even though this one isn't bad. But I'm not looking for new. I'm looking for nostalgia."

Beckett couldn't wrap his head around this. Grayson beat him to the question that popped into his brain, asking, "What about renovations or updates on the cabin?" His brother looked around, gestured to the current state.

"Again, we can help each other out." The older man smiled. "You'll be giving me a deal on the sale because it's not in great shape though the bones are solid. I'll pay for the renovations myself."

Damn. It sounded too good to be true.

"Would you be part owner?" Jill asked. Another great question.

"Yes and no. I'd be full owner of this cabin only."

"I don't even know the logistics of how I could do the paperwork for that," Grayson muttered.

"You could do it like a percentage so on paper it would look like he is part owner but add in whatever clauses make it clear that he only has ownership of this piece. You'd have to decide if he paid a rental fee on the land or if he owns outright," Presley said. She looked at them all then pressed her lips together. "Sorry."

"No. Please don't be," Beckett said. "That's an excellent point."

"What happens if you change your mind?" Gray asked. "If this place stops being special, if you need more updates, want to add on?"

Dropping his shoulders, Mr. Dayton sighed. "I'm good at reading people, Grayson. You're going to get on your feet with or without me. This is a way to do some of it without an uphill battle. If I wanted more, I'd have asked for it. Truth is, I thought of buying the whole lodge, but I'm glad I didn't get the chance. I don't want to run this place or make money. I just want to have a home away from home that reminds me of things I once had. A place I can feel comfortable and connected to my family even though they aren't here."

It would mean they had one cabin less, if Dayton owned it, but the benefits could far outweigh the drawbacks.

Jill smiled at Beckett, then Gray, who shoved his hands in his pockets.

"We need to discuss this as a family," Grayson said.

The words stuck in Beckett's chest, like a sliver in his rib cage. He couldn't leave his siblings for a stake in Brian's company. He didn't *want* to. He needed to tell Gray and Jill about the bike rental idea. It would tie in perfectly. Especially now. With Dayton's money and the business loan Beckett had been preapproved for, the road was stretching out in front of him with an obvious sign saying: THIS WAY.

"I'd think less of you if you didn't," Mr. Dayton said.

"We need to get ready for dinner," Jill mentioned.

"I didn't even get to tell you guys about my trip to the mainland." Beckett realized there was a lot of good news to share.

"Maybe we should meet up after dinner," Grayson said, sending a smirk to Jill. "We could close down the hot tub again."

Presley laughed, holding up her hands. "Not because of me this time."

"But you're welcome to join us," Jill said. "You have valuable contributions, and Beckett's never brought a woman home before, so we need to get to know you."

"Enough. That was all you, but I'm not sorry. Those women treated me like meat. Happy to be off the market," Beckett said.

Presley laughed, pretending to fan herself. "This is all moving so fast."

"Maybe you guys need some time to chat as well," Grayson said, matching his sister's smirk.

"It's not a bad idea. I'd like to know more about our relationship," Presley said.

Mr. Dayton laughed. "You set the rules, Presley. He's lucky to have you."

Beckett smiled at Presley. "We've barely begun and I think I owe you flowers."

"If that Gabrielle woman sends me dagger eyes at dinner, you're going to owe me a lot more than that."

They all laughed. Grayson and Jill walked out first. When Beckett and Presley started for the door, Mr. Dayton asked if he could stay for a moment.

Beckett grinned at the man who'd asked so many questions the other day that he couldn't have imagined then feeling the fondness for him that he currently did.

"Stay as long as you'd like," he said.

When Presley took his hand on the walk back to his own cabin, he wanted to say the same to her.

Twenty

Oh boy. There was some serious activity happening in her stomach—like a flock of chickens pecking around and getting all worked up. The closer they got to the cabin, the more sensitive her skin felt, like even the breeze registered. Her chest tightened, her lungs shrinking. His girlfriend? It had taken Emmett three months and an argument to introduce her as something other than his "gal pal." That should have been a hammer-to-the-head clue. She really hadn't wanted to see what was right there before her.

Beckett pulled his phone out of his back pocket as Presley shut the door.

"Jilly will bring your bags down. We left them in the lobby." He looked at her; she leaned her back against the door, unsure, unsettled, unbelievably attracted to him.

Whatever words she'd had ready vanished as they stared at each other. Beckett came closer, stopping just before their toes touched.

"You okay?"

She nodded. Presley felt like she'd had one too many drinks, like the old version of herself was watching the new version of herself, egging her on. *Be bold. Take what you want. You have less than a week to be whoever you want to be with this man.*

"Just staring at my boyfriend," she said with a smile, fluttering her lashes playfully.

Beckett laughed, ducked his gaze. When he looked up again, she recognized the heat in his eyes. Felt it between them like something tangible she could hold. He stepped closer, the fronts of their bodies touching.

"I'm sorry. I did warn you about Jill's matchmaking."

Presley put her hands on his chest. His went to the door, caging her in. "It's fine. I don't blame her for protecting you. The mom was a little frightening."

"Yes!" He laughed, but the sound cut off quick when he rested his forehead against hers. "I wish time would slow down."

"Something tells me this brief relationship is going to be better than even my longest one." Her fingers curled into his shirt.

"Presley." He said it like a curse and an oath in one.

"You're okay with this?"

His breath was shaky, which made her feel better about how worked up she was. She was quite certain she'd never wanted anyone—possibly anything—this bad.

"I'm more okay with it than I am with walking away," he said, his finger sliding lazily up her arm, leaving a trail of goose bumps.

"So, all in?" She wanted the words. She wanted to hear what he was saying with his eyes, his hands.

"I can't imagine anything less." Beckett's mouth opened as if to say more but Presley cut him off with a kiss. No more waiting. If their days were limited, she wanted every single second of every one. A low growl left the back of his throat, spurring her on, making her want more. His hands came to her hips, gripped them as she went up on tiptoes, wrapped her arms around his neck like she was his life preserver and he might drown if she loosened her hold even a fraction. *Not on my watch.*

One of his hands streaked down her side, up, played with the hem of her shirt, his fingers grazing bare skin. The need to get closer pulsed inside of her. His other hand burrowed into her hair, pulling little tendrils, but she didn't care. This moment was burning itself into her brain like a permanent Etch A Sketch.

A heavy knock made them both jump. He moved back but she had nowhere to go. She bit her lip, could still taste him.

"That'll be Jill," he said, his voice low.

"Right." She inhaled a sharp breath, let it out quickly, smoothed down her shirt. Turning, she pulled the door open and was met with only her bags. Peering out, she saw the back of Jill, who was heading back to the lodge. She picked up her things, brought them in.

"I'll put those in the bedroom," he said.

When he took them, their fingers brushed and she wondered if this electricity between them was stronger simply because of the timeline. At the moment, she didn't care.

She moved to the couch, sat down, tried to collect herself, but his kisses had shifted something inside of her, making her realize how ready she'd been to *settle*. For so much less than she deserved.

Beckett returned, joined her on the couch. She shifted so her knees were tucked to the side and she was angled toward him. He took her hand, ran a finger over her knuckles.

"You're a very special woman, Presley Ayers."

She watched him trace over the light veins on the back of her hands. "You're pretty cool, yourself, Beckett Keller." *Understatement.*

The intensity and the feel of his hands on her lingered like a ghost but she liked this, too. She liked sitting with him, chatting, touching, and looking at each other. Being seen. She was very interested in taking their combustible chemistry all the way but she also wanted to know him. Learn more about him. Laugh with him. Make him smile.

"Do you have a deck of cards?" she asked.

His eyebrows drew together. "Yes."

"Grab it," she said, smiling at his suspicion.

Beckett got up, went over to a dresser against the wall next to his bedroom. The drawer squeaked when he pulled it open. He was back quickly, handing her the cards and taking his seat.

"It's not strip poker," she said.

He plucked them from her hand. "Never mind, then."

She laughed, took them back. Taking the cards out of the package, she shuffled, then laid the deck on the cushion between them.

"Ace to six, you ask me a question, seven to king, I ask you."

"How come you get an extra card?" Beckett stretched his arm along the back of the couch, pulling one knee up so he was angled like her.

"Women always get more. It's polite."

He laughed, played with a lock of her hair, sending a shiver over her skin. "Hmm. That sounds right. Okay. You draw."

She turned over a four.

He grinned. "Why did you book a trip that involves hiking?"

That was fairly safe. "I thought it would show Emmett I could enjoy some of the things he likes; that it might strengthen our relationship."

Even when he frowned at her, he still had little happy creases at the corners of his eyes. "Some things aren't worth the work."

True. "But people should be, right?"

"Sure. If they're willing to meet you halfway." His gaze went to the cards. "My turn." He turned over a two, met her gaze with another grin. "If someone were to plan a trip for you, what would be your ideal?"

She rubbed her hands together. "Oh. I like that question." She tapped one finger against her chin. "I actually really love looking at the water and I don't really mind the boat. So, maybe a pretty place on the water but with access to cute mom-and-pop eateries and gift shops. I love to shop. I love to browse, try new foods, and get a feel for the character of new towns. Especially small ones where everyone seems to know everyone."

"Hmm. That sounds like fun. Not what I expected."

"You thought something with a spa package?"

He laughed. "It crossed my mind."

"Don't get me wrong, I'd be all over that."

Beckett's gaze heated. He leaned forward, used the hand on the back of the couch to cup her neck and pull her closer for a kiss.

Before it could make her forget she wanted to know him, she pulled back. "My turn." She flipped over a king. "Finally!"

"Question you've been dying to ask?" His laughter made her smile on the inside.

She set the card down in the discard pile. "What's your dream?"

Something she couldn't label shadowed his gaze. "Wow. That's a deep one." He tapped his hand against the back of the couch. "I've always loved the outdoors. I like camping, any water sport available, I've been on a few weeklong hikes."

Presley gasped. "Were you lost?"

"No," he laughed.

"Did you trace 'HELP' in the sand and hope for rescue?"

He laughed harder. "No."

"Then why did you go for so long?"

Beckett reached out, tapped her nose with his finger. "It was fun."

"Lies," she said. "But carry on."

"Unlike a lot of people I went to school with, I always wanted to come home after university. When Brian, my boss, offered me a management gig at his sports store, it seemed perfect. Combined the things I loved. But for a while now, I've been feeling like I wanted more. Then Gray got this place and we got busy."

On paper, they couldn't be more different. But his answer proved they were more alike than either of them could have guessed.

"You didn't answer the question."

He laughed, nodded, as if he had just realized she was right.

"And the bike shop?"

Running a hand through his hair, something he did when he wasn't quite sure how to respond, he looked straight ahead, out the window. "Right. I shared that with you." He turned to face her. "I've always had this idea that opening my own bike rental shop in Smile would be really fulfilling." He looked down, tapped his finger against his thigh before meeting her gaze again. "I've always wanted to be part of what makes Smile a cool place to visit. This would let me do that."

"So, the second store?"

He shook his head. "I've taken that off my list. I don't want to be away from my family. I want to watch Ollie grow up, see what Gray does with this place."

She loved that. Something stretched tight inside of her chest. Longing?

"It's good to be sure. Where are you at with the bike shop?"

His gaze went past her again. "I actually got preapproved for a business loan this morning. I've been researching bikes for years, so I know which ones I'd start with. Singles, doubles, and some family ones. I'm still undecided on a location, but I have it narrowed down. With everything going on here, I haven't told my siblings yet."

She waited until he looked at her again. "You sound happy when you talk about it. I think it's a wonderful idea. You and your siblings seem to not only love each other but *like* each other. I'm sure they want to support you just as you've done them."

He nodded. "I know. You're absolutely right. They would. But it feels selfish to start my own business while Gray is getting this one up and running."

"You have to know the two businesses would complement each other."

Beckett leaned into her, making her feel like he was sharing his secrets. Which he was, but she wondered if that was wise, given their expiration date. But maybe it was easier for them to talk because neither of them had any obligation to the other.

"I love your business brain. I think the two would work perfectly together. But again, Gray is barely staying afloat. Now he's got Dayton's idea running around in his head. I could just go, do my own thing, but . . . I hate missing out when I'm gone. I love it here, but it's his, not mine, and I want my own thing. Maybe that's ridiculous. I'm not sure. My parents will be here soon. I miss them. They're touring the country in an RV. Once I see them, maybe I'll feel less like I'm abandoning my brother. Sorry. My answer was really long."

"I liked it," she said quietly, playing with the fabric of the couch, her hand nearly touching his fingers. "I think you should give your brother and sister more credit. They might be learning the ropes, like you, but you could present your piece of this in a way that might ease your brother's mind. The idea that you're part of it might actually be a weight off of his shoulders."

Beckett's brows scrunched and it made her smile to see him actively considering her thoughts.

"My turn." He flipped an ace, making her groan. "Where's your family?"

"In Great Falls, like me. They're happy, good people. They love me but we're not close like you guys. They raised me to live my own life." She'd always thought it was because they wanted her to have her own sense of self, but seeing Beckett with his family made her wonder if it was more that they didn't want to let her in, let her be a part of what they considered theirs. The thought hurt.

His brows moved together. "That sucks."

She shrugged. "It's fine. I have Rylee and she's got a great big family that she shares."

"I'm glad you have that."

She flipped a card and groaned when a three showed. This wasn't working out in her favor even with the advantage.

Beckett's fingers danced along the back of her neck, drifting aimlessly while inciting little fires along her skin. "What's your dream?"

Her pulse stuttered. She'd been so focused on her goals, on checking things off her list, she hadn't actually thought about her dreams. When she was little, she always made the same wish on her birthday cake candles: for someone to love her like her parents loved each other. But now, she wondered if they were too consumed in themselves. She hadn't considered that before this trip. They all got caught up in their own lives, so Presley assumed it was normal. But Beckett, Jill, and Gray had their own lives and yet still found time and room for each other.

She picked up Beckett's hand and told him the truth. "To be happy." She wasn't entirely sure why her throat felt tight.

He flipped over a ten, then slipped his arm around her shoulders, pulling her closer.

"Is this . . ." She gestured between them with her free hand. She didn't have words to describe what she was feeling, so if he felt it, he'd know. "Have you ever . . . before . . ." She didn't know how to ask.

Beckett released her, picked up the cards, and stacked them on the table. Then he turned so he was facing her, staring straight into her eyes like she was the only thing he could see.

"Is this normal for me? Have I felt this way?" His brows rose.

A breath of relief whooshed from her lungs. *Yes.*

He took both her hands. "No. Nothing like this, Presley. It might break my heart a little when you leave but I've never wanted anyone to be my fake girlfriend more than you."

She laughed, appreciating the way he tried to lighten the moment but kept it real. Her heart might break more than a little, but he didn't need to know that. She was a big girl and could deal with the fallout later.

"This isn't typical for me either. I'm not generally a big fan of spontaneity," she said, getting up to move so she could reposition herself, this time on his lap, her legs on either side of him. "But besides being for a good cause . . ."

His hands gripped her hips. She loved the feel of it. Like they were fused together or he didn't want to let go. "Protecting me?"

She nodded, kissed his chin. "Yes. Aside from that goal, this feels right. In a way nothing has for so long. Maybe I was meant to come here on my own."

He nodded, his fingers kneading. "If for no other reason, to guard my virtue."

When was the last time she had laughed this much? She couldn't remember. Presley ran her fingers through the sides of his hair. "Aw. Poor Hot Mountain Man is afraid of a cougar."

He snorted with laughter. "I don't have a lot of experience with the breed. Best to stay close during dinner. And it's good you're staying here again, in case any of them get loose, wander the grounds."

She lowered her mouth, whispering against his, "I can do that. I'm very good at indoor pursuits."

One hand moved up into her hair, pulling her so close their mouths touched when he spoke against it. "Then we're a perfect match."

For now. She pushed that thought away. She'd tried the whole planning-it-out thing. For now, *right* now felt great.

Twenty-One

Beckett had approximately zero seconds to feel guilty about Jilly calling Presley his girlfriend once they entered the main lodge. Like homing pigeons, two of the three women spotted him and immediately began throwing out comments about where he could sit.

He wanted to turn around and head back to his place, but that seemed cowardly. He may have gripped Presley's hand a little tight though, if her amused smile was any indication.

Jill, earning sister bonus points, announced dinner as soon as she noticed the mother trying to shoo Morgan to the end of the table so Beckett could have that seat. When he sat, Chantel moved beside him, and if Presley hadn't been glued to his side, he had no doubt Gabby would have parked herself in that chair. Instead, she sat directly across from him and stared like he was ice cream on a sickeningly hot day. Was this how women felt? The thought that anyone ever made his sister or Presley feel this . . . objectified sat like cement in his gut.

Libby sat next to her sister, arguing across the table with Morgan about whether Pink Floyd or Fleetwood Mac was the more influential band on today's youth. Presley picked up her napkin, laid it in her lap. Beckett sent her an appreciative gaze. God, there was something about this woman he'd never felt before. Looking at her was like fishing on a perfect day, an awesome bike ride, a cold beer at the end of the night before crawling between the sheets. She *calmed* him. Made him feel a sense of ease with just a glance, a smile, a touch. Yeah, she was pretty. More than. It didn't seem like a strong enough word to describe her, and it damn sure didn't explain the clutch in his chest he felt sitting next to her. "Pretty" didn't accurately convey the curve of her lips when she almost smiled, the way her lashes stretched impossibly long and her skin flushed when she was happy.

"What?" she whispered, making him realize he was staring.

He shook his head, giving her a smile he was sure hadn't existed before she came into his life. *Get a grip.*

The scent of roasted chicken made his mouth water, and it felt good to focus on something other than how much he liked Presley.

It wasn't until Ollie sat in Gray's seat instead of her usual one that he noticed his brother's absence. There were a lot of damn people around this table.

"Where's Grayson?" He lowered his voice, asking as he grabbed the basket of rolls from Jill.

"He said he needed to go back to the mainland and pick up a few things." She shrugged. "I think he has a closet addiction to karaoke duel night." Beckett snorted, trying to imagine his brother belting out some Lady Gaga or Jonas Brothers.

"What's a karaoke duel?" Libby asked. "I love a good competition." She blinked like she had something in her eye.

"Really, it's just karaoke night at the local pub, but Liam and Leo are brothers who had a falling-out. They decided to split up the pub like they split their room when they were teenagers and got in a fight. They each run half of it and are constantly competing for customers," Jill explained.

Presley's gaze widened. "You've got to be joking?"

Beckett shook his head. He put a scoop of potatoes on his plate. "Nope. Everyone thought they'd make up, but instead, they built a flimsy dividing wall straight down the middle of the pub. People try to visit both pubs equally."

The guests laughed. Gabby added a ridiculously small amount of meat to her plate. They had vegetables, but maybe there should be a full vegetarian option. She smiled at him. "That sounds like fun. Any chance of visiting?"

"Grayson makes daily trips over to the mainland," Beckett said. Though not usually back-to-back.

"We try to keep to a schedule. We're stretched a little thin right now." The corners of Jill's eyes creased in worry. He didn't like it.

"Things are going to ease up. It'll be fine," Beckett assured her.

"Providing you don't kill him," Ollie said from the other end of the table.

All eyes flew to his niece, who looked proud as hell, up on her knees, scooping potatoes onto her plate.

"Ollie!" Jill's voice was atypically sharp.

She stopped, looked at her mom, her nose scrunching. "What? That's what you said when Uncle Gray said he started a TikTok count and put Uncle Beck on it."

Beckett's roll smooshed in on itself in his grasp. "Excuse me? What the hell? You have a TikTok account?"

Ollie pointed. "Uncle Beck sweared."

"Swore," Jill corrected.

"He did." Ollie dropped her hand, her mouth pursing into a pout.

"Ollie, stop." Jilly slapped her hand on the table.

"Which one is TikTok?" Beckett spoke through gritted teeth.

Several of the guests became very interested in their plates. Muffled laughter tied Beckett's stomach in knots. Presley put a hand over his, plucked the roll from his hand and set it on his plate.

"People get creative with short video clips."

"If it helps," Gabby said, meeting his gaze with a sultry smile, "you look great on there as well. The one I saw was a compilation clip put to Justin Timberlake's 'Sexy Back.'"

Beckett groaned.

Libby looked up from her plate, sent her sister an irritated glance. "Don't fan the flames." She looked at Beckett. "There were a few others we saw with links to the lodge. Your breakfast photo acts like a backdrop. Very tasteful."

Presley squeezed again. "See?"

He didn't want his photo to be the backdrop for anything. The conversation shifted, awkwardly, like driving over unexpected potholes, but smoothed out as the guests told each other about themselves, asked questions about the lodge, and complimented the meal.

"How long have you guys run this place?" Libby asked.

"Less than six months," Beckett said. He frowned when something hit his shin.

"Why are so many of the rooms closed?"

"None of the rooms are actually closed. We just don't have all of them up and running. The cabins are being updated." Beckett stabbed a baby potato with his fork. A foot. It was a foot on his shin. His knee. His lap. What the actual—he choked on his bite while Gabriella smiled sinfully across from him, raising her brows.

"Are you okay?" Presley looked at him with concern.

Shifting his chair back, he nodded, spoke around the coughing. "I'm good. Fine. Went down the wrong way."

"Best to be careful," Gabby said.

Beckett stood up. "I think I'll get started on cleanup."

Jill looked at him with a question in her gaze. What was he supposed to say? *The woman next to you is using her foot to feel me up?* Nope. He was done. Had it been Presley? Hell yeah. Which made him realize: he wasn't a casual hookup guy. It wouldn't have been just any good-looking guest who turned his head. Just Presley Ayers. Grabbing his plate and a few empty serving dishes, he headed for the kitchen.

Chef was wiping down the counters, and the dishwasher was open, waiting to be loaded.

"Finished already, Hot Mountain Man?"

Laughter seemed like all he could offer at the moment. "You, too?"

"You're not my type, but I see the appeal," he said with a grin.

Beckett shook his head, added the plates to the dishwasher. "Thanks. I think." He leaned against the counter as Chef carried on. "I don't think I've ever been so blatantly hit on."

Chef chuckled. "Presley doesn't seem all that forward. Friendly. Outgoing. Definitely part extrovert."

Beckett shook his head. "No. The other women."

Closing the dishwasher, Chef went to the fridge and grabbed two bottles of water, handing one to Beckett.

"You're realizing something we all do at some point," he said after opening his and taking a sip.

Beckett turned the top. "If I am, I'm doing it without knowing I'm realizing it."

Chef chuckled. "At some point we realize we're tired of the game. We don't want a night here and there. I thought I'd want easy and casual for the rest of my life. Then I met Louis."

Just the way he said the man's name warmed something in Beckett's chest and reminded him of how Presley said she liked the sound of her name on his lips. He liked *her* lips on his.

Taking a long swallow of water, he measured his words. "That's just it. One night or forever. None of it has been on my radar."

Chef smiled. "It never is until it is. Speaking of which, I'm going to finish cleaning and go meet my forever at the dock."

"I can finish up if you want," Beckett said.

Chef shooed him away. "Time goes too fast for you to waste it in here with me."

Laughing, Beckett started for the door. "Oh, the others loved the idea of doing a reel of you and Presley making French toast sometime this week."

"Excellent. I look forward to it," Chef said, a sly look on his face.

"Everyone involved will be fully clothed. And I won't be there," Beckett said with a mock glare.

"Spoilsport."

❧

At least he was smiling and more relaxed when he joined the others again. The dining room conversation had turned lively between several of the guests. The Pink Floyd conversation had escalated, with Morgan pointing his fork at Libby and telling her the songs she had to listen to. Beckett's heart gave a happy wobble, like it was dizzy, when he saw Presley chatting with Jill. *Why? Doesn't matter if your family likes her.*

She's not staying. If they were doing this six-day thing, he needed to keep his heart firmly locked up. It was fun. Sexy. A fling. Something to look back on when he was Mr. Dayton or Chef's age. He walked behind her chair, leaned over to speak to her, inhaling the subtle fragrance he knew he'd never forget.

"I'm going to head back to the cabin. You okay here?"

She turned her head. "I am. I'm going to help clean up."

"You don't need to. You're a g—"

"Girlfriend?" she interrupted with a laugh.

"Yes. You are that. I'll see you in a bit." He stroked a hand down her silky hair, the feel both comforting and stirring.

Beckett strolled out of the lodge, taking in the changes they had made in the short time they'd been there. The grounds had resembled a small jungle, complete with a variety of wildlife. They'd trimmed, cut, and planted, checked all the trails, cleaned up garbage, taking loads to the dump—a pain in the ass when using a boat. But it was coming along. If . . . no, *when* he opened the shop, he wouldn't be here as often, but it was only a short commute away. Grayson was walking up the path, hands weighed down with cans of paint. Beckett hurried forward.

"Is there more?"

Gray nodded. "Yeah. We need some sort of cart so we can just load it up and bring everything in one trip."

"I'll take a look next time I'm on the mainland." He hurried to the boat, grabbed the bags, and caught up with his brother. "We've got a full house, man. Jill said two more day after tomorrow," Beckett said.

Grayson stared straight ahead, said nothing as they carried everything to the lodge steps. When his brother dropped his stuff, he huffed out a breath, ran his hands through his hair. Beckett recognized the frustrated gestures, waited it out.

"Listen, I'm not trying to exploit you," Gray started.

Beckett worked to keep his expression neutral. "You sure? I was starting to wonder if you wanted to put a stripper pole up in the lodge. Maybe do one of those 24–7 cameras."

Grayson's jaw dropped. He started to talk but only managed to sputter incoherently. Beckett rescued him, clapping him—hard—on the shoulder.

"TikTok? What the fuck, dude?"

"Would you believe Ollie showed it to me?" Gray's ears turned a soft shade of pink. "She was showing me these dances and I saw one that had ten thousand views."

"That's a lot of views. But I think we need to rein it in. Or at least regroup and think about what we want."

Gray stared at him, his smile coming slow. "We?"

The spot just between his shoulder blades started to itch. Beckett shrugged. "Yeah. Always we. We're in this together for now." He backed up. "I gotta go, but I need to talk to you about something soon. You and Jilly."

"Everything okay?"

Beckett felt confident with his nod. It would be. "Yeah. Just want to run something by you guys."

He was only a few feet away when Grayson called him. He turned to face his brother.

"I like your girlfriend. She's cool."

Beckett held up his hand, lowering all fingers but one.

Around his laughter, Gray said, "Thanks, man."

Beckett nodded. "Family first. Always."

It'd been drilled into their heads from a young age that they all needed to look out for each other. As he headed back to his cabin, a restless energy nearly consumed him. He pulled his phone out and looked through the app store but managed not to download anything.

Instead, he thought about what he could do to make the following few days with Presley special. An idea popped into his head, one he knew would make his "girlfriend" smile. He did his best to focus on the night, not the idea of tomorrow or the next day. The intensity he felt for her had to come from the finality of it. There was no future so it was okay to go all in. Or maybe Presley was the kind of woman where he would have had no choice regardless.

Twenty-Two

Presley walked back to Beckett's cabin slowly, savoring the sweet scents of the night air, the sound of the lake ever so gently lapping at the edges of the shore, and the feeling of peace. She spent so much time running around, getting things just right, making arrangements, organizing events, and seeing to others' needs, she'd pushed aside her own. Not that she minded. She loved her job, her life. Rylee, her family. She thought, for a brief moment in time, she'd wanted to love Emmett.

In the distance, the sun sank low, bursts of color shooting out from its center, shimmering across the ripples of the lake. It was breathtaking. So different from the sights and sounds of her own neighborhood. Traffic, people, and activity were background music where she lived. There was an energy in her city that made a person feel like anything could happen at any moment.

This place felt . . . still. Presley wasn't actually sure how she felt about the quiet overall, but right this second, as the cabin loomed, it made it possible to *hear* her pulse shifting into overdrive, echoing loudly in her own ears. There was nothing tranquil about the way it picked up its pace. All her planning and she never could have foreseen this path. Never would have imagined herself taking it. Time was a funny thing; hers here was limited, and it made her braver.

When she entered the cabin, Beckett nearly jumped out of his shorts. His phone flew from his hand, fortunately landing on the couch.

Presley paused by the door, brows raised. "Am I interrupting?" She pulled her bottom lip between her teeth, watching the flush of color rise up his neck, over his cheeks.

He glanced at his phone before his gaze darted back to hers. "I . . ." That was it. His sentence ended there, and he sighed, heavily, his shoulders sagging even as he reached for his phone.

Gliding his thumb over the screen, he held it out to her. Her stomach turned into an active beehive—too many things buzzing around inside of her—as she stepped forward. She didn't truly know this man, and how much could she trust her gut, given how she'd ended up here alone? Was he going to show her something that would send her running? Definitely not how she'd planned to spend the evening.

Their fingers touched as she took the phone, sending a little thrill through her from that simple connection. Taking a deep breath, she forced herself to look down at the screen. When she did, she laughed. Loudly. Looking up, she saw the embarrassment in his hunched shoulders.

Hurrying over, she sat beside him on the couch, setting his phone down on the coffee table.

"You jumped like that because of this? I seriously thought I was about to see something kinky or perverse."

His gaze flew to hers. "What? Like what? Never mind. I don't want to know. This is bad enough." He gestured to his phone.

"Instagram?"

"I downloaded it, Presley. I joined." He lowered his chin. "I followed you. And my sister, the lodge, a bunch of people in town. Even Gramps, the mayor of Smile, has an account."

She bit her lip, hard, because she sensed this was a serious issue for him and not one he found nearly as amusing as she did.

"That makes sense. People use it as a way to connect. It can be whatever you want it to, Beckett. You don't have to use it, but really, if you're going to start your own business, you should be on social media. It's a great way to advertise and connect with your audience."

He shook his head, took her hand in his like it was the most natural thing in the world. Like holding hands on the couch was an old habit of theirs.

"I don't have anything to share or post. I don't want to waste my life staring at someone's best moments online when I can be *living* my best moments for real. My brother's ex posted daily about their incredible relationship and it was all lies. Jill was shocked by the split because once a day, minimum, she'd get notified that they were still in love. These sites, they're a way for people to perform. You lose who you are to become someone followers want to see."

He wasn't entirely wrong. She inhaled deeply, thinking about her next words. "I don't think that has to be true. I think we have the potential to lose ourself in anything. But it doesn't mean we *have* to. It's another choice we're offered in life. No one is asking you to be anything you aren't. It's truly a great marketing tool and a wonderful way to keep up with people you couldn't otherwise see face-to-face."

His brows arched. "Is that what you use it for?" He picked up his phone, brought up her account. He scrolled through her most recent photos, turning his phone so they could both see. She'd gotten a beautiful shot of the water from their hike. "'Connecting with nature'?" His lips quirked.

"Okay. Yeah. You decide how you want people to see you. Especially when you know people are looking. But that's almost more power. You control the narrative." She thought about the photo she *hadn't* posted; the one where she and Beckett looked like they were about to get lost in each other. She hadn't shared it because it felt too . . . real. Too honest. Too personal. Maybe he had more of a point than she wanted to concede.

"I like focusing on what's real," Beckett said. It seemed like he wanted to say more. He set his phone down, turned his body toward her. "I think it's hard to decide what to share and what not to. Then it becomes hard to decipher what's real and what isn't."

She sensed they were moving into new territory here. Her breath caught. "That's fair. You can't always do that from a picture. So just use it for your business." His gaze had lit up when he spoke about it. She needed to spend some time in his hometown. He clearly loved it. And his family.

His thumb moved over her hand, increasing in pressure. They

shared the same air without moving and she envisioned pressing "like" on this moment a million times. "It's human nature to be curious about the lives of others. But you're right in that those snapshots into their worlds can make us question our own. Make us miss out on our own moments."

Beckett's free hand moved up to her face. He traced the line of her jaw with his index finger, then sank the rest of his hand into her hair. The way his fingers tangled in it mirrored the way *he* was tangling himself into her heart.

He lowered his chin. "I wouldn't want to miss this. Not that I would mind a picture of us."

She leaned forward, scooted his phone forward, turned it toward them, leaning in, not for show but because he was someone she wanted to be close to. He smiled. There was nothing pretend in either of their gazes. She snapped the photo, set his phone down.

"Not everything has to be for someone else."

His fingers continued to dance over her skin, slow and seductive like an unhurried waltz. "No. That one can be just for us."

Presley wrapped her hand around his wrist, squeezed his other hand tight. "Then we don't have to hashtag or caption it."

He laughed, but the sound was rough and heavy. His fingers pressed into the back of her neck, making her skin feel alive.

"Could you?"

She laughed. "Not without getting put in Instagram jail."

His face moved closer. "There's such a thing?"

Her body shifted. "Oh, yeah. Most of what I'm picturing, along with the thoughts running around in my head, is definitely social media jail worthy."

His other hand came up to mirror the one already in her hair. "Hmm."

She thought he was going to kiss her, press his mouth to hers, but instead, he ran the tip of his nose along her jaw and trailed it up to her ear, his breath warm and seductive.

"How about the caption: 'you might ruin me for anyone else'?" The whispered words slid over her, curled like vines around her heart, which she was trying to keep out of the entire situation, and filled her with a longing that was so much more than physical.

She gripped his other wrist, pressing her body closer, tilting her head so he could trail his lips over the sensitive skin of her neck. She closed her eyes, let herself just *feel*. "That's a good one," she said, her voice unrecognizable. "Maybe I'd comment 'God I hope so' or 'that only seems fair.'"

He pulled back to press his forehead against hers, and their eyes locked. "You're sure about this?"

Her throat went dry. Her whole life, she'd *worked* for the results she wanted. With Beckett, it felt effortless. Like jumping off a cliff with a guaranteed safe landing. "I feel like you're the first thing I've been sure about in forever."

It was as if all he needed was to hear the words from her lips. His mouth slanted over hers, their lips meeting with an urgency she'd never felt. Never known existed. He was right about one thing, she thought as their hands roamed over each other. There was no way to caption this moment, no picture that could truly encapsulate how much she felt or how badly she wanted this. Wanted *him*.

He whispered her name like a sacred prayer, his hand stroking down her back, up the side of her body, over her ribs, his thumb grazing, exploring. When he pulled her up, their bodies locked together, their breath mingling as he boosted her up so she could wrap her legs around him. He walked them toward his room, slowly, like he was trying to hold on to the seconds, memorize the moments. Nothing existed outside of this man, his words, the feel and taste of him. It amazed her that something could feel so dreamlike and real at the same time.

He lowered her to the bed, covering her with his body, and it surprised her that someone so large could move with such grace, such care. Such gentle precision. He stroked her hair back from her forehead with both hands, pressing featherlight kisses along her hairline, her jaw, to the spot just under her ear. The sound of his breath in her ear, the feel of his muscled arms surrounding her, pulling her nearer, like he couldn't get close enough, the way his hands moved against her skin scattered her thoughts.

Presley pushed at his T-shirt, eager to explore him, learn him, consume him. Beckett pulled away only long enough to reach behind him, tug it over his head, and toss it away. Back and forth, she thought with a smile. Push and pull.

Then his lips found hers again and Presley was lost. She'd been so worried about the future, she'd forgotten about now. She'd come to the middle of nowhere, sad and alone, and ended up feeling more seen, more connected, and more valuable than she ever had in her life.

"Presley," he whispered.

Her breath caught on the depth of emotion in his voice, his gaze, his touch. No, she couldn't capture this with words or an image, but she could memorize every second. As they sank deeper into one another, tangling themselves up physically and emotionally, that's exactly what she tried to do.

Presley burrowed into the crook of Beckett's arm like the space was created for the shape of her body. A little shiver erupted over her skin as he trailed his finger along the dips and curves while their breathing evened out. She had a newfound appreciation for the great outdoors. If that was what gave this man his six-pack abs, sun-kissed skin, and agility, she was now an outdoor enthusiast.

"You're quiet," he whispered, kissing the top of her head.

"I'm appreciating what the wilderness has done for your physique," she said.

He laughed, leaning back to look at her. "I love how you just say whatever is on your mind."

"It's actually not a good thing. But in this case, I'm okay with it."

His hand skimmed down, rested on her belly. "Well, whatever workout regime you follow is working for you as well."

Presley turned on her side. "Oh, it's brutal. A daily grind that includes at least one trip to Starbucks and one meal out. It's commitment, but if it matters, you do it."

He smiled against her mouth, pulling her into another kiss that made her brain hazy. When he lifted up, he ran the tip of his nose along the bridge of hers before he grinned at her, his hair tousled, his gaze slumberous.

"I applaud and approve of your commitment. Also, I have a surprise that I think will fit right in."

Curiosity and desire warred with each other. When he hopped from the bed with far more energy than she felt, she followed. They pulled on sweatpants and sweaters. She pulled her hair into a ponytail, doing her best not to worry about checking her makeup or wearing something that flattered her more. He didn't care. He looked at her and she could *see* and *feel* that he liked what he saw.

"Come on," he said, taking her hand.

She laughed at his excitement, wondering what he wanted to show her. When he led her outside to the backyard, her body filled with happiness.

"When did you do this?" She took a step forward, her gaze moving over the setting. Under the cover of trees that shrouded his yard, allowing only miniature windows into the night sky, he'd strung more lights, crisscrossing them overhead, looping them on the fence posts and draping them like an aisle on either side. Before this, the twinkle lights on the porch had been cute. Now, the collection of bulbs, the warm light of all of them shining together, was nothing short of breathtaking. He'd done this for her.

"Before I got sucked into Instagram. TikTok scared me or I'd probably still be on my phone."

Presley threw her arms around his neck. "I think I could have rescued you."

His gaze went hot and serious all at once. "I think you already did. I just don't know from what."

He kissed her with hundreds of lights dancing around them while the music of water lapping against the shore played softly in the distance.

When he pulled back, he pressed another kiss to her forehead before leading her down the few stairs. They walked to the cozy camp chairs. He'd set blankets on them, moved two of the chairs so close they were touching. Beckett lit the gas firepit, adding more dazzle to the night.

A cooler sat beside one of the chairs.

"Have a seat. I'm making s'mores."

Presley's laugh seemed to echo into the darkness. "Your trick to making me like the great outdoors is chocolate and marshmallows?"

He turned from his squatted position, where he was loading marshmallows onto sticks. "And twinkle lights. Did it work?"

With him beside her? Oh yeah. "I think it did."

He grinned, went back to his task. "If it doesn't, I also have a cooler full of beer and snacks."

"I think just being with you might do it." She said it so low, she wasn't sure if he heard her.

But when he stood, he left the treats on the tray he was using, put his hands on either side of her face, and met her gaze.

"Let's pretend we have all the time in the world."

A lump lodged in her throat, from both his words and his bittersweet tone. "What will we do with all of that time?" She hoped her attempt at flirting would distract her from the ache in the center of her chest.

They lost themselves in a kiss that made her sure of exactly what they'd do with every moment of that time. Until he pulled back, tapped her on the nose, and stepped back.

"We'll eat s'mores."

She laughed as she made herself cozy in one of the chairs, a blanket tucked in around her, the lights twinkling everywhere.

"You better watch out, sexy mountain man. If word gets around that you provide chocolate in addition to a great view, you might never get time alone again."

He handed her a stick that she held over the fire. "Good thing I have you to protect me."

Good thing. But was it? Presley could tell herself, repeatedly, that this was temporary. In her head, she *knew* that. But her heart wasn't listening. It'd gotten a taste of what it was like to really *feel,* without parameters or a to-do list, and reining that in was going to be harder than she could have imagined.

Twenty-Three

The sky shook like a furious fist, sending ribbons of light through the dark gray clouds. Thunder bellowed on the heels of lightning. The rain had started during the early hours of dawn when Presley and Beckett were awakening each other with gentle glides of their lips and hands.

After getting up, showering, and pulling on warm clothes, they'd made a run for the lodge to join the others for breakfast. The day's plans had taken a sharp turn thanks to the weather. The morning's hikes and fishing excursions were canceled.

Richard and Mel took the weather as a sign to spend the day reading, curled up in front of the fireplace in their room; so they said over a breakfast of oatmeal, berries, and incredibly fluffy pancakes. While Bo and Morgan were easy enough to appease with the promise of setting up Ollie's Xbox on the big screen, Libby and Gabby decided a rainy day meant going back to bed. Chantel was watching a movie in her room, and Jill had promised a comfort food lunch for everyone.

Beckett and Grayson had already left for cabin four, intending to use the day to get as much done on the repairs as they could. Presley was trying to eat her last pancake at a normal speed rather than scarfing it down so she could head to cabin four. Not only did she want to soak up more Beckett time but she loved projects and jobs like they were taking on. Sure, she'd never done anything substantial. She'd gone to a sign-and-wine night with Rylee and had come out of it with a gorgeous three-foot piece of wood that she'd sanded, painted, and lacquered. It read: SET GOALS, WORK HARD, SUCCEED. It hung in the hallway of her apartment.

She was doing her best *not* to clue Beckett's sister in to the fact that last night had been incomparable to any she'd ever had. Which meant not choking on her pancakes or smiling like an idiot.

"Can I go help Uncle Beck and Uncle Gray?" Ollie asked as she cleared her plate from the table and set it in the stack on the trolley.

"Sure. But be careful. There's lots of tools and stuff down there right now."

Ollie tilted her head, gave her mom a look that was entirely too mature for her age. "Mom. I know. I'm not a baby."

Jill's lips twitched. "No. You're not. I'll be down soon. I just have to make sure everyone is settled and make a few phone calls."

When Ollie ran from the room, Presley met Jill's gaze and they both laughed.

"She's a handful sometimes, but she makes me smile and laugh every single day," Jill said, setting her cutlery on her plate.

Presley felt a sharp pinch in her heart. She wanted that. Bone-deep-all-the-way-to-the-core. Being with Emmett had quieted that piece of herself, or at least distracted her from taking a hard look.

"Listen, Presley," Jill said, pulling her attention from her inner revelations. "I wanted to apologize again for putting you in the middle of things. For calling you Beckett's girlfriend. You're clearly so good at your job. I can't imagine you ever doing something so unprofessional."

Presley smiled warmly at this woman who, if life were leading her down a different path, she could definitely see herself being friends with. She got up, moved to a seat closer to Jill.

Her long, layered hair was somewhat similar in coloring to her brothers', with reddish undertones. Her eyes were a soft blue and added to her approachable nature. She fidgeted with her napkin.

How did she thank a woman for doing something when she didn't want to reveal how much it had given her in return? Without this week, Presley wouldn't be realizing that all of the things she thought she wanted might not be what she needed. That she'd been settled so heavily into a path, it hadn't occurred to her to check if she was *happy* being on it. All that had ever mattered was moving forward. Progress. Succeeding.

"Please believe me when I tell you that this week is nothing like I expected and everything I never knew I needed. I don't regret any of it. Least of all, you pairing me up with Beckett to save his virtue."

Jill held her gaze for a solid ten seconds before bursting into laughter, which made Presley do the same.

"Okay. Maybe not his virtue," Presley admitted.

"I'll say," Jill said through her laughter.

"But honestly," she said, catching her breath. "There's nothing to apologize for."

She'd need to remind herself of that when she returned home; alone. She wouldn't let herself be sorry either.

❧

Presley was no slouch. She worked her butt off in three-inch heels every single day. No one clocked more hours moving across the hotel lobby and back than Presley. But *this* was not *that*. What they were doing here—painting, sawing, sanding—this was backbreaking work. She was sweating more than she had on the stupid hike. Nothing ladylike about it. Moisture dripped in uncomfortable spots, her chest felt tight, and the air was muggy and sticky in the worst possible way.

"How you doing?" Beckett passed her an ice-cold bottle of water. The sound of hammers and laughter echoed behind them.

She wasn't sure if the way she moved her mouth passed as a smile or a grimace, but since muscles she didn't know she had hurt, it was the best he was going to get. "Fantastic. This is turning out amazing."

He grinned, ducked his head. *His* sweat managed to look sexy. That hardly seemed fair. "It is. Thanks to all of you."

After breakfast, she'd joined them along with Jill. Morgan and Bo had grown bored of the Xbox and had several helpful skills. Though the siblings said it wasn't necessary, they'd joined in, and it felt more like one of those fun home renovation shows than work. Well, except for the work part.

Beckett leaned in. "You can take a break, you know."

His hair was a bit damp, his shirt sticking to some of his more defined muscles. He was definitely her favorite view at the lodge.

She sent him a haughty look, the one she threw at coworkers who doubted her ability to get last-minute reservations at the hippest new restaurants. She stiffened her shoulders, stretched herself taller, pretending her blistered feet—stupid shoes, stupid hiking—were in heels rather than runners. "Do I *look* like I *need* a break?"

Beckett stepped even closer, and the scent of him combined with the sweet after-rain summer air messed with her head. "You *look* sexy and adorable."

Her stomach flip-flopped. So far, her fake boyfriend was better than any real ones she'd had. He made her feel more alive. More fun.

Presley opened her water and took a long drink, appreciating the way his eyes never left her. When she lowered the bottle, she smirked. "Try to keep up."

He laughed, following behind her when she went back to the wall she was painting a creamy beige color. With so many people working in one space, things came together quite quickly. The rain had only lasted through the early morning, leaving soft, gray clouds in its wake. Everyone had migrated toward the cabin out of curiosity but ended up sticking around to help out. The sun started to peek out of the clouds in the late afternoon. Presley took a moment to stare at the rainbow. She'd always loved them for their fleeting beauty and colorful magic.

Presley did a quick live on her Instagram to show the progress. The others, including Beckett, smiled and waved in the background as she scanned the space.

"As you can see, things are only getting better here at Get Lost. They're hard at work to make this place your go-to summer spot."

Several people joined the feed, sending waves, hearts and comments. Many of them asked about her Hot Mountain Man.

"I see you guys asking about Beckett." At his name, he looked back over his shoulder with a somewhat shy grin. He waved and Presley's heart nearly catapulted out of her chest.

"Can I be on it?" Ollie asked, standing beside her.

Presley looked over at Jill, who nodded, before crouching so Ollie could take the phone.

"Hi. I'm Ollie. Get Lost is the best fishing place around."

She handed the phone back to Presley, who laughed at the abruptness. "There you have it. Okay, that's all for now. I'll share the end result when it's all finished and put a link to the booking site."

Her notifications and messages were hitting triple digits, so she could only imagine what the lodge's numbers looked like.

When she put the phone away, she saw Jill talking quietly with Grayson.

Grayson turned to the group and got their attention.

"We really appreciate all of you. You're a special group of guests. You truly didn't have to pitch in this way, and we can't thank you enough."

Morgan lifted a can of beer. "Place looks great. We'll have to bring some buddies and book this next time. Wish we weren't leaving tomorrow."

Grayson gave him a grateful smile. "As to that, as a thank-you, we'd like to offer you a free night as a small show of gratitude. If you'd like it to be now or sometime in the future, that's up to you, but we'd love it if you'd stay another night on us."

"Betcha Beckett's girl stays more than one night," Bo said, shooting an exaggerated wink in Presley's direction.

She laughed. Morgan shoved his friend in a good-natured way.

"Let's stay tomorrow, then. Hell, if you got room, let's stay two more nights."

Bo shrugged, slugged back the rest of his beer, and started cleaning up.

In those few minutes, as they started cleaning and went back to laughing, singing, and chatting, Presley felt something she hadn't in a really long time, if ever: She felt like she was part of a family. A motley crew of a family, one no one would think of piecing together, but a family nonetheless.

Beckett walked up to her, a speck of paint on his cheek. She reached up, hoping her heart wasn't flashing in her gaze, and swiped it away with her thumb.

Before he could say anything, she went up on her tiptoes and pressed her mouth to his in a kiss that likely shared too much about her real feelings.

As he angled his head, bracing the back of hers with his hand, she pushed away her worry that there was something phony about the way she was falling.

When she pulled back she smiled up at him. "Thank you."

He laughed softly. "For the kiss? Thank *you*."

Presley shook her head, her throat thick, her chest tight with emotion. "For that and so much more."

She was grateful when Ollie started chatting about the things her mom needed to pick up on the mainland and how she couldn't wait to be older so she could do karaoke.

Presley was squatting down, touching up some paint on the baseboards, the last of her jobs. Without looking, she brushed her thumb against the rim, getting paint all over her skin.

In her crouch, she reached forward for the rag she'd set aside. Her hand was already on the speckled cloth when it moved, coming toward her. Presley didn't know what was happening until she saw the big eyes and long spotted body. Whatever it was looked right at her as it brushed its body over her hand, scurrying in her direction. Presley's scream of surprise only made the creature faster, so she crouch-walked backward, hitting the leg of a sawhorse that propped up a freshly painted cabinet door.

The door fell, landing on the hand she'd used, poorly, to brace herself. Everyone in the room turned, but it was Ollie who showed up at her side first. The . . . thing? *Amphibian? Lizard? Is that its own species?* Whatever it was, it moved like a sprinter. Maybe it smelled fear.

"You found a salamander!" She hurried forward, unaware of Presley's distress.

Presley's hand throbbed, her butt hurt, and her eyes stung with unshed tears.

"It's so cute," Ollie said, cornering it with a speed that rivaled its own. She picked it up as the adults came forward.

Beckett crouched, putting himself in her space like a much-needed distraction. He touched his hand to her face. "Hey. It's okay. It's just a salamander."

Presley's gaze widened. It could have been an alligator for how badly it had scared her. Her heart was waging a war, trying to bust out of her chest. All of a sudden, she flashed back to that one night she'd spent on the balcony of her family's apartment. She hadn't thought about it in years, but aside from the cold and the eerie sounds, she'd woken just before dawn, after having a very restless sleep, to find a bird perched on the rail. It'd startled her, but not nearly as much as the squirming mouse in its beak. The one that it dropped *on* Presley, terrifying her and almost sending her through the glass. She'd screamed then, too, as the mouse fell, the bird swooped, and her dad, an early riser, caught the commotion and came to open the window for her.

He'd told her she was fine and told her to go catch up on sleep in her own bed. *That ought to cure your newfound love of the great outdoors,* he'd said with a chuckle.

Beckett was rubbing his thumb along her neck, murmuring softly to her, bringing her back to the present. "Hey. Hey. It's okay."

"I'll go put him near the forest," Ollie said, showing the creature proudly to the crowd that was now gathering around them.

"Thanks, sweetie," Jill said. Jill came forward. "Beck, her hand is bleeding."

Presley looked down to see that the top of her hand was cut. Not badly—mostly just broken skin from the weight of the cabinet door.

"Shit. Come on, sweetheart, let's get you up," he said softly, helping her to stand.

"I'm fine," she said, her voice shaky. Though she'd be a lot better if everyone wasn't looking at her.

"We'll clean this up," Morgan said, looking at Presley with concern etched in his features. "Think we have time for another round of *Mario Kart* before dinner?"

Grayson nodded, his brows knitted, his frown deepening. "Absolutely. I'm sorry you got hurt, Presley." Regret slithered through his words.

"I'm fine," she said again, feeling silly for freaking out. Though, *hello*, it was not every day that she saw a salamander. In fact, that counted as another first. One she could gladly do without an encore of.

"If it makes you feel better," Beckett said as he led her away, toward his cabin, "they feel just like the fish you caught the other day."

She looked up at him as they walked. "It does not make me feel better about that but it does make me feel better that I didn't touch the fish."

He laughed. She thought about who she'd been all those years ago. There'd been two people who loved her in that apartment. And she realized now that she'd never felt as cared for as she did in this moment. It wasn't solely her parents' fault. They'd been good to her, giving her what she needed physically. It just hadn't occurred to her that there was more people could give.

❧

Inside his cabin, she sat at one of the kitchen chairs while Beckett grabbed the first aid kit. He pulled the other chair close to hers, setting the kit on the table and opening it.

"Hmm, that's interesting," he said, staring at it.

Presley looked up from inspecting her hand. "What?"

Laughter lit up his eyes, making them crinkle in the corners. "Could have sworn I had a brand-new box of fifty Band-Aids in here."

He picked up the two Band-Aids she'd left in the kit, rubbed them together between his thumb and forefinger. Presley averted her gaze.

"That is weird." She so owed him some Band-Aids. The extra padding of them helped in her shoes.

His laugh brought her gaze back to his. "Let's get you cleaned up."

It was on the tip of her tongue to say she'd do it herself and take the Band-Aids from his fingers. It wouldn't do her any good to get attached to the way he naturally cared for her. It was enough that she could acknowledge how much she enjoyed his attention. She couldn't come to *need* it as well.

Beckett gently wiped her hand with a warm cloth, then lifted her hand close to his mouth, blowing gently. Presley said nothing, letting the moment happen. He wasn't being sexual in any way. He was just taking care of her, and somehow, that was about the sexiest thing she'd ever seen.

Her skin tingled with awareness. His gaze lifted, meeting hers. Just one side of his mouth turned up. "You okay? Missing the city today?"

She smiled. She wasn't missing anything at all. She shook her head.

Beckett kissed each one of her fingertips before turning her hand gently and placing a kiss in the center of her palm. Heat radiated outward from that spot.

"We've worked everyone hard today. I think Jilly has a thank-you dessert planned after dinner tonight. You've done so much." He ripped open the Band-Aid wrapper, set it carefully on her skin. "You already have a bruise forming."

Presley leaned forward to smooth the wrinkle between his brows. "I'm fine."

Beckett took her hand again, used it to pull her closer, kiss her gently. When he pulled back, he brushed her hair from her face. God. When a man looked at a woman the way he looked at her, did it last? She wasn't sure anyone had ever looked at her the way he did. Maybe it was too much. It was all fun and games until salamanders and hearts got involved.

A quick knock sounded before Jill poked her head in. "Hey. You okay?"

Presley pushed the chair back and walked toward the door. "I'm absolutely fine." It helped that they were mostly finished.

Jill stepped all the way into the cabin. "I was going to see if you wanted to come to the mainland with me to grab a few things. Also, the bedding from that site you showed us is in." Jill's grin widened, making it easy to see where Ollie got her happy smile from.

Presley sucked in a breath. "I think my heart just skipped a beat."

Both Beckett and Jill laughed. He came up behind Presley, put his hand to the small of her back. When he kissed her temple, her heart skipped again. Or danced, more accurately. Shopping was a good idea.

"I'll go help with cleanup," he said.

The move was so . . . couple-ish, it almost made her ache. *Almost.* "Can I have a few minutes to clean up?"

"Of course," Jill said. "I'll meet you at the speedboat."

Presley hesitated. "It doesn't *have* to speed though, right?"

Her cheeks warmed at the belly laugh Beckett gave. "Maybe you two should take the dinghy."

Presley poked him in the hard stomach, making him laugh again. "Maybe we should. Then you'd have longer to stay here and play host through dinner, Mr. Hot Mountain Man."

Jill tipped her head back with her laughter while Beckett frowned, which wasn't all that effective with amusement in his gaze. They made it so easy to belong. Presley walked away with a throbbing hand, an almost achy heart, and a feeling that if she didn't have a time limit on this whole thing, she could be in big trouble.

Twenty-Four

Presley hung on for dear life with one hand and, not for the first time, wondered why the boat had no seat belts. Jilly cut through the water like she was in a Porsche on the Autobahn. Not only that, but she looked like it thrilled her. The throbbing in Presley's left hand was a welcome distraction to the way her heart pounded.

Forcing herself to breathe in through her nose, breathe out through her mouth, she went through a list of reminders that she used when her stress was high: *I'm okay. Everything will be okay. This moment does not define me.* Though her stomach suggested differently. It jumped with the boat.

The good thing about Jilly's speed was they arrived at the mainland quickly. She parked the boat with ease and jumped out, saying hello to an older gentleman who immediately came over to help her tie the boat to the dock.

"Oh, no. I'm so sorry," Jilly said, looking at Presley. "Are you okay? I should have gone slower. I'm sorry."

Presley unclenched her fingers from the side of the leather seat and waved that hand dismissively. "I'm fine."

Jill tipped her head to the side, compassion shining in her gaze. "If I run into Anderson, I'm having them make you a shirt that says just that: I'M FINE. It's your catchphrase."

"Let me help you, miss," the gray-bearded man said, offering a hand to Presley.

"Thanks, Gramps," Jill said.

Presley stumbled as she stepped onto the seat to climb out. *Ah,*

Gramps. How could she feel like she knew these people when she'd never met them? He caught her arm.

"Here we go," he said when she was firmly on the dock.

Her stomach settled almost immediately. "Gramps but not related right?"

The older man's smile poked through his beard. "Oh, you never know. But no, that's just what people call me." He put an arm around Jill. "Nice to see you. Where's my Ollie?"

"She's helping her uncles. We're trying to get one of the cabins up and running."

Presley walked beside them as Jill told the man what they'd all been up to.

"I caught a bit of it on your Instagram. Ollie is a good little publicist," Gramps said.

Jill shook her head, gesturing for Presley to go ahead of her on the ramp up to the road. There was a parking lot to the left, while more boats and a couple of shops lined the right side.

"Grayson is happy to let her be our spokesperson. He's just scared to do it himself," Jill said with a laugh.

"And this pretty woman here who's still getting her sea legs is our Hot Mountain Man's girlfriend?" Gramps's bushy brows waggled.

Presley ducked her chin, not sure how the mainland knew about that. "Presley."

"Pleasure to meet you," Gramps said. "Okay. I'll say goodbye here. You bring Ollie next time."

"You got it." Jill pressed a kiss to the man's bearded cheek.

"My car is in the lot, but for now we can walk. It'll help steady you," Jill said.

"I'm okay now," Presley said, hitching her bag higher on her shoulder. The ramp led to a road with homes and green space. Obviously, they'd driven right by this area on the day she arrived, but none of it looked familiar.

They walked along the sidewalk with the sun hitting their shoulders.

Presley tipped her head up. The water was now on her right, small, single-family homes on her left. Other than bird squawks, boat motors humming in the distance, and their feet hitting the concrete, the world was . . . quiet. Peaceful. *Odd.* Presley was one of those people who loved the sound of traffic, the chatter of people. But this was nice, too.

Jill pointed to the crosswalk. "We'll head up this way. Are you hungry? Middle Street hosts street markets every week, so there's lots of options."

A small laugh left her throat. "Middle Street?"

Jill nodded. "Yes. It's a contentious topic in town." They crossed the street. "When Smile was smaller, two roads up was the middle of town. The whole place was only five blocks each way."

"It's literally the middle of the town?"

Jill laughed. "Exactly. Or it was. It grew, with Ernest Simel buying up more land. Half the town wants to change the name to something different, but the other half says if they do that, we might as well just call it Simel as it was meant to be, and then that stirs up a whole other hive of bees."

Presley laughed at the expression. Sure enough, one street over and the town came alive.

Booths and people filled both sides of the street that was cordoned off with long sawhorses much like the one she'd painted on. Music pumped from tall speakers that were set up farther down in front of the General Store. An actual general store.

"Oh, this is wonderful," Presley said, pulling her phone out to take pictures.

Turned out, the street market was more than just a chance for the town to socialize. Whatever people created, baked, cooked, or barbecued was offered at the kiosks lining the sidewalks. People walked down the center of the street, ambling back and forth from one side to another, chatting and shopping, snacking and sharing. Children chased each other, couples kissed and held hands, neighbors and friends visited. It was like walking through the set of a Hallmark movie. And she'd know, as she had the chance to do that once when they filmed one near her work. The hotel was in the background of several scenes.

People called out to Jilly. She waved and kept walking. "If we stop, we're stuck. I love it here, but no one can chat like the folks in Smile. They'll give you their life history if you ask their name. You got off lucky with Gramps because he had to go help with the boats."

Presley snapped dozens of photos. She'd post some later, but for now, she wanted to capture everything. For herself. As they neared the General Store, the music got louder, but she managed to overhear bits and pieces of conversation. Nothing showed a town's heart like the people in it. That got lost in big cities like Great Falls, but there were always pockets just like this one.

"Jill!" someone called through the crowd.

A tall, broad-shouldered man made his way over to them. He was dressed in a soft blue sweater and khaki pants. Presley immediately pegged him as a professor or a lawyer. It was a little game she played with her staff during check-ins.

"Graham," Jill said when he stopped in front of them.

"Hi. How are you?" He shifted his shopping bags and leaned in for an awkward hug that Jill returned.

"I'm good," she said when she pulled back.

"We were just talking about you at the office," Graham said, glancing at Presley.

"I'm so sorry. Where are my manners? Presley, this is Graham. He's a senior accountant where I work."

Accountant. Lawyer. Close enough. She was giving herself the point. "Nice to meet you. You're on leave, right?" Presley asked Jill.

"She is. We're all eagerly awaiting her return," Graham said.

Presley got the distinct impression that Graham, in particular, might be the most eager.

"I can't leave Gray during the summer. I'm due back at the end of September," Jill said.

"I need to check out the lodge one day. I haven't been over there since I was a kid," Graham said.

He reminded her a bit of Emmett. He didn't look like an outdoorsy guy, but Presley was learning first impressions didn't always tell the whole story.

"Well, it was nice to see you," Jill said, sidestepping his suggestion to check out the lodge. "Say hi to everyone for me."

"Will do. Nice to meet you, Presley."

"You, too."

Presley waited until he walked off to send Jill a questioning glance.

Jill shook her head. "We can talk about Graham another time over a glass of wine. For now, let's pick up my packages and grab something to eat."

The interior of the General Store was clearly updated, but they'd kept its old-timey feel. A long checkout counter with pale blue shiplap lined one wall while the rest of the store was split into rows of shelving. There were three people behind the counter, each serving customers. Presley loved that there were shelves of glass jars filled with candy on the wall behind them.

A middle-aged woman with her hair pulled into a large bun wound with intricate braids on top of her head waved to Jill. "Look who left the island. I was getting worried your brothers were holding you hostage."

They walked over to the counter, where the woman was putting a gray-haired woman's purchases into a paper bag.

"You have a great day, Mrs. Carmichael," the cashier said to the lady who lifted her bags.

"You, too, Maureen. I'll see you Tuesday night when I beat you at Hearts."

The cashier, who must have been Maureen, laughed, tipping her head back. "We'll see about that."

The older woman turned, saw Jill, and smiled widely. "Oh, Jill. How are you doing, dear?"

Jill gave her a hug. "I'm good, Mrs. Carmichael. How are you?"

"I'm good. Not too many complaints. How's the lodge coming? I see Beckett is keeping himself in good shape—and oh, aren't you the girlfriend?"

Before Presley could say anything, the woman carried on. "How's Ollie and Grayson? You tell us if you need anything."

"We will, and everyone is fine. I'll bring Ollie to visit next time I'm here."

Mrs. Carmichael patted Jill's cheek with obvious affection. "You do that. You tell that brother of yours, Beckett, that I sure do appreciate him keeping an eye on Adam."

"I will, but you know he loves hanging out with him. They get to talking about bikes and everything else disappears," Jill said.

The woman nodded. "Don't I know it."

When the woman left, Jill turned to Maureen. "How are you?"

"I'm good, girl. How are you? And Mrs. C was right, you're the girl-friend," Maureen said with a hint of mischief in her gaze.

Jill laughed. "This is Presley. Presley, this is Maureen. She's actually Chef's sister. I'm happy to hear people are checking out our social media."

Maureen extended her hand, showing long, bright blue nails that reminded Presley she could use a manicure.

"It's so nice to meet you, Presley. Feel free to post a little more of Beckett's abs any time you feel like it."

Presley laughed. "I'm not sure he'd like that."

Jill nodded her head. "I can guarantee he wouldn't, but I'm glad people are seeing our posts."

"Seeing them?" Maureen asked. "Oh, Jilly. The brothers are running competing specials at the pub. Mountain Man Burger is up against the Hot Mountain Man Platter."

Presley looked back and forth between the two women. "Excuse me?"

"Leo and Liam? The brothers who split their pub? They're always doing things like this. One does a promo and the other tries to tank it," Jill said.

Presley remembered something about dueling karaoke.

"I've been trying to get those two in a session together, but so far, they'll only come see me separately," Maureen said, disappointment making her tone heavy.

Again, Presley was lost. "Session?"

Jill's phone pinged. She checked it, then pocketed it, grinning. "Yup. Maureen here is also the only licensed psychologist in Smile."

"You're kidding. And you work at the General Store?"

"I own it," Maureen said, her shoulders squared, her pride obvious.

"That's incredible. I can barely keep up with one job," Presley joked.

"Most people around here have a couple specialties. In fact, your Beckett is one of the best hiking guides in town, a sports equipment specialist, and a sexy Instagram model."

Presley liked the sound of "your Beckett" more than she should, but she skipped over the feeling to comment, "I'd cross that last thing off his résumé."

Maureen and Jill both laughed.

"That's my favorite one," Maureen said.

"Mine, too," said one of the other cashiers.

Presley shrugged. "Okay. Mine, too."

Jill grabbed a couple of items off of the shelves and stuck them in their basket. When they made their way to the other side of the store, Presley noticed the wall. She'd sort of seen it when they first walked in, but the glance had not done it justice. It was one of those chalkboard walls, and it was huge. It was also jam-packed with the most random things.

ANDERSON AVAILABLE FOR CUTS TUESDAY & THURSDAY

CELEBRATE LOUIS' RETIREMENT AT COMMUNITY HALL
AUG 11

CARPLY FAMILY RENTING OUT HOUSE BOAT FOR ALL OF
JULY. TAKERS?

THE WILSONS NEED HOUSE SITTERS.

TWO LAWN MOWERS, STILL WORK, NEED A HOME. CALL TEVIN.
CAMP COUNSELOR POSITION JUST OPENED UP. TALK TO MAUREEN.
WHO IS GOING TO RUN HIKES THIS SUMMER?
CAN WE ADD A MAP TO THE TOWN WEBSITE?
TOWN MEETING: JULY 8, 6:00.

Dozens and dozens of messages. Presley was captivated.

"We'll be here all day if you read them all," Jill joked.

"What is this?"

"It's the community chalkboard. You want to sell something, find something, schedule an event, whatever. It's usually all here."

Presley shook her head, staring. "Just . . . everybody just writes down what they need?"

Jill nodded like this was standard operating procedure. "About four years ago, Gramps made a text thread with the eldest of like thirty families. He wanted to be more efficient in how we sent out community news. It was a pretty big mess. Let's just say Smile may not keep secrets well, but if there's a large text thread going, there's no such thing as secrets. We shut it down."

Presley laughed but she couldn't wrap her head around it. There was nothing efficient about it but she absolutely loved it. "Doesn't it make things hard to keep up with? I know you guys have a website, I checked it out. Wouldn't it be easier for people to go there on their phones or Facebook?"

Shrugging, Jill picked up a bag of chips from one of the end shelves. "It's more of a social thing and habit at this point, I think. Plus, I don't know who would run it. Gramps is working on his book about the town and our city council is always short a few members. It's slow, probably inefficient, but it works."

Presley couldn't stop grinning. This town was like nothing she'd ever seen. It was impossible not to be charmed. She was still in awe as they made their way to the back of the store. An older man was sitting on a high-backed chair, a toothpick in his mouth, laughing at something on his phone. He glanced up when they approached.

"Hey there, Jilly." He stood up, set his phone down.

"Hey, Miles. This is Presley." Jill pointed at her, then added, "Miles is Maureen's husband."

Chef's brother-in-law. She was drawing a flowchart in her brain, connecting all the people together. "Nice to meet you," Presley said, reaching out her hand.

"You, too. You've got a lot of packages," he said to Jill. "You go on a shopping spree?"

"Something like that. We're renovating one of the cabins sooner than expected, so we needed a few things." Jill pulled her phone out of her pocket, opened up her to-do list.

"I'm thinking of bringing my dad and brother over for a weekend," Miles said, flipping through an accordion file box.

"We'd love to have you," Jill said, leaning on the counter.

When his cell phone rang, he used one hand to answer and shook some papers out of the file with the other. "Miles here. Yes. You bet. They came in this morning. Sure thing." He hung up. "People know their packages have arrived because they get a confirmation email, but they phone anyway." He shook his head but one side of his mouth tipped up in a grin. He set the papers in front of Jill, who checked them while he wrote something on a well-used pad of paper.

Jill looked through the papers, slid them across the counter, then leaned on it and turned to Presley. "Smile residents tend to put the General Store as their address because things show up quicker. Plus, drivers get frustrated by the funny street names and the random way they're laid out."

"We like to keep them guessing," Miles said. He walked through a swinging door, leaving Presley and Jill at the counter.

"If I wasn't here myself, I'm not sure I'd believe some of what I'm seeing. The owner of the General Store does therapy on the side, pubs are split down the middle, the community chalkboard has everything from singles ads to flower sales, and the entire place is named after a misspelling." Presley was mostly musing out loud to herself, but Jill grinned.

"Charming, right?"

"Ridiculously so."

Miles came back with stacks of boxes. "You want me to get Anderson to take these to the dock?"

"I didn't realize there were so many. I thought they'd package more together," Jill said.

"Maybe we should have brought your car," Presley commented.

In the end, they decided to have Anderson pick up and drop off the items at the dock.

When they left the store, they sampled some of the vendors as Jill said hello and chatted with what felt like every single person. Presley took it all in, half listening to conversations, chatting with people, and eating delicious food that just kept appearing in front of her. She didn't even get a chance to pay for anything, because everyone knew Jill and wanted her to try a bit of everything.

As they strolled, Presley realized the marketing opportunities for the lodge were huge. They could cross-promote and piggyback with dozens of other Smile businesses. And Beckett's bike business? He was absolutely right. Smile needed something just like that.

Stop working. You're on vacation. She took pictures, bought a cute scarf for Rylee, and posted a few shots on Instagram of the adorable scenery.

Rylee texted, asking for Hot Mountain Man content. She laughed at her phone screen, and when she lifted her gaze, she saw Jill looking at her.

"My best friend is also a fan of your brother's abs."

Jill cringed. "Trust me when I say that of all the things I thought might put the lodge on the map, it was not Beckett's abs."

A delicious shiver traveled along every inch of her skin. The internet didn't even know the half of it. They'd just gotten a tiny glimpse. A barely there peek. As someone who'd been up close and personal, she could confirm they were worth the buzz. In fact, Beckett as a whole was an unexpected treat. A perfect remedy for her dented heart. If anything, it'd not only bounced back, it had grown fuller. Happier.

And you're leaving. Why wasn't she spending every minute with him? The thought sent a jolt of panic through her. She couldn't become attached, because she was leaving on a boat, bus, and airplane in less than a week. Needy much? Beckett was probably grateful for the break. They'd spent 24–7 together.

She stopped walking, looked down at her feet. *Breathe.*

"You okay?" Jill's feet came into sight.

"Yes. Just trying to focus on now. I learned it at a meditation retreat. When my brain starts spinning with too many things, I look down at the ground, remind myself that I'm right here, right now."

Though she didn't look up, she sensed that Jill was copying her and it felt oddly comforting to know that instead of laughing, she just joined in.

"Huh. This really does work. I like it."

Presley looked up and smiled, fighting the urge to hug this woman. "Your family is something special."

Jill's eyes widened in surprise right before she threw her arms around Presley. "So are you. Don't forget that."

Presley hugged her back tightly, hanging on to her words like a lifeline.

Jill pulled back, squeezed her arms and then gave her a teasing smile. "Okay. One more stop. I think you'll like this one best."

Twenty-Five

Beckett was nervous. Not the kind of nervousness he felt about telling his siblings about what he was now sure he wanted to be his professional future. No, this was different. Like a restless energy simmering inside of him that he didn't know what to do with. As he sat in Brothers' Pub—or, more accurately, Leo's side of Bros', which is what the locals called it—his leg bounced up and down. The evening crowd of regulars shuffled in, saying hellos and setting themselves up for a night of karaoke and pull tabs. He hadn't touched the beer he'd ordered while he waited for Jilly to bring Presley to the pub.

When the Tiger Trio, his new nickname for Gabby, Libby, and their mom, asked to come to the mainland for a little fun, he'd offered to bring them before he could think it through. It took about two seconds to realize that the reason the offer sprang from his mouth was because he wanted to be where Presley was. *You're on a timeline with this woman. It's fine if you want to spend every moment possible with her.* He could do that and not get attached. His leg bounced faster.

Finally, he saw her come through the door with his sister. They stopped in the entrance, and he had a chance to just look his fill. On the surface, she was stunning. The graceful line of her neck, the way her hair fell over her shoulders, the smile that lifted her lips. But what shook him to his core was the fact that it wasn't any of those things making his heart race. It was knowing she hated hiking even though she pretended not to. The way she picked up a hammer, a brush, or whatever else—as long as it wasn't a salamander—as though she didn't want to miss out on anything. It was the way she pushed through her fears, and how she looked below dozens of twinkle lights. The way she woke up early and smiled about it. Her eyes scanned the room with an openness and approachability and fucking lit up when they landed on him. Oh yeah. He was in big trouble. But really, how far could a person fall in one week?

They walked toward him, with Jill saying hi to several people. They didn't move far without seeing someone Jill knew. But Smile was growing. There were more people he didn't know than he did these days. Maybe it was because he kept so busy that it had taken him a while to notice, but their little town was expanding.

"Hi," Presley said with a breathtaking smile. "So, this is the famous Brothers'. Whose side is this?" She leaned down to kiss him as he went to stand in greeting, making their heads collide.

"Shit. I'm so sorry," he said.

Presley put a hand to her forehead, laughing.

"Smooth, Becks," Jill said. She pulled her purse over her head, set it on the table, grabbing her wallet out of it. "I'll grab drinks while you two figure out how to say hello."

His chest tightened like a damn schoolkid who'd asked out the popular girl on a whim. "Are you okay?" Beckett tipped her chin up, looked into her eyes. Aside from her irises being a gorgeous hue of blue, like the sky on a perfect day, her pupils checked out okay.

"I'm good. A little dazed, but I think that's par for the course, being around you," she teased.

They stood facing each other, staring, and even though Beckett knew people were looking at them, whispering *about* them—he didn't care. Five days.

"Very funny. Also, did you just make an outdoor sports reference?"

She went up on her tiptoes, pressed a soft kiss to his lips, making him wish they didn't have an audience. When she dropped to flat feet again, she grinned. "Just because I can't and don't play sports doesn't mean I don't love a good cliché."

"Sit," he said. "People are watching us." He didn't love being the center of attention, but this time it was his own fault.

He held a chair out for her. She'd barely sat down when Liam came out of a back room with a box of alcohol weighing down his arms. Well over six feet, he was two minutes older than his brother and the funnier of the two. Leo was much more serious.

"Hey, Beck. You brought your girl," he said, moving the box to one hand so he could shake Presley's.

Beckett noted the subtle shade of pink that darkened Presley's cheeks, but she held her hand out. No matter how big Smile grew, gossip would always run like water out of a faucet.

"I'm Presley," she said.

With his short hair and stocky build, Liam reminded Beckett of a pro wrestler. He'd certainly gone many rounds with his own brother over the years.

"I'm Liam. Nice to meet you. You two here for dinner? Folks are loving the Hot Mountain Man Platter."

Beckett's jaw dropped, right along with his stomach. "Excuse me?"

Jill joined them in that moment. Beckett didn't miss the way Liam looked at his sister, but he was still stuck on what the pub owner had said.

"I can't stay tonight, but I'm coming back for that one," Jill said. "How's it going, Liam?"

"I'm good, Jilly. You know I'd be happy to take you out for a meal somewhere other than here any time you want."

"Maybe you stop hitting on my sister and tell me what the hell a"— Beckett stopped, looked around, and lowered his voice—"Hot Mountain Man Platter is."

He also didn't miss the amusement in Presley's gaze. "Didn't you see the chalkboard sign? It's a sampler of all the appetizers on the menu. It sounds delicious. I definitely want one."

Liam and Jill laughed.

"Lot of women do," Liam said.

Jill sat down, pushing a fruity-looking drink toward Presley and taking a sip of her own pint of beer.

Presley took a sip. "Mmm. That's great." She looked up at Liam and then at Jill and Beckett. "You know, you could work together on some promotions. The lodge could offer ten-percent-off coupons for this place. Liam, you could share some social media posts, maybe have some flyers for the lodge by the door?" She had to raise her voice, because with the cheap separation down the middle, the music and noise from Leo's side of the bar bubbled over.

Beckett couldn't believe that even in the midst of . . . too many things . . . she had marketing strategies. Good ones.

"I love that idea. Connecting the local businesses and building off of each other is a great idea," Jill said.

"I'm on board. Maybe you and I could meet up and talk?" Liam smiled at Jill.

"Liam, you're walking a fine line, man," Beckett said, unable to control the subtle growl in his tone.

The others laughed.

"Why don't I tell Grayson to call you?" Jill said.

"Sounds good. I'll send a waitress by for your food orders," Liam said, winking at Jill and heading toward the bar.

"I don't like him," Beckett said.

Jill laughed. "You do so. I think we're about fifteen years past when I needed my big brother to watch out for me."

Presley put her hand on Beckett's forearm. The touch somehow soothed something inside of him. Settled him. Grounded him.

"Don't worry. I won't order the platter," she said.

His shoulders loosened. He could laugh at himself even if he didn't like the stupid name. "Order whatever you want. Jill isn't staying for dinner."

Jill almost choked on her drink. "Subtle. Really nice. I do need to get back soon. Anderson brought all of the packages to the boat."

"The cabin is nearly finished. It looks fantastic," Beckett said.

"Everyone seemed to have fun taking part," Presley said, her hand still warm on his skin.

"They did. Richard and Mel came down and said it made them want to do some home renos of their own. And Dayton is following Gray around like Ollie does, telling him what he could do with the money he'd happily throw his way for his cabin."

The music grew louder, making people raise their voices to carry on conversations, but it didn't detract from his enjoyment. Beckett hadn't come to the pub in far too long. They'd all been so busy with the lodge, they'd hit the ground running every day. He and his siblings needed to remember to take more breaks. Together or separately. It couldn't all be about the lodge.

"Is there anyone you could talk to about the idea? Maybe an accountant at your firm would have some insight?" Presley asked, looking at Jill.

Jill stared back at her, something passing between them that Beckett didn't understand.

"If Gray wants me to, I will. I think it's a good idea. What do you think, Beck?"

He shrugged. He *thought* he'd like his sister to leave so he could hang with Presley. "I like the old guy. I don't see a downside as long as the conditions are made clear. If Gray lays down clear guidelines, it could be the influx of cash he needs."

A screech came from the speakers, making people groan. Up onstage, a waitress spoke into a mic. "Sign-up for karaoke is open. Let's not do the same songs tonight, okay? We have new people in the house, visiting from Get Lost Lodge. For those of you who haven't spotted him, we also have our very own Hot Mountain Man here. If you haven't tried his platter, it's our special tonight."

Beckett resisted the urge to drop his head to the table as the crowd whistled and yelled.

Presley stroked his back. "Tomorrow we'll do some posts that are more lodge focused, get some of the attention back on that."

"On that note, I'm heading out. You two have fun, and I'll see you when you get back."

"Thanks for a nice day," Presley said, standing to hug Jill.

Beckett liked how easily they got along. His sister kissed his cheek, patted his shoulder. "Don't let the attention bug you," she whispered.

He nodded. Not much he could do about it. He'd just have to focus on Presley and drown out the rest of the noise.

When Presley looked at him, heat simmering in her gaze, he didn't think that would be too difficult.

She leaned in, kissed him, making him forget about everything else. "Sorry I deserted you earlier."

He took her hand, stroked his fingertip around the Band-Aid. "Is your hand okay?"

"It's fine. Just a bruise and a small cut."

The waitress who'd announced the karaoke stopped by their table. Her name tag read JENNA. Beckett didn't know her, so either she'd seen him on social media or Liam had pointed him out.

"Hey. How's it going, you two?" She pulled a pad of paper and a pen out of her Bros' apron.

"Good, thanks. We haven't looked at the menu yet," Beckett said.

"Well, like I said up there," she said, hooking a thumb over her shoulder, "you're our special tonight."

Just then, Libby and Gabby came to the table. Gabby stood too close when she announced, "We had the platter. You were delicious."

Libby smacked her sister's arm. "Knock it off. Sorry. She's had one too many already. Hey, Presley. Beckett."

They exchanged greetings, the waitress offering to give them a minute and telling them they could scan the QR code on the table for the menus.

"Mom went over to the other side of the pub," Libby said. "Is your hand okay? We heard about it when we surfaced from our movie marathon."

Presley nodded, smiling like the sisters weren't interrupting their time together. *Get it together. You don't need every second of her attention. If you do, this was the wrong place to have met up with her and*

Jilly. He just wanted to show off a bit of his hometown. It was small and quirky, but the people were great, and he knew every corner of it.

"It's not too bad. Are you having fun?" Presley asked even as she scanned the code.

"So far. We're going to do some karaoke and then someone named Anderson said they'd give us a ride to a club just outside of town."

Beckett gave a rough laugh, picking up his beer. "'Club' is a generous word for Birdie's."

Gabby pointed at him. "That's what it was called. Does it suck?"

He shook his head. "Not at all. There's a younger crowd, so you girls will fit right in. There's dancing, but it's not a big-city club, if that's what you were thinking."

"Doesn't matter. Just something to do. We're heading home soon and want to do as much as we can," Libby said.

"We're glad you came to stay," Beckett said. They weren't the expected clientele—not avid fishermen, that's for sure. But this was good. Opened things up. And honestly, he appreciated any business his brother could get. Plus, them being there had pushed him and Presley closer.

"I want to sing Lady Gaga," Gabby announced.

The girls waved goodbye and wandered through the growing crowd. The antsy feeling Beckett had before Presley showed up returned.

"You have a place here?" she asked when he looked her way.

"I do." He wanted to spend the night with her there. He hoped she'd like his surprise.

"Why don't we take our food to go and hang out there? If that's okay. I don't mean to be presumptuous. You might not want company." Her gaze widened.

"I very much want *your* company, and you can be as presumptuous as you'd like."

They ordered burgers and fries to go, then took twice as long getting out of the pub as he wanted to. Everyone had a hello, a quip about the Hot Mountain Man hashtag, or a question for Presley.

When they finally made it out onto the street, Beckett pulled in a deep breath.

"You're a popular guy," Presley said, her hand in his.

"Not usually. That would be your fault," he said, teasing her.

"I don't think so. I'll take the blame for the photo, but those people care about you and your family. You have an untapped support system and you don't even know it."

There was a hint of wistfulness in her tone. With the food in one hand, he pulled her close with the other, tucking his arm around her shoulder. "Maybe."

But he wasn't thinking about his own support system. Even without the town—and she was probably right there, his family was well-liked—he had his siblings, his parents, even Ollie. Who did Presley Ayers have?

Twenty-Six

Strolling through Beckett's hometown was more fun than she had expected. The street kiosks had shut down for the night, but people, mostly younger ones, were still hanging out. She'd been to beachside towns before, but this one felt different. Like a hidden cove of magic. Or maybe she felt that way because of the man beside her.

"What's it like where you live?" Beckett asked. He kept his arm around her shoulder while she held the hand that hung down.

It was a very couple-like position, and Presley didn't want to think too much about how right it felt.

"I live close to the hotel. About a fifteen-minute walk. My apartment is on the seventh floor of a fourteen-story building. It's your typical downtown neighborhood. Starbucks on every corner, great shopping close by. It's a lot busier than this. I can't believe how quiet the streets are. There's no traffic."

"When you can walk to everything you need, it tends to cut down on that," Beckett said.

They'd reached the end of the main strip. They turned left, walking away from the water. Most of the homes were one and two stories, but Beckett pointed out that some of them, like his, had been converted into apartment units.

"That's a great way to keep the character of the town but address the growing population," Presley said.

When she looked up at him, he was grinning down at her.

"What?"

He shook his head, kissed her quick. "Nothing. I just like the way you talk."

She laughed. That was a new one.

They walked in comfortable silence along a quiet, tree-lined street. Gulls carried on in the distance. The air had cooled but she was comfortable in her light sweater. It felt like time moved in slow motion here.

Beckett stopped at a two-story that resembled the rest of the street. A black wrought iron gate sat closed between two cement-block pillars. He unlatched the gate, held it open.

"I'm second floor, left," he said.

He used his key in one of the building's double doors, letting her precede him again. The house opened into a small foyer with stairs directly in front of them. There were two apartments on the lower level and two on the second. They took the stairs to his place. Before they got inside, the door across the hall opened.

"You're back sooner than usual," his neighbor said. Tall and thin with messy red hair, he stared at Beckett. "Is everything all right?"

Beckett smiled at him. "Everything is fine, Adam. I wanted to show my friend Presley where I live. Presley, this is Adam."

Adam said hello, his lips quirking in an almost smile. "You posted on Instagram and made Beckett famous."

Presley laughed. "I think famous is a bit of a stretch but I did get him some attention by accident. It's nice to meet you, Adam."

He nodded his head, his hand on the doorknob. "I'm going in now. We'll still go to Crinkle's?"

Beckett smiled even though Adam didn't look at him. "Just like we usually do. Have a good night, okay?"

Adam nodded once. "Okay." He let himself into the apartment and shut the door.

Beckett unlocked his door. "Adam's twenty-two. He's been living on his own for a long time now. His parents died in a car accident, so it forced him to grow up sooner than he should have."

"Oh, that's terrible." She should phone her parents. Her mother had been texting, but Presley was too in her own head right now to deal with her mom's thoughts on her breaking up with Emmett, visiting a fishing lodge, and even taking a vacation.

Beckett nodded. "He likes routine."

She nodded. "And you take him to Crinkle's every week?"

He shut the door behind them. "It's a comic book store at the other end of town."

He shrugged it off like it didn't say anything about the kind of man he was. Like the fact that she was now standing in his very cozy and charming home that he rarely got to use didn't show his family loyalty in a way words couldn't. Beckett Keller was a really good man.

"Adam's grandma was a teacher. She taught all of us. Mrs. Carmichael expects the town to keep an eye on him without getting in the way of his independence. It was a hard loss for everyone." Beckett started unloading their takeout onto a tall countertop that separated the living area from the kitchen.

"I met Mrs. Carmichael today. At the General Store," Presley said, her gaze traveling over the room, taking it all in.

She loved seeing a person in their own space. The large, open room, which had the living, kitchen, and dining all in one, had two hallways, one on either side of the living area. The smell of burgers and fries made her mouth water.

"If you spend any time in Smile, you'll meet a lot of people. They're a friendly bunch."

Presley looked at him. "They certainly are." She continued to wander, running her fingers over the spines of his Grisham novels. "I like your place."

"Thanks. I do, too. Tell me about some of the people in your life," he said, bringing over two plates full of fries and mile-high burgers. Setting them on his coffee table, he came up behind her at the bookshelf, pressed a kiss to her cheek. God, she loved those random touches, kisses, moments. "Pop, beer, or wine?"

"Pop is good."

They were settled and partway through the meal when he reminded her she hadn't answered his request.

"So? You have your friend Rylee. What does she do?"

"She's a chef. She works at this ultra-fancy downtown restaurant that is booked months out."

"Does she try out recipes on you? I could be a best friend to someone who needs a taste tester," he said, then popped a fry in his mouth.

Presley finished chewing. "Sometimes. But not a lot. Honestly, when we get together, which is usually every week to binge whatever series we're watching, we get copious amounts of junk food."

"Nothing wrong with that."

She pointed to the hallway right of the kitchen. "What's down there?"

He looked over his shoulder as if he didn't know what she might be pointing at. "Bedroom, closets, half bath." He pointed to the other side of the room. "That way is the primary bedroom, en suite, and a . . . spare room."

Presley set her plate on the table. "I'm full. What's in the spare room?"

Beckett's gaze drifted down to the last bite of his burger. He gave it far too much attention.

"Uh-oh. Do you have a naughty room?"

His gaze zipped up to hers. "A what?"

She smiled at the surprise in his expression. "You know, like a Christian Grey Red Room?"

His brows nearly touched as lines formed on his forehead. "Who the hell is Christian Grey?"

Presley laughed. "An eccentric billionaire who likes a lot of props."

"Did you date him?"

She nearly choked on the sip of pop she'd taken. Coughing, she set her drink down, her cheeks turning red. Beckett rubbed her back, concern etched into his features.

Laughter and coughing combined made ridiculous sounds, but Presley needed to catch her breath before she could truly soak in her embarrassment.

"You okay?" Beckett regarded her carefully.

"I'm good. I just like to make a fool of myself around you."

He continued rubbing her back. "Who knew fools turned me on so much?"

She laughed again, her chest tight. "First, Christian Grey is a fictional character. Second, how about a tour of your place and secret room?"

Beckett stood up, took her hand. When he pulled her into his arms for a hug, she all but melted against him. His arms held her tight, his chest making the perfect landing spot for her cheek. She closed her eyes, breathed in the scent of Beckett. She hoped she'd never forget it. One day, she'd be walking along and something would trigger her memories of this moment.

"Come on."

He led her down the right hallway first, then showed her his bedroom, which was masculine, welcoming, and comforting with its dark gray tones. When he hesitated in front of the spare room door, butterflies tickled the inside of her stomach.

"Show me your secrets, Beckett," she teased.

Laughing, he squeezed her hand. "This town has no secrets." He pushed open the door.

Presley walked into the room and took it all in. There was no furniture. Only bikes. She hadn't been on a bike since . . . forever. A friend had taught her to ride in the field behind their elementary school in about fifth grade.

She recognized one as a tandem and another as a cruiser but only because she'd helped a few guests rent them over the years.

"This is quite the collection," she said, warmth spreading through her chest. This town had a few secrets, and he'd shared his with her.

Beckett walked to a regular-looking bike and put his hand on its red handlebars. "This one is actually mine. It's called a crosstrail. It's good for around town or riding through some of the bike paths in the woods."

"Are you one of those adrenaline junkie bikers? Do you jump ravines and ride across thin rails?"

He laughed. "No. I love a good trail ride, but I'm not into extreme biking. That's a whole different sport. These are some of the bikes I want to have available at my place. I want to get a couple more tandems. Those are fun for families and couples. I'm looking at a bulk order of cruisers. I'm hoping to stock six of those."

She wondered if he realized what he'd just said. "That means you've made a decision. You're doing it?"

A slow, almost reluctant smile tilted his lips up like he was finally accepting the truth. "I am. I definitely am."

"This is so cool, Beckett. Your family must know you love biking." She watched as he ran his hand over the rubber handle grips.

"They do," he said, meeting her gaze. "We all do. It's fun. I'm going to tell them about my idea."

"From what I've learned about them, they'll be in full support," she said quietly. It wasn't her place, but she'd already crossed and tangled lines in unknottable ways. What was a few more knots? "They love you. It's so clear all of you want the best for each other. I understand the timing isn't perfect, but you'll make it work."

Beckett came to stand in front of her, taking both of her hands. "I know you're right. I just don't want to add to the chaos. Not yet."

She removed her hands from his, slid them up his shirt, around his neck. She loved the way his immediately shifted to loop around her hips. Speaking of tandem, she'd never felt so in sync. Because of course. Life was full of ironies like that. She hadn't even realized she was lost until she came to a lodge with that very name.

"I wanted to take you for a bike ride tomorrow. We don't have to though. Biking probably isn't your thing." He gave her a lopsided grin.

"You have no evidence that it isn't." She tried to keep a straight face.

He returned the look. "Great. So, we can take two of the trail bikes? The inclines aren't too bad."

She broke first because there was no way she was getting on a trail on a bike. This was an either-or situation.

"It's been a while. How about we ease in?"

He nodded. "I was hoping we could stay here tonight. Maybe tomorrow, too." He kissed her forehead.

Presley's heart sighed inside of her chest. Just them, no others around? She loved people, and his family in particular, but time alone with him sounded like a fantasy come true. "I'd love that. Well, the staying-over part. I'm reserving judgment on the biking. Won't they need you at the lodge?"

Beckett pulled back, one of his hands finding the skin beneath her shirt and rubbing small circles. "Tevin owes me a favor. He's pitching in for a night or two."

Presley moved her own fingers into his hair. It was soft and felt good against her skin.

"You didn't have to do that," she said, though she was glad he did. When was the last time someone other than Rylee had put her first?

Softly nudging the bridge of her nose with the tip of his own, he pulled her closer. "I wanted to. I wanted to be alone with you. Away from everything else."

"I'm glad. The lodge is great, but I like seeing where you live. Being in your space." She trailed her lips along his collarbone, smiled against it when his fingers pressed into her hips. A low, rumbly sound left his chest.

"I have something else you're going to like, a lot."

An unexpected giggle left her mouth. Beckett pulled back, amusement dancing in his brown eyes. "Nice. But not what I meant. Well, that, too—but come with me."

Taking her hand, he led them out of the room, into his bedroom, and then into the en suite bathroom. A large soaker tub took up one wall, and she thought maybe he was going to suggest that. She didn't have time to be disappointed though, because he led her to the glass-enclosed shower and pointed up.

Presley sighed. There were two huge rainfall showerheads hanging from the ceiling. Another smaller, removable showerhead hung from the wall.

"It's like a spa shower," she said, leaning back into him.

"With excellent water pressure. Basically, the exact opposite of the lodge," he said, kissing her neck.

Letting her go, he opened the shower door, turned on the water, and then pulled her back to him.

"Unless you'd rather go for a night bike ride?" He was already lifting her shirt over her head.

Presley laughed. "It's unlikely you'll get me out of this shower." She pushed at his shirt, heart hammering against her ribs when he reached back, tugged it off himself.

"I can work with that."

The lighting here was also better than the lodge or cabin. In the soft, warm glow, with steam rising around them, Presley took her time exploring the lines and muscles of his chest, kissing the spots her fingers touched, listening to their combined breathing.

His hands tangled in her hair, his next kiss consuming. It was a whole-body experience, the way he wrapped himself around her like he couldn't get close enough. She lost herself in the feeling of being wanted, needed, cherished. They parted only long enough to remove the rest of their clothing and tumble into the shower together. He whispered words that heated her more than the water slicing over them. Words that made her feel seen.

He stroked her hair back from her face, stared at her with an intensity, a desire she'd never experienced. She told herself the heightened, unfamiliar need came from having an end date. But as she went up on her tiptoes to close the distance between them, she knew, without a doubt, that it was him. A week or a lifetime, the sensation would be the same. Because it was Beckett.

Twenty-Seven

That lovely, hazy moment in between sleep and waking was one of Presley's favorites. In those precious seconds, waking in Beckett's bed, she imagined this was more than a brief interlude. She ran her fingers over his soft sheets—the man did not scrimp on thread count—only to find his side empty.

Her eyelids fluttered open as her body came awake, including her mind. Which had the annoying habit of counting down, good or bad. Four days. She'd be going home in four days.

Stretching, she got out of bed, visited his bathroom, made sure her hair wasn't pulling an Einstein. *Not too bad.* She smoothed it out a little before grabbing her toothbrush. Beckett had brought some of her things over. Thoughtful with great sheets was something a girl didn't find every day of the week.

She found coffee in the kitchen, but not Beckett. Her phone, which she'd left charging on his counter, came awake when she unplugged it. There were several emails that she didn't bother to open, a check-in text from Rylee, and a text from Beckett saying good morning, have some coffee, and he was just outside getting the bike ready.

"I hope that means you're adding extra padding to the seat," she said aloud as she poured herself a cup.

When she was a little more awake and caffeinated and had checked her socials, she posted a photo of her coffee with the caption: Second-best way to be awoken in the morning. Just for fun, she added the hashtag #GetOutside, because why not be optimistic? It got likes even before she closed the app to go find the internet's current Hot Mountain Man.

He was outside, pushing on the back tire of the tandem bike that had been in his spare room.

Beckett's eyes came to hers when she came outside. "Good morning."

He left the bike as she walked down to the bottom step, leaning into a kiss like they'd rehearsed it. Like it could become a habit. Taking her hand, he pulled her toward the bike.

"Thought we'd take the tandem. I can take the front, or, if you'd like to, you can," he said, turning her so she faced the bike and he was behind her.

"Definitely you in front. Then you won't be able to see when I don't pedal," she said, approving of this plan.

She felt his rumble of laughter against her back, enjoyed the way his couple of days of stubble rasped against the skin of her shoulder.

"You know I'll be able to tell if you're not pedaling, right?"

Turning in his arms, Presley kissed his chin. He lowered it so she could kiss him again, on the lips. "Flat surface?"

Laughing again, he nodded. "No hills."

"Then I'll do my share."

❦

On the very short bike ride to a little diner just one street up from the water, Presley counted eight people who said hello to Beckett. It was barely ten A.M. She worked with over a hundred people at the hotel, about twenty-five on any given shift, and that many people barely greeted her by the end of the day.

They parked the tandem in front of Pete's Place, a retro-style diner that reminded Presley of her used-to-be-favorite pie shop. There were a couple of other bikes in the rack, but the tandem stuck out the farthest by a long shot.

"Everyone in this town is so nice," Presley said as she unclipped her helmet. The short bike ride wasn't nearly as bad as she'd worried it would be.

Beckett hung both of their helmets on the handlebars. He laughed, glanced at the diner doors. "Funny timing on you saying that. You might change your mind shortly."

A couple came out of the diner, hand in hand. "I'm not going back," the woman said, all but stomping down the three concrete steps.

"You say that every week." The guy nodded at Beckett and Presley as he followed the woman.

"Am I missing something?" Presley looked through the diner window, but a checkerboard pattern was painted on the lower half, making it hard to see much.

Beckett took her hand. "Best breakfast in town. Pete's an amazing chef. He's a bit rough around the edges. He's got a big heart, but his words aren't always—how should I put it?—measured." He held the door open for her.

She walked into the smell of vanilla and deliciousness. Seriously, something smelled incredible. Her stomach rumbled while her brain conjured images of funnel cakes and county fairs. She immediately wanted waffles with a side of pancakes.

A curly-haired waitress in a T-shirt and jeans waved from the cash register even as loud voices shouted from behind the pass bar.

"No one is stopping you from leaving," a burly voice said.

"You'd be sorry if I did," a flippant, clearly female voice replied.

A man's face appeared in the rectangular opening between the front of house and the kitchen. He looked like a cross between a biker and a grumpy Santa Claus.

"Sorry you didn't go sooner," the guy said. His dark hair had patches of gray that matched the gray of his beard.

"Hey, Pete," Beckett called, lifting his hand as he nudged Presley toward one of the booths along the window.

"Hot Mountain Man," the man said.

Beckett groaned, but the waitress and chef shared a laugh. Presley bit back on hers as Beckett led her to a table. "Hey, Annabelle," he said to the woman cashing out a customer. The customer left, the bells over the door jingling.

"Hey, Becks. Be right with you."

Presley started to slide into the booth but was caught off guard by the tabletop.

Beckett pressed his hand to her lower back. "I thought you'd like this."

He was clearly referring to the way the tabletop had been painted to resemble Van Gogh's *Starry Night*. She ran her hand over the slightly textured surface, her breath stuck in her throat.

"This is incredible." Instead of sitting down, she glanced around. To the left of the door were eight booths, four by the windows, four across the aisle. Same to the right of the entrance, with a long counter-top at the front. There were two customers at the end of the counter, a single person sitting in the booth farthest from them, and a couple on the other side as well.

All eight of the tabletops on their side depicted famous paintings. Monet's *Water Lilies*, a Picasso abstract of a woman's face, Andy War-hol's Marilyns, and several she recognized though she couldn't name the artists.

"A newcomer," the waitress named Annabelle said, menus under one of her arms as she leaned against one of the padded booths, watching her take it all in. "Gets them every time."

Beckett slid into the *Starry Night* booth. Presley turned to face him and the waitress, whose hand was resting on the *Mona Lisa*.

"This is incredible. Who makes them?" She desperately wanted to see the rest of the tabletops but resisted. After breakfast. By then, hope-fully the other side would be clear of customers.

"It started when Pete and Gwen's daughter used acrylic on that ta-ble Beck's sitting at. She was only five at the time. She goes to art school in New York now. Instead of getting mad at her, Gwen, who's also an artist, showed her how to make it into something special."

Presley slid into the booth, across from Beckett. "What about the rest of them?"

"Gwen's been experimenting with other mediums. The ones on that side of the diner are now vinyl stickers of images," Beckett said.

More grumbling, something about making substitutions to the menu, sounded from the kitchen. Presley's eyes widened when she heard Pete call, "I'm the chef. Why can't people just trust me that it comes best the way I say it does?"

The swinging door pushed forward, a tall woman with her hair bundled on top of her head coming through with two plates.

"Swear to God and the patron saint of diners, I'm going to beat you with your spatula, Peter," the woman said.

Annabelle laughed, setting the menus on the table. "Don't worry, she won't," she said to Presley. "Get you two some coffee?"

"Actually, could I have some orange juice, please?" Presley asked, curious how the waitress could be so sure. The other waitress's tone suggested she'd really like to follow through and smack the chef.

"Of course. Beck?"

"Coffee, please," he said, an amused grin brightening his face.

Presley traced her finger along the swirling groove of a star in the night as Annabelle went to get their drinks.

"Breakfast and a show," she said.

"Yeah. Pete's all bluster. Like a moody artist, only his medium is food. He's actually pleasant when Gwen or Courtney, their daughter, are around. Half the time, I swear it's mostly for the show. The customers sort of expect it now."

The swinging door behind the counter flew open again and Pete came through. He wore a white chef coat and held a large glass in his hand. He was a big man, one who would be attractive in a silver fox sort of way if he wasn't grumbling to himself.

Going to the soda fountain behind the counter, he pressed one of the buttons. Annabelle brought over their drinks, but Presley was too busy looking around and watching Pete from the corner of her eye to be ready to order.

"Pete makes the best waffles on the East Coast," Beckett said.

"Damn right I do," Pete called.

"It's true," Annabelle said.

"Sounds perfect," Presley said.

Beckett ordered the same. When Annabelle walked away, Pete came to the side of their table.

"Beckett."

Beckett smiled. "Pete. Pleasure as always. This is Presley Ayers. She's staying at the lodge."

His lips quirked. "Doing more than staying there from what I hear, hot guy," Pete said.

"Now you're a comedian?" Beckett frowned.

"I have my moments. How do you like the lodge, Presley?"

She glanced at Beckett, not sure why her cheeks felt warm. "It's been a wonderful adventure." There. That was safe. Didn't reveal too much.

Presley couldn't help herself. "Have any of your waitresses ever actually smacked you with your own spatula?"

Pete's gaze narrowed a split second before a rough, rumbly laugh left his mouth.

Beckett nearly spit out his sip of coffee. "Holy shit, did you just laugh?"

"Shut up," Pete said, his mouth flattening again, but Presley noted the slight sparkle in his gaze. "That one has." He hooked a thumb over his shoulder. "But she's my younger sister, so it's not a surprise, and to be fair, I probably deserved it."

"No doubt you did," Beckett said.

"I repeat, shut up," Pete said, his tone almost friendly.

"You coming to make this food?" his sister called, waving at Beckett and Presley.

"Welcome to Smile, Presley," Pete said, heading back to the kitchen.

She folded her arms on the tabletop, leaned toward Beckett. "He sounds grumpy but I think he's secretly nice."

Beckett leaned forward. "Not when you beat him at poker."

Her laugh turned to a contented sigh when he laced his fingers with hers and stared at her across the *Starry Night* table.

Beckett gazed out the window. "See that spot right by the marina?"

Presley looked to where he pointed. "The empty lot?"

"Yeah. I'm thinking about that as the rental space for the bikes."

Grinning, she turned her head to face him. "It's a great location. Close enough to the action. Lets people pedal around the lake or through town."

"Exactly." He nodded and smiled but Presley noted the reluctance in his gaze.

"Grayson and Jill are going to be really happy for you." She was sure of it.

"I know I'm building it up in my head. I just need to do it. But I worry it's not the right time."

Treading carefully since it wasn't really her business, she folded her hands together. "I think we fool ourselves into believing there's a 'right time' for all of the things we want. But really, life does what it wants, and we need to seize the opportunities we have when they present themselves." Wasn't that exactly what they were doing here?

Beckett's gaze turned thoughtful. "I've got the loan plus my savings. It's enough for bikes, space, and to float me through the first year. I mean, it's a fairly seasonal business, so I'd keep my job for now."

Which meant he'd be spread even more thin. "That's probably a good plan."

He tapped his fingers on the tabletop. "Part of me wants to give the money to Gray. It would help him a lot. He needs this to work."

Presley didn't know many people who'd literally put aside their own dreams for someone else's. *You've surrounded yourself with the wrong people.* Other than Rylee, the people in her circle did what was best for them first.

"I don't think he'd want it to replace your own goals. You should at least talk to them."

Annabelle brought them their breakfasts. Presley's mouth watered at the stack of waffles.

"Let me know if you need anything else," she said with a smile, dropping extra napkins on the table.

Probably for the drool. They smelled better than any waffles she'd ever had.

Sensing Beckett's need to change the subject, Presley was quiet while she cut into the little squares of yumminess. Pete shouted at his sister again.

"I'd like to meet the woman that married him," Presley said.

"You will," Beckett said with confidence, cutting into his own waffles.

Presley didn't question him on that. If she didn't meet the woman today, she likely never would. But she liked the way it sounded when Beckett said it; like there was no end date on the possibilities.

Twenty-Eight

The short ride to the diner had fooled her into believing getting back on a bike would be like, well, just like riding a bike. It took Presley less than a half hour to realize riding a bike in her thirties did not produce the whimsy and freedom she'd felt as a child. It did not *feel* the same either. *Why do people do this?* Hard seat that had no business being called a cushion, hunched over to reach the bars . . . this couldn't be good for a person.

Beckett pedaled like he did everything else physical; with ease. He might struggle to make life choices, preferring Presley's least favorite approach--ignoring them—but if it involved fluid motion and balance? No problem. He lifted his hand more than once to wave and return greetings. He didn't even look uncomfortable, and she was pretty sure if she could see his face, he'd be smiling.

"You okay back there?"

"Of course," she said. A person probably shouldn't be out of breath when the course was flat.

"Okay" was a relative term. She'd be signing up for some spin classes when she got home, but sure, she was okay. Would she rather be cuddling with Beckett on a shaded patio with fruity drinks in hand? Hell, yes. But she could do this, too. The benefit of all of the things that had happened recently was learning she could do a lot of things she hadn't known she could.

At the edge of town, they entered a trail marked OUTER LIMITS. There was what seemed like a narrow opening between towering trees. With the sign and lack of visibility, Presley found it a little sci-fi/horror movie-ish, but she trusted Beckett. *With more than the route.*

"Smile gets a lot of tourists starting soon. This is one of our hidden gems. People love it," Beckett called back.

People loved narrow trails away from civilization? *To each their own.*

Curling into herself so the trees didn't brush up against her arms, she breathed a sigh of relief when the path widened enough for a biker to pass them going the other way. When Beckett simply waved while the other rider just nodded his chin, Presley smiled, put her feet up on the bars. He wouldn't notice if she took a small break.

"Did you not know that person? Is there someone in this town that you don't know?" she called up.

Beckett's laughter floated back to her. "If you can imagine, yes. There are almost five thousand people in Smile now. I don't know them all. Though Jilly might. My sister is the social butterfly of the three of us."

A small bump dislodged her feet, so she put them back on the pedals. Probably safer.

"She passed that on to Ollie."

Beckett's chuckle drifted back to her. "And then some."

Yesterday's flash storm was nowhere to be seen, but everything looked fresher and brighter as a result of the rain.

Presley started to say more, but the path opened up into a surprising view. In front of them was what felt like a mini-town inside of the town. *Hidden gem indeed.* Beckett slowed them to a stop when the path turned to cobblestone. On the right was a row of multicolored shops with adorable awnings displaying names. On the left was a stretch of beach, the water, and a wide pier. Along the edge of the pier was a row of houseboats that mirrored the look of the shops. The rainbow of colors made the town name absolutely perfect.

"This is Tourist Lane," Beckett said when they dismounted. Once the kickstand was up, he smiled, like he was waiting for her reaction, like he *knew* how much happiness this would bring her.

How could he *know* her already? The shops were open with a few people strolling along the sidewalk, a few more up ahead on the cobblestones, and several on the beach, in chairs, and even a few on the dock with fishing rods. A couple of people were on the flattop roof of one of the houseboats.

Presley walked forward, happiness surging through her with such speed that she couldn't stop the little bounce in her steps.

"It's like a rainbow!"

Beckett laughed. "It's pretty cool. The main street in town has all of your basic needs, but this area was carved out by a few local artisans, including Gwen. Years back, there were just a few people living on the houseboats, but then a couple of locals got permits to build shops here. It's been growing steadily over the years."

The array of colors, the canary yellow, meadow green, and sky blue of the buildings, felt like architecture imitating its surroundings. From where she stood, Presley saw a fish and chips shop, a couple of jewelry stores, an art store, and a few other food shops.

She pulled out her phone, opened Instagram, and pressed the LIVE button. She waited for it to connect while Beckett watched with patience and a sexy smirk. "I keep thinking I've seen all there is to see of Smile," she started, turning so the camera pulled Beckett into the shot. He ducked his head and pressed a hand to her hip, like holding on to her made the attention more bearable. "But then a certain tour guide goes and surprises me. Put Smile on your list of places to visit, and when you get here, stop by Pete's diner, Bros' Pub, and Tourist Lane before settling in for a cozy night at Get Lost Lodge."

Beckett nuzzled his face into the crook of her neck, making her stomach spin faster than the wheels of the bike zipping past them. When she ended the live, tagging the businesses she'd mentioned, she took a selfie of them, knowing that she'd never forget the feel of him against her like this, the quiet, solid strength and acceptance in his touch.

She posted the photo on her feed with a caption: Bicycle for Two. Hashtags could be hit or miss, but she tagged the lodge and added #RainbowTown #grateful #smile

"What? No 'Hot Mountain Man'?" Beckett asked as she tucked her phone away. Notifications pinged immediately so she silenced it without looking.

She kissed his cheek. "Not this time. Besides, you're more than that." *And I don't want to share you.*

He laughed. "Thanks. I think."

Yeah. He was a hell of a lot more than that.

Needing to distract herself from those thoughts, she leaned into his side. "This wasn't in any of the brochures I saw online."

"No. It wouldn't be. It's a word-of-mouth sort of thing, but people come from all around to visit. Several of those houseboats are vacation rentals."

"I'm not sure how I'd feel about sleeping on a boat," Presley admitted. She looked up at Beckett. "Speaking of online, your website is really outdated."

He nodded. "I know. Jilly was working on it, but with all of the renos and updates, and, honestly, repairs, it just hasn't been a priority. Before us, the owners hadn't been renting it out or using it much."

She didn't want to push him on the ideas she had brewing in her brain. It was their family, their business. Today, and for the next few days, she wanted to live in the moment. She wanted to get lost in this mini-town, lost in Beckett. She wanted to twirl around with her arms open. Instead, she let the happiness course through her, hoping she'd remember the feeling long enough to pull it out on lonely days back in Great Falls.

He leaned down, his lips finding hers in a soft, sweet kiss. "Want to start at the end? How are you feeling?"

Her butt and lower back hurt, but she was too excited to care. "I feel wonderful. The bike ride was good but this is better."

His hand slid down her back, then he laced his fingers with hers. "Did you enjoy the ride at all?"

"Of course." They walked toward the row of shops.

"Was it better when your feet were up?"

Presley stopped, looked at him.

He arched his brows and she felt her cheeks warm.

"I don't know what you're talking about."

She could get drunk on his laughter. It lit up his whole face. "Mm-hmm."

"That's my story." She pulled him forward.

The smell of fish and chips made her forget they'd eaten not too long ago, but she pushed off the feeling. Shops first, more food later. Presley found an ornate bracelet for Rylee at one of the end shops. It was aptly named: This and That. She also found a little something for Ollie and Jill in that store. They tried samples of homemade candy at Sugar Rush, bought postcards at a stationery shop called The Write Place, and stopped at Waterfront, a tiny bistro with only six tables, to share a flight of locally brewed craft beers. They strolled by the water, and part of Presley wished they had their suits. She wasn't much of a swimmer, but the day was growing warm.

She was thinking about trying the fish and chips when they got to Inspiration, a small, eclectic art store. It was like a museum of gorgeous items, but everything was for sale.

Within minutes, Presley had her heart set on the beautiful, shallow bowl in gorgeous shades of purple and blue that was part of a window display. It was a for-sure purchase, but then she fell in love with a knitted gray blanket, a painting of the General Store, and a glass-bead bracelet. Beckett laughed when she picked up a stack of hand-drawn postcards.

"There's only so much room in my backpack," he teased.

"Everything is so pretty and well crafted," Presley said, running her hand over a watercolor sketch of the lake.

"All of it is local, as well." The blond woman who'd been helping a customer when they entered joined them at a hutch displaying trinkets and stationery.

"It's incredible. All of it. I love your store," Presley said.

"Thank you. I'm Gwen. How are you, Beckett?" she said, reaching out a hand.

Presley didn't think she could smile wider. "Gwen."

Beckett and Gwen shared a glance, and the woman laughed. "Uh-oh, did my reputation precede me?"

Beckett took Presley's hand when she'd shaken Gwen's. "We had breakfast at Pete's this morning."

Gwen nodded in understanding. "Ahh. You'd be surprised to know he's quite the romantic."

Beckett laughed over Presley's dreamy sigh. "Pretty sure Pete would deny that with every breath in his body."

"He's harmless, and the man can cook," Gwen told Presley.

"That's certainly true. He's ruined me for all other waffles."

"How long are you here?" Gwen asked.

Presley wondered if Beckett realized his grip tightened briefly at the question. "Just a few more days."

Giving Beckett a somewhat motherly look, Gwen brushed her long blond hair back over her shoulders. "Well, I'm glad you're making the most of your time here and seeing all of the wonderful things Smile has to offer." Her gaze settled on Beckett as she spoke.

Pressing her lips together, Presley nodded, quite certain Beckett would not want to be described that way any more than Pete wanted to be labeled a romantic.

"I'll let you finish looking. It was lovely to meet you, Presley," Gwen said.

It was so hard to choose. Beckett was more than patient, giving her time to peruse, second-guess, and try to see every little thing. In the end, she chose the bowl because its bright colors would always remind her of this day. Gwen wrapped it in several layers of paper. She also chose a small pewter statue. It had a squat, square base to hold the little sign that read SMILE.

Outside the store, Beckett carefully packed Presley's purchases in his backpack.

"You showed great restraint," he told her, his lips twitching.

"You have no idea. I could have spent a month's paycheck there."

Settling his backpack on his shoulders, he pulled a small paper bag out of his pocket.

"What's that?"

His smile was soft and sweet, intimate in a way she'd never felt. The kind she hadn't seen him give anyone else since she'd arrived. "Something you missed."

She took the bag, opened it. Inside, wrapped carefully in tissue paper, was a tiny silver charm of a hashtag. Tears filled her gaze when she looked up at him.

"I love it."

He shifted his stance, ran a hand through his hair. "It's nothing. Just something that reminded me of you. I don't know if you have a bracelet or anything."

Presley wrapped her arms around his waist, settling her head on his chest, breathing through her nose so she didn't cry. She clutched the hashtag charm in her palm, listening to the gentle thud of Beckett's heartbeat under her ear.

"It's perfect."

His hands rubbed up and down her back like he was soothing them both. After pressing a kiss to her head, he cleared his throat, stepped back. "How about a late lunch?"

She nodded, sniffled just a little. "Sounds great."

After a delicious meal of fish and chips, they walked back to the bike where they'd left it at the entrance of the strip.

He grabbed her helmet first, tucked it onto her head.

"You okay?" He grabbed his own helmet.

Fastening the chin strap, she nodded—not a smart idea. She nearly pinched her chin. "I'm good. I think Rylee would love it here."

"She means a lot to you," he said, pulling the bike from the rack. "Any other best friends back in the city?"

She shook her head.

"Any close cousins?"

"No cousins at all, actually. Both of my parents were only children."

Beckett pursed his lips, stared out at the water. "My siblings both drive me nuts. Less so now that we're older, but growing up, man, they drove me crazy." He grinned at her. "Don't tell them, but I like them both quite a bit now."

Laughter replaced the almost-gloomy feeling in her chest. "I won't tell. Where to now?"

"Thought we'd head back to my place?" His phone rang before they could get on the bike.

He slid his thumb across the screen. "Hey, Jilly. What's up?"

Presley could hear murmurs through the phone and knew immediately from Beckett's expression and words that something was up and he'd once again change his plans for his family. Why did that make him sexier? He paced away from the bike, staring out at the water.

"We're at Tourist Lane. What happened? Is he okay? We have to grab our stuff from my place, but we'll be back within the hour."

He hung up and sighed, still looking out at the water. She gave him a minute, wringing her hands together with the need to help however she could.

"Beckett?"

He turned to face her. "Chef had an accident. Dropped a knife, grabbed it out of reflex, sliced his hand and knocked a pot of hot water onto himself. They're airlifting him to Mackinaw City Hospital right now."

Presley sucked in a sharp breath, her hands flying to her mouth. "Oh my goodness. Will he be okay?"

Beckett nodded, running a hand up and down her arm. "I think so. Jilly thinks so. Louis is already on his way to the hospital. Maureen's taking him so he doesn't have to wait for the ferry. Gray was in town when it happened, so he's waiting at the dock for us to come back."

His forehead and around his eyes wrinkled with tension. Presley put her hands on his chest. "Let's go."

He shook his head. "Jilly doesn't love blood, so she's shaken. She said she's okay on the phone, and Gray's heading back, but I'd rather see for myself that she's all right."

She tilted her head to the side. "You don't have to explain it. Of course you want to be with them."

"I'm sorry our day got cut short."

Presley curled her fingers into his shirt. "Beckett. This is your family. All of them. Jill, Grayson, *Chef.* It makes sense you'd want to be there with your siblings right now."

He stared at her a moment like he was unsure how to take her absolute acceptance of his need to be with his family. She felt a slight tremble under her hands.

"You're torn on showing me a good time and being there for them. There's no either-or here, Beckett. We need to go."

Relief washed over his features right before he crushed her to his chest in a tight hug. "Thank you."

Emotions pulled tight strings around her heart. It wasn't even her family and she felt the urge to be there every bit as much as he did. Beckett released her, moving to the bike to nudge the kickstand up. Presley's butt ached with only the thought of getting back on.

"Maybe it would save time if Grayson picked us up at this dock?"

Beckett looked at her for a full beat before he grinned. "I'm pretty sure you're the only person other than Ollie who could make me smile at this moment."

She tipped her head to one side. "Is that a yes?"

He chuckled, the tension in his shoulders easing just a bit. "Get on the bike, Presley. Everything will be okay."

Twenty-Nine

Beckett wasn't sure why the universe chose this particular snippet of his life to show him what perfect felt like when he couldn't fully immerse himself in it. They'd returned the night before, and Beckett had immediately told his sister to take a break and hang with Ollie while he and Gray cleaned the kitchen. The guests were more than accommodating and worried on Chef's behalf, but Louis had called later that night saying the burns on Shane's hip weren't too bad and though he'd needed nine stitches in his hand, he was in good spirits.

Beckett insisted Presley head down to the cabin. She'd done so much for them already. He didn't want her to spend her last few days working. Plus, he had so many worries, ideas, and thoughts swirling in his brain, he needed to get inside his own head and clear the space. Figure shit out.

❧

He'd left the bed before she woke up. Maybe he'd watched her sleep for a few minutes, reveling in the fact that she was in his bed. Ignoring the fact that she was leaving in a few days. Also ignoring the contradictory way his chest tightened in her presence even though his breath came easier when she was there. Feelings were weird.

Beckett hung up the phone after confirming for a guest that, yes, this was the Hot Mountain Man lodge, because really, he didn't have time to correct them. It would die down, and for now, the money coming in from the bookings was keeping them afloat. Living here wasn't free for any of them.

"Hey," Jill said, pulling her hair up into a high ponytail as she walked into the room and came behind the counter. She looked well rested if a little pale. Mrs. Angelo had heard the news about Chef through some secret Smile gossip network and sent a month's worth of muffins and casseroles with Gray so they didn't have to worry about food more than necessary.

"Thanks for taking care of the front desk. And for last night. I hate to say this, but we might need a more powerful dishwasher," she said. She hooked a thumb over her shoulder. "I'm running the same load for the second time."

"Add it to the list," Beckett said even as he pulled his clipboard out from beside the computer to add it himself. "Where's Ollie?"

"She's in the garden. Mel is helping her plant some herbs. I can't believe how much I'm going to miss her and Richard. I hate that they're leaving tomorrow."

"They're special. This whole group was. Is it wrong that I'm really hoping things go well for Mr. Dayton and Grayson at the meeting? I know Gray wants to keep it in the family."

Jill opened her laptop. She was obsessed with the site Presley had shown them. "No. I think it's a great option as well. It was nice of Graham to agree to meet with them today."

Beckett tapped the clipboard against his thigh. He wasn't the only one whose life was in flux right now. "Wonder why he'd drop everything and fit them in? Maybe he really likes Grayson." He couldn't stop his smile. Gray and Graham had gone to school together, but the accountant's interest was definitely in Jilly.

"I'm going to sidestep that with a question for you," Jill said, looking up from her screen. "What are you going to do about Presley?"

Setting the clipboard down, he tidied up the counter while answering. "Nothing. Nothing to do. She's here for a few more days. Right now, I'd be happy if I have time to hang out with her, but I need to check the dishwasher, fix another spot on the dock, confirm a bunch of equipment orders that I need to deliver next week, prep a hiking route that isn't really a hiking route at all so the Tiger Trio can feel like they had an outdoor experience, and pack up for a night hike with the two guys in room eight."

"She's special, Beck. The kind of special that doesn't come along every day," Jill said, stepping in front of him so he would stop fidgeting.

"She's a guest."

Jill frowned. She was a foot shorter than him, but somehow, she managed to look down her nose, making him feel small.

"Family first." Once Grayson's life was sorted, they could all move forward.

"No one will question your loyalty, Beck."

He patted his sister's shoulder, moved around her. They might when he said he couldn't be here, at Brian's, *and* start the bike rental shop. "I know that. One issue at a time. Let's focus on the lodge." Because focusing on Presley would turn him inside out even more than she already did.

Libby, Gabby, and Chantel came down the stairs, laughing loudly. Gabby lit up when she saw him, but not the way Presley did. That warmed him from the inside out. When Gabby did it, he just felt like he was stuck in a crowded space with no way to get out.

"We are so excited about our hike this afternoon," Gabby said, leaning on the front desk.

She wore boots, but they were pink, shiny, and had heels on them. He should take them to the little stream through the woods in the back or he'd have to find Band-Aid alternatives, since Presley had run through his supply.

"With no chef, is there anything to eat?" Libby asked, looking up from her phone.

"Of course," Jill said, going into full hostess mode. "We have fresh fruit, granola, and muffins that one of the delis sent over. This afternoon, we'll have sandwiches, and tonight, we're having lasagna and Caesar salad. It's not Michelin-star caliber, but I promise you won't go hungry."

Gabby's eyes trailed over him, making him frown. Presley walked through the door at that moment, and he had to thank the universe once again for the timing.

Dressed in a pair of lounge pants that cinched at her ankles, a pale pink T-shirt that read #DREAM across the front—her and her hashtags—she looked beautiful to him. His heart felt like it was being squeezed in the fist of a giant when she smiled at him.

"Girlfriend alert. Behave, Gabs," Libby said.

"Leave your sister, darling. She's harmless," Chantel said.

"Why don't we grab breakfast," Jill said. She ushered the women toward the kitchen even as they waved Presley's way.

Presley waved back, coming to the front counter. "Good morning."

Coming around the counter, he kissed her hello. "Good morning."

He'd never thought much about those little things. Over the years, he'd had several girlfriends. Some long-term, some not. He'd been sure he was doing the right thing when he proposed to his high school sweetheart. When she left for New York, he was crushed, but deep in his heart, he'd known they weren't meant for forever. His proposal was a last-ditch effort to avoid change. He'd felt love, lust, and several things in between. But nothing like the feelings Presley brought out, like she was part of him. Being around her was like he'd painted the gray sky with color. Like the rainbow that appeared after the storm. It was overwhelming, and he didn't know if he could handle *feeling* this much on a regular basis, and something told him his feelings would only intensify with time if she stayed.

Good thing she's not. Right. That's what he told himself. This kind of connection wasn't sustainable long-term. If she stayed, he'd be so wrapped up in her, everything else would fall away. *Or you'd live the life you always imagined.* But she wasn't staying. And he needed to tell himself that was a good thing, because if he thought he'd been crushed at eighteen, trying to convince Presley to stay and having her leave anyway might demolish him.

Beckett sighed. *Focus on what you can control.* It didn't seem like there was much on that list, and the realization made him want to hide out. Preferably with the woman standing next to him.

"Hungry?" he asked, already knowing the answer.

Her stomach growled. "Maybe." She smiled. "How about breakfast on the porch? You have a busy day today, right?"

He did, but all he wanted to do was hang with her while he could. "I do, but I'd love for you to take part in whatever you're up for." Leaning in for another kiss, he let his hand glide down her back, then farther. "How are you feeling?"

She laughed, poked him in the chest. "Like I spent too long on a bike."

"You get used to it."

"Sure. You probably say the same thing about hiking."

He loved making her smile. "No-time-to-think question," he said quickly. "Biking or hiking?"

She blinked rapidly. "Biking."

He grinned. "Fishing or biking?"

"Biking."

"Vanilla or chocolate?"

He loved the way her eyes crinkled when she was caught off guard, but she rolled with it immediately.

"Chocolate."

"Neck kisses or collarbone kisses?" He knew both sent subtle shivers through her body.

She sucked in a breath, stepping closer. "Both?"

He laughed, kissed the tip of her nose. "I'm sorry I don't have more time today."

Her hand on his arm felt so natural. "Don't apologize. I'll go on the easy hike with you so you don't have to be alone with the trio."

"You're my hero," he said, meaning it. He kissed her again; lingered.

When she pulled back, her eyes were hazy, sort of like his feelings. "Your turn to be my hero. Feed me."

His laughter came easily around her, something that surprised him. It was something he knew would be all too easy to get used to.

After the walk—no one could actually call it a hike—and lunch, Beckett went to check on the progress of cabin four. The smell of paint hit him hard, so he opened the windows, looked around.

They'd done well in a very short period of time. *The power of accepting help.* Tevin had brought a friend with him when he'd come to stay the night for Beckett, and the two of them had finished the final touches while Gray had a campfire and s'mores for the guests.

The walls were a forgiving gray, the furnishings simple, the fireplace welcoming. It looked awesome. He opened the door to the bedroom, pleased with the way Jill had made the bed appealing with a dark gray throw blanket resting on top of the dark blue comforter. Pillows she'd had made weeks ago had clearly arrived, because they sat on the bed, staring right at him and making him smile. Stitched into the white covers were the words GET LOST.

The cabin was definitely guest ready. If they could sort things out with food and amenities, Gray would pull this off. He shut the cabin door on his way out, pulling his phone from his pocket to set a reminder for himself to come back and close the window.

He'd set his phone on silent during the walk but now saw three missed calls and a number of texts from Mrs. Angelo. When he slid the screen to unlock it, he saw they were actually from her daughter.

Mrs. Angelo

> Hi Beckett. It's Elizabeth Angelo. Mama wanted to make sure you have enough food until Chef's return. No time like the present to tell you this will be a good trial run for us working together if your family is on board.

Sorry to bug you again.
Your brother came in for lunch with
the nicest older gentleman.
We talked to him about breakfast
and lunch options.

Mama says to tell you lunch is on us
next time you're here. Also, my cousin,
Mateo, will be here in a week. Mama
said to tell you she'll send him your way.

Beckett laughed and sighed at the same time while he typed up a response.

Beckett

Hi Elizabeth. Thank you for the texts.
Thrilled you guys can work with us.
Your food is a lifesaver.
Jill received Mateo's resume. Gray is
excited to have him on board.
Looking forward to that lunch. Thanks
again to you and your family. In case
you haven't heard, which is
unlikely given where we live,
Chef is doing okay and insisting
he'll be back in a couple of weeks.

A pleased, optimistic energy rushed through him. Things were going to sort themselves out. They'd all land in a good spot.

He had a bit of time to spend with Presley before this evening's hike. Maybe just the two of them could share a meal in his cabin rather than going up to the lodge. Immediately, guilt tapped on his shoulders like an annoying acquaintance. If he didn't go up to the lodge and Gray wasn't back, it would be too much for Jill to handle alone.

Beckett stopped short when he saw Presley on his front stoop, staring at her phone like she didn't understand what the ringing was for.

She glanced at him, a strange expression on her face.

"You okay?"

"That's a pretty relative term," she said, her voice sounding distant.

"I figure if you can't say yes, then it's got to be no," he replied, coming to sit beside her on the step.

One glance at her phone gave him an explanation. The face of a blond guy with too much gel in his hair flashed on her screen, the name "Emmett" displayed on the bottom.

"The ex," he murmured, a strange, uncomfortable feeling impacting his easy and steady breaths.

"We could call him that. I also like idiot, jackass, and asshat."

The phone continued to ring.

"'Asshat' is an entirely underused term," Beckett said.

When Presley leaned into his side, her head on his shoulder, his breath returned to normal. "You're not wrong. He saw the posts. Wants to know what I'm trying to prove."

"You could decline the call. Block him."

She tilted her head back to look at him. "That's my gut reaction, too, but on the other hand, I want to tell him off. I'm just not great at that sort of thing."

He understood the desire to want to say things to another person and being unable to do so.

"Want some privacy?"

Her smile was sweet and soft. He knew he'd see it every night when he closed his eyes after she left.

"Not from you." She pressed IGNORE.

"I wish we could curl up on the couch and hang out, but I need to help Jill with dinner and I have a night hike."

"I can help with dinner, too. You're on your own for the night hike," she said.

Taking her hand, he traced his index finger over the back of it. The cut wasn't too bad. It would heal nicely as long as she didn't do anything to make it worse.

"Battle scar," she teased.

"Outdoor pursuits can be hard on the body," he agreed, moving his hand up to cup her cheek.

"You're telling me. Even sitting on this step hurts a little."

Beckett laughed, lifted her easily into his lap. "Better?"

"Much." Her arms looped around his neck. "Can we just stay like this?"

Their foreheads met, pressed against each other, making him think he wasn't the only one who needed as much contact as possible in these next few days.

He closed his eyes, breathed her in. Breathed out, "I wish."

Thirty

Presley spent a lot of time trying to prove herself, only to be overlooked. When she was in the middle of living her life, eyes on the end goals, she'd been unaware. Now, in a place where the hours felt like days, she realized it was true not only personally but professionally.

She'd once stayed up all night, something she hadn't done since college, to perfect a presentation for La Chambre—i.e., Ms. Twain— only to have her decide to "go another way." *And Emmett.* That experience needed to go in the "hope you learn from this" column. She'd tried to fit him into her premade timeline, ignoring signs, letting plans override feelings. What she wanted to see overruled reality.

But as she finished up the Canva slideshow, she knew these people, the Kellers, who'd only known her a week, would welcome her ideas, appreciate her, and take her seriously. Validation. Genuine belief in her abilities. From herself and others around her. She needed that more than she'd known. And now, maybe she wouldn't settle for less.

A parting gift. "Don't think of it like that," she chided herself.

She glanced around the cabin, her gaze touching on the couch where Beckett had slept at first, the table where she'd shared a lovely meal with him and his niece, the door to the backyard wonderland he'd made to see her smile.

Beckett had gone out early to take a couple of guests fishing. Mel and Richard were leaving today. Grayson was due back. He and Mr. Dayton had stayed on the mainland so they could visit the bank that morning.

She was surprised, when she left the cabin, to find Mr. Dayton coming up from the dock.

"Clearly, you're back," she said, smiling.

He smiled back. "Have been for an hour or so. Are you just getting up? It's nearly lunchtime."

Presley laughed, checked her phone. "Not quite, but no. I've been up for a while. How was the mainland?"

His gaze sparkled with excitement, making him seem younger. They walked the path side by side. At some point, Beckett had fixed the loose stones. She was pretty sure he had twenty-five hours in his day instead of twenty-four like the rest of them.

"It was very productive. Your mountain man is due back soon. Jill is setting out lunch options for the guests so the five of us can chat."

Presley nearly missed a step. "Five of us?"

Mr. Dayton stared at her a moment. "Of course. You're part of this. Have been from the beginning."

She wasn't entirely sure why that made tears well up. *You know. Stop denying what you don't want to face.* She was part of this. Part of something special. Something important. A family of sorts, actual and found.

"Mel and Richard are leaving today. I'll be sad to see them go," she said as they resumed walking.

"And how will you feel when you go?"

Huh. Apparently, Mr. Dayton wasn't into breezy conversation this morning. "I don't want to think about it."

He gave a low, raspy chuckle. "I suspected as much."

When they reached the lodge steps, he put a hand on her arm. She turned to face him. He dropped his hands, stuck his thumbs in his pockets casually.

"Life flies by alarmingly fast, my dear. You don't always get a second chance to seize what makes you happy."

Presley pursed her lips, a lump forming in her throat. "No. But sometimes those feelings of happiness aren't reciprocated." She'd learned that well enough.

His brows lowered. He made a "tsk" sound. "You don't believe that."

She hadn't known her grandparents but if she had, and had been close to her grandfather on either side, she imagined he'd give a look like this one. A don't-try-that-on-me look.

"It's not always practical. Or manageable."

He patted her arm. "You'd be surprised how things can work out if you want them badly enough."

Balloons of hope and want surged in her chest. But she couldn't put herself in that position again. When she went home, there'd be no Emmett, but she'd have her job, her promotion, her apartment. *Empty apartment. Possible promotion.*

She might not be sorry she and Emmett were over, but misreading their relationship had left a mark that hadn't healed yet. She couldn't do the same with Beckett. They'd said a week. He hadn't asked for more, and neither had she. The memory of this trip would be magic she'd sprinkle over her life when she needed it most.

Her gaze dropped. "Wanting isn't always enough."

Ollie came flying out the door at that moment. She nearly skidded to a stop on the porch when she saw Presley and Mr. Dayton.

"Hi. Mom and me made a cake to say goodbye to Mel and Richard. We're going to have it for lunch! Instead of boring sandwiches or something. The other guests get the sandwiches."

"That sounds wonderful," Mr. Dayton said, clapping his hands together.

"We gotta wait for Uncle Beck but Mom said to come see if you needed anything, Presley."

"Who could need more than a dose of your smile?"

That smile grew. She bounced like an animated woodland creature. "Me. I need cake."

Presley and Mr. Dayton laughed, following her inside, listening to her steady stream of chatter. The lodge was quiet, other than Ollie, when they entered, and Presley looked around, memorizing it. Her arrival felt so long ago. *You're not gone yet. Stop.*

When Ollie's hand slipped into hers, she didn't know what to say so she just squeezed it.

"We're eating in the library."

"There's a library?" Mr. Dayton asked, following their mini-hostess.

Ollie looked back quickly, making her hair whip around. "That's what I call it. There's lots of shelves and books. I play games and watch TV in there."

To the left of the front desk was a small hallway that Presley hadn't been down. They passed a powder room on the left, and on the right was a large rectangular archway. Two pocket doors blocked the room from view.

Ollie pushed against the left one, sliding it open, then the right. The room in front of them was something between a sunroom, a tearoom, and, like Ollie called it, a library. There was a round table by the wall of windows. The blinds were drawn, likely to keep out the rising heat and glare.

On the right wall was a television and surround sound system with a couch facing toward it. The left wall housed the shelving, and it was magnificent. Like something out of the Beast's private study.

Presley took a step in, almost reverently. This room was tranquil and inviting, and more importantly, she suspected it was only used for family.

Ollie went running in, bouncing onto the couch.

"Ollie. We don't jump on couches," Jill said, coming in at the exact right moment. *Must be a mom thing; they see and know all.* Though her own mother hadn't. Her own mother had sent a text asking if she was on a reality show of some sort because she didn't understand why she'd subject herself to the conditions she was "vacationing" in.

"Sorry," Ollie mumbled.

"Presley. How are you? I feel like it's been nothing but chaos since you got back. I'm sorry about that."

The cake she held looked absolutely delicious. Chocolate frosting and large enough to feed them all.

Presley smiled. "If that chocolate cake is in my future, I'm wonderful."

Jill set it on the table. "It is. A goodbye and celebration of sorts." She looked at Mr. D as she walked past, patting his arm. "Be right back with plates and forks."

Mr. D walked to the window, adjusted the blind slats so he could see. There was a view of the hot tub and the woods.

"Beautiful place," he said, almost to himself.

"It really is."

Presley went to the bookshelf, looked at all of the titles. Unlike the rows of hardbound classics with perfect spines that they displayed in the meeting rooms at La Chambre, these books were well read and loved. Paperback novels, children's books, multiple genres. More intriguing were the framed photographs that broke up the rows.

Jilly and Ollie, the three siblings, the entire family. Beckett and Gray looked like their father. Jilly, their mother. Presley searched her brain for memories of family photos. She had old holiday ones, but most of them were of her with one parent or her parents together in some and her alone in others.

"Both of my brothers hate that their photos are up but since this is typically a private room, I told them too bad," Jill said, joining them again.

Grayson, Mel, and Richard joined them at nearly the same moment. Ollie's excitement ratcheted up several notches, and while Presley was happy to see everyone, it was Beckett's arrival that, for her, made the group complete.

He walked right to her, his hand going to her shoulder, like he wanted to touch her as quickly as he could, then reel her all the way in.

"Hi," he said, looking down at her, both arms coming around her back.

"Hi, yourself." He smelled a bit like fresh air, the start of summer, and happiness all rolled into one.

"I texted to let you know we were meeting up here."

She grinned, looked past him to where Ollie was chatting nonstop at Mel and Richard. "I had a personal escort."

He didn't even need to look to match her grin. "We here at Get Lost pride ourselves on our top-notch hospitality."

"As you should."

The slight red of his cheeks suggested they'd gotten some sun, or at least some wind. She ran her hand over one shoulder, smoothing it down to his pecs. He wore a blue Henley that seemed to make his eyes darker, and his hair was still a bit windswept.

"Fishing was good?" she asked.

"It was. Julian and Chuck caught a couple of big ones. I told Grayson he has to barbecue them." Julian and Chuck were the two newest guests. They were about Gabby and Libby's age and had hit it off well with them. Presley had joked that maybe the lodge should be called Get Love, then realized what she'd said out loud and covered it with cringeworthy laughter.

"They can barbecue them," Grayson called over, lifting his can of pop.

Beckett leaned in, the corners of his eyes creasing. "Cleaning and cooking fish grosses him out."

Presley laughed at the irony but also at the way Beckett's face transformed with his smile. He looked young and carefree when he was happy.

"Okay, everyone, please join us over here," Jill said.

Since everyone other than Presley and Beckett was already there, they moved that way.

Presley smiled at Mel, her chest feeling like the time she'd tried a weighted blanket. Rylee had gotten her one because sometimes she struggled to turn her brain off and sleep. They had rave reviews but she'd felt like there was a Saint Bernard sitting on her chest. She couldn't move, which stressed her out more, making her sure she couldn't breathe.

Sadness and being crushed felt similar.

"I wish Bo and Morgan could have stayed," Jill said, looking at the people who formed a circle around the table. Grayson had basically swapped them out for the two new guests. Those goodbyes hadn't been easy either.

"We've been treading water since day one here, and we still have a lot of work to do, but you are a very special group of people. You feel like more than guests, and we are beyond grateful for your help, your support." She cleared her throat, looked at Mel. "Your kindness. We will miss you and hope that you will visit again."

Mel pulled Jill into her arms. "Oh, honey. You aren't getting rid of us that easily. I already followed you on Instagram and requested to be your friend on Facebook. We'll be back next year for sure."

"Absolutely," Richard said, smiling at the way his wife embraced Jill. He looked at Grayson. "You're going to be just fine, son."

"Thank you," Grayson replied, his cheeks turning a bit ruddy.

Presley almost expected him to shuffle his feet. They were a stronger family than they knew. They were used to stepping up for each other and were still learning how to accept help from the outside. Hopefully, her little parting gift would be well received, in the spirit she intended.

"Can we have cake now?" Ollie asked, her index finger stretching toward the chocolate.

Jill grabbed the finger and pretended to chomp on it, making Ollie squeal with laughter.

Everyone else joined in.

The cake was delicious. One layer of vanilla, one of chocolate, with chocolate frosting. Everyone chatted about cabin four, the hiking, how the fishing had gone. No one talked about goodbyes or leaving. It was almost like Presley could pretend it wasn't happening. Until it was.

Jill checked her phone. "Tevin is here to take you guys to the mainland."

There were hugs and some tears, promises to stay in touch. Jill and Ollie walked them to the dock. Grayson, Beckett, and Mr. Dayton were chatting about one of the boats, and Presley was stacking the plates when they came back in.

"You don't have to do that, Presley," Jill said, sending an admonishing look toward her brothers.

Presley laughed. "I don't mind. I'd rather do this than talk about boats."

"Will you come back next year like Mel and Richard?" Ollie asked her quietly, looking up at her with her big brown eyes.

Presley crouched down. "Maybe I will. That would be fun."

She didn't dare look at Beckett. What if she came back one day and he was married? Settled down? Riding tandem bikes with a woman who loved fishing and hiking?

She stood up, tempted to unstack the plates so she could stack them again and keep her hands busy.

"Do we have some time?" Grayson asked.

Jill nodded. "Guests have been made aware of lunch options and told they are free to explore the grounds or lodge, sign up for the hot tub, or hang by the lake."

She walked over to an armchair beside the couch, sank into it. Her hair was still in a perfect bun at the back of her head. She wore dark blue jeans and a light sweater. She looked like she belonged here, or anywhere else she wanted to be.

Beckett's eyes met Presley's. He gestured for her to join him, so she did. They sat side by side on the couch, with Mr. D at one end of it. Grayson grabbed a chair from the table and set it on the other side of the coffee table.

"Can I play on the iPad?" Ollie asked, picking it up off the table.

"You sure can. We're going to have a meeting, then I thought we could go check your plants," Jill said, giving her daughter a hug.

"Okay."

They all sat quietly for a minute, like they collectively needed a breath. A lot had happened in the last week. Beckett's fingers found hers, settling on his thigh.

"I could sleep for a week," Jill said with a sigh.

Grayson frowned. "You've been doing a lot." He looked around, smiling at Beckett, Presley, and Mr. D. "You all have. I've taken advantage of your generosity in time and help."

Beside her, Beckett's body tensed. She wished he could share his happiness about the bike rental. Maybe with Grayson's news, he'd be able to.

"What happened at the bank?" Jill asked, looking between him and Mr. D.

"Well," Grayson said, his smile low and controlled, "we had a substantial deposit put into the lodge account. We have a silent partner."

Mr. D laughed. "Don't think anyone has ever called me 'silent' before."

Everyone else laughed, but Presley felt the strain in Beckett's posture. This was very good news, a relief for everyone, but was it enough for him to take the step he was scared to? He said his hesitation was about wanting to be there for his family, but part of her recognized something in him that he didn't see for himself: fear. Presley saw it because she'd shown up on this island after realizing the life she'd been living was a facade. Presley believed that Beckett's deeper issue, the one pulling at the reins more than the lodge, was making a concrete decision and sticking with it. Not that he didn't have the ability to do so, but more as though he was afraid to choose wrong.

Sometimes, life didn't show you what you were supposed to see until you took the first step. He needed to do that. She knew how hard it was to do it without knowing what the path ahead would reveal. But she believed in him. His siblings and niece would as well. He just needed to be ready to do it himself. If she could help him see that his own dreams were worth the risk, she'd leave knowing she made an impact. Left an impression. That, maybe, they—he—wouldn't forget her.

Thirty-One

Beckett's jaw dropped like a cartoon character's. He couldn't form words. Not only had Mr. Dayton bought in, paying Grayson current market value for the cabin, agreeing to all of the terms and conditions, he'd loaned him enough money to make things a success. Or at least to give it their best damn try.

"I can't believe you accepted a loan," Jill said.

Those were the words running through Beck's head.

Mr. D laughed, pointed a finger at Grayson. "He didn't want to. That's for certain. Now, everything isn't signed by a lawyer, but the money is there, and I know he'll pay me back."

"With interest," Grayson said, his expression somewhere between happy and uncomfortable.

"This is fantastic." Presley reached over and squeezed Mr. D's hand. "I'm so happy you get a piece of your past in your future."

He patted Presley's hand with a look of fondness Beckett completely understood. "Me, too, dear. I plan to spend a lot of time here. You kids might get sick of me."

"No chance of that," Jill said, tears in her eyes.

"We're going to winterize all but two of the cabins for now. Three if we include Mr. Dayton's. It'll mean we don't have as much vacancy—hopefully—but what we do have will be in good shape." Gray's voice was lit with an excitement Beckett hadn't heard in far too long.

"You kids are spreading yourselves too thin. Condensing this place will allow you, Beckett, and you, Jill, to have more of your own lives, and it will give Grayson a breather as well. Quality over quantity," Mr. D said.

Presley turned her chin in Beckett's direction. It scared him, just a little, to interpret her look as easily as if he could read her mind. Yes, he could tell his siblings about the bike rental idea. If they were smart, got some advice, his brother wouldn't need any of the seed money Beckett had earmarked for his own venture.

She gave him the most imperceptible nod and it infused him with strength. Courage. *Faith*. In him.

"I have some news as well, while we're sharing," Beckett said, the words feeling sticky in his throat.

Jilly picked up her water glass, gave him a bratty-sister wink. "You and Presley are the real deal? No more pretending just to guard your virtue?"

The words "real deal" would have knocked him on his ass if he hadn't been sitting. Jesus. Had anything felt more real in his life than her? When he looked at Presley, her cheeks were pink, her gaze a little wild. He tried to smile, pretend he wasn't affected by Jill's words.

Gray didn't often use his oldest-sibling look, but he gave it to Jilly now. "Knock it off. She's still a guest."

Jill bit her lip and Beckett knew her well enough to know it was because she was trying not to laugh.

Presley's thigh pressed against his. He needed to move or he'd never get the words out. Squeezing her hand, he hoped the gesture expressed his gratitude for her encouragement. Grayson gave him a strange look when he chose to pace the room rather than sit in front of them.

"What's going on, Beck? Is everything all right?"

When he turned to face them, he caught the immediate note of worry in Jill's gaze.

"Everything is great. I've been thinking about something for quite a while, working toward it, actually, but unsure if I'd be able to pull it off."

They said nothing. His stomach spun like a coin on a tabletop. Presley smiled at him, her eyes shining with pride that rippled through his chest. He took a deep breath.

"Brian offered me my own store a couple hours from Mackinaw

City. I considered it, but I've realized I don't want to be that far away from you guys. But I'm tired of being a store manager and I've had an idea in my head for way too long. Now seems like the best time to finally see it through. I want to be part of the growing tourist industry in Smile, and one of the things this town is lacking is recreational biking. We've got boats, kayaks, and Sea-Doos over by Tourist Lane, but no one is capitalizing on the easiest way to get through Smile and see it all. I want to rent or buy the lot beside the marina and open up a bike rental shop. I'll have tandems, singles, and, if I can find good prices, a couple of quadracycles."

His lungs tightened in his chest. "I've got several bikes. I just need to talk to Gramps about the rental lot."

"A bike rental?" Gray asked, his words slow.

"It's actually really smart. We could use something like that in town," Jill said, nodding.

He gave a rough laugh. "Thanks. Sometimes my ideas are good."

"Your ideas are fantastic, and a bike rental could actually complement the lodge in a very real and profitable way," Presley said.

He nodded in agreement. They hadn't discussed ways to cross-promote but he knew she had a talent for that sort of thing. Maybe he could stay in touch with her, pick her brain for ideas. A sharp tug pulled at his heart. Staying in touch with her wouldn't be easy. Not if he wanted any chance of moving on. Presley was all about connections and lifting others up while doing the same for yourself. She was, without a doubt, the coolest, strongest, most beautiful and kickass woman he'd ever met.

And she's leaving. And you have no right to ask her to stay.

Grayson rubbed his palms against his jeans. "You're not locked in here, Beck. I know I've taken a lot of your time."

He wanted his dream, but he wasn't abandoning his family. "I'm still going to be here, Gray. I'll have time. I've got a loan of my own and savings. I'll be cutting my hours back at Brian's. I'll need to be in Smile for rentals, but it's such a quick trip here, I can probably be here more."

Once he got things up and running.

"I was going to tell you guys sooner, but I was still on the fence. Then I thought maybe I should offer you the loan. But now . . . well, I think we can both have what we want."

Grayson stood up, walked to Beckett, and pulled him into a tight hug, clapping his back a couple of times.

"Goes both ways, man. We'll do what we can to help you as well."

A little overwhelmed, a lot happy, he pulled out of his brother's embrace to give his sister, who'd joined them, a hug.

When his siblings sat back, he noticed Presley all but bouncing on the seat cushion.

"You good?"

She beamed at him. Damn. He'd miss that smile more than sunshine on a gloomy day.

"I'm great. I have something for you guys. A parting gift, if you will," she said cryptically. She got up and turned on the television and Apple TV.

"Have a seat," she said to Beckett.

Taking his seat next to Mr. D, he looked her way along with the others.

The screen came alive with a pale green slide. As he sat there, his siblings flanking him, his niece now asleep on the floor, he watched Presley's slideshow—beautifully and painstakingly made—tie everything together. Their goals, their mission, ideas for improvement and local businesses they'd either connected with or could connect with. There were ideas on merchandising and marketing, and several ideas to reduce cost. One of the slides spoke to the bike rental shop, and Beckett grinned.

The slide looked like a coupon and read:

Get Lost on Beck's Bikes. Take ten percent off your rental if you're staying at Get Lost Lodge.

It was nothing short of amazing. He got up again when the slideshow stopped and she stood there staring at the group.

Taking her hands in his, he gripped them, unsure how he could feel so much for someone in such a short period of time.

"Thank you," he said, his voice a rumbly growl to try and stave off the emotion building in his chest.

"I absolutely love this, Presley, and it's such amazing timing," Jill said, pulling their attention.

Beckett pulled Presley to his side and tucked her beneath his arm, where he wished he could keep her as part of him.

"That was excellent. It'll almost make us look like we know what we're doing," Grayson said. He looked at their sister. "You're right. I know exactly what you're thinking, and it's perfect."

"Want to fill us in?" Beckett asked, feeling like he did as a kid when they shared something between just the two of them.

"I was researching grants and it turns out Smile offers a few every year to local businesses. You have to give a presentation to city council. If you're okay with us using your presentation, Presley, it might sway things our way. Especially now that we have a sizable investment." Grayson spoke with a note of reverence, like he couldn't believe it was all coming together.

"Of course you can use it—and what a fantastic idea."

He'd never had anyone outside of his immediate family be so invested in their well-being and happiness. This last week, there'd been Presley, Mr. D, Mel, Richard, Bo, and Morgan. Hell, even the Angelo family had jumped in when they'd needed help. Tevin. That was a long list. Loyalty ran through Beckett like a river to the ocean. Family first. Always. But he hadn't understood how that word could have different meanings.

Everyone talked over one another with their ideas and excitement until it was time to return to helping guests, organizing dinner, going through the to-do list. When they went their own ways to do their own things, him with Presley at his side, he wondered what it would feel like to have his dreams come true with her beside him. Because he was doing this. He had his family's support. It was happening.

And in two days, he'd feel alone. Successful. But alone.

Thirty-Two

Presley wasn't good at goodbyes. Maybe that made her good at her job. She did everything she could to make a guest's stay as delightful as possible. In return, she had several that returned to the hotel frequently. It was always satisfying to see them, knowing that of all the choices they had for lodging, they'd chosen La Chambre. Some of them maybe even because of her, because she'd enhanced their stay.

She never said "goodbye." She said "see you soon," "see you later," "so long." Rylee noticed it once and called her out on it, saying she belonged on a TV show. When Presley had shown confusion, she told her that on TV, characters never said goodbye when they hung up the phone. After that, Presley had watched all her favorite shows closely, and sure enough, no goodbyes. Technically, the conversation, the connection, never ended.

The day had been long and wonderful, spent helping Beckett with ideas and plans for his rental shop. He'd shown her quadracycles with the same excitement children had for Santa Claus. Everyone seemed to be riding high on yesterday's news. She'd helped out with closing down the cabins they'd get to in the future, giving ideas on how to utilize the items that could be repurposed for other guest rooms.

She'd helped him and Jill choose weekly menu options for the next month from a list of options Mrs. Angelo's daughter sent. Presley was able to give Jilly a break by "supervising" Ollie as she got an upstairs king suite ready for her grandparents to arrive.

Basically, the entire day had been about getting from one moment to the next without thinking about tomorrow. As the air cooled and she got up from the wide couch in the library—she was unabashedly in love with this room—where she'd been rereading a favorite Nora Roberts book, she checked the time on her phone.

Emmett had stopped leaving voicemails but was now sending way-too-frequent texts. He'd texted her more in the last few days than he had in the last few months of their relationship.

Intending to go help Jill with whatever she might need before finding Beckett, she ran into him, literally, as she rounded the corner from the hallway.

His hands came to her shoulders, his laughter coming easily. "Not often a beautiful woman falls for me."

She laughed at his corniness. Something happened yesterday when the good news unfolded—the invisible weight on his shoulders had lifted. He'd traded worry for mirth without even noticing. She could see it in his smile, his eyes, and the way he hummed, just a little, while he worked today.

"I think the accurate thing to say is it's not often you *notice*," she said, wrapping her arms around his waist. He had blinders on when it came to his own attributes, which, of course, made him more attractive.

Sweeping her hair back from her forehead, Beckett pressed a kiss to her left eyebrow. It was such a sweet and unintentional gesture, Presley's body tensed with need.

"I was hoping you wouldn't mind if we skipped dinner with the guests tonight. I have plans. I can tell you if you'd prefer but I'd rather show you."

She regarded him suspiciously. "Plans, huh? Naked plans?"

His laughter filled the hallway. "Definitely later. But no. That wasn't the whole of it. Trust me?"

"Completely." Another one of those ironies. She trusted a man she'd known less than two weeks more than one she'd been willing to merge her life with.

❧

She thought she'd be cold with the almost-dusk chill permeating the air, but plastered to Beckett's back, arms around his middle, bundled up in an undershirt, sweater, and jacket and with a helmet on, Presley was overheated. She felt every bump, the vibration of the motor, the safe and solid feel of Beckett. He'd taken the trail they'd walked in those first couple of days, but many trees back, he'd veered right, taking them up higher. The gentle smell of gasoline mixed with the freshness of the cool air, the scent of the trees.

The path narrowed some but nothing like the one they'd biked. *Who are you? You've hiked, biked, and now ATV'd in the last week.*

Beckett slowed the vehicle as he entered a clearing. When he pulled to a stop, her body felt like it was still moving. He smiled at her, helped her off the ATV. They both removed their helmets and hung them on the handlebars. He unhooked the backpack he'd attached to a rack behind the seat. It was handy because it made her feel like if anything was going to fall, it'd be the bag first.

"First time on an ATV?" His smile shone even in the waning light.

She didn't want to think about how they were getting back. She trusted him.

"How'd you know?" She shrugged. She could do breezy.

Slinging the backpack over one shoulder, he took her hand with the other.

"Besides the look on your face when I told you to hop on, I'm pretty sure I'll have imprints of your arms and hands on my waist."

Nervous laughter bubbled. "You're welcome."

They walked over the uneven incline and beyond the receding tree branches to a spot that stopped her in her tracks. It felt like she could see the whole lake from here.

"It's like an enormous bowl of ink," she said quietly, her voice sounding louder than she'd spoken.

Beckett laughed. "It does look pretty dark from up here. Those lights there?" He pointed to the right. The lights he referred to were a barely there glow. "That's the lodge."

She turned, looked up at him. "That's amazing. How did you find this place?" A thought hit her like a branch to the head. "Are there animals up here?"

Smoothing one hand down her hair, which had to be somewhat haywire, he shook his head. "They won't bother us."

Presley narrowed her eyes. "That wasn't a no."

More laughter. "They're more scared of us. I promise. Come on, let's set up."

Another thought hit her. "Are we sleeping here tonight?" She tried to keep her tone casual I'm-cool-with-that calm.

Beckett set his backpack down, faced her fully. "You said you trusted me, but your words and the look on your face suggest otherwise."

"No. I do. I really do, but . . . well, *are we?*"

"No. I promise we'll sleep in the almost-comfortable bed in my cabin. Tomorrow, you'll wake up there and I'll pretend that this hasn't been one of the best weeks of my life."

Stepping into him, she went up on tiptoes. "Don't pretend that. Don't forget me, Beckett Keller." Because she damn sure wouldn't be able to forget him.

As he closed the distance between them, he whispered, "I couldn't."

Though she sensed he didn't want to pull back, he did. He set up a surprisingly cozy seating area, along with a few little lanterns that buzzed with electricity.

He looked up from his tasks. "Bugs get worse in the summer, but this will keep them from snacking on us."

She did her best not to cringe. She preferred to do the snacking. She must not have hidden her concerns well.

"Give me five minutes, city girl. I'll make sure you're comfortable."

The backpack of wonders continued to produce a wealth of goodies. A small mason jar–shaped container turned into a miniature fire. He unrolled another sleeping bag that she felt certain would never go back in its carrier, then put a bento box and two juice boxes beside the setup.

Next, he settled himself on the seating, gestured for her to sit between his legs, which she did, then pulled the sleeping bag over their laps.

"Cozy?" His breath brushed her ear.

"Surprisingly, yes."

The sky was growing darker, and she spotted a random sparkle here and there.

"Remember the twinkle lights?"

How could she forget? It was etched in her heart, along with all of his other sweet gestures.

"Yes."

His arms held her tight. "You're about to see how they pale in comparison to the real thing."

She laughed, tipping her head back on his shoulder so she could see his face. "We do have stars in the city, you know. I've seen them a few times."

His gaze pierced hers. "Not like this."

Refusing to break eye contact, not knowing if she could, she whispered, "Is tonight going to ruin me for all other stars?"

"God, I hope so."

Their mouths met like crashing waves, unexpectedly harsh, pulling her under, drowning her in the best possible way. His hand cupped her cheek, his body surrounded her, and Presley forgot they were outside, that there was anything outside of this moment, this man.

She wasn't sure how long they kissed. It felt like seconds and hours. Forever and not nearly long enough. He pulled away slowly, millimeter by millimeter until just the tip of his nose was touching hers. She loosened her grip on his shoulder, her breathing uneven, her heart unsteady.

"Look up, Presley."

Like coming out of a sleep-infused fog, she turned her head slowly to see the darkness lit up by more flickering stars than she could ever count or wish upon. From this spot, it felt like she was part of the sky, dancing among the stars with Beckett. It was an image she'd never unsee. If she was lucky.

"It's incredible," she finally whispered.

"Like you."

"No. I mean, it's really amazing."

"I know. So are you."

She laughed softly. "I've never seen anything like this."

I've never felt anything like this.

"It's the kind of view you could see every day for the rest of your life and never tire of."

A massive fist squeezed her heart. Just one, tight squeeze. She turned back to him, knowing he'd be looking at her.

"Beckett," she whispered.

He held her gaze so long, the words rushed from her. "I'm so happy you're moving forward, that you made the right decision for you. I think your bike rental shop is going to be perfect for Smile. I'm so happy for you."

His grin was tinged with sadness. *Say it. Say the rest.*

Before she could, he spoke. "For a minute, I thought I might take Brian's offer. I thought it might put me closer to where you live. That it might give us a chance at something long-term."

She sucked in a breath. Did he want that? Did she? She'd trusted her own feelings before, and look where that had gotten her.

"But I think what's so special about this, about us, is that it's defined by us giving everything we have without changing our entire lives. A lot of couples have to do that to accommodate the other's dreams. We knew going in we'd have to be over. So, I can do the bike shop, and you'll end up the manager of some swanky downtown hotel, and when we look back, we'll both know we were a part of making each other's lives, even if only for a little while, better. Something special."

She swallowed down the tears and disappointment his words brought. She knew, in her mind—because, strange or not, she knew *him*—that he was trying to rationalize, make this easier on both of them. But that didn't make it hurt any less.

He kissed her again, and in her mind, he asked her to stay, even though she knew she couldn't. He was right. Here, they'd had no demands on their relationship. None of the real-world struggles that life threw in the path every day as people worked toward their goals. What made this special was the fact that it was fleeting. All of the stars in the sky could be forgotten for the chance to see a shooting one. It was rare and precious *because* it couldn't last.

🌹

That night, on the side of a mountain, she saw and felt a beauty she'd never known before and suspected she'd never know again. The bookends of time would make it unparalleled. She told her weeping heart that just because a love could last a lifetime didn't mean the relationship would.

Thirty-Three

That thirty seconds between dreaming and waking. That was the sweet spot Presley wished she could live in. Especially now. Right before everything rushed back; good and bad. The sound of movement in the kitchen made her smile.

Part of her was tempted to steal a pillowcase—tuck it away in her luggage and see how long it could retain the Beckettness. Maybe a T-shirt. She debated it with Rylee, reluctant to get out of the bed and face the day.

Rylee

This is just a thought but maybe you don't steal any of his stuff

Presley

It's not stealing. Not, like, the traditional definition of stealing.

Rylee

Oh. I'm sorry. I didn't realize stealing had a multiple definitions. I can't keep up with the way kids talk these days. Tell me how it's different.

Presley

I'm positive he'd let me have either his pillowcase or his shirt. If I asked.

Rylee

Ask

Presley

That would be so pathetic.

Rylee

You're right. Stealing makes you seem cool.

Presley

Not aiming for cool.

Rylee

Are you okay?

Presley

...

Rylee

I know you hate goodbye.
You won't even say it on the phone to me.

Leaving won't erase him.

Presley

Goodbye sounds so
final.

Rylee

But sometimes it's okay for
things to be over. Look what being
over with Emmett did for you.

Tears burned her eyes. She didn't want to do this, but for the first time in her life she also wanted to do it. Properly. Rylee was right. Letting go of Emmett, going on this trip without him, had shown her new pieces of herself. Ones she would take back into her regular life. She didn't want to say goodbye to the Kellers. To Beckett. But she wanted to thank them for everything they'd given her: their support, laughter, the feeling of being included. When she went home, she'd look for those things in any new relationships. She'd be stronger. She'd put more value in her own ideas and worth. Goodbye didn't have to be an end. It wasn't with Emmett. It could be what this whole experience had been: a beginning.

Rylee

Take the shirt. It's more useful.

Presley laughed. She was going home a new version of herself. Surer of who she was and who she wasn't. She didn't like the bikes, but she enjoyed the walks, the subtle scent of the water, and the stars. God. She could close her eyes and still see them. She felt like she was the tiniest particle in this huge galaxy. But she was part of it, and she hadn't truly felt that way before now.

Presley

I'm better having met him.

Rylee

I'll be at the airport
when you get there.

Presley

My car is there.

Rylee

No, it's not. I had Avi
help me pick it up with your
spare keys. I didn't want
you to come home alone.

Presley

You're the best.

Rylee

Things we already knew.

She threw back the covers. Big-girl pants. "Goodbye" was just a word. She could go out there and say a whole slew of words. It was always going to be hard. It was hard to come and, ironically, harder to leave. But she could do that. She could do a hell of a lot more than she'd given herself credit for.

Having packed last night, she threw on her cozy leggings and oversized sweater, then shoved her pajamas in her bag. They only had about a half hour before she needed to head over to the mainland and catch the bus.

When she put her hand on the doorknob, she looked back at the bed. She'd pulled the covers up, set the pillows on top. It was juvenile, but if she had to say goodbye, she was doing it. A person could only handle so much growth in one day.

Hurrying back to the bed, she stripped Beckett's pillow of the pillowcase, shoved it in her bag, and left the room. Hoping her face didn't give away her transgression and her heart wouldn't betray her sadness, she pasted on a smile.

Jill turned to face her from her spot at the sink. "Good morning."

The smile held. "Good morning." Something tightened inside of her, coiling like a spring. She looked around the cabin. The bathroom door was open. There was no sign of anyone other than Jill.

"Presley," Jill said, and she knew.

Unable to face his sister, she said the words to make them true. "He's not here."

"He had an early hike come up."

Swallowing past the lump in her throat, she nodded, wrapped her arms around herself.

"Of course. Um, any chance I can get a ride to the mainland early?"

Jill came over to stand in Presley's space, forcing Presley to tighten her grip on herself.

"Ollie and I want to take you," Jill said.

Presley nodded. It was hard to breathe.

Jill's hand touched her shoulder. That coiled spring wanted to snap.

"He couldn't say goodbye," Jill whispered.

Presley pursed her lips, breathed slowly. In and out. One breath at a time. "I understand."

"Let's have something to eat and then we'll go."

"Could we go now?"

She couldn't eat. She needed to go home. So much for goodbye.

The air whipped through her hair, and unlike on the first speedboat ride, Presley didn't feel scared. Ollie snuggled up to her side, chattering over the sound of the engine and the water. The choppiness was oddly soothing, like Ollie's voice.

Gramps met them at the dock, offered his hand to Presley. "How you doing?"

"I've had better days, Gramps," she said quietly, surprising herself with her own honesty.

His sun-weathered face showed understanding. "The good thing about that is you know they exist."

Presley bit the inside of her cheek.

"How's my Ollie-girl?" Gramps lifted Ollie up in the air, making her laugh with the kind of carefree abandon people grow out of.

"I'm good. Except Presley's going home and we're going to miss her."

If she bit the inside of her cheek any harder, she'd draw blood. She switched sides.

"Is she going somewhere without internet?"

Presley grinned as Jill smoothed out her hair. "I'm not."

"In my day, I had to mail letters, and we could only do it once a week when a boat came over from the mainland for pickup and drop-off. You kids have all the gadgets to make it feel like there's no distance between you."

"That's very true. Just because someone has to go doesn't mean they're gone," Jill said, leaning into Presley.

"We will definitely keep in touch," Presley agreed, the words like marbles in her mouth. It wasn't the same. But it was something.

"I know where the bus is, so you guys can say goodbye here." Presley held her arms out. Ollie rushed into them.

"The bus. Don't be silly. You're one of us now whether you live here or not. Anderson is waiting to drive you. They'll take the ferry over with you and drive you to the airport."

She hadn't met Anderson officially. "I can't ask that."

"You didn't ask. It's been arranged. We're going to miss you, Presley." Jill wrapped her in a hug while Ollie kept her head against Presley's waist, her arms too short to wrap around Presley's body.

Tears pushed. Presley pushed back harder. "Okay. I'll let you know when I'm home. Thank you for so much more than I can say."

Jill nodded against her shoulder, pulled back, brought Ollie with her. Unshed tears shone in her eyes, but Ollie didn't hold back. The silent tears the little girl cried threatened to completely unravel Presley.

How could she feel so much for so many people in such a short amount of time?

Because you knew it wouldn't last. Everything is more intense. It'll fade when you go.

"Come on. I'll walk you up to the parking lot," Gramps said, taking her bag.

Presley and Anderson didn't speak much during the ferry ride over, but once they were back in Mackinaw City, Anderson chatted in a soothingly monotone voice about the history of Smile. By the time she arrived at the airport, Presley knew she'd left a little bit of her heart in Smile. The weird thing about that was, somehow, the wobbly organ in her chest felt fuller going than it had coming.

Thirty-Four

Beckett stared at the daylight view of what he'd shown Presley the night before. He'd actually been able to see the speedboat leave. At least he thought that's what that speck heading away from the lodge had been.

Picking up a handful of rocks which was mostly just dirt, he tossed it over the cliff. He wished he could do the same thing with the ball of emotions eating him up from the inside out. What the hell had happened to him this week?

You fell in love, you fucking idiot. Yeah. He was an idiot. But not for falling in love. He was an idiot for not telling her, for not spending every single last second that he could with her, but he truly didn't know if he had the ability to say goodbye to her.

The night before, as she'd slept in his arms, he kept imagining saying goodbye, and it had felt like there was an elephant holding a piano sitting on his chest. He didn't know why the elephant was holding a piano, but he also didn't know why the first time he'd felt this way, it had to be for a woman he couldn't have, so who the hell was he to question it?

"Hiding won't change how you feel," Grayson's voice said from behind him.

Beckett didn't turn. He kept staring into the distance like somehow it would heal him.

"What are you doing up here?"

"The guests came back two hours ago. Ollie would kill me if I left you up here to die. I don't have time to be dead, so I thought I'd better check."

He felt his brother's presence beside him and it eased a little weight off his chest.

"I'm alive." Just didn't feel like it.

"Feels like you're on the brink though, right? Like a painful almost-death."

Beckett turned his head. "A little bit. Is this how you felt when Lana left?"

Grayson tipped his head side to side. "Not entirely. It's how I would have felt if she'd gone while I was in the beginning of falling on my ass for her. By the time it was over, I felt hurt and sad but also a little relief because I knew it couldn't keep going. It was harder to be together than apart."

"So, it's a good thing I got out now." There. He did feel better. Yeah. Sure. It hurt, but damn, how much would it suck to have this moment five, ten years from now after building a life together?

"You're an idiot." Grayson punched him in the arm.

Beckett shoved him. "What's that supposed to mean?" He turned to face his brother, too many feelings boiling inside of him, ready to overflow and leave a mark.

"It's not code, man. You. Are. An. Idiot."

"You think it'd be better if I declared myself only to have her say 'thanks and see ya'? Or maybe we figure something out. Both fall in love and then five years from now, we realize we were stupid to think we could make it work and I'm you, living with regret on an island I didn't want?"

The surprise in Grayson's expression almost covered the hurt. Almost.

"I'm sorry. Listen, this is why I stayed up here. I'm not fit to be around humans right now."

"I don't regret my marriage." His brother's words were below a whisper, like he'd just admitted the sentiment to himself for the first time.

"How is that possible? She tore your heart and your life apart."

He nodded, turning to stare out at the view like Beckett had. "She did. It sucked. I always thought when I got married, it'd be the real, forever deal, like Mom and Dad. It's what I wanted. Even when she didn't, I kept fighting for us. But there were moments that I'll never forget, moments that made me a better version of myself. Things I like about myself now that only exist because of her." He laughed without humor, ran a hand through his hair. "Don't get me wrong, there are a lot of things I don't miss about her. And you're right, I didn't want this place, but it brought me back to you and Jilly. Ollie. It reminded me a bit of who I am and who I thought I'd be. As much as I loved Lana, as much as it hurt to have it all fall apart, I wouldn't take it back. I can honestly say, I hope she's happy."

Beckett didn't know what to say to all of that. They'd done the brotherly thing, gotten stupid drunk when the divorce papers were signed. His brother had been so angry. Broken. Which was why it mattered so much to make the lodge a success. Working on it, working toward something had rebuilt his brother. Rebuilt all of them, really. Seeing it come together not only made him more certain about his own career goals, it made him sure of what he'd wanted: to stay in Smile. He'd have been miserable managing, even part-owning, a second store for Brian. He wanted something that was his own. But now that he was getting it, everything felt empty. It made him wonder what the point of it all was.

"Just happy? You don't hope, even just a little, that she moved next door to a punk rock band that practices, badly, at all hours of the night?"

Grayson laughed, a hearty, real laugh that carried through the air. "Dude, that's the best you could come up with?"

Beckett shrugged. "You loved her. I didn't want to be a total dick."

"That ship sailed when you let Presley leave without a goodbye."

Fuck. Direct hit, center chest. The shot pierced him, stuck there like a sharpened arrow digging into his heart, making pain radiate from the center outward.

He buried his face in his hands, scrubbed them up and down, letting out a harsh groan.

When he looked up again, he gave his brother the truth. "I couldn't stand to watch her leave."

Grayson slapped his shoulder. Hard. "On some level, I get that. But you still should have been there."

"I know. Did everything go okay?" he asked after a while of just standing side by side, staring out at the water.

"Ollie and Jill got back about an hour ago. Ollie was crying. Jill went right into cleaning mode. Remember when she got divorced? Everything within a fifty-foot radius was cleaner than it'd ever been."

Beckett chuckled. "Yeah. I came home from a trip and she'd painted my bedroom."

"What are you going to throw yourself into?"

At least he had an answer for that. "The bike rental. Called Gramps, asked if I could talk to him about the lot."

"And?" By unspoken agreement, they turned, started down the path.

"And what? I'm meeting with him in a few days. I'm heading to Indianapolis for a few days to visit a bike manufacturer."

"What if you went to Great Falls?"

Beckett stopped walking. "What?"

Grayson turned so they were facing each other. "No matter where you go, we're still family, man. You sure a bike rental is your dream now that you've met Presley?"

Beckett shoved his hands in the pockets of his jeans. "They're hardly the same thing."

"No. One will let you do something you enjoy, close to the home you've always known and the safety of your family. The other could change your entire life and bring you a happiness like you've never known."

Irritation rose in his chest. He tried to tamp it down. Gray's job as an older brother was to be annoying and play devil's advocate. "It was a weeklong fling, man."

"Oh yeah?"

That irritation simmered. "Yeah. She was a guest. It happened. It's over."

His brother nodded. "Of course. Because anything different would be scary and you don't do scared. You don't do hard or tough."

Beckett pulled his hands from his pockets, and they clenched into fists. His chest heaved. "What did you just say?" Stupid question, since he'd never forget the words.

"The truth."

It was hard to resist the urge to shove him like he would have as kids. "I've been busting my ass for you, putting aside what I want, living in a stupid cabin like a frat boy to help you. I'm so exhausted some nights from being here, traveling back and forth to my actual job, and trying to have a life, I fall into bed without even meaning to. And you think I can't handle something hard?"

Grayson's body braced like he was ready for whatever Beckett gave. "I appreciate the hell out of you, man. I've never doubted your loyalty. You are the most kickass brother a guy, or Jill, could have. You're a great uncle and a great son. Sometimes, you're not even that bad of a fisherman."

"Screw you." Beckett brushed past him, intentionally knocking his shoulder against Grayson's. "Screw you, man."

Not taking a hint, Gray fell into step beside him. "But all of that is the safe path. Remember when we used to play Life as kids? Jilly made us play that stupid game all the time. She and I would switch it up. Go to college, get a job, have twelve plastic babies, bet big, quit a job. Not you. You chose the same damn path, the same job, the same wife, and two point two creepy, plastic kid pegs every time until you got to retirement."

Beckett stopped again, his breath sawing in and out. "You're being an ass because I beat you consistently at a kid's game?"

Grayson laughed but stopped short when he realized Beckett saw no humor in what his brother had said.

"No. I'm saying you've always chosen the same path because—I don't know. Maybe you're not scared. Maybe you have a misguided sense of loyalty and feel like you don't deserve whatever dream you want to chase. Why'd it take you so long to tell us? You didn't think we'd back you? You telling me there isn't a spot near Presley, some little park or something, where you could rent out bikes or sell them or do whatever the hell it is you want in a place where you get to go home every night to her?"

"What self-help book are you reading?"

Grayson grabbed his arm, swung him around. "Stop. Stop fucking walking. Stop running."

"What the hell do you want from me, Gray?" Beckett hadn't meant to shout.

"I want you to think about what you really want and go for it no matter who gets left behind. I want you to be happy and fulfilled. I want you to not be so scared of things being different that you walk away from love. I've never seen you light up like that, man. I want you to go for it even if you fail. Even if you do end up back here, living in a cabin like a frat boy. You'll know you gave it everything."

Beckett's chest felt like a wall of rocks, carefully stacked on top of one another. One rock shifted. Another. And the whole damn thing came tumbling down. He was a fucking idiot.

He loved Smile. His family. His dream of the bike shop and even his apartment. He loved routine and seeing Adam when he showed up at home. He loved bike riding through town and hanging out with Ollie. He loved Jill's laughter and the way she fussed over guests. He loved back-porch beers under the stars with Grayson. He loved his mom and dad and couldn't wait to see them.

But being away from them wouldn't change his feelings. It would make it more special when he *did* see them or get to do those things. Because staying here to live out his goals didn't feel like it would fulfill him anymore. Without Presley, it didn't feel like enough. It felt like a vital piece was missing. If he wanted to be the best version of himself, he needed to do everything he could to make himself feel whole again. Presley might not take him back, but he couldn't move forward until he tried. Until he gave it his all. She deserved that and more. It was time he proved it.

Thirty-Five

The trip home was a lot like the trip to Get Lost: Presley got through it by putting one foot in front of the other, keeping her head up, and blocking her own thoughts. By the time she got into her apartment, she was ready to fall down, maybe right there on the entryway carpet. Rylee had gotten her inside and said she'd be back, but Presley assumed she meant in the next couple of days.

Presley texted Jilly to say she was home safe and saw several emails from Ms. Twain and some texts from Emmett. But because she could only do so much, she turned her phone off the minute she texted Jilly.

It was time to readjust, compartmentalize. She had to be at work at seven A.M. She had a management conference—not just the promise of one—to attend the day after. If she were scanning the skies for silver linings, one was that her absence had made Ms. Twain more aware of Presley's value.

She showered, curled up on the couch, and stared at her phone like it was an enemy. She set out her clothes for the next day, tried to eat some dry, stale cereal, made a grocery list.

When the buzzer for her apartment went off, she figured Rylee was checking on her even though she'd promised her friend she was fine and just needed to sleep. Glancing at the retro-style clock sitting on her bookshelves, Presley frowned.

It was late even for Rylee, and especially for her, since she had to be at work in only six hours.

She pressed the speaker button near the door. "Hello."

"Pres. It's Emmett. Let me up."

Presley's head fell forward, hitting the wall just above the speaker. She pressed the button again. "Why?"

"It's cold out here. We need to talk."

They didn't need to talk, but Presley wasn't the kind of girl who left an ex standing out in the cold at one A.M. any more than Emmett was the kind of ex who would go quietly.

She buzzed him in and waited by the door while moments in their relationship slipped through her mind like an Instagram reel. He knocked. She opened the door, stood in the doorway.

His hair was gelled into submission, not one strand out of place. It was practically the middle of the night and he looked like something he definitely wasn't: perfect. Nothing about him appealed to her as she looked at him. It was as if the false front had fallen away and all she saw were the reasons he wasn't good enough for her rather than the other way around.

She could thank *bleep* for that. That's right. She was bleeping out his name in her head.

"What do you want?" All the feelings she'd been so sure about were gone. Like she'd imagined them. She realized, *now,* that real love didn't disappear that way. It sank its roots into your soul, changed you. Whether you wanted it to or not. Emmett had changed her. More importantly, he'd never change.

Emmett's expression softened, the way it used to when he was willing to give a little. *Sure, babe, we can have pizza if you really want it. I had my heart set on Thai, but let's go with what you want.*

"You."

Presley's brows would have hit her bangs if she had any. "Are you drunk?"

"Can I come in?" Had she ever thought that tone was seductive?

"No."

His mouth flatlined. "Be reasonable."

"Be gone."

"Presley. Come on. We had a fight. We've cooled off. Let's talk."

She realized, even as her buzzer sounded again—who the hell was here now?—that he fully expected her to give in. Because she would have. With him. Her parents. Her boss. Her friends. Shaking her head, she pressed the intercom button beside her door, still blocking his entrance.

"Hello?"

"Tell me that isn't dipshit's car in front of your building," Rylee's voice said.

Emmett scowled.

"I'd never lie to you," Presley said, buzzing her friend up.

"Great. Never mind. We'll talk tomorrow."

She shook her head. "No. We won't. We won't talk again. Don't show up here, stop texting. Go away." She wanted to say *get lost,* but it hurt to even think.

The elevator opened and Rylee stomped down the hallway, a brown paper bag from Presley's favorite ice cream parlor tight in her grasp.

Emmett, who finally got some sense and picked up on the tone, put his hands up. "I'm leaving."

"Damn right you are," Rylee said, shooting Presley a glance. "What the hell are you doing here in the first place?"

Emmett was stupid enough to roll his eyes. "My mistake. Thought maybe I could have a reasonable conversation with Pres."

She laughed, not quite as maniacally as she had when the Tiger Trio showed up that day, but it was close. Rylee stepped closer and Presley soaked up the strength and support she knew her friend was giving without question. She had her back.

"*Presley.* Jesus Christ, *Em,* how hard is that? It's two syllables. Presley. I should have known that you were too lazy to be worth my time when you couldn't even say my whole name."

"Uh, sweetie," Rylee said quietly, moving closer. "Maybe we should go in." She glared at Emmett. "*You* should go home. Or far, far away. And never return."

Good idea. Presley stepped into her apartment and closed the door, but not before she heard Emmett yell through the wood, "I don't know what's gotten into you but I'm glad we're done."

Rylee started to reopen the door, ready to go mama-bear on Presley's ex, but Presley's unsteadiness must have concerned her more. She turned and caught Presley as she swayed. The bag crinkled and Rylee dropped it to the ground.

"Hey. He's not worth it."

"I know. I know that now. I'm so tired, Rylee."

"I know. I got you." Rylee wrapped her arms around Presley and held tight.

"I found everything I wanted, what I didn't even know I needed or craved, and I can't have it for stupid reasons. I learned what it was like to feel cherished and cared for, to feel like I was part of a family, to feel like I was part of *something*. Something good and beautiful and special and real. I didn't just fall for him. I fell for the whole family. Jilly, Ollie, Grayson. Even Mr. Dayton and the town itself. And now it's gone. Because what other choice is there? I fell in love. The real kind that won't go away. And it hurts. My heart feels like it's really broken. Like I sliced it right up the middle and now the two parts don't know how to fit back together." She felt the tears but didn't stop. "I woke up and realized that everything I've been working toward is nothing like what I truly want. And I don't know what to do, I had a plan. Veering from the plan temporarily is one thing but aborting it altogether? How can I do that? How can I trust myself when I'm just now figuring out who I am and what I want?"

"The plan is whatever you want it to be. It could change a hundred times but all that matters is that it makes you happy. Does Beckett make you happy?"

"He does. And I know I made him happy while I was there. There was no room for smoke and mirrors. He saw me. All of me. And he liked me anyway."

"Of course he did," Rylee said fiercely. "He'd be a damn fool not to."

Presley's laugh was watery. Her tears were getting all over Rylee's shirt. Presley leaned back, sniffled indelicately. "The best part? He made *me* see myself. But it wasn't enough. I just wasn't enough."

Presley sank down to the floor with Rylee holding her tight, telling her she'd always be enough. Presley had enough presence of mind to know that her friend was right. It was just hard to believe in this moment.

When she calmed down, they crawled into her bed with the ice cream and two spoons. Rylee distracted her with stories of the worst dates she'd ever been on. There was a woman who had brought her grandmother's engagement ring, saying if Rylee didn't like it, there was no point going any further.

Presley wished her heart could freeze like her throat as she swallowed another bite of ice cream.

"The thing was gaudy," Rylee said. "I'm talking 'gothic rocker with a penchant for flowers' ugly."

Despite herself, Presley laughed. "Maybe it was a test."

Rylee shook her head before leaning it on Presley's shoulder. "I failed. Happily."

Presley groaned when she saw that the clock read after two. "I need to work in the morning. You didn't have to come back."

Rylee turned, took the container of ice cream and spoons. "Don't be an idiot. Where else would I be? You're my girl. No matter what. I'm going to clean up, then sing you to sleep."

Presley laughed and pulled the pillow over her head. Rylee, for all her wonderful qualities, had the worst singing voice. Ever. It was painful.

"I'm already asleep."

Rylee laughed, leaving the room. Tears threatened again but Presley forced them back. She'd be okay. She knew her time with Beckett was just a moment in time. A snapshot. Something to look back at with the fondness it deserved. It wasn't his fault she fell in love.

Rylee crawled back into the bed, turned out the lights.

"You'll be okay," she whispered.

"I know," Presley whispered. "I didn't mean to fall in love."

"No one ever does."

Thirty-Six

The following day, Presley went through all of the motions that had been her life with the energy of a half-drunk zombie. But she did it with a smile on her face. The good news was she was so tired when she got home, she went to bed and didn't wake up until the next day. She went to the three-day management course she'd been promised countless times over the years. She threw herself into it, absorbed everything she could, took notes, jotted down ideas, networked, made connections, maybe even some possible friends.

When she got home to her apartment after those few days, she thought she'd feel different. Since she didn't, she took a long shower and crawled into bed.

Rylee showed up early the next day and, best friend that she was, brought not only pizza but more ice cream. There were no food rules when it came to breakups.

"Hey. How was it?" Rylee asked, putting the pizza on the counter and grabbing spoons for the ice cream.

She handed Presley a pint and took the other for herself. They went to the living room and sat down on the gray sofa Presley had picked out three years ago after painstaking research on couches. She shook her head at herself. It was just a couch. More time she'd wasted. Her notebooks mocked her with their ideas between the pages. Dreams and plans and goals. She'd spent three days at a seminar she'd dreamed of going to and didn't have one thing to add to her notebooks. Not for the hotel anyway.

Rylee waved her spoon in Presley's face. "Hey. Zombie. How was the conference?"

Presley's lips wouldn't move into a smile. She tried, but the truth was, she'd pasted it on for the last few days, and with Rylee, she didn't have to pretend.

"It was everything I hoped it would be. If Ms. Twain actually gives me a promotion, I definitely feel prepared to take it."

"Good. I'm glad it was good. How are *you?*"

Presley shrugged. "I met several people who gave me their cards. Existing management who work outside of Michigan. Some bigger places right here in Great Falls."

Rylee fixated for a moment on getting a clump of cookie dough out of the hard ice cream. Once she had it, she popped it in her mouth. "Oh yeah? Any in, say, northern Michigan?"

Presley decided it was a great time to do her own cookie dough dig. She stared at her ice cream.

"Avi and I broke up," Rylee said.

Presley scrunched her nose. "I didn't know you were still seeing her. Your first date was over a month ago."

Rylee shrugged. "Yeah, so? Anyway. It didn't work out."

"I'm sorry. What did she do?"

"The usual. Accepted me as I was, didn't put pressure on me to spend more time with her. Was great in bed."

"The horror. Who wants that?"

It was usually a running joke, Rylee's string of wonderful partners, women and men, who could have been the one if only Rylee believed in happily-ever-afters for herself. As a child who'd sat on the sidelines watching her parents go through a nasty divorce, she'd always said she didn't care who she dated as long as they knew forever wasn't an option on her menu. More than once, Presley wished she had her friend's resilient, wandering heart. But this time, she wondered if maybe Rylee was opening herself up to more.

"You do, sweetie."

Presley looked down. "This was about you. He hasn't texted. It's been five days."

"That's rude. And he left your texts on 'read'?"

Presley scooped up some ice cream. Sometimes the only way to get to the good part was to weed through the okay part. No one really bought cookie dough ice cream for the ice cream. They should just make and sell bags of the cookie dough in the freezer section.

"I didn't text him," she mumbled around her bite.

"He could be sitting on his couch right now, with his best friend, pretending to like cookie dough ice cream for more than the cookie pieces and saying the same thing."

Genuine laughter fluttered through her for the first time in days. "I think his best friend is Ollie. Though Mr. D is making a play for the role, I think."

"You remember the big wedding party we had at the restaurant last year?"

Presley narrowed her gaze. It seemed like a topic shift, but she knew her friend too well. Somehow, a lesson would be layered into this story. "Sure. Hysterical mother of the groom. Drunk bride, crying groom. Fighting parents on the bride's side. A reality-show-worthy event."

Nodding, Rylee scooped up another bite, then put the lid on her ice cream container. She walked to the kitchen, which was through a tiny attached dining room and around the corner of a random wall that worked as a separator for the space, and came back with the pizza and napkins.

"The only thing that went well that night was the meal."

Presley smiled. She'd heard this story before. The meal had been written up in the *Michigan Tribune* because the bride had invited her uncle who wrote for the newspaper.

"You got your promotion. Head chef. You rock. Things we already knew."

Rylee pulled a piece of pizza from the box. "I don't think I ever told you how close I came to losing my job that night."

Presley stuck with the ice cream. "What do you mean?" She put her feet up on the coffee table, wondering again why she hadn't just moved in with Rylee when her lease had been up a year ago. *Because you'd hoped to be moving in with someone else.*

Rylee finished a bite of pizza, grabbed a napkin. "I was in charge of ordering the meat. I did it. I always do my job. But someone on the other end screwed up the order. The morning of the wedding, the order shows up, but it's about fifty filets short of feeding the entire party."

Presley's eyes widened. "I thought you served salmon."

Rylee nodded. "We did. But that wasn't the plan. It was supposed to be three courses, the entréc being filet mignon. My boss wanted to fire me on the spot, she was so mad, but she couldn't afford to be short-staffed. So I called in a favor, had the salmon delivered, came up with a kick-ass recipe for it that complemented the filet mignon and told the wedding planner about the honest mistake and we did a quick survey of who would prefer salmon. We almost didn't have enough for those who wanted it. The bride clearly should have had an option on her RSVP card."

Presley sat with the story for a few minutes, trying to figure out its significance. When she couldn't, she went to the freezer, put her own ice cream away, and grabbed a couple of cans of pop.

When she sat down next to her best friend, she stared at her for a moment. "I know you're trying to do some Yoda thing here where I figure out the deep thought myself, but I'm tired."

Rylee laughed, went for another piece of pizza. "No matter how much you plan, things happen. You roll with it, you adjust, and sometimes the thing that knocked you down is the thing that wakes you up. What you think might be the worst moment in your life can show you exactly what you were missing."

Picking up a slice, Presley weighed this in her brain. "So, Emmett was the filet mignon and bleep is the fish?"

Rylee rolled her eyes. "Stop bleeping his name."

"Nope." Her phone buzzed, but she didn't check it right away.

"There's nothing tying you here, Presley."

"There's you."

Rylee smiled. "I work so much you hardly see me. And I'm not a reason to stay."

Presley chewed her bite, wishing it didn't taste like paste in her mouth. Her eyes watered. When she swallowed it down, she gave her friend the truth. "I don't have a reason to go. He said it was probably good we were going back to our own lives because a real relationship would have been harder. He didn't ask me to stay. He didn't even stick around to say goodbye."

"I know. But all that tells me is that he couldn't. Some people are too hard to say goodbye to."

Presley's heart squeezed. She'd been so sure it was just the opposite: that she was too easy to say goodbye to, leave, or get over. Too easy to be without. But what if she was wrong? What if, for Beckett, she *was* the one person he couldn't say goodbye to? She shook her head, clearing the thought—the hope—from her brain.

"I can't put myself in that position again. I know it's stupid and childish, but I need to be the one someone can't live without." She'd never had that. Even Rylee, who loved her and who she knew needed her on some level, could live without her. Her parents hadn't returned the two phone calls she'd made since returning home. "I need someone who asks me not to go. Someone who, at the very least, can say goodbye even if they don't want to."

Rylee reached out, squeezed Presley's hand. "You're going to be okay."

"I know." Because what other choice was there.

When she reached for the remote to turn on the TV, she tapped her phone. Notifications lit up her screen. *What the?* She picked it up, sliding open her texts first.

Ms. Twain

High profile client coming
at 4 P.M. today. Needs
personal concierge. You are

> best one. I know it's your day
> off but it should just be a few hours
> for tonight.

She sighed. Shit. She wanted just one day to collect herself. It was already two o'clock. So much for moving up. She showed Rylee her phone, and her friend frowned and pulled her in for a side hug.

"Okay. So you still have to do the lower-level stuff, but once a management position opens up, you're ready. You're next in line. That's huge."

Rylee was right. That was what Presley had been working for. So why the hell wasn't she more excited?

Another notification buzzed on her phone. It didn't make any sense.

"I'm getting a notification that Hot Mountain Man is going live. I'm tagged specifically."

Rylee bolted upright. "Open it."

Presley rolled her eyes. "It's not Beckett. For one thing, he would never refer to himself as that. Second, he hates the idea of being live."

"Well then, let's see who the copycat of his moniker is." Rylee pressed the notification for her and Instagram opened.

When the little circle on the top of her feed showed "Hot Mountain Man is live right now," Presley clicked it herself.

She sucked in a sharp, painful breath when Beckett's face filled the screen. The Wi-Fi cut right at that moment, freezing his face in an almost smile. Freezing her heart and maybe even time.

The video resumed. Rylee squeezed the hand not holding the phone.

"I don't know if this was the best idea, but it's a start," Beckett said into the camera.

Several comments popped up.

You got this, Mountain Man.

♥

♥

♥

🔥

I want you, Hot Mountain Man.

Go get your girl.

Beckett stared at the camera, leaned back against what looked like a brick building.

"Ollie, that's my niece. You guys have seen her on the lodge videos. Anyway, she showed me how to do this live thing and I started a new account just to use the nickname y'all are so fond of. Jilly said she told our lodge followers I was going to do this so thanks for being here and supporting me. Ollie told me not to mess this up, so I'm going to do my best. I don't know if Presley will see this, but I tagged her. God, that sounds weird. The internet is weird, but I'm grateful for it right now." He paused.

"He doesn't know how to see who's listening," Rylee whispered.

Beckett ran his hand through his hair. "I know there's lots of comments, but if I try to answer them, I'll mess it up. Presley, if you're, I don't know, listening."

His face scrunched adorably. "One sec, my sister is texting. Come on, Jilly. You knew I was doing this." His finger reached for the screen and then his lips formed a perfect O.

"Jilly says Presley's listening. I'm not sure I completely understand the internet but I'll trust my sister."

He dropped his hand, stared at the camera like she was right in front of him. "Presley. I'm an idiot. I let you go without saying goodbye.

I couldn't face it. I'm a coward. How do you say goodbye to the person who you want to say good morning and good night to every day for the rest of your life? You don't. You head up a mountain and hide until your brother hauls your ass back and tells you to smarten up."

His smile made her insides go squishy. She wasn't alone, if the comments were any indication.

"I did. I'm smarter now than I was five days ago when you left. I'm here. I'm in Great Falls. I'm coming to you because I didn't know how else to show you that I'd do anything for you."

Presley couldn't feel her fingers and her heart was ticking like an overactive clock.

"He's here, Presley. He came for you."

She laughed. "Why the hell is he doing it this way?"

Like he heard her, he stretched his arm out, showing where he was. "You went out of your comfort zone for someone who didn't appreciate it. Then you did it over and over again like a fucking champ. Sorry for swearing, Ollie. Presley, you're amazing. I'm crazy about you. I'm here, doing this live, because that's not *my* comfort zone. You make me brave. You make me laugh. You make me want to take chances. I'm staying at your hotel, Presley. If this is too much for you, then I'll just beg to see you one more time to say a proper goodbye." He brought the camera a little closer, making Presley's breath hitch. One side of his kissable mouth tipped up. "You do owe me about fifty Band-Aids." The look in his eyes turned serious, nearly soulful. "But if it's not too much, if you can forgive me for being an ass, I'm here. I won't leave without saying goodbye."

He was silent for a bit except for the noise and traffic in the background. A couple of people walked past him now that he'd moved away from the building. He gaze was thoughtful and just a little sad.

"I have no idea how to stop a live video. Thanks for listening, guys. I guess you'll want to know how things end up. If this works, if Presley meets me, forgives me, gives me a chance, I will put up my first Instagram photo. It'll be a reflection of all the things to come. An honest picture of a moment of true happiness. I'm hoping there'll be more of them."

Then he clearly figured out how to end things, because the live feed stopped. Presley's notifications did anything but.

Rylee turned her body to look at her. "Holy shit. That guy is bananas for you. He's an entire fruit freaking cocktail. Get dressed. Go."

"But—" Presley said, then stopped.

"Yeah, I can't wait to hear this," Rylee said, standing up. "But what? But you don't love him, too? But he isn't everything you ever wanted?"

Her best friend was right. She hurried into her room, pulled on a pair of jeans and a sweater. Rushing around, she ran her hands through her hair as she pulled on a pair of shoes. Rylee went into the bathroom, came out a minute later, and tossed something at Presley.

It knocked into Presley's hand, falling to the ground. As she bent to pick it up, she laughed.

"Band-Aids."

Rylee grinned. "Yes. Pay the guy back."

Giving her friend a hug, she took the Band-Aids, grabbed her purse and her jacket, and headed for the door.

There was no plan other than get to Beckett. And that was all she needed.

Thirty-Seven

Beckett was flying by the seat of his pants. He hated that part. Gray was right—being scared and doing it anyway was hard. Facing the fact that it didn't matter if he ran a bike shop, a sports store, or a fucking chicken coop, he wouldn't feel complete without Presley Ayers by his side, was a hell of a thing. It didn't mean he didn't still want things. It just meant things were better *with* her. He could hike in the rain. Might even enjoy it. But when the sun shone, it made the entire experience better. Presley was like his sun. She made everything that much better.

He'd been a fool to let her leave without telling her that, but in all fairness, it'd taken an almost-fight with his brother to knock that thought clear. Now he stood outside La Chambre Hotel and went through the list of items he'd requested for his room. He'd received confirmation from Presley's boss that it was all there, waiting for his arrival. Did she know? Suspect? God. He couldn't wait to see her face and only hoped he'd get the chance. He'd called her ex names, but right now, realizing there was a chance Presley might tell Beckett to leave, that she might not even give him a chance to explain, he knew he was the asshat in this scenario.

He took a deep breath, leaned against the aged brick. He could do this. It could only go one of two ways. She'd want him back or she wouldn't. He could deal with whichever outcome, but he couldn't deal with not knowing. Beckett wouldn't be able to move forward without knowing, without a doubt, that he'd put it all on the line and told Presley how much she meant to him. Even if she turned him away—*please don't let her turn me away*—it'd be better than not trying.

His phone buzzed. He smiled when he read the message.

Ollie

You got this Uncle Beck.

He could use even a tenth of her confidence.

Beckett

Thanks, kid. Love you.

Ollie

Love you, too. Mom says don't screw it up.

He laughed out loud, ignoring the look he got from an elderly couple walking their dog along the sidewalk.

Now or never. He texted Presley.

Beckett

Seems I'm missing a pillowcase.

Presley

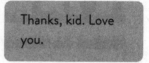

Anticipation flooded his veins.

Beckett

Wondering if you've seen it?

Presley

I can look. Maybe it accidentally got mixed up with my things.

Beckett smiled. *"Accidentally," my ass.* Pillowcases didn't fall off the pillows. Plus, she had responded. That was a good sign.

Beckett

Guess you owe me more than Band-Aids

Presley

I'll FedEx you some

He laughed. He did that more with her in his life. Enough playing.

Beckett

I miss your face, Presley.

Presley

I miss yours, too.

Relief swamped him in such a rush, he felt light-headed. Okay. If she missed him, too, he could work with that. They weren't finished. There was still a chance, and this time, there was no way he wasn't taking it.

He left the text on "read." There were things to do. In about an hour, he'd know if he was the biggest idiot ever. He could always go back to Smile. It wasn't going anywhere. But if Presley felt the way he did, it wouldn't matter where he was; he'd always be home.

Thirty-Eight

Presley was nervous. She all but ran into the hotel, hoping she could see Beckett before starting her shift. But Ms. Twain caught her before she could even ask the front desk about a Mr. Beckett Keller staying with them.

"You're early, and so is he. Good job."

Presley stared at her boss. "What? No. I came in early to take care of something."

Ms. Twain didn't even look up from the computer screen. "Yes. Your client. I've already checked him in for you. He's here on business. Resting at the moment—but I'm sure he'll want to meet you."

Fine. She could juggle both. She'd go meet the client, address his immediate needs, then she'd just call down to the front desk, hope Breanna answered, and get Beckett's room number.

Ms. Twain glanced up, frowned. "You're not in uniform."

She resisted the urge to roll her eyes. Or quit on the spot. This woman grew more infuriating with every interaction. "Again, I'm early, so I was going to change once I got here."

"No time. Mr. Simel. Room 404."

Presley felt a jolt in her chest, like her stomach and heart had collided. The dots connected and created a panicky feeling of hope. She did her best to maintain a professional expression. "Okay."

She turned toward the elevators but Ms. Twain called her name. She bent behind the counter, her voice muffled as she spoke. "He called down, requested the concierge bring these up."

Presley's heart slammed into her throat when Ms. Twain held out a box of Band-Aids. Unable to breathe or move, she stared at it.

"Problem, Ms. Ayers?"

Something was blocking her airway. Hope was one thing, but this confirmed it. He was really, truly here for her.

"Ms. Ayers. Are you up for this or not?"

Her breath whooshed out. The answer was easy. "Yes. Yes, I am."

The elevator ride to the fourth floor was perhaps the longest of her life. This went against everything she thought she knew about him. Beckett didn't love spontaneity any more than she did. His life was in Smile. He'd thought the bookend dates for their time together were a *good* thing. He'd told her so under the stars. He hadn't asked her to stay. He hadn't said goodbye.

On the fourth floor, she walked to the doorway, stared at the pale white molding that needed a paint touch-up. The little peephole was right below the gold numbers: *404*.

She knocked, squeezing the Band-Aid box in her other hand. The door swung open.

"You brought Band-Aids. Perfect. I got a paper cut," Beckett said, holding his index finger up to show her a barely visible mark.

Tears and giggles welled up at once. She had to breathe through her nose for a second to keep herself in check. "You might want to clean that up so it doesn't get infected."

He nodded. "Smart."

They stared at each other and she wondered if he could hear her heartbeat tap-dancing in her chest.

"Why did you do a live and pretend to be a high-profile client?"

His cheeks darkened with embarrassment. "Covering my bases in case you didn't see my live or weren't swayed by it."

A heavy breath whooshed out of her lungs and she had to ask:

"What are you doing here, Beckett?"

The easy humor fled from his gaze. "You took something of mine."

She laughed. "Yes. Fine. I admit it. I stole your pillowcase."

Stepping closer, he reached out, took her hand. Just that simple touch was like he'd shocked her back to life. He pulled her into the room, the door floating closed behind them.

"Not my pillowcase, Presley. My heart. You took it, and it's really freaking hard to function without it."

She pressed her hand against his chest, trying not to cry. "I left mine for you."

He settled his forehead against hers and everything in Presley's body settled like it was finally all back in the right spot.

"I have a feeling they might only function properly together," he whispered, running his hands up her arms and cupping her face. His thumbs stroked just under her ears and his gaze swam with vulnerability, honesty, and love.

"You didn't say goodbye." That part still hurt.

"I wouldn't have been able to."

"You didn't ask me to stay." She realized now she'd hoped he would.

"I didn't think I had the right."

Swallowing past the lump in her throat, she moved her hands to grip his wrists.

"Then what are you doing here?"

"I'm here for you. I'm here because I want to be wherever you are."

Her fingers tightened on his wrists. "What does that mean?"

He smiled. "It means I love you, Presley Ayers. I love you in a way I didn't know was possible. Definitely not after a week. I don't care if you don't like the outdoors, if you never want to fish, if you want to stay here in the city or move to California. Wherever you are is where I need to be. I didn't say goodbye because I didn't want to. I don't want to. I don't ever want to say goodbye to you, Presley. I want to say good night and good morning every day. But never goodbye."

She couldn't wipe the tears trickling over her lids because she couldn't release her grip.

"What about Smile? Your family? Your bike shop?"

He shrugged. "You tipped the scales. You matter most. The rest of it—it still matters, but not the way you do. I can work around all of that, but I don't work without you. I love you."

Her heart may have flatlined for one second, but it came back with a vengeance, beating strong and loud. She let him go so she could wrap her arms around him.

"I love you, Beckett. I didn't think you felt the same. These last few days have been hollow. Nothing looks or feels the same without you."

Beckett's lips moved against her cheek, kissing her teardrops, one cheek, then the other. Then his mouth found hers and he kissed her, held her close in a way that she'd dreamt about for the last five nights. She kissed him with the same passion, clinging to him, running her hands through his hair, wanting this moment to never end. Wanting the kiss to never end.

Even when it did, they didn't pull back from each other. They spoke with their faces so close, they shared the same air.

"What now?" she whispered.

"I'll open the second shop here for Brian."

"You'd move here for me?" Her heart puffed up.

"I'd do anything for you."

She grinned. "Clearly, you would. You came all this way, booked a reservation and a personal concierge, all not knowing how this would end. You went on Instagram *live*. Willingly."

He pulled her to the bed, down onto his lap. When he brought her hand to his lips, he kissed each finger. "I just focused on it not ending. We're not over. Whatever you need for us to make this work, I'll do it."

He meant it, she realized. She'd always been the one to bend, accommodate, adjust. She stared at him, running her hands over his strong jaw, the subtle rasp of a few days' growth.

"You know what I want?"

"God, I hope you say me."

She nodded. "Definitely you."

She saw the hesitancy in his gaze. "Done. What else?"

Taking a deep breath, she let it out, realizing she'd known since the minute Gramps helped her onto the dock, maybe even before that, what she wanted. It had definitely not been part of the plan.

"I want to go home. With you. To Smile."

His gaze widened and he sucked in a breath. "What about your job? Your promotion? Your life here?"

Holding his face in her hands, she smiled at him, love and energy coursing through her body in a way she'd never known. "My life is where you are. Where your family is. Where there are colorful surprises at the end of winding paths. Where we can see the stars at night. Where we can be part of the lodge and make your bike shop thrive. The truth is, I fell in love with you, Beckett Keller, but I'm also pretty fond of where you come from."

"They're your family, too, Presley. They miss you. Everyone misses you."

Little cracks that had formed in her heart at a young age, when she had realized she wasn't the most important person to anyone, filled with Beckett's love. With knowing she'd found a place to belong.

"Then let's go home."

Epilogue

Presley eased her pale pink cruiser to a stop in front of the General Store. Rather than using the bike rack, she left it resting on the kickstand. She wouldn't be long. Unless Maureen and Miles had some tea they couldn't wait to spill. It'd only been a few days since her last visit, and Smile residents hung on to gossip about as well as Presley would a slippery fish. She pulled her phone out, checked her texts first, then pulled open her Notes app, where she'd made a list of what she needed.

"Hey, Presley," Gramps said, coming out of the store.

She looked up, grateful her wide-brimmed hat (a gift Mel had sent Jilly, Ollie, and Presley when she'd returned home) blocked the brightness of the sun. It didn't stop the heat, but it helped with seeing who she was talking to.

"Hi, Gramps. I was going to call you later and talk about the website," she said as he moved down the steps and stopped in front of her bike.

Beckett had been so nervous to give it to her, promising that if she didn't like it, he'd buy her something else as a, as he called it, thanks-for-moving-to-Smile-loving-me-and-being-the-best-thing-to-ever-happen-to-me gift. After assuring him she loved the thought he'd put into it—it had an adorable little basket for her to carry things, a specialty seat with extra padding, and wide, lifted handles so she didn't hurt her back—she'd been thrilled to learn it was a lot more comfortable to ride than the tandem.

Gramps transferred his cloth bag full of groceries to the other arm and tugged at the collar of his T-shirt. "It's hotter than the surface of the sun today."

Presley laughed. "I'll take your word for it, but it's definitely warm."

"Council voted unanimously," Gramps said. "Not only are we

thrilled you'll take over the marketing and social media for Smile, we'd like to offer you a position. 'Director of Tourism' was floated around, but you can pick the label."

Excitement made her stomach swirl. In addition to this, she was taking over the social media and marketing for the lodge, as well as for several other businesses in Smile. She would be able to work from home—be it the cabin or the apartment—for now.

"I love that title."

"The pay isn't much, but with Smile growing, I think we'll see more revenue coming in. We can revisit the salary at next year's general meeting."

Individually, none of the jobs she'd taken on paid all that much, but when she pushed them all together into the same pot, she was doing just fine. Especially since she no longer paid exorbitant rent, food, Uber, or other city prices. Once she and Beckett got more settled, she was going to set up her own website and offer more marketing and social media services.

Unable to resist, she gave Gramps a side hug. "Thank you. I know you put in a good word for me with the council."

His chuckle was deep and booming. "You're pretty easy to say nice words about, Presley. You're good for our town. For Beckett."

She liked to think so. The town and Beckett were certainly good to her. "Thank you. Okay, I've got to pick up a few things I ordered."

"I heard Beckett's bikes are all rented for the rest of the week," Gramps said with pride in his tone.

She nodded. "A large family is staying over on Tourist Lane. They rented all four houseboats and they wanted access to the bikes the whole time they were here. The insurance is in order even if we don't have anywhere near the full amount of stock he wants."

The past three weeks or so had been a blur. Since she still had banked vacation days, she'd used them as part of her two weeks notice. Ms. Twain had accepted her resignation but continued to text frequently with random queries. Rylee had taken over Presley's lease since she wanted to be closer to work. She'd taken care of selling Presley's furniture on Marketplace for her since she and Beckett had wanted to return to Smile as quickly as possible—though not before Rylee grilled him over drinks and dinner. He passed the bestie test so well, Rylee agreed to come visit as soon as she could.

Once they'd returned home, they both made a list of what needed to get done first. Even if Beckett hadn't finally admitted to himself how much the bike shop meant to him, it was evident in how prepared and ready he was to open it. With Beckett having five bikes, he was able to do a soft launch, which ended up making him busier than he'd expected.

"How'd you know about the rentals?" Then it clicked. "He got his hair trimmed this morning."

Gramps nodded. "Right after me. Anderson was relieved. They worried he was growing it out to perfect his Hot Mountain Man look."

Shaking her head, she wondered if Beckett would ever escape that nickname. "No worries there. He's happy to never be called that again."

She hurried into the store, saying hello to Maureen as she turned down the aisle that led her to the chalkboard.

"There she is," Miles said, toothpick between his lips. "Good thing you're here. You have enough deliveries to open your own store."

Presley knew he was exaggerating, but he wasn't entirely wrong. "Beckett and I are doing some renos on his apartment so it feels more like ours. I wanted to add some pops of color."

Miles started stacking Amazon packages on the counter. "No doubt you do that, Presley."

Warmth swamped her chest. Picking up the chalk, she wrote her note beside the "community BBQ" and "jet ski for sale" notes.

JOIN US AT GET LOST LODGE FOR A CELEBRATION DINNER TO WELCOME CHEF SHANE BACK TO WORK. SATURDAY, 4 P.M. WE'LL PROVIDE THE BURGERS & HOT DOGS. BYOB PLUS A SIDE OR DESSERT.

Chef had needed almost three weeks off, and now, as it neared the end of July, he was scheduled to come back part-time. They'd worked out an arrangement with the deli to provide low-cost breakfasts, easy lunches, and a variety of snacks. Chef would work afternoons, providing only dinners. He'd need physiotherapy for a few months still to regain strength in his hand, but he was eager to get back to the kitchen.

Miles was grinning at her when she set the chalk down. "Is Beckett's place big enough to hold all of this?"

Presley laughed, unsure, now that it was in front of her, how she was going to get it all to the dock. "Some of it's going to the lodge, but he's cleared out the spare bedroom, so it should." She'd come back for the apartment items later.

"I'll call Anderson?"

Presley nodded. "Thank you. But I need . . ." She trailed off, looking for a specific package. It wasn't from Amazon, so it was easy to find. The small box gave nothing away.

"See you Saturday?" Presley asked.

"Wouldn't miss it," Miles said.

Back on the cruiser, her special package in the basket with the few items she'd picked up, she rode toward the dock, waving at people along the way. Mateo had joined the lodge as a part-time hiking guide, which freed up Beckett's time to get as much as he could in order for the rental shop before going back to Brian's part-time.

Getting off the bike, she walked toward Beckett, who saw her almost immediately. The large, garage-style doors of what had once been an auto shop were open. Tevin and a friend were finishing up the last of the interior.

"This looks great," she said as she came closer.

Much like the cabin, it was coming together quickly. After a conversation with Gramps, Beckett had decided he wanted to rent an actual building. It would make storage easier. When Gramps suggested the former auto shop across from Pete's would work well, Beckett wasn't immediately sold. Presley had doodled her ideas of what it could look like once they painted and added a counter and a seating area. From there, Gray and Jill suggested adding bike racks in front for easy parking and maybe offering easy-to-travel snacks and drinks for the riders.

"It's coming along," Beckett said, taking her hand. He pulled her in for a soft kiss that made her sigh with happiness. "What's in the box?" he asked when he leaned back.

"A surprise," she said.

"For who?"

She poked his chest. "You." She held it out to him.

Music pumped from the back office, where the guys were painting.

"You didn't have to get me anything," he said, looking at her with so much love she could *feel* it. He said it often, and so did she, but it was the little things he did—bringing her coffee in the morning, anticipating her needs, taking her hand or putting one on the small of her back like he couldn't stand not touching her. Now that she knew what it felt like to be someone's person, to have someone return her feelings fully and completely without reservation, she wondered how she'd thought she could settle for anything less.

"I did," she said on a breathy sigh. "It's a thanks-for-loving-me-back-and-making-me-the-happiest-woman-in-Smile-I'm-so-excited-about-our-life-together gift."

Beckett's laugh echoed in the freshly painted, empty space. He yanked her into a one-armed hug, swinging her around.

"God, I love you."

When he set her down, her heart was racing. Now she knew how he had felt giving her the bike. "I love you, too," she said quietly, nudging the box. "And I hope you love these. If you don't, I won't be offended."

With care, he opened the box, pulling the lid off. Inside, nestled under some tissue paper, were business cards.

He pulled one out, looked at it. The 3.5 x 2 cardstock paper looked small in his grasp. She was pleased to see it'd turned out exactly as she'd designed it with her own personal doodle of a tandem bike in one corner and a cruiser in the other. In the middle, it read:

BECKETT'S BIKES

SMILE'S ONE-STOP SHOP FOR ALL YOUR RENTAL NEEDS

The address, phone number, and website were listed below the tagline they'd created together. She clasped her hands, resting her chin on them, waiting for him to say something.

His gaze moved over the words slowly before rising to meet hers. "You've believed in me from the second I told you about this."

Her heart gave a nervous flutter. "From the second you told me, I could feel your excitement and passion for doing this. For doing this *here*, where you grew up."

Emotion made her throat feel tight. "I can't believe you were willing to give that up for me."

He tilted his head to one side, his thumb brushing over the embossed lettering.

"You gave up everything for me."

"No. I gained everything because of you. Because you showed me what it feels like to belong. To be needed *and* wanted. To be part of a family. A community." She took a deep breath. "Do you like them?"

After carefully setting the box down on one of the stepladders they'd been using for painting, Beckett pulled her into his arms, the place where she felt most at home.

"I love them. Everything about them. The thought behind them, your adorable doodles that I think you should find a way to market and sell at This and That. I love that you wanted to surprise me, that you made something that shows your faith in me. You make me stronger. Happier than I've ever been." He lowered his chin, pressed a featherlight kiss to her temple. "Mostly, I love that I get to spend my life with you, showing and telling you how happy I am that you came to Get Lost and decided to stay."

Presley's breathing hitched as she pushed her arms through his, up around his neck, going on her tiptoes to be just that little bit closer.

She pressed her mouth to his neck, heard the intake of his breath, and smiled. "I found a lot more than a Hot Mountain Man."

There was laughter in his groan as he tightened his hold on her waist. "Maybe you ought to add 'taken' or 'off the market' to the hashtags."

Before she could reply, Tevin cleared his throat from behind them.

"Sorry to interrupt, even though I know you don't mind putting on a show, Becks," he said, not hiding his laughter.

Beckett moved, pulled her into his side as he turned to his friend, who was standing behind them with a paintbrush. "That's me. Next thing you know, I'll be doing karaoke at Bro's."

"I'd pay good money to see that," Presley said.

Beckett shot her a glare. "Absolutely not. What's up, Tev?"

"Just wanted to tell you we're all done in here. You're ready to go. Furniture can start moving in tomorrow."

Tevin and Drew left quickly, leaving Presley and Beckett alone in the space. He turned, looking around, and she wondered if he was imagining what it could be. She'd done a lot of that in her own life, and as it turned out, what she ended up with was nothing like she had imagined. It was so much better.

She touched his shoulder. "We should go. I grabbed marshmallows for Ollie."

Beckett's eyes were bright, full of wonder and happiness, and Presley loved that more than staring at the stars.

"Now she's got you supplying her with them," he said with a grin.

"I can admit to being slightly wrapped around her finger."

Beckett's bark of laughter echoed in the space. He picked up the box of business cards. "Slightly? I think she's got all of us secured around a separate finger each."

They walked out of the building that would soon house Beckett's Bikes, waited while the doors slid down to the ground. Presley grabbed her bike and walked it alongside Beckett as they headed for the dock.

"You know, she asked me if she could call you Aunt Presley," he said casually.

Her heart didn't do casual with him. It bounced right up, painfully, longingly against her ribs. "Oh yeah?"

He looked over, his gaze so steady and genuine. Just like him. "Yup."

"What'd you say?"

It wasn't like they weren't planning a future together, but it also wasn't like he'd proposed. Presley wanted that, and she knew Beckett did, too, but there was no rush. If only she could tell her heart that.

"I said that I'd ask you."

"Oh. I mean, if you're okay with it. If your sister is." Definitely not a proposal. *Which makes perfect sense. Maybe focus on one or two major life alterations at a time.*

Beckett shrugged. "Of course. She'll call you that after we get married, so I figure, what's the harm in starting now?"

Presley nearly tripped over the bike pedal. She stopped in her tracks. "Did you just throw out getting married like it was no big deal? Like, oh, well, we're going to sleep at the cabin instead of the apartment tonight?"

He stopped, turned toward her slowly, put his hands on the handles of the bike, right next to hers, linking their pinkies.

"It's a big deal, Presley. One I'm surer about than I've ever been about anything else in my life. When the time comes, I'll do it right. I promise. Make sure I'm down on one knee, that there's no salamanders or bugs, it won't be on a boat, and there'll be chocolate close by."

She sniffled. For a non-proposal, it was pretty damn romantic. She wasn't sure how she'd make it through the real thing when the time came.

"But, like, Ollie calling you her aunt, I figure, why not start getting used to the idea, the sound of it, now?" He lifted his hand, cupped her jaw, smoothed his thumb over her skin. "The night before you left, I said some stupid things about how we knew, going in, we'd be over. I hated that I said it. I did it more to cement it in my mind because I didn't think I had the right to ask you to stay."

He moved closer, the bike leaning against them as he placed his other hand on her shoulder. Presley's fingers circled his wrists as he brought their faces closer.

"I want to put it out there as often as possible, so that it just becomes something you expect, you know, you can count on, that I love you now and I always will. I don't ever want to be over. I didn't want to then, and now, I can't imagine my world without you."

Tears pushed at her eyelids, but she fought them. "You don't have to. I love you, too, Beckett. That night, I wanted to believe your words to protect myself, but I knew, even then, it was too late. My heart was already yours."

His forehead touched hers, pressed like he couldn't get close enough. "When it happens? I was thinking we could get married at the lodge."

She grinned. "You really have thought about it."

"I think about you and us far too many times in the run of a day."

She let her hands drop, slip around his waist. "Might be hard to secure the venue. That place is pretty popular now."

"Thanks to you."

She grinned, moved her hands to his stomach. "Partially me. But mostly because of these."

He let out a low growl as he kissed her. When he pulled back, his gaze narrowed. "My abs are never going on social media again."

Presley's entire body lit up with her smile. She *felt* the happiness coursing through her. "Agreed." She kissed him again before adding, "Unless there's a lull in bookings."

He shook his head indulgently, and she knew she had a lifetime of this to look forward to: smiles, happiness, ups and downs that they'd weather together. Beckett slung one arm around her shoulder, walked the bike with the other.

As they approached the dock, Beckett said her second set of three favorite words: "Let's go home."

Acknowledgments

While it's absolutely true that books are magic, writing is hard. But, like so many other great things in life, it's worth the effort, self-doubt, uncertainty, highs and lows. I'm so excited to share this book with you all. Presley and Beckett are, in my mind, absolutely wonderful. Even as I'm filled with anticipation, counting down the days until release, I'm terrified that people won't love it. Or worse, that they'll actively dislike it. The truth is, you can't know. There's so much about writing that mirrors life in general. We can't control everything. We aren't in charge of what happens when we put something out into the universe. All we can do is put our heart and soul and best intentions into the things we love and hope for the best outcomes. Of course, while we do that, we (hopefully) all have our own support systems propping us up, talking us down, reminding us to focus on the good and learn from the rest.

This book, like every other I've written, is more than just words I typed on a page. It's more than some cute characters I developed with the intention of making them kiss as often as possible. This book is my family supporting me by giving me the time to write—my husband, Matt, making me all of my favorite foods and believing in me even when I'm arguing with myself. It's my agent, Fran, telling me I can do this even though she's said it before and I should really just believe her. It's Alex, and this time Cassidy, taking the time to answer my questions and concerns and soothe my uncertainties while simultaneously making my words shine. It's a whole team of people at St. Martin's Publishing Group who want the very best for this book and show this through their marketing, publicity, amazing covers, and incredible support.

This book is my best friend, Bren, telling me I'm not a fluke; my daughters, Kalie and Amy, working hard to achieve their own dreams because they see me chasing mine. It's their hugs after long days or ones that don't go as planned. It's them inspiring me with their attitudes and determination, their grace and beauty. It's the result of so many people pushing me forward and filling my heart with kindness and gratitude and making me feel like there's room for me and my words. There are so many moments when you write books that you stop and go, "What am I doing?" Then there are people you ask that very question to and they take the time to remind you that you belong here, we all feel this way, and it's all going to be okay. That kind of support, whether you reach out frequently or intermittently, is priceless. Thank you to Sarah Fox, Sarah Adams, Courtney Kae, Elle Cosimano, Austin, and Emily for being approachable and so kind. There are just so many people when you do something like this. It's overwhelming, but in such a wonderful way. Thank you Amy Lea for agreeing to blurb even though you were busy with a newborn baby (and also Elle and Courtney for their time and blurbs). Thank you Brendan Deneen for your hard work opening doors for me that I might not have even known were there without you.

Most importantly, thank you readers for taking your precious time and choosing my books. Reading makes me so happy, and I always think, *that's* what I want: to make people smile and fall into my words, my worlds, and my characters. Thank you for letting me do that. I'm beyond grateful. If I forgot you, it's not because you don't matter. I'm just forgetful. I really need to start making a list as I go.

About the Author

Shelley Bell

SOPHIE SULLIVAN is a Disney-loving Canadian author who lives on the West Coast with her sweet family. Reading and writing romance has been her favorite hobby since she was twelve years old, bingeing on Sweet Valley High novels. Her debut rom-com, *Ten Rules for Faking It,* won the Canadian Book Club Award for best romance. Also the author of *How to Love Your Neighbor* and the most recently released *A Guide to Being Just Friends,* she hopes her rom-coms make you laugh, smile, and swoon. Along with her St. Martin's Griffin titles, she's had plenty of practice writing happily-ever-afters as her alter ego, Jody Holford.